THE
Gifted
ONE

Jacob Z. Flores

Dreamspinner Press

Published by
Dreamspinner Press
5032 Capital Circle SW
Ste 2, PMB# 279
Tallahassee, FL 32305-7886
USA
http://www.dreamspinnerpress.com/

The Gifted One

Cover Art by Reese Dante
http://www.reesedante.com

ISBN: 978-1-62380-462-6
Digital ISBN: 978-1-62380-463-3

Printed in the United States of America
First Edition
April 2013

To my earthly guardian angels:
my mother, my grandmother, my husband and my love.
Because of you, I am truly a gifted one.

AUTHOR'S NOTE

While trying to learn as much as I could on angelic lore during my research for *The Gifted One*, I came across a mostly abandoned religious text called the *Book of Enoch*. Labeled apocryphal, or not a part of the Biblical canon, Enoch's testaments were considered by most Jewish and Christian scholars not to be the word of God. Several reasons were cited for its exclusion from the canon, but one was the reference to the fallen angels. At the time the canon was created, it was inconceivable that angels would ever sin or revolt from God.

In Enoch's writings, however, it became clear that God granted angels free will, just as He did for mankind. The difference, however, was when angels fell into earthly sin, the consequences, as Enoch noted, were devastating for both heaven and earth.

And it came to pass when the children of men had multiplied that in those days were born unto them beautiful and comely daughters. And the angels, the children of the heaven, saw and lusted after them, and said to one another: "Come, let us choose us wives from among the children of men and beget us children." And Semjâzâ, who was their leader, said unto them: "I fear ye will not indeed agree to do this deed, and I alone shall have to pay the penalty of a great sin." And they all answered him and said: "Let us all swear an oath, and all bind ourselves by mutual imprecations not to abandon this plan but to do this thing." Then sware they all together and bound themselves by mutual imprecations upon it. And they were in all two hundred; who descended in the days of Jared on the summit of Mount Hermon, and they called it Mount Hermon, because they had sworn and bound themselves by mutual imprecations upon it. And these are the names of their leaders: Samîazâz, their leader, Arâkîba, Râmêêl, Kôkabîêl, Tâmîêl, Râmîêl, Dânêl, Êzêqêêl, Barâqîjâl, Asâêl, Armârôs, Batârêl, Anânêl, Zaqîêl, Samsâpêêl, Satarêl, Tûrêl, Jômjâêl, Sariêl. These are their chiefs of tens.

And all the others together with them took unto themselves wives, and each chose for himself one, and they began to go in unto them and to defile themselves with them, and they taught them charms and enchantments, and the cutting of roots, and made them acquainted with plants. And they became pregnant, and they bare great giants, whose height was three thousand ells: Who consumed all the acquisitions of men. And when men could no longer sustain them, the giants turned against them and devoured mankind. And they began to sin against birds, and beasts, and reptiles, and fish, and to devour one another's flesh, and drink the blood.

—From the *Book of Enoch* (great-grandfather of Noah)

Whilst thus to ballast love I thought,
And so more steadily to have gone,
With wares which would sink admiration,
I saw I had love's pinnace overfraught;
Thy every hair for love to work upon
Is much too much; some fitter must be sought;
For, nor in nothing, nor in things
Extreme, and scattering bright, can love inhere;
Then as an angel face and wings
Of air, not pure as it, yet pure doth wear,
So thy love may be my love's sphere;
Just such disparity
As is 'twixt air's and angels' purity,
'Twixt women's love, and men's, will ever be.

— Excerpt from "Air and Angels" by John Donne

PART I: CONVERGENCE

CHAPTER 1

THE weather went crazy the day Mateo Cruz was born. It was Thursday, January 17, 1985, and an unusually strong storm system spread across the skies in Victoria, Texas, covering the town of 60,000 underneath a blanket of darkness and gloom. The resulting downpour quickly flooded the streets, and the Guadalupe River, which cuts a path through the city, crested over its banks and swamped the low-lying areas.

The night air was unseasonably warm, even for south Texas, and uncharacteristically somber, almost as if the town were holding its breath in anticipation. Most residents avoided the streets, seeking shelter from howling winds that turned the rain into stinging pebbles. With each passing hour, the rain turned ever more oppressive, ceaselessly pelting the windows of houses and the windshields of motorists who had no choice but to brave the storm.

Carlos Cruz silently cursed the storm as he fought to see through the sheets of rain that distorted the view of the road before him. The windshield wipers of his 1972 Cutlass Supreme failed to wipe away the steady deluge, though they whirred frantically back and forth in vain. The tired motor and worn rubber linings couldn't hold back the steady onslaught.

"Aiiieeeee!" His wife screamed in the passenger seat. Perspiration covered her face, and her typically dark brown hair was matted black from sweat. Her delicate hands roamed protectively over her swollen belly, hoping her touch would slow her son's hasty entrance into the world.

"Just breathe, *mi amor*," he advised, but Veronica Cruz's cold stare told him his counsel was neither needed nor wanted.

"Just get me to the hospital, Carlos," she commanded through gritted teeth. "He's coming."

"I'm trying," he said, hoping he sounded more apologetic than frantic. "The rain is falling in buckets."

Veronica responded not in words, but in the panting short breaths they learned in the Lamaze classes she made him take with each pregnancy. Since this was their seventh child, Carlos had hoped their previous experiences would somehow grant him clemency from the weekly classes of panting like dogs. His wife, however, had been adamant they attend, and when she was with child, she was more headstrong than ever.

With six healthy boys at home, delivered by the same doctor and brought into the world using the same Lamaze techniques each time, Veronica's superstitious nature and maternal instinct were two forces Carlos vowed never to challenge. He begrudgingly agreed then.

Now that their progress was slowed by the weather and the streets flooded like a river, he was glad he had consented. The breathing exercises and lessons accumulated over the years might make a difference.

"Where are we?" she asked, concentrating on her breathing. Carlos knew she was using the short, focused breaths to draw attention away from the waves of crashing pain. Done correctly, the controlled breathing could alter her pain perception as well as reduce her heart rate and anxiety. He hoped it was working because he was about to lose his mind to fear, and his heart felt ready to burst from his chest.

"We're at Five Points."

"Five Points? That's still over twelve blocks away."

"I know. But the rain's flooded the streets. If I go too fast, the engine might choke."

"Damn you and this car," she said and a loud clap of thunder punctuated her curse word in a mighty explosion.

"God doesn't like it when you cuss," he playfully scolded.

"He'll forgive me. A cantaloupe is trying to exit my po-po, and it hurts."

Carlos laughed. Despite his gnawing fear that he might have to stop the car and deliver the baby himself, his wife's polite word for her vagina made him forget his mounting worry.

At least until the car behind them slammed into their rear end.

"What the…?" Carlos began, almost allowing the cursed F-word to escape his lips. Luckily, he stopped himself before Veronica could stare at him in disapproval. She hated the F-word more than any other in the English language, even more than its Spanish counterpart.

"Just drive," she told him. "It doesn't matter. Your brother can fix the damage later."

"But what if you're hurt?"

"Just drive!"

But before Carlos could apply pressure to the accelerator, a man tapped on his window.

"Sorry about that, buddy," the stranger said. "My car skidded when I braked."

Carlos stared at the man with the broad smile. His features were dark and hidden, but his teeth were exceptionally white. If Carlos had to pick him out of a line up, he would only be able to identify him by the wide grin and large teeth. Carlos had no idea what color the man's eyes were. Or his hair. And his clothes were impossible to describe, as they were drenched in more than just rain. Inky shadows spread across the fabric, making it difficult to discern both the color and material.

He knew he had to offer some response in order to get going again, but his throat tightened. For some reason, terror gripped him.

"Hey, buddy, you okay?" The man's concern sounded forced and hollow. "How about your wife? She looks to be in lots of pain."

At the mention of Veronica, Carlos shifted his gaze to her. Her eyebrows were knitted together, and a look of worry seized her normally radiant features. She obviously felt it too. Something was wrong.

The door to his car flung open, and the stranger's hand wrapped around his left arm and jerked him out into the pouring rain.

"Carlos!" Veronica shouted from inside the car as the stranger violently flung him into the street.

He wanted to yell for help, but the stranger was too fast. His left hand covered Carlos's mouth while his right arm wrapped around Carlos's neck, and tightened. Carlos then found himself lifted off the pavement and dangling within the crazed man's death grip.

Carlos kicked wildly against the stranger. His feet connected with the man's left shin and right knee. The man made no cry of pain. Carlos knew he struck him hard enough to at least loosen the man's grip somewhat, but his hold around his neck was still vice-tight. And getting tighter.

"When I'm done with you, I'm going after your wife," the stranger whispered. His breath felt fiery hot against Carlos's cheek. Almost as if he were standing before an open flame. "And your son will be no more."

Carlos struggled more violently. He never cared what happened to him. He was unimportant. His wife and children were the world to him. Without them, he would be nothing, and he would not allow some deranged lunatic to take Veronica or his unborn child away from him.

He dug his fingernails into the man's forearm. Instead of breaking the man's flesh, Carlos broke his fingernails. Each one of them cracked and splintered as if he clawed at stone instead of skin and bone. His arms flailed, and his eyes darted about, hoping and praying that a car's headlights would spring into view and be their salvation.

"I like it when they struggle," the man chuckled, sending waves of searing heat against his neck. "It's sweeter that way."

Carlos felt his grip on consciousness loosening. The fog of oxygen deprivation blurred his vision, and his lungs desperately tried to pull air into his body, which was shutting down.

His stunted vision was fading to black. Blood no longer rushed noisily through his ears. All he heard was silence. Carlos knew he was mere moments from departing this world and leaving his Veronica and their baby at the mercy of this wicked man.

Without warning, Carlos felt the man's body unexpectedly stiffen before releasing his stranglehold around Carlos's neck. His lungs gulped for air as his body crumpled to the hard, slick pavement.

His vision still hazy, he managed to make out another pair of legs behind the stranger. Although he couldn't see the newcomer clearly, he watched as his savior pulled something long and shiny out of the stranger's back before flinging him across the street the way a child might toss away an unwanted toy.

"Are you alright, Mr. Cruz?"

Still unable to talk, Carlos nodded as the man helped him to his feet. The newcomer was tall, somewhere over six foot five and Carlos felt dwarfed by his presence. Rivulets of rainwater washed down the man's head, which was covered in black, short-cropped hair. Unlike the stranger who tried to kill him, this man's features weren't covered by shadow. They were clear and easy to read. His rugged jaw looked granite strong, but his smile and tanned face held tenderness and concern along with an edge of urgency. There was also a radiance about him that glowed from within, making his blue eyes look like patches of clear sky.

"Thank you," Carlos finally said, through a strained voice. It hurt to speak, but expressing his gratitude was more important than favoring his tender throat.

"We need to see to your wife," the man said.

Carlos cursed himself. He had almost forgotten about Veronica, who was now screaming at the top of her lungs. He had become so entranced by his savior that everything else around him disappeared.

Now that he was properly focused, he sprinted toward the still open driver's side door. When Veronica saw him, she cried out in both relief and extreme pain. During the struggle, she had positioned her back against the inside passenger door and spread her legs onto the front leather seat.

The yellow dress she put on before leaving the house was now stained black with blood. And it was everywhere. Pools of thick blood coated the seat, and her hands looked painted red. She had been reaching between her legs to deliver her son.

"He's stuck," she pleaded. Her eyes looked at him frantically, expecting her husband to know what to do.

"I'll get us to the hospital," Carlos said.

"There's no time," a voice behind him added. "Your wife is about to deliver, and the baby is breech."

His savior gently moved Carlos aside and climbed into the car with his wife.

"Veronica," he said, his voice soothing like music. "I'm going to have to deliver your baby."

She nodded quickly, as if the man's words were not to be questioned.

"Wait a minute," Carlos said, placing his hand firmly on the man's shoulder. "Are you a doctor?"

"No, but I'm more than capable of delivering your son, Carlos."

"How do you know our names? Who the hell are you?"

Thunder once again exploded overhead, and lightning flashed brightly through the night sky.

His blue-eyed savior turned around to gaze deeply into Carlos's eyes. "We don't have time for this," he said. "Your wife and son are in danger." Even though he didn't know why, Carlos believed the man's words.

So he let the stranger get to work.

HOMER RODGERS hid in the darkness across the street. Twenty feet away from him lay the body of the one sent to end the life of the infant. The man's failure wouldn't go unnoticed, and he would suffer eternally for it.

"The boy will live," hissed a voice from the darkness around him.

Homer nodded. He knew enough not to speak.

"You will not fail us. Will you, Homer?"

Homer shook his head in response.

"Good," the voice purred. "You know what happens to those who fail."

Homer nodded again.

"When you're called to act, you shall succeed. Or you will learn the true meaning of never-ending torment."

Homer swallowed, hard. Since he'd first heard the voice call to him from the cistern on his property, his life had been nothing but fear. And waiting.

He didn't want to do the unthinkable, but he gave up that right to save his wife. In order for her to live, in order for her cancer not to return, he made a covenant. To go against that now would damn them both.

CARLOS watched Veronica bear down one final time as his son was born into the world. The stranger worked busily between his wife's open legs to readjust his son's birthing position before gently guiding him out of her protective womb.

When his son let out a wail that shook the heavens, tears freely flowed down Carlos's cheeks. His son was safe. He was going to live.

But as his savior handed Carlos his son, he watched his wife's eyes turn dreamy and look off into the distance. "Veronica," he called to her. His voice cracked with fear.

Her beautiful hazel eyes rested on him for a moment before turning to her son. "He's so beautiful," she cooed.

"Yes, he is. He looks just like you."

"Take good care of him, Carlos. He must be a good boy."

"Of course he'll be a good boy. We'll make certain of that."

Veronica smiled at him. She looked drunk and unable to focus.

"My beautiful gift from God," she said. "My Mateo."

Then, Veronica's head fell back against the window, and she was gone.

Carlos pleaded for her to come back as he clutched his son to his chest. He tried to reach her, but his savior was in his way. "Do something," Carlos commanded. "She's my Veronica. She must be with me. With our sons."

The eyes of the man who saved him and his son looked at him with sadness wider than the deep sky hue of his eyes. "There's nothing to be done. She's gone home to be with God."

Carlos stood there in the pouring rain, unable to move. In his arms, he held the last gift his wife gave him. Their son. Their Mateo.

The man exited the car and patted him on the shoulder before walking away.

"Wait!" Carlos cried out. "Where are you going?"

His savior never turned around. Instead he kept walking until he blended with the rain and disappeared into the night.

CHAPTER 2

THE forecast for Tuesday promised no rain and clear skies, and most citizens of Houston, Texas, were enjoying the unseasonably warm weather for the middle of January. The first sixteen days of the year would go down as the longest cold snap in the city's history, and the chill of those first few days of 2012 seemed already forgotten.

All throughout the city, arrows of light invigorated all they touched. The warmth brought people to life, awakening them from the peaceful slumber of winter's cold embrace. Recharged and revitalized, most people embraced the light of the sun with open arms. They packed the city in droves with their postponed errands, or they sought the many public parks to bathe in the warming rays. There were a select few, such as Matt Westlake, who tried to block out the light in favor of a few more precious moments of sleep.

But the sun wouldn't be ignored.

Matt opened his eyes to the insistent light pouring through the half-shut wooden blinds covering the bedroom windows of his apartment. Through drowsy eyes, he squinted at his alarm clock. It was 9:00 a.m., and if he didn't get up and get ready soon, he was going to be late.

He hated being late, but his body ached and refused to emerge from the cool covers wrapped around his naked frame. Dee and Shane had taken him out drinking the previous night to celebrate his last hours as a twenty-six year old. He tried to get out of it. He told them about his late morning appointment with Dr. Owens followed by a twelve-hour shift at the hospital. He didn't have the time, much less the energy, for a night of binge drinking with his best friends, but when Dee launched into how little they had seen him recently, it was just easier to go.

So they did. They headed straight for South Beach, where Dee and Shane purchased drink after drink for him. Within the first thirty minutes, he had two rum and cokes and three shots of some random alcoholic special of the night brought around by hot men clad in only underwear.

Matt hated drinking those "shots of death" as he called them. They always gave him a fantastic headache the next day, but Shane was susceptible to the hard, barely covered bodies of the wait staff. Every time one sauntered by and offered him a drink, he bought three.

And as he predicted, when he downed the first one, his temples throbbed in angry retribution.

Today was going to suck.

On his nightstand, his cell phone rang. He picked it up and saw it was Dee.

"Morning, Deeds," he answered, his voice still thick with sleep.

"Would that be a good morning or a I-feel-like-I-just-puked-up-my-kidneys morning?"

His mouth was dry, and his tongue felt wrapped in a fur coat. Still, he didn't feel sick. "It's good," he answered with a yawn. "At least for now."

"Good," she replied. "Then get yo' skinny white ass out of bed and meet us for breakfast, biatch! We's gonna have a birthday breakfast."

Matt laughed. Since Dee was currently in ghetto mode, that meant she was feeling fine and feisty. A deadly combination.

"I have…"

"An appointment and work," she interrupted. "I'm not a stupid ho, ya know? I can remember shit people tell me the night befo'."

"Do you always rhyme this early in the morning?"

"Do you want a sista to come drag yo cracker ass outta that bed?"

He sighed. It was useless to argue with Dee when she was being all ghetto. "Fine. I'll be there in fifteen. The usual place?"

"Is there any other?" She answered before laughing and hanging up the phone.

Matt flung back the covers and walked into the bathroom with a sigh. Since he'd met Dee five years ago, he'd rarely slept late after a night out with her. She enjoyed reliving the events of their adventures at breakfast the day after. It was how they learned who got lucky and who didn't as well as fill in any gaps created by excessive alcohol. Still, he had hoped to get a reprieve on his birthday.

He should have known better than that.

As he turned on the water to brush his teeth, he looked at his reflection. He immediately wished he hadn't. He looked like something even death wouldn't want. Bloodshot, puffy eyes surrounded by sagging eyelids. Skin that looked pale yet jaundiced, and disheveled hair that made Medusa look like a beauty queen.

He spit out the last of the toothpaste and made a beeline for the shower. It was the only thing capable of making him feel slightly human again. After he turned on the water and adjusted the water temperature to a few degrees less than boiling, he hopped into the stream and let the water wash the ugly away.

While he was soaping up, his mind shifted to his appointment with Dr. Owens. On the mornings of his weekly visits with his therapist, he mentally prepared himself for the visit.

They had been working for a few months trying to understand the nightmares that had come to plague his sleep. He hadn't wanted to see a therapist, but his grandmother thought it would be a good idea in light of everything Matt had been through in his life. He consented only because it made his grandmother feel better, and he would do anything for her.

While he might not have wanted to see Dr. Owens at the beginning, he ended up being glad he did. Dr. Owens was an unusual looking man who reminded him of Mr. Bean. Plus, he had a strange bedside manner, but their talks had been beneficial. The dreams stemmed from his childhood trauma, not that that was any big surprise, but Dr. Owens had recently suggested the dreams might also be suppressed memories trying to work themselves into his waking consciousness.

If they were memories, he wanted them to come out. Although he knew what his adoptive parents looked like, he had no memories of them. According to Dr. Owens, the memories were there, but they were hidden underneath the pain.

If Matt wanted to access those memories, and he did, he had to work through the pain first. It was a task he dedicated himself to achieving.

Feeling human again, he shut off the shower and grabbed his towel. Within moments, he was dressed and ready to meet Dee and Shane for a quick breakfast. But before he left, he glanced at himself in the bathroom mirror.

Sometimes, when he concentrated really hard on his reflection, he saw a figure, just beyond his peripheral vision. It appeared as a faint shimmer more often than not. Once, he caught a glimpse of what appeared to be a full-grown man, but whether shimmer or man, it always disappeared whenever he turned his head to look.

While such a sighting would frighten most people, Matt never felt fear. Instead, he felt safe, special. And since it was his birthday, the day was all about his feeling special.

But whether it was the alcohol he consumed last night or his burning need to make haste, no shimmer and no man appeared.

"Hopefully, I'll catch you later," he told his reflection before heading out of the bedroom, out of his apartment, and onto the streets of Houston.

FIFTEEN minutes later, Matt walked into The Beanery and found Dee and Shane sitting at their usual wooden table along the front window. The two loved being on display more than they loved men, if that was possible, and with Dee's current outfit, she was bucking to be noticed.

Her pink shirt—with the words FCKH8 printed in white letters—stretched across her ample bosom, which made the words pop out like a 3-D movie. She had ordered the shirt in December and promised to wear it as soon as the weather allowed. Since today was considerably warmer than the past week or so, she made good on her promise.

When Dee saw him, she flashed her trademark grin, a full set of white teeth and a head tilt. In response, Shane turned around and waved him over.

"What's up, ladies?" He asked while taking the seat next to Shane, who was wearing a black cashmere sweater and jeans. Even though it was warm outside, Shane, as usual, was cold.

"Same old, same old," Shane replied while flipping a stray blond curl out of his eyes. "Gossip."

"Who's the subject of your derision this bright Thursday morning?"

"Karl," replied Shane with a scoff.

Karl was Shane's ex-boyfriend. Though they had dated only a month, Shane claimed to have loved Karl more than any other boyfriend, of which there were many. As was typical for Shane's romances, he fell hard fast and then was hurt when the relationship didn't survive the passion of the first weeks.

In fact, that was how he and Dee had first met Shane three years ago. They found Shane, crying into his beer at the Brazos River Bottom bar, during Shane's country-western phase. Matt initially thought the scene comical, a man sitting alone on a barstool while a cowboy crooned about his lost lover over the speakers, but Shane had looked so pathetic, Matt's amusement didn't last. Instead, he and Dee offered Shane two shoulders to cry on, and since then, they had been inseparable.

"What did Karl do now?" Matt finally asked.

"What didn't he do?" Dee asked, incredulously. In Dee's typical fashion, she came to her friend's defense whether there was reason or not. "He called Shane last night."

Matt arched his eyebrows in surprise. "Really? And what did the bastard want?" Although he didn't really think Karl was a bastard, he had to be equally as supportive of Shane's pain as Dee was. It was what they did.

"He wants his Nasty Pig T-shirt back."

"The one he gave you?" Matt asked.

"The very same," Dee answered. "Can you believe the nerve of that guy? He gave that to Shane the night they first met, and now he wants it back?"

"The audacity," Matt said in feigned repulsion. "What's he want it back for anyway?"

"Who knows?" Shane replied, throwing up his hands in overexaggerated exasperation. "He just won't rest until he rips up what's left of my heart."

"Maybe he wants it because it smells like you now," Matt offered as an alternative. "Maybe he wants you back."

Dee kicked him under the table, and he yelped in pain. He grinned wryly at her, but Shane pondered the possibility while being oblivious to their exchange. "Do you really think so?"

"I don't," Dee replied quickly while giving Matt the stink eye. "Besides, he's a jerk. You wouldn't want him back anyway."

"But I loved him so much," complained Shane.

Dee continued her argument against a Karl-and-Shane redo. Having already heard this conversation at least a dozen times, Matt sipped the latte Shane had purchased before Matt's arrival, and stared out the window of the coffee shop. Beyond the store's small parking lot, cars zoomed down Montrose and joggers ran by, most with white iPod buds nestled in their ears.

He was certain Gaga or Britney were currently on the playlist. The gays loved their exercise almost as much as they loved their divas, and Matt was no exception. When he exercised, he set his Pandora station to the divas and let them belt it out while he sweated it out.

But his love of Gaga and Britney faded to the background as his eyes took in the world outside the window, and as he typically did on such beautiful days, he got lost in Montrose.

Dubbed the gay district of Houston, Montrose wasn't the most spectacular looking gayborhood, but to him it was home. Quaint shops lined the street, and gay-friendly people populated the area. It was sometimes easy to forget that beyond the borders of Montrose life was not as idyllic.

Life was hard enough without fear and hate corrupting people's hearts. He didn't understand how love between two consenting adults could ever be wrong. Love was the great cure-all, even though he had yet to find love for himself.

As he scanned the many couples in the coffee shop, Matt's thoughts turned to his inability to settle into a long-term relationship. Most of the men he dated were jerks, perverts, or both. They wanted one-night stands, not something lasting longer than a few short sweaty hours in bed. He wasn't averse to hooking up, but he didn't do it often. It just wasn't his thing.

He wanted romance. He wanted a man to sweep him off his feet and carry him into the sunset like Richard Gere did for Debra Winger in *An Officer and a Gentleman*, his favorite romance of all time.

That's the kind of man he wanted, but he didn't seem capable of attracting the man he envisioned.

Dark-haired and dreamy. Tall and muscular. Sweet yet badass.

His standards were high. He knew that, but he was incapable of lowering them, no matter how many times Dee or Shane told him that his expectations could never be met. He just knew the perfect man was out there somewhere, just out of sight, like the shimmer man he sometimes saw in his reflection. His perfect man was simply waiting for the right moment to enter his life.

If he had to wait forever to meet him, he would.

"Fine," Shane replied to something Dee said. "I'll give him back his shirt and move on. But that means tonight, we go on the prowl."

"Agreed," Dee said with a nod of her head, at which point they both looked to Matt for his answer.

"You've got to be kidding me?" Matt asked. "We partied last night. I can't do two nights in a row. I do have to work, you know?"

"It's yo' birfday, you silly cracker. We's gots to par-tay!"

"Oh Lord" was Matt's only response.

"You didn't think a quick breakfast would suffice, did you?" Shane asked.

"Although I wouldn't call a free latte breakfast, I was kinda hoping this would be the extent of the celebration after last night."

"Well, you hoped wrong, my friend," Shane replied before giving him a peck on the cheek. "Tonight, we celebrate your actual birthday and my official re-entrance to the party scene!"

"I wasn't aware you exited the party scene."

"Don't be hating," Dee wisecracked.

"Fine," he replied while looking at his watch. "I'll meet you after my shift, but I've got to go or I'm going to be late."

"Okay, honey," replied Shane. "We'll see you tonight. And dress to be molested."

"Naturally," he commented while crossing over and kissing Dee.

Dee said good-bye, and Matt exited The Beanery heading for his car parked on the side of the building. If he didn't haul buns, he was going to be late.

MATT parked his car in the garage across from Dr. Owens's office complex and surveyed the sky. During his drive down Montrose, the blue grew increasingly darker. He smirked at the thought of every meteorologist in town scratching their heads in confusion at the obvious storm front moving across the city. They might have forecasted no rain today, but God had other plans.

Thunderheads gathered in the enormous mountain ranges overhead, blotting the morning sun from the sky. Their sudden appearance threatened more than rain. Their massive proportions and dark, menacing crowns promised to unleash a veritable hell storm.

Lightning flashed brightly and was followed by an explosion of thunder that caused the windshields of the surrounding cars in the garage to vibrate. Then, the heavens opened up and released the contents of a small lake all at once.

Water fell in huge sheets that appeared more solid than liquid and almost immediately pooled about the road and sidewalk. The wind whipped up into a steady breeze before blowing with the fury of a small tornado. Trash and other small, unsecured items became airborne and disappeared into the storm.

"Great," Matt whispered to himself. "And me with no umbrella."

He stared at his watch. He had fifteen minutes till he was officially late for his appointment, and while he contemplated waiting out the storm in the garage, he doubted the storm would let up any time soon.

"Looks like I'm getting wet," he announced and then dashed into the rain.

His clothes were immediately soaked within the first few steps. By the time he was halfway across the street, he was sopping wet. Dr. Owens usually kept his office colder than was necessary, so he anticipated an hour of teeth chattering and shivering.

What he didn't foresee was the slick condition of the road. Before he could prevent it, Matt's feet lost traction and he fell backward; his ass and then his head struck the pavement hard.

DARREN STANLEY sat in his black Ford F-150, watching his target. He followed him from The Beanery on Montrose to a parking garage on Kirby. He didn't look like anything special, but he had orders to follow. If he didn't, well, the alternative proved unthinkable. As far as he was concerned, there was no other option.

It was either this man or Darren's son, and he would do anything for his son. Even this.

The man he observed looked to be in his late twenties and no more than 150 pounds soaking wet. His slight frame told Darren he would have little trouble doing what needed to be done. Darren went to the gym six days a week and had the body to show for it. It would be a simple task, and it would mean the difference between life and death for his boy, who was losing his battle with leukemia.

The man stared tentatively at the sky, which suddenly began to pour buckets. Darren hoped the guy would head back to his car to grab his umbrella, where he could easily knock him out and then take him somewhere else, somewhere private.

Instead, his target darted into the street. It looked like Darren would have to wait for another opportunity. But then his target slipped and fell.

Dazed, he lay in the middle of the road and didn't move.

This was what Darren had waited for. He couldn't be blamed for running over someone lying down in the middle of the street.

Darren started his truck and gunned it, aiming his vehicle straight at the prone figure. In a few minutes, the deed would be done, and his boy would live to be an old man.

THE minute his head hit the street, Matt's breath left his body and stars suddenly rocketed into his field of vision. The world spun around and made him dizzy.

Rain continued to fall around him, splashing his face and getting in his mouth and nose. Each splatter of rain felt more like a slap across the face. Never before had rainfall hurt so much. It reminded him of what he sometimes did to unresponsive patients at the hospital. Gentle smacks to rouse the patient to consciousness.

The sudden sound of a car peeling toward him grabbed his attention. Even though it hurt to move, he turned his head to the left and watched as a black truck barreled down the road toward him.

He needed to get to his feet and get out of the way, but when Matt sat up, the world spun around even faster and he almost lost consciousness. He had a concussion and that meant he was going nowhere without someone to help him up.

Now only a few feet away, the truck continued toward him. Matt knew this was it. His number was up, and it was time for him to meet his maker. He just hoped his death wouldn't break his grandmother's heart. She had suffered enough loss in her life already.

Matt braced himself for the impact, but instead of metal slamming into him and tires crushing his bones, a blur of movement darted toward him through the rain. Someone he couldn't see through his hazy vision lifted him off the pavement, before sidestepping the oncoming vehicle.

A flash of something bright flew from the stranger's hands and hit the rear tires of the truck. In response, the vehicle skidded and lost control. It spun to the left before lurching forward and careening into the intersection, where an eighteen-wheeler T-boned the truck. The resulting impact caused the truck to split in half with a deafening crunch of metal.

"Good God!" Matt exclaimed as his vision cleared enough to see drivers exiting their cars in an attempt to rescue the man in the truck. It wasn't until his feet once again touched the ground that he realized he had still been safely cradled in his savior's arms.

Matt looked up at the man who saved him. When he saw him for the first time, his breath left him for the second time that day.

The man was stunning. His eyes looked like chipped fragments from the heavens. The radiant blue filled Matt full of awe and made him want to soar like a bird on the uplifting currents emanating from the man's stare. Rivulets of rain fell from his jet-black, short-cropped hair, which matched the stubble that spread across his face. It made him look brooding, serious, and intimidating.

Matt, however, wasn't fooled. Hidden behind the strong, chiseled face, that most would find unapproachable, he sensed only kindness and compassion. A rough exterior existed, no doubt. His chest was expansive, framed by massive shoulders and muscular arms. Packaged inside a black leather jacket and dark blue denim, he looked tougher than diamond, but Matt instinctively knew he had nothing to fear from this man.

He had risked his life to save him, and Matt knew he would do it again, if necessary.

"How's your head?" the man asked. His voice sounded like a symphony.

"It hurts," he replied. Although he forgot the pain for a few moments, the throbbing returned with a vengeance. "Good thing I'm a nurse. I know what to do."

"I have no doubt." The man reached up and placed his sizeable hands on each side of Matt's head. After a few moments, the pain ebbed to a dull ache before disappearing all together.

"The pain's gone. What did you do?"

"I did nothing," his savior said before turning to leave as the heavens abruptly shut off the rainstorm.

"Wait a minute. Come back here."

But before Matt could chase after him, a voice behind him spoke.

"Excuse me, sir, but are you okay?"

Matt turned to face a police officer. "I'm fine," he told the officer. "But I have to go."

"I'm afraid I can't allow that. You need to answer some questions. And see a paramedic." The officer glanced back across the street, where the man's partner dealt with the accident.

"Listen, Officer Belton," he said, reading the name on his tag. "I have to go find the man who saved me and thank him."

Officer Belton's eyes narrowed in concern. "The man who saved you?"

Matt nodded in reply and turned around only to find his savior had disappeared as suddenly as the rain.

"There wasn't anyone else here, sir. I was in my patrol car across the street. I saw you fall down and the truck headed toward you. I tried to make it here as fast as I could, but you jumped out of the way at the last second. There was nobody else."

Matt turned back to face Officer Belton. "That's absurd. I know what I saw."

"And I know what *I* saw," he told Matt. "And I'm not the one who hit my head."

The serious look on Officer Belton's face told Matt that the policeman believed he was telling the truth. The problem was that Matt knew it wasn't.

How was it possible for him to be saved by a man no one else could see?

CHAPTER 3

AFTER a thorough evaluation by the paramedics who agreed that he didn't need to go to the hospital, Matt contacted Dr. Owens. Luckily, the doctor had no appointments scheduled after his and agreed to push Matt's appointment back an hour in order to give Matt time to recover, answer police questions, and get into dry clothing.

Now, he sat in the reception area in fresh apparel and waiting for Dr. Owens to return from lunch. Once he did, they would likely begin with his near-death experience instead of his dreams.

He knew he should be as freaked out as everyone else was by the accident, but he wasn't. He felt sorry for the man driving the truck, who had been pronounced dead on the scene. But Matt was fine. It was an accident. Nothing more. He certainly didn't need the constant texts from Dee and Shane checking on him or the worry he heard in his grandmother's voice when he spoke to her shortly after it all happened.

It had been no big deal.

It's true the timing of this could have been better. His birthday, like Friday the thirteenth, had enough tragedy associated with it. The day didn't need any more. That was why he hated when people made a fuss about January 17.

Whenever the first of the year rolled around, Dee and Shane plied him with alcohol a few days before his birthday and for a couple of days afterward. His grandmother took him for long weekends to Austin or created elaborate homemade dinners at her place. His friends and his grandmother were the people who loved him the most, and they worked in concert to keep him from thinking about his tenth birthday.

Nothing could do that, however.

He appreciated their efforts, and he loved them for it, but what had happened that day hung about him like an invisible weight. Distractions couldn't lift that two-ton pachyderm from his neck.

At the moment, though, neither the accident nor his tenth birthday dominated his thoughts. His mind toiled over the man who had rescued him.

He had appeared out of thin air to save Matt from becoming roadkill and then disappeared just as mysteriously as he had arrived. Though their contact had been brief, a sense of familiarity had resonated between them. He felt as if he had somehow known his savior his entire life. Being in his arms had felt like being home, which was something Matt wasn't accustomed to feeling.

For him, home ceased to exist the day he turned ten.

The fact that Officer Belton hadn't seen his six-foot-five-inch knight in shining black leather boggled his already jumbled mind.

"Matt, I'm ready for you."

He looked up from his place on the taupe leather couch in the waiting room and saw Dr. Owens, looking like Mr. Bean's identical twin, smiling at him from the open office door. The doctor's eyes were wide with concern, and his bushy eyebrows arched well into his forehead, which was a typical Mr. Bean facial expression.

"Are you hurt?" he asked while rubbing the five o'clock shadow already visible on his cheeks and chin. As a testament to cosmic irony, Dr. Owens's hair growth didn't extend to the top of his head.

"Not a scratch," Matt replied while crossing into the office and settling into his usual chair. The cool plaid fabric stretched across the overstuffed chair instantly put him at ease. Sitting in the chair was like resting on a cloud.

"What a miracle!" Dr. Owens replied as he proceeded to the leather-backed office chair that sat behind his cherry wood desk.

"If that's what you want to call almost being run over."

"I'd call that a horrible misfortune. *Not* being hurt is the miracle." Dr. Owens studied him for a few seconds. His previously wide-eyed expression of amazement quickly turned to a squinty glare of inquisitiveness.

At only about a squeak above five feet, Dr. Owens lacked physical intimidation, but his penetrating eyes scared the fool out of Matt. The man had the ability to peel back the layers of Matt's soul and discover problems Matt avoided or overlooked. His keen psychiatric perception caught a hint of distress. "So, tell me. How are you?"

"I'm good."

"Really? You've been through quite an ordeal today. It would bother most anyone."

"I'm not most anyone, considering what I've already been through," he reminded Dr. Owens.

Dr. Owens nodded. "And the day's significance hasn't occurred to you?"

"Of course it has. It's my birthday, a day that continues to live in infamy."

"How do you feel about that?"

"Besides the fact that it sucks to have awful things happen on the day I was born, I'm just dandy."

"We've talked about avoidance," Dr. Owens scolded. "It's counterproductive. I thought you wanted to work through the trauma of your childhood? To reach the memories of your parents that have been buried along with the pain?"

"Of course, I do."

"Then let's get to the heart of the matter, shall we?"

Matt nodded.

"Did you have the dream again?"

He hated talking about the dream. It scared the living crap out of him. Unable to say the word, he simply nodded yes.

"Tell me about it."

"It's the same every time. Why do I have to relive it each week?"

"Because every time you talk about it, you remember more. The first time you told me about the dream, there was just the door. A few weeks later, you remembered the room. The time after that..."

"I remembered the date," he finished.

"Yes," Dr. Owens replied. "Your birthday. That's when we realized the source of your dream was the night your parents were murdered. And that the dream..."

"Was most likely a memory."

"Correct." Dr. Owens laced his fingers together and sat back in his chair. He stared at Matt in silence, something he often did when he was through talking and waiting for Matt to fill the silence with words.

Matt sighed and closed his eyes. It was easier for him to remember the dream that way. The simple act of shutting out the here and now somehow made the dream, or the memory, more vivid. It cleared the cobwebs of denial from his eyes and blew away the fog of time.

Unlike most dreams that faded after waking, this one sprung to life in the darkness behind his eyelids. Instead of disconnected images and surreal backdrops, the visions crystallized, becoming as real as images playing across a television screen.

"There's the door," he told Dr. Owens. "It's right in front of me. Something's on the other side."

"Something?" Dr. Owens asked.

"Yes, some*thing*. I can hear it breathing. I wonder if it can hear me breathing. So I try to hold my breath. But my lungs hurt. They burn so badly. I want to take a breath, but I know as soon as I do, he will hear me. He will come for me too. But I have to breathe, so I inhale and whatever's on the other side stops. I put my hand on the doorknob. I want to lock it, but I can't. There's no lock. The doorknob starts moving, and I feel the door open. I push back, hard. And the thing on the other side pushes back even harder. I'm screaming. I'm throwing all my weight into the door, but the door keeps moving. It opens a little and then closes. It opens wider but then closes again. It's playing with me. It knows it can get in. I scream for my parents. I scream so loud my throat hurts. And I start coughing. The door opens wider and I try to close it. I see only darkness around the door's crack, but I know something's there. It's coming for me. It's getting closer. I fight against the opening door, and the door starts to shake. It's vibrating like in an earthquake, but it's only the door that's moving. Nothing else. The door opens wider. The shaking gets stronger. I'm having trouble holding on. But something's happening… something different."

"What is it?"

"The door… it's breaking apart. Like paper. Huge holes are opening up in the door. It's disintegrating. Where the holes form, there looks like fire and smoke. But it's not. It's something red like fire but not fire. The smoke is different. Like thicker. Almost like a volcano venting underwater. There's more holes than door now, but I'm still holding onto the doorknob. Now, the door's gone and…"

Matt opened his eyes and sat bolt upright. His body, drenched in sweat, shivered uncontrollably. He rubbed his arms to try and warm himself, but the cold coursed through his veins like an ice flow.

"What did you see?"

"I don't remember," Matt replied. "I just remember the door falling completely away until I was only holding the doorknob, and there was only a black void in front of me. But inside the blackness, there was something… bad waiting for me."

Dr. Owens nodded and then wrote in his legal pad. Matt hated when he did that. The scratching of his ballpoint against paper made him feel insane, as if the words he spoke were being documented and would be used against him later.

"What is it?" he asked, annoyed. "Did I say something different this time?"

"Yes," Dr. Owens replied. "*Two* things this time."

"What were they?"

"We'll discuss the second difference first." He got up and sat in the chair next to him. This was a typical Dr. Owens move whenever progress had been made. For some reason, he closed the physical distance between them to symbolize the ground Matt had covered. "This time, the door disappeared."

"Disintegrated," he corrected.

"Correct, disintegrated," he paused before continuing. "It fell apart in your hands while you were trying to keep it shut."

"What does that mean?"

"I think it means the door to your past is finally swinging open. Enough for you to pierce the darkness of repression that waits on the other side." He sat back in the chair, obviously pleased.

Matt wished he shared Dr. Owens's enthusiasm. The door falling apart in his hands didn't exactly inspire him with confidence and neither did the feeling of something menacing waiting for him on the other side. It terrified him. What if whatever existed on the other side *shouldn't* be remembered? What if he was opening a door better left shut tight?

"You don't seem pleased by this," Dr. Owens said, stating the obvious.

"I'm not."

"Why not? It's a breakthrough."

"Whatever's on the other side scares the hell out of me, Dr. Owens. I don't know if I want to remember it."

Dr. Owens nodded in understanding. "And you don't have to. If that's truly what you want. You've lived with that door closed for almost twenty years. I'd imagine you could go your whole life *without* remembering it."

"But then I wouldn't remember my parents."

"True," he said, shifting his position in the seat. He stared off in the distance before starting again. "You'll have to decide which of the two you can live with. Keeping the door closed and not accessing the memories of your parents or opening the door, dealing with whatever pain exists on the other side, and retrieving the memories that are rightfully yours."

Matt let out a long exhalation. The prospect of discovering what lay on the other side of the door in his dreams petrified him more than words could express. However, the thought of continuing to live without the memories of his parents frightened him even more.

Every time he visited his grandmother or looked at the photographs in his albums at home, he felt like he was staring at strangers. He knew they were his parents, and he felt an emotion akin to love. But the sentiment was dulled, hidden within the anesthetizing numbness of pain.

He owed it to his parents to remember them. The stories his grandmother told him proved they were loving people, who took him in when no one else would. They gave him love and security, but more importantly, they gave him a family.

As far as Matt was concerned, there was no other choice.

"I'm willing to open the door," he finally told Dr. Owens, who smiled broadly. He was obviously expecting that answer. "Now that that's settled, what else did I say?"

"Well, instead of saying someone was outside the door, you said some*thing*, and you were very positive about that."

Matt thought about it. He recalled saying something not someone. And he remembered that feeling right. He had no idea what that meant though. "Why would I say that? If this is the memory of the night my parents were killed, I already know that it was a *who* on the other side of my door, not a *what*."

"You're referring to Clifford Crouch?"

The mention of the man's name made Matt instantly angry. Of course, he meant Clifford Crouch. What other man was arrested and convicted for killing his parents? There was no other *who* he could be referring to.

"I didn't mean to upset you," Dr. Owens said as he sat forward. His eyes were soft and warm. "I know how much you dislike hearing the man's name, but I wanted to be absolutely clear to whom we were referring."

"It's fine," Matt replied through gritted teeth. He took a deep breath to calm his anger. Once a semblance of composure returned, he asked, "So if I already know who it was on the other side of the door, why did I say some*thing*?"

"I believe in your dream, you've made that man a monster, demonized him if you will. That's why you sense something malevolent on the other side. He's responsible for so much pain in your life that it's easy to conceive why the childlike part of your personality has done this. It makes the experience less real. More fantasy."

"There's nothing about my parents' deaths that I would consider a fantasy."

"Of course not. I'm not saying fantasy like a dream vacation. I refer to fantasy as something that's easier to dismiss, to compartmentalize. This would explain why you have difficulty recovering memories of your parents. They became wrapped in that fantasy. And to access the memories of your parents makes the fantasy too much of a reality for your conscious mind."

Strangely enough, the psychobabble made sense to him. Clifford Crouch was the monster who murdered his parents, and it was he who was outside his bedroom door. Clifford wanted to kill him too, according to the news reports that documented the trial, but he couldn't get the door to his bedroom open. By some act of God, the door had stuck. If Clifford had been able to get inside, Matt would have suffered the same bloody fate as his parents.

That was why Matt was still apprehensive about opening the door in his dream. The closed door had saved his life once.

Would opening it now somehow change that and allow the evil in his past to flood into his present?

CLIFFORD CROUCH hated prison, especially during the day. At night, relative quiet descended upon the cellblock. Sure, some loony fuckers howled all night; some moaned and grunted while they fucked, but at night, all you had to worry about was your cellmate.

If you had a bad one, all twenty-fucking-four hours of prison were a living hell. But Kenny, his cellmate for the last three years, proved to be all right. Sure, he was in for murder. Kenny killed his girlfriend and the guy she had been whoring around with, but who was Clifford to judge?

He was serving life for murdering two rich white folks, even though he didn't remember doing it. He vaguely remembered voices telling him what to do, and then his doing as told. But it never felt like he was doing it. Whenever he did something bad, it always felt like someone else was in the driver's seat.

He told his court appointed attorney that. That admission, along with what he told the arresting officers, was supposed to get him into a mental health facility. Not jail.

But, of course, that didn't happen for poor black men who murdered rich pillars of the community. All that mattered to the attorneys and the judge was payback, so almost twenty years ago they convicted him and sent him down the river, where he served out his life sentence instead of getting the death penalty. The sentence was the prosecuting attorney's concession for Clifford's fuzzy recollection of the murders. As if that somehow made up for being fucked over by the system.

Since then, he settled into the routine of prison, trying to avoid getting shanked or becoming someone's bitch. Not many people messed with him, considering the crazy circumstances of his conviction. On the outside, what he did made him a pariah. In here, it earned respect, and he used it to his advantage.

He even shared that respect with those worthy of it. Like Kenny.

Kenny was just some dumbass kid who made a big mistake, and if it weren't for him, Kenny would be dead by now. But he made it known that Kenny was his friend, and messing with Kenny meant fucking with the "Devil Dude," as they called him.

They left Kenny alone.

Even though Clifford was relatively safe and had a few close convict buddies, he still hated prison during the day. It wasn't the routine or the constant threat of danger from cocky assholes trying to prove their shit didn't stink.

It was seeing the sun beyond the bars. Outside the walls, life went on without him, and the world couldn't care less. His fiancée dumped him. His parents didn't visit. And the friends he had on the outside all disappeared after the first few months in here.

Seeing the sunlight peek through the bars reminded him how alone he was and how abandoned he felt by those who were supposed to always be there. While he was rotting away in prison, his fiancée Wendy had no doubt married and spit out a bunch of kids. His parents were likely retired, living the high life on some cruise, if they weren't rotting corpses by now. And his friends, the guys he thought of as brothers, probably all moved to the suburbs, had good jobs, and hot wives with even hotter snatches.

All he had was his reputation. And Kenny.

Daytime in prison didn't bother Kenny. Right now, he was out in the yard playing basketball and showing off, something Kenny enjoyed doing. If he didn't hate the outside world so much, Clifford might be out there, but he did, so he wasn't.

It was better to stay in the relative quiet of his cell during the few hours off detail or routine. It left him alone with his thoughts, which didn't bother him as much as it once did. The voices disappeared from the moment he entered the walls of the Texas State Penitentiary in Huntsville.

So far, that was the *only* good thing to come out of prison.

CHAPTER 4

MATT didn't have time to think about his appointment with Dr. Owens. By the time he got to work, the place was a zoo. The emergency room of Ben Taub Hospital was packed. Apparently some street war had erupted, causing mass casualties to flood the area hospitals, and since Ben Taub was county run, most of the injuries were routed to them.

Matt no longer worked in the E.R. as a trauma nurse, having transferred to intensive care three years ago, but he predicted many of the victims would wind up on his floor.

Experience proved him right, when Arnold De Hoyos became his second patient for the evening. Arnold was admitted with a gunshot wound to the chest, which collapsed his lung. The emergency room doctors fitted him with a chest tube to re-inflate the lung and then transferred him upstairs to be monitored.

Although Arnold needed close observation, as vital signs for a patient with a collapsed lung could sometimes be touch-and-go, the assignment was run-of-the-mill for the Trauma Intensive Care Unit.

Run-of-the-mill or not, Matt insisted his patient care remain stellar and personable. It was what he was known for and why many on the unit called him Flo. They meant the reference to Florence Nightingale as a joke, but Matt took it as a personal compliment. Being Flo meant he had fulfilled what he had set out to do by becoming a nurse.

He went to nursing school because he wanted to help patients in a way that was different from the care received from doctors. Physicians tended to be cold and logical in their diagnoses and treatment. He felt it was the job of the nurse to add humanity to medicine, something Florence Nightingale did and something he prided himself on emulating.

But becoming a nurse also accomplished another important goal for Matt: it allowed him a certain amount of control. Sometimes, Matt felt as if he were a passenger in his own life, navigating a charted path that continually led him through turbulent waters, where things happened *to* him. At work, though, the ship was his to command, and the path was his to set.

Here, he was the captain. He was Flo.

And so far, Matt had accomplished a lot on his voyage of healing. The majority of his patients seemed to recover, no matter the illness or wound. From severe coronary problems to brain stem injuries, his patients typically left his care on a positive path toward recovery.

Some of the other nurses thought he had a magical touch, but Matt didn't think so. He was just in tune to what his patients needed; he instinctively saw the ailment or virus when others couldn't see it or when diagnostic tests proved inconclusive. It was almost like a sixth sense. He wasn't some miracle worker who healed the dying, he knew that much. He was only a man who happened to love healing those who needed it, and right now, he had a patient who required his attention.

"How's my patient?" Matt asked upon entering Arnold's room for the third time in the past thirty minutes.

"I've got a tube sticking out of my fucking chest," Arnold complained. "How the fuck do you think I'm doing?"

After a quick check of the monitors, he replied, "Well considering you aren't dead, I'd say you're doing fantastic."

Arnold mumbled further curse words under his breath to which Matt didn't reply. He understood that his patient's machismo was currently in the driver's seat. Though he was only seventeen, he possessed the gruff attitude of a jaded adult. Matt didn't hold that against him.

Life in a gang and in Arnold's part of Houston was rough. Based on his admission records and what the police officer shared with Matt, Arnold had no parents and was responsible for the care of his younger siblings. He had dropped out of school and turned to a life of crime to support his family.

He wasn't a bad kid. He was a kid having to cope with a bad life, and he was doing the best he could with what he had. He didn't ask for the lot he received in life, but he hadn't abandoned his family. Matt respected that.

After all, he knew from personal experience that sometimes life crapped all over you.

"Is there anyone you'd like me to call for you?"

"What the fuck for?" Arnold asked, the anger in his tone razor-sharp.

"Most patients enjoy having someone at their bedside. I'd be happy to contact whoever you want."

"I don't got nobody," he replied. "Except my brother and sisters."

"Is someone watching them?"

"What the fuck do you care?" Arnold asked, sneering at him. "You work for social services too or something?"

"Nope," Matt replied, trying his best to sound like a friend and not the enemy his patient obviously perceived him to be. "But if they need someone to watch them, I'd gladly call someone to help you out. A neighbor, perhaps? Or one of your friends?"

"Don't do me no favors, man. I can take care of my own, you hear?"

"I'm not implying you can't. I just wanted to help you out if you needed it."

"Yeah, well, stay out of my business, *cabron*," Arnold warned while calling him a bastard. "My life is none of your concern."

"But it is," he replied while pulling up a chair and sitting down. Matt hoped a more casual, friendly posture such as sitting eye-level would ease the tension. "You're my patient. It's my job to make sure you live, so your life *is* my business, don't you think?"

"Your job is to stay the fuck out of my business. You can check my blood pressure or whatever else you fucking *maricón* male nurses do, but that's it. I don't want you sniffing around trying to recruit me to be a buttfucker."

Matt now understood where some of Arnold's hostility toward him came from. Arnold suspected he was gay and hated him for it. That wasn't the first time that had happened to Matt, and he doubted it would be the last.

"So your problem with me is that you think I'm gay?"

"Well, yeah. Aren't you?"

"Guilty as charged."

"Fucking faggot," the young man mumbled and averted his eyes in disgust.

"Listen, Arnold…"

"Lolo. No one calls me Arnold. Not even a cocksucker like you."

The animosity Arnold, no, Lolo felt was palpable. There was no way he could do his job if Lolo didn't trust him enough to care for him. Matt had to find some common ground between them. For reasons he couldn't explain, the pure contempt Lolo held for him was preventing Matt from doing his job, and there was something there, something Matt could sense but not see that needed to be brought to light before it was too late. "Okay, Lolo," Matt began, hoping to bridge the gap between them. "To me, it makes as much sense for you to hate me for being gay as it does for your rival gang to hate you for being Latino."

"Latino?" he said in disgust. "*Soy mexicano!*"

Lolo's exclamation that he was Mexican, not Latino, caught Matt off guard. "What does that mean?"

"Latino is what you polite prissy bitches call us, so you don't hurt our feelings. You think saying someone is Mexican is an insult. Well fuck that! Being Mexican is who I am. It's who my parents were."

Inwardly, Matt sighed in frustration. He was getting nowhere fast, and he somehow knew time was running out. After a few moments, he said, "I didn't mean to insult you, and I apologize for that."

Lolo rolled his eyes in response.

"I'm Mexican too," he offered, hoping to have found some common ground in their shared culture. "At least I think so, so I'm not one of *them*. That makes me one of you."

"You *think* you're Mexican? What the fuck does that mean?"

"Well, I'm adopted, so…."

"Adopted by white people?" Lolo interrupted.

Matt nodded, already knowing what direction Lolo planned on taking this conversation.

"Then that doesn't make you one of us. That makes you a coconut. Brown on the outside but white on the inside. I'm brown inside *and* out."

"Being raised by white parents doesn't change who I am. It doesn't make me any less *mexicano* than you."

"It makes you *less* than me," he told Matt. "That's what *I* think."

So much for common ground, Matt thought, but he wasn't done yet. He never gave up that easily. After a few moments of silence, he thought perhaps he might have found the angle he needed to make some headway. "Does not having a father and a mother make you and your brother and sisters less of a family?"

The man tensed, ready to fly from the bed and attack him. Matt didn't flinch. Though Lolo put up a good front, Matt still saw the hurt young boy on the inside.

"It doesn't," Matt answered for Lolo. "No matter what anyone else thinks." Lolo's body relaxed, and Matt noticed his blood pressure spike a bit before returning to normal. He needed to keep Lolo calm. Riling him up wasn't good. He didn't know how he knew that, but he did. "All I'm saying is that what you or anyone else thinks about me being gay or raised by white parents doesn't make me anything less than what I am."

Lolo snickered. "You've got this lily-white version of the world because you've never lived the life I did. You've never suffered what I've suffered."

At last, Matt found the common ground he needed. The one thing he understood all too well was suffering.

"That's not true. I've suffered."

Lolo's narrowed eyes told Matt his patient remained unconvinced, but the young man was at least looking at him now. Matt had gotten his attention. That was a start.

"My parents, the ones you dislike for being white, raised me when no one else would. They were also murdered in our house when I was ten. I was almost killed that night too." The rigidity in Lolo's face lessened a bit, and in his face, Matt detected sympathy, as if his patient had suffered something very similar in his troubled past.

Lolo only grunted in reply, but this time it was different. Some barrier had fallen, and with the first walls down, Matt sensed there was something *very* wrong with Lolo, something that had been missed in the emergency room. But the continued animosity prevented Matt from figuring out what that was.

Matt rose from the chair and scanned the monitors. Based on what he saw, everything looked normal, but he knew better.

"I know you're rich. I can smell it on you," Lolo sniffed while Matt checked his vital signs once again.

"Does that matter?" Matt asked, still trying to locate the source of his distress for Lolo's health. "Would money really make all your problems go away?"

"It would be a start."

Matt shook his head in disagreement while staring at the EKG. He somehow knew that the problem would reveal itself there. "Having some money hasn't brought my parents back to life or returned the memories I've lost about the people they were."

"Are you trying to make me feel sorry for you?" Lolo asked. He crossed his arms and glared at Matt. "Because it's not working."

"I don't want you to feel sorry for me," Matt looked away from the machine for a moment to stare into Lolo's eyes. He wanted the young man to feel the sincerity of what he said, not just in his words but also in the soul that brought them to bear. "I want you to see that money isn't the answer. The love for your brother and sisters is the key."

"What the fuck are you talking about?"

"I can tell how much you love them, and they need you, Lolo. Without you, what will happen to them? What happens to them if you're killed during the next shoot out? Where are they going to go? Will they be separated in foster care? Have you thought about that?"

From his faraway look, Matt could tell he hadn't. For the first time in his life, Lolo seriously contemplated the life he currently led and how that could seriously affect his siblings if it went bad. He had been masquerading as the man in his family before this point, doing whatever needed to be done even if it was illegal. Now that he thought about his actions, his face changed from a boy trying to be a man to someone who might no longer be trying.

Then, another change fell across him.

When Lolo tried to speak, his mouth went slack and his eyes turned dreamy. Matt crossed over to him and felt for his pulse. It was thready. Lolo's head fell back against his pillow, and his neck appeared to swell.

Matt already knew the problem before looking at the EKG. Lolo was suffering a cardiac tamponade.

A glance at the EKG confirmed Matt's diagnosis. Lolo's heart rate turned rapid, and as he watched the machine, its waveforms became smaller indicating a cardiac tamponade.

Lolo was in grave danger. A cardiac tamponade meant fluid was collecting in the pericardium, which was the sac surrounding the heart. Most likely, a stray bullet from the gunshot wound nicked the pericardium, causing blood to slowly fill the small gap between the heart and the pericardium. Since a cardiac tamponade was rare, it was easy to miss. But if the fluid wasn't removed immediately, it would constrict the heart and prevent it from beating.

Matt hit the code button that would immediately alert everyone on his floor that his patient was near death and needed assistance. Though doctors would soon arrive along with the crash cart, he couldn't wait any longer.

If he did, Lolo would die.

Fortunately, Matt knew what had to be done.

He sprinted into the hall, where an emergency cart sat outside every other room. He returned with a large bore needle and inserted it at the point of the sternum and into the pericardium. When he pulled back on the plunger, it immediately filled with blood.

Loud voices suddenly filled the room as two other nurses and a doctor ran in with a crash cart.

"Patient suffered from a pericardium tamponade," he reported while pulling out the needle. With the excess blood removed, Lolo's vital signs returned to normal, and he began to regain consciousness.

Dr. Phillips studied the EKG before examining the patient. "Good call, nurse. You just saved this man's life."

Matt watched Lolo's eyes settle on his in what seemed to be gratitude. "It's my job," he said.

"Sheila," Dr. Phillips told the nurse next to him. "We need to take the patient to surgery for a pericardial window to relieve the pressure on the heart. Call Dr. Mehan and have him meet us in surgery."

She nodded her understanding and quickly left to complete her task.

"You owe Flo your life, Mr. De Hoyos," Dr. Phillips told Lolo.

"Flo?"

"That's what we call Matt. He's a regular Florence Nightingale."

"Thanks, man," Lolo finally said with his chin up in a reverse head nod before two orderlies came in to cart him to surgery.

"I'd say any time, but I don't want to see you back here again. And neither do your brother or sisters."

Lolo nodded once in reply before being wheeled away.

CLIFFORD stared into the darkness of his cell. He couldn't fall asleep. Usually, he blamed it on Kenny's loud ass snoring in the bunk above, but tonight Kenny's sleep was peaceful. For once.

In fact, an unusual quiet settled on the entire cellblock. No crazies howled at the moon or snickered beneath their breath. Not even the sound of an ass being brutally fucked pierced the stillness.

A dead calm settled over everyone and everything. It made him edgy.

Like everything else in prison, the night had a set routine. Guards scuffled up and down the cellblock, shining their flashlights in everyone's cells. They ordered guys who were fucking their bitches to get into separate bunks. While they patrolled, the guards talked about their wives or the girlfriends they banged. They chatted about sports and about how much they hated their jobs. Their conversations provided a running commentary of life outside the walls that kept him confined.

While no one admitted it, the prisoners looked forward to those nighttime conversations. They learned how their favorite sport's teams faired, what new movies were playing, or jacked off to the guards' reenactment of their latest sexual conquest.

Tonight, no guards patrolled, and no conversations wafted through the cells. They were just as quiet as the prisoners.

Clifford knew something was up. He didn't know what it was, but he could feel it looming in the darkness. It crowded the space usually filled with the nighttime rhythm of prison, and it pushed everything else aside until silence was all that remained.

"Clifford."

The sudden sound of his name being uttered startled him. Even though the word was spoken in a soft whisper, the surrounding quiet amplified the word like a bullhorn.

He sat up quickly and looked around. No one stood outside his cell.

"Clifford," the voice whispered. This time, the voice came from inside his cell.

"Kenny?" He asked, looking up at the mattress above his head. In response, Kenny mumbled and farted.

"Over here, Clifford," the voice murmured again.

Clifford looked toward the corner of the cell, where the toilet sat underneath the sink.

"Yes, Clifford. Over here."

Even though he didn't want to, he swung his legs out of bed. The cold pavement quickly bit into his bare feet, and his toes wiggled in protest. His body switched to autopilot, and he crossed the few feet to the toilet and stared into the bowl.

"It's you, isn't it?" he asked, staring into the small pool of water within.

Though he hadn't flushed or touched the commode, the water swirled once to the left and then twice to the right. "Have you missed me?"

"No."

"But we've been good friends for so many years." The voice attempted to sound hurt. Clifford only heard mocking.

"If we're such good friends, where have you been all these years?"

"Busy. Planning."

"Planning what?"

"Your escape."

The words shocked Clifford. He didn't know whether to believe what he heard or not. Over the years, the voice had promised him many things. Some it even delivered. When he needed money, he got it. If someone crossed him, he got revenge. And all the voice ever asked in return was the one thing that landed him in prison.

He wondered what freedom cost.

"Don't you want to get out of this place? To live your life in the sun again and do whatever you please?"

"What do you want?" Clifford asked. The price would likely be high, but if it meant his freedom, he might be willing to pay anything.

"Reach into the water."

"You've gotta be fucking kidding me?"

"Reach into the water and you'll find the key."

The toilet water splashed three times before turning still.

Clifford had no intention of sticking his hand in the crapper, but he bent forward anyway. As usual, whenever the voice spoke, he felt compelled to obey. His will and his body stopped answering to him and only followed the commands of the voice.

His fingers tentatively pierced the skin of the cool water. He half expected some hand to reach up and grab him. When nothing happened, he let his hand sink beneath the water until it rested against the cold metal at the bottom.

"Deeper," the voice returned.

"I can't go no fucking deeper," he replied.

"Deeper," it commanded before falling silent again.

Clifford balled his hand into a fist and jammed it against the metal, twice. On the third attempt, the metal gave way and his hand somehow pushed past the material. He reached so far into the toilet, he had to get on his knees to reach his arm all the way inside.

Then, something cold and hard pressed into his hands. He wrapped his fingers around it and withdrew his arm from the water.

When he stood up, he held a shank.

"What the fuck kind of key is this?"

"It's the way out."

"And what kind of damn door do I use this on?"

"On Kenny," the voice replied coolly.

"Kenny? What the fuck's Kenny gotta do with this?"

"He's your way out. Use it on Kenny and you'll see."

"Kenny's my friend," he told the voice. He sounded pouty like a child, but he didn't care. In the past three years, he had grown to care about Kenny, and he had no intention of harming him.

"You have the key. The choice is yours. Use it and be free. Don't and die in here."

The toilet water splashed one final time before moving no more. And then, as if someone flipped on a switch, the nighttime noise of prison returned.

Guards laughed in the distance. Someone hooted in a cell to his right while someone else moaned as he dumped his load in his prison bitch. His world returned to normal. The only abnormality was the shank in his hand, and the decision that weighed heavily on his heart.

CHAPTER 5

IN THE unseasonably temperate night, warm pockets of wind sent fallen leaves scurrying down the street and chasing after each other like children at play. The brown vegetation and bare trees proved to be the only lingering reminder of January. The chillier weather of winter had vanished almost twenty-four hours ago, when warmer weather claimed dominion.

The people of Houston embraced the abrupt change. Couples walked arm in arm, leisurely strolling through the streets, enjoying the night and each other. Families were out in abundance, exiting ice cream shops, which reaped the benefits of the warm evening and sold ice cream cones and sundaes by the dozens.

The south Texas climate rarely followed traditional patterns of the nation. Most people who lived here accepted that and rarely raised an eyebrow at such drastic changes in weather. What they didn't comprehend was that Houston was the only city in the state enjoying such warmth. Even Brownsville, at the southernmost tip of the state, was over twenty degrees cooler.

Local news programs pointed out the aberration, but most viewers simply scratched their heads and went about their business, oblivious to the storm, which brewed about them.

But Gabriel couldn't be troubled with the everyday concerns of the many. His job proved more singular in purpose and far more precious to him.

Whenever he closed his eyes, his mind summoned Matt's face. It fueled his strength and doubled the wealth of courage in his heart.

Though he knew what gathered out in the darkness, for he had seen it far too many times, he would willingly spend eternity wrapped up in the shadows if it meant one more day enjoyed in the light that Matt brought to his world.

AFTER his shift and a quick run home to change into club clothes, Matt entered the newest club in Houston, the F Bar, to meet Dee and Shane. He squeezed his way between the throngs of men packed tighter in the club than they were into their jeans before finding his best friends standing by the outside patio bar.

Both obviously took Shane's advice from earlier. They were dressed to be molested.

Dee wore a low cut white blouse that barely contained her breasts. Her girls were on display and ready to party, and if she were any place other than a gay bar, she would definitely be getting some action. Not to be outdone, Shane sported a black tank top, which clung to his slim frame. His jeans looked painted on, which exposed his kibbles and bits to all who wanted to see.

"There she is!" Shane exclaimed and opened his arms for his hug.

Matt pulled Shane into an embrace and kissed his cheek before repeating the routine with Dee.

"How are my sisters?"

"Forget us!" Dee exclaimed. Her hands rested on her full hips, which meant she was not amused. "How are *you*? We've been crazy worried about you all damn day. You've barely responded to our texts after the accident."

"I was with Dr. Owens. Then went to work," he reminded Dee. "Some of us work for a living."

"I work," pouted Shane before taking a sip of his bright green appletini.

Matt rolled his eyes at Shane. "Calling in sick every other day at the Gap doesn't constitute work."

Shane's mouth opened wide while his left hand rested on his slim chest, clutching at nonexistent pearls to express his faux pain. "You wound me."

"Did you call in sick today or not?"

"That's beside the point," Shane answered. "You're mean and spiteful and should be destroyed."

"Will you both cut it out?" Dee asked. Her arms were now crossed. She had moved from being unamused to the edge of pissy.

"Look, I'm sorry," he told her while wrapping both arms around her. Although she pretended to still be mad, her body relaxed. Dee could never withstand the power of a hug. "I was real busy. I even saved a life today."

"I'm glad, Matty. I really am," she replied before pushing out of his embrace. "But you were almost killed today. And your grandmother's beside herself. She's been calling Shane and me all day. She hasn't heard from you or seen you, and she's worried."

Matt turned to look at Shane, whose serious nod confirmed the worry he caused his loved ones. "I'm really sorry," he told them, hoping he sounded as sincere as he felt. "I didn't mean to worry everyone, much less The Duchess."

"Well, The Duchess is ready to have you drawn and quartered, and you know she'll do it!"

Matt knew his grandmother all too well. There was no other person more loving and compassionate in the world, but when she was perturbed, that sweet old woman disappeared. In her place stood The Duchess, which was what his grandmother's society friends called her whenever she was cross.

He was twelve the first time he heard the nickname used. Since then, it was how he lovingly addressed his grandmother.

"I'll set up lunch with her tomorrow. I promise," he told Dee and Shane. "She certainly doesn't need any more aggravation today. Of all days."

Dee and Shane looked away self-consciously. As with most people who knew about his past, they grew uncomfortable at the mere mention of the day's significance. Matt thought it silly. Too many people avoided the subject, and he found it increasingly annoying, especially considering the progress Dr. Owens felt he was making.

If he was going to make further progress, his tenth birthday could no longer be a taboo subject.

"Good," Shane replied while handing Matt a rum and coke. "Now drink up. It's your birthday."

He took the offered drink and was about to take a sip when a strong hand rested on his shoulder from behind. From the look on Dee and Shane's faces, the guy was smoking hot. Matt secretly hoped it was the guy who had carried him off the street this morning.

When he turned around, it wasn't his mysterious savior. Instead, he gazed into the handsome face of the first police officer to arrive at the scene of the accident. "Officer Belton?"

"How about you call me Craig?" he answered. "At least when I'm not in uniform."

And Officer Craig Belton was most certainly *not* in his police uniform, unless official H.P.D. attire consisted of a form-fitting blue V-neck tee and jeans tighter than Shane's.

"Craig it is," he answered while shaking the officer's extended hand. "Thanks for all your help this morning. I was pretty shaky for a while."

"That's understandable. You'd just been through quite an ordeal."

"Tell me about it. I'm just sorry the driver didn't make it."

"Yeah, sad story. Family took it hard too. Left behind a wife and son, who's battling leukemia."

"That's awful," Matt replied. He felt terrible that the man's family now had to cope with the loss of a husband and father on top of what they were already dealing with. "I feel like I should do something for them. It was my fault after all."

Craig's green eyes narrowed in confusion. "How is it your fault?" he asked while running his hands through his wavy blond hair. "He almost ran you over."

"Well, I *was* the idiot lying in the middle of the street."

"Not by choice," Craig reminded him. "I saw you slip and fall, remember?"

"Yeah, but if I hadn't been such a darn klutz."

Craig placed both his hands on Matt's shoulders, rubbing them in consolation. His touch felt warmer than the night air. "Accidents happen. Believe me, I know. While it was a tragedy, you weren't at fault. Try to remember that."

His touch reassured him, and Matt found it comforting. Few people had such sway over him, especially people he didn't know. It felt good, even if a little foreign. Finally, he nodded in response.

Then Dee tapped him on the shoulder. "Remember us?"

Matt turned to Dee and Shane who smirked at him, eliciting a blush on his cheeks. He knew what his friends were thinking and that they were going to make his life miserable for this. "Sorry, guys. This is Officer, um, Craig. He's a police officer and was…"

"With you at the accident," Shane replied, cutting him off. "We heard." Shane reached out and patted Craig on his forearm. "I'm Shane," he told Craig. "And this hot piece of ass next to me is Dee."

"Nice to meet you both."

"Do you mind if I ask you a question?" Shane asked.

"Go right ahead."

"You boys pledge to protect and serve, right?"

"That's the motto."

"I don't do protect very well, but I'm great at servicing," Shane replied with a wink.

Matt wanted to die. Shane always came on too strong, and he was constantly embarrassed for him, though his friend rarely seemed to notice.

"Don't pay attention to him, Craig," Dee said while smacking Shane on the ass. "He's just had a boyfriend-ectomy, so he's suffering the usual symptom of excessive sluttiness."

Craig laughed, and when he did, his eyes sparkled. "Been there and done that," he told Shane. "How long ago was the break up?"

"One week," he replied, then jutted out his lower lip. Shane thought it made him look sultry. Matt didn't have the heart to tell him it made him look ten years old.

"Mine was six months ago." Craig put his arm around Shane's shoulder, not out of sexual interest but out of brotherhood and camaraderie. Shane apparently realized the gesture for what it was because he stared blankly at Matt and Dee. "What we need to do is find you a Mr. Right Now, who's not only hot but who only wants to use you for sex. Then your friends can take a pic of you and this guy making out on the dance floor and upload it to Facebook."

"Facebook?" Matt asked. "Why?"

"I assume you're still Facebook friends with your ex?" Craig asked Shane.

Shane nodded, and then a huge grin stretched across his face when he realized the merits of Craig's plan. "I love it!" Shane said while wrapping his arm around Craig's waist, no longer out of lust but out of a burgeoning friendship, born out of spite and vindictiveness. Both traits Shane worshipped.

Shane quickly scanned the crowd, searching for the perfect specimen.

"Not bad," Matt whispered to Craig. "You handled that well."

Craig winked at Matt and placed his hand on the small of his back. "I'm excellent at diffusing tense situations. Comes with the job."

Matt stopped paying attention to what Craig was saying. All he could focus on was Craig's hand on his lower back. It had been a long time since someone touched him so intimately without being gross or disgusting, and Matt liked the way it made him feel.

FROM across the crowded patio, Gabriel watched the man touch Matt. He didn't like the familiarity the man took for granted. When his hand wasn't on Matt's lower back, it rested on his shoulder. They held hands when they walked through the crowd, and the man leaned against Matt at the bar while Matt's friends pretended to be engaged in conversation.

He was powerless to do anything about it. Matt wasn't in danger, so he couldn't intervene. But if it even looked like the man might pose a threat, he would be immediately sorry.

"Hey, sexy, can I buy you a drink?"

Gabriel quickly looked left at the man standing beside him. He was tall, not taller than Gabriel was, but around two inches shorter. His dark hair was long and slicked back, fastened into a greasy looking ponytail.

"No," he replied without warmth, hoping the guy would get the hint.

"Aw, don't be like that," the guy persisted. He took a step closer, and Gabriel immediately tensed. He didn't want to hurt the man, but he wouldn't shy away from doing so if it was warranted.

Gabriel locked eyes with his aspiring suitor. This would be the man's final warning. "I'm not interested, so keep moving along."

"What? You think you're better than me? Or are you some fucking homophobe?"

While the man's attitude infuriated Gabriel, the curse word angered him more. In one quick motion, Gabriel had the man's right arm pinned back under his shoulder blade and slammed him face down on the bar. "I said I'm not interested, and I don't like it when people cuss."

The crowd around them grew quiet and stepped backward. He immediately realized his mistake. One of his objectives was never to draw attention to himself, something he had just done. He released the man from his grip and met the gaze of those staring at him in fear or anger.

"Nothing to see here," he told them. "It's just a minor disagreement. Go back to your drinks and your conversations."

Instantly, the crowd returned to their previous activities, quickly forgetting a disturbance ever existed.

"Now, you," he told the man whose arm he had almost dislocated. "When a person tells you they're not interested it means they're not interested. Got it?"

The man nodded.

"And *no more cursing.*"

"No more cursing," he repeated dreamily.

"Now go home."

The man nodded one final time before heading for the back patio exit.

"You need to be more careful," said a voice Gabriel immediately recognized.

When he turned around, Gabriel gazed into eyes tinted with the same blue as his own. That was where their similarities ended. Where Gabriel had short dark hair, the man before him had long golden locks. Gabriel's features, both physically and emotionally, were always harder, while the face he hadn't gazed into for decades was softer, more soothing just like his personality.

"Michael!"

The men embraced for a long time before finally parting.

"It's been too long, brother."

"It seems like centuries."

Michael sat on the stool next to him, and Gabriel ordered them both a drink.

"To what do I owe the pleasure?" he asked Michael, though he had a clue.

"I think you know," was all he responded when the bartender returned with two bottles of water.

"What's the problem? I'm doing my job, aren't I?

Michael unscrewed the cap and took a drink from the bottle. "Yes, but you're becoming too invested. The lines are blurring, Gabriel. That cannot be."

"Am I supposed to not care? I thought that was part of the reason I was assigned as a GA?"

"Partly, yes. You'd grown too gruff, too eager to fulfill your primary responsibility."

Gabriel remembered all too well. Unlike the rest of his brethren, he carried a burden they did not. They could never understand the weight of his appointed duty, and they often judged him too harshly for it, especially

Michael. He was the gentlest of them all. There was no way he could comprehend the gravity of his ultimate function.

"I'm not so eager anymore," he announced.

"But not for the right reasons," Michael said. "You know that. We all do."

"It comes with the job."

"No, it does not. I know what the job entails."

He was growing angry. Michael was the only being in creation capable of rousing Gabriel's ire so quickly. "How would you know? You've never held GA status. You don't know what it's like. All you know is what's been reported to you."

"By other GA's," Michael retorted.

Gabriel took a deep breath. Not only would getting into a fight with Michael not be productive, it would be, well, extremely bad for everyone in the general vicinity. "I'm doing my job, and I'm doing it well."

"You've done better than well. You've been phenomenal."

He smiled at Michael. Praise from his brother meant the world to him. And just as quickly as Michael had made him angry, Michael's smile cooled his raging blood.

"It's going to get a lot worse, you know," Michael admitted.

"I know," he replied. "The forces are gathering."

Michael nodded. "Minor forces have been called, but we fear the summons for the more powerful players has already been sent."

Gabriel nodded. "I can handle it."

"You must. There are no other options." Michael turned to stare at Matt, who was laughing with his friends. "He's more important than even *we* realize."

Gabriel wanted to respond. He wanted to tell his brother how important Matt really was, but he remained silent. Expressing his feelings, whether Michael sensed them or not, would do him no good. In fact, if he spoke them aloud, he ran the risk of throwing Matt into even more jeopardy than was currently headed his way.

CHAPTER 6

MATT hadn't been this happy on his birthday in a long time. The day typically held too much sadness, too many reminders of his parents' deaths, which usually marred whatever celebrations his loved ones planned. And considering the way he had started the day, he figured his twenty-seventh birthday would prove no different.

He had been wrong, and he had Craig to thank for that.

For some reason, Craig had the uncanny ability to make him feel better. He was friendly and got along with Dee and Shane, something that was rather difficult to accomplish. Previous boyfriends complained about his best friends, hating their constant interference in Matt's life and their rather domineering personalities.

But Craig took it all in stride. He had proficiently disarmed Shane's flirtations by refocusing Shane on being spiteful. The two found a hottie for Shane, snapped pictures, and then laughed while they uploaded the pictures to Facebook for Shane's ex, Karl, to see.

Craig even gushed over Dee, playing to her vanity. Not only did Dee enjoy being told how beautiful she was by hot gay men, she also enjoyed the spectacle of dirty dancing. Craig gleefully supplied her with both. In fact, Matt was still recovering from their gyrations to Lady Gaga's "Edge of Glory."

After being nearly run over, he never imagined he would enjoy Officer Belton's company at the F Bar, but he was. And though he got involved in his friends' conversations and interests, he never ignored Matt. His hand lingered on Matt's back or his shoulders when he talked, letting Matt know he hadn't been forgotten. He even held Matt's hand as they did laps around the bar.

Obviously, Craig Belton was interested in him, and the feeling was mutual.

His green eyes were warm and kind, not the cold fixed glare typically associated with someone in Craig's profession. Matt didn't find men attractive who viewed the world through eyes of confrontation or mistrust. He always suspected the reason men like that were so jaded was because they weren't any better than the world they didn't trust and wanted to fight.

Craig was the polar opposite of those men. Though, as a police officer, he saw people at their worst, his wide, cheery eyes revealed no such cynicism. He was gentle without being soft, a combination Matt found difficult to resist.

"I like him," Dee said, nodding to Craig who was paying the tab.

Shane leaned against the bar next to Matt and agreed. "And if he wasn't so damned interested in you, I'd be all over that."

"You really think he's interested?" he asked his friends while he eyed Craig's well-muscled arms and broad chest from across the bar.

"Girl, please," Dee replied. "He's been hanging all over you like white on rice."

"I'm sure he'd rather be inside you," Shane added.

Matt glared at Shane. "Not all of us are like you, Mr. Vanslutten."

"It's pronounced Vanslooten," Shane corrected with a grin. "Besides, it's your birthday. You're entitled to a piece of cake, you know? I'd say cut you off a slice and eat up!"

"You disgust me," he playfully replied.

"I'm not one who usually gives away the candy for free, but I agree with Shane." Dee's comment caught Matt by surprise. Although Dee loved to flirt, she rarely indulged in one-night stands. She found them degrading. Like Matt, Dee preferred the passion associated with a relationship not the come-and-go action Shane frequently enjoyed.

"Are you serious?"

She nodded her head. "You need to cut loose, sweetie. You're always so uptight, so proper. After the day you've had, I say go buck wild. There's nothing wrong with that. Besides, I've got a feeling Craig's interested in more than just a booty call."

"I don't know."

"You don't know what?" Craig asked, suddenly standing in front of them.

Matt blushed instantly. He wasn't certain if Craig overheard the rest of their conversation, so he didn't know what to say. When faced with embarrassment, Matt turned mute.

Luckily, his best friends always took up the slack.

"We were just wondering if we should hit the hay or move the party to another location," Dee replied.

"I vote for more partying," Shane said. "We can go back to Matt's place. It isn't far from here."

Matt glared at Shane. His attempts at getting Craig back to Matt's apartment were pathetic and transparent. He only hoped that Craig didn't think the idea was his.

"I'd join you guys if I didn't have a shift tomorrow, but I do," Craig said. "So, it's bed for me."

"Me too," Matt echoed. Although he was disappointed Craig didn't jump at the chance to go back to his place, he was also relieved. It meant that Craig might not be a fan of hooking up either. That in itself was better than getting naked with him. Well, almost better. "It's been a good birthday, guys, but I need to get some sleep."

"I didn't know it was your birthday." Craig stared at him, wounded. "Why didn't you tell me?"

"I try not to make a big deal about it."

"You should! Someone's birthday *is* a big deal. At least to me."

"Amen," Dee replied.

"Have you had any cake?" Craig asked.

"It's not really on my diet."

"Aw, come on," Craig said, wrapping his arm around Matt's neck. "You gotta have cake."

"That's just what I was telling him," Shane said. "Lord knows he could use a slice."

Matt glared at Shane while Dee snickered.

"Then it's settled," Craig said. "Let's get you some cake."

"Cake at this hour? On a weekday? Where on Earth are we going to go?"

"Where else?" Craig replied. He stared at Dee and Shane whose eyes lit up with the answer.

"House of Pies!" They both exclaimed excitedly.

Craig nodded. "There's no place else."

It was true. There was no other place in Houston like The House of Pies. Not only could customers get decent food after a night of drinking, but their desserts were famous city-wide. Most gays who packed the club ended up there to soak up the alcohol with some sustenance.

As he stared into three pairs of eyes begging him to say yes, Matt finally agreed. There was no way he could say no to such a pathetic display. Besides, he enjoyed the fuss Craig was making over his birthday. It made him feel special, and feeling special on his birthday hadn't happened for quite some time.

SHORTLY after arriving at the surprisingly empty House of Pies, Craig promptly ordered a thick slice of chocolate cake, which was Matt's favorite, for everyone. When the waitress set their order before them, they all sang "Happy Birthday" to him and then set to task devouring the dessert.

As usual, the cake was scrumptious. Even though cake wasn't something Matt enjoyed regularly, he inhaled almost the whole piece. Now, he felt stuffed and miserable, but the look of satisfaction on Craig's beaming face was well worth the gastrointestinal discomfort.

"Good, huh?" he asked from the booth seat next to Matt.

"It was sinfully good," Matt replied. Craig then stretched his arm across the booth back until his arm rested around Matt's shoulders. The gesture made him feel giddy like he was a cheerleader sitting next to the high school quarterback.

"Well, there goes my diet," Dee griped while looking at her empty plate. "And I wanted to lose five pounds this week. I just know when I wake up tomorrow that cake will already be sitting on my thighs."

"Lucky cake," Craig replied with a wink.

Dee grinned at Craig and tilted her head to her left. "My God, man, if you were straight, I'd be spinning you like a top by now."

A slight flush of red tinted Craig's cheeks, and he coyly looked away.

Shane laughed out loud. "I think you've embarrassed the man, Deeds. Good job." A devilish twinkle flashed in his eyes. Matt knew further torment was on its way. "I wonder how embarrassed Officer Belton would be if I told him what I'd be doing to him right now. That's if he was even *at all* interested in me." His eyes then followed Craig's arm around Matt's shoulders. "But, alas, he's not. He's attracted to far simpler fare!"

Craig's cheeks now bloomed a deep red, and he quickly withdrew his arm from Matt's shoulders. "All right, that's enough," Matt scolded. "I think poor Craig's been subjected to enough of your teasing to last a lifetime."

"I'm a big boy," Craig responded after he recovered from his mortification. "I can take good-natured ribbing just fine, but I think it only fair to point out that my tastes are far from simple." With that, he scooted closer to Matt in the booth.

Dee and Shane oohed in unison before shifting their gazes to Matt. Now, it was his turn to blush. Never before had a man so boldly staked a claim for his affections. It made him truly wonder if his life might be taking a turn in a more positive direction.

"You have good taste then," Dee told Craig. "Especially if you can turn down sampling Shane's tired old pie."

The table erupted into laughter, except Shane who sulked.

"My pie's not tired."

His response only made things worse. Tears streamed down Matt's eyes, and his already full belly ached from the heartiness of his laugh. Dee and Craig didn't fare any better. Dee's mascara trailed black, fuzzy snakes down her ebony cheeks while Craig held his stomach in painful merriment.

The wait staff and customers around them eyed them suspiciously. The raucousness of their behavior no doubt caused worry. No one could tell if they were drunk, crazy, or both. Matt hated drawing attention to himself, and he wanted to calm down long enough to no longer look the fool, but the laughter felt too good to be bottled up.

It made him forget the pain.

Then, he detected a figure out of the corner of his eye. He turned his head to the right and looked out the wall of windows viewing the side parking lot. Who he saw made his laughing fit cease almost immediately.

His savior from earlier this morning stood on the other side of the parking lot. Though the man was more than thirty feet away, Matt recognized him. It was the same dark hair and tall frame wrapped in leather and denim. But what Matt found more surprising was that even from this distance, the man's blue eyes were easily distinguishable and still as amazing.

No one else noticed Matt staring out the window. Shane was asking everyone to stop laughing at his pie while Dee and Craig burst out into another fit of laughter.

He hadn't told anyone about his mysterious stranger since Craig informed him that no one else had been on the scene. Although it felt real at the time, Matt allowed Craig's words to convince him that he had simply hallucinated as a result of the fall.

But his mysterious stranger was real and staring back at him from across the parking lot.

Matt wanted to get up from the table, to talk to the man who rescued him, but his body wouldn't cooperate. It wasn't out of fear; he felt struck dumb, as if the man's mere presence nullified his ability to move, much less think.

Then as if acknowledging Matt's presence, the stranger nodded his head before turning and walking away.

Matt wanted to cry out and plead with the man not to leave, but instead he half knelt and half stood on the booth. "I need to get out," he told Craig who blocked his path.

The urgency in his voice halted the laughter, which Shane appeared to appreciate. "You okay?" Craig asked. Concern for Matt quickly replaced the amused sparkle in his eyes.

"I'm fine," he replied, his voice still urgent. "Excuse me." When Craig still didn't move, he repeated with more force. "Please."

Craig nodded and stood up from the booth.

Matt dashed away from their table, and despite the cries of his friends, he sprinted through the restaurant and out the front door.

A wall of oppressive humidity slammed into him once he exited the restaurant. Some time since their arrival, the night had grown warmer, and now felt more like mid-August than mid-January.

Matt, however, had no time to ponder the weird weather patterns of Houston. All that mattered to him at the moment was finding his savior. He darted through the parking lot in the same direction he had watched the man walk, but he was nowhere to be found.

The cones of yellow light falling from the street lamps illuminated only patches of empty asphalt stretching out to the fence more than fifty yards away. Like this morning, the man had again vanished into thin air.

Matt wasn't about to be so easily deterred. He trotted the length of the building toward the rear. Perhaps his savior had ducked behind the restaurant. As far as he knew, there wasn't a way out in the back, so unless he could leap a nine-foot wooden fence, that meant Matt would find him once he rounded the building.

When he turned the corner, he ran smack into a man who was not his savior. The force of the collision made the tall, thin man dressed in a tan overcoat drop half a dozen small bags filled with powder. When Matt stared down as the pouches hit the pavement, he immediately knew they were drugs. He also noticed the man wasn't alone. He had a friend with him, who looked antsy.

Oh crap! Matt thought as he stared into the dangerous men's annoyed faces. He knew he was in big trouble. *Here I go again!*

"What the fuck?" the man he ran into cursed. His face, inked with a tribal tattoo, darkened with an angry scowl.

The man he was doing business with backed away, shaking his head. "Forget it, Blade. I don't need no trouble tonight." Then, he ran down the parking lot in the direction from which Matt had just come.

"I'm sorry," Matt stammered. He tried to turn around and head back toward the front door, but the man named Blade stepped in front of him.

"Sorry?" he growled. "You just fucking cost me a sale. You don't just get to say sorry and leave."

"I'll pay you for the inconvenience," he replied, hoping that the promise of money might save his life. "You can even keep your product."

Blade shoved him backward, and for the second time that day, Matt found himself sprawled on pavement. "Oh, you'll pay. With more than money."

Matt immediately grew angry. Life seemed to push him around enough, and he wasn't going to allow some drug dealer named Blade to jump on *that* bandwagon. It was high time Matt took control of his life beyond the hospital, even if standing up to this man proved to be the dumbest move he ever made.

"You won't get anything more from me than money," Matt challenged as he tried to stand.

Blade kicked Matt back onto the asphalt before pulling a switchblade out of his pocket. "Oh yes, I will," he snarled before lunging at Matt.

A wall of denim and leather suddenly appeared before Matt, blocking Blade's path. When he looked up, his savior stood between him and his assailant. They scuffled for a few seconds before Blade flew backward and landed hard against the green dumpster sitting outside the restaurant's rear exit.

His savior pulled the knife jutting from his stomach out of his body and tossed it onto the pavement without a second glance. Matt instinctively knew the wound wasn't serious. In fact, as hard as it was for him to believe about a stab wound to the abdomen, Matt suspected the knife didn't do much, if any, damage at all.

And before Matt had time to register how he could possibly know that, the man then leaped toward Blade, who was scurrying to get to his feet.

"Matt!" a voice from behind him called.

He looked over his shoulder and saw Dee, Shane, and Craig turning the corner of the building. When they saw the two men fighting, Dee and Shane stopped in their tracks. Without thinking, Craig rushed into the fray.

"Stop!" Craig cried, while trying to pull his savior off Blade. "Police."

Neither man took notice of the warning.

Craig raised his fist to punch the man who had twice saved his life, and Matt immediately sprung to his feet. He rammed into Craig, knocking him over. Dee and Shane shrieked in response.

"What the hell?" Craig asked, when he hit the pavement with Matt on top of him.

"Don't hurt him," he replied. "He saved me."

Suddenly, Matt found himself lifted from Craig and safely scooped within the arms of his savior.

"Don't touch him," his savior warned Craig.

"He's getting away!" Dee shouted.

They all turned to watch Blade jump on top of a car and then bound over the wooden fence to safety beyond.

After he was gone, everyone stared at Matt, who was still safely cradled in his savior's protective arms. Matt gazed deeply into the man's blue eyes. Where once a storm of rage blew, they were again as calm as a windless day.

"Are you hurt?" he asked Matt.

Unable to speak, Matt shook his head no.

His savior then, reluctantly, set him back onto the pavement with great care as if he were the most fragile, special person on the planet. And though his friends and Craig stared at the two of them in bewilderment, Matt wanted nothing more than to return to the comfort of the arms that seem destined to protect him from harm.

THE last police car pulled out of the parking lot. As Matt watched the spinning red and blue lights head off in the distance, he added yet another tally to the horrendous events that had happened on his birthday.

This time, though, a sense of perpetual dread didn't overcome him. For reasons he couldn't explain, an air of positivity wrapped itself around him equally as strong as the oppressive heat that still clung to the night.

Even with almost being killed for the second time today, he found himself looking on the positive side of the awful events for once.

The day had brought Craig into his life, a handsome man, who was obviously very taken with him. He had spent the evening getting to know the police officer, and so far, he liked everything he knew. Craig was a good man with a kind heart and quite attractive to boot. He had been a hit with his friends, and throughout the evening, Matt fantasized about getting to know Craig Belton even better.

He made Matt feel special without trying. When Craig looked at him, Matt could tell he saw no one else, not even the many men in the bar who tried desperately to get his attention. Either Craig didn't notice or he didn't care. Whatever the case happened to be, Matt enjoyed the way it made him feel.

But Craig wasn't the only man who had walked into his life today.

There was also Gabriel.

He didn't know his name because Gabriel had told him. He only knew it because he heard Gabriel identify himself to the police. He had no idea what Gabriel's last name was because at that moment, Craig had come over to check on him, and the rest of Gabriel's conversation with the police was swept away by the shared concerns of Dee, Shane, and Craig.

Now, the police were gone, and the lot was practically vacant. Only the four of them remained. And Gabriel, who stood apart from them, stared at Matt.

If anyone else watched him the way Gabriel was now, with such singular intensity and focus, he would be creeped out. But there was nothing ominous or threatening in his dazzling blue eyes. Even after seeing the storm of determination with which Gabriel sought to protect him, Matt instinctively knew that swirling tempest would never come his way.

"You ready to head home?" Craig asked. He was talking to Matt but eying Gabriel suspiciously.

"Almost," he replied before crossing the pavement to Gabriel.

Gabriel watched him approach, a slight smile stretched across his lips. Matt didn't know why it was there, but he immediately knew he would do anything to see that smile again.

"Are you well?" Gabriel asked in a voice more lyrical than the everyday spoken word.

"Yes. Thanks to you."

"Thanks are unnecessary."

"I beg to differ. He would have killed me if you hadn't stepped between us."

"Always best not to find out."

"I agree," Craig said, standing beside him. He placed his arm around Matt's waist. "I can't thank you enough for what you did."

Gabriel's eyes left Matt's to acknowledge Craig's presence before looking down to where Craig's hand rested protectively around Matt. The smile, which previously lit up his face, vanished quickly. "As I told Matt. Thanks are unnecessary."

"Fuck that!" Shane said. Matt watched as Gabriel bristled at the curse word. "You're a hero." He crossed over to Gabriel and gave the man a big hug. Gabriel's body tensed, and Matt could tell Gabriel wasn't accustomed to being touched so easily by another. But Shane, always oblivious to body language, didn't notice.

"What's your name, sweetheart?" Dee asked. She was being questioned by the police at the same time Gabriel was, so she hadn't heard him like Matt. "I want to know what to call the man who saved my best friend. Lord knows I'll be telling everyone about you."

"I'm Gabriel," he told her, pronouncing it gay-BREE-el before taking Dee's hand in his and brushing a small peck on the back of her hand.

"How gallant," Shane commented, extending his hand out to Gabriel. "Do I get one too?"

"If you so desire," he responded and then kissed Shane's hand in the same manner as Dee's.

"That's fucking awesome."

"Awesome by itself would be sufficient," Gabriel said. "The cursing tarnishes the experience."

Shane apologized. Matt had never heard Shane be contrite for cursing in his life. Since the day he met him, Shane had always been a potty mouth.

Craig extended his hand to Gabriel. "I don't need a kiss, but I would like to shake your hand."

Gabriel nodded and took the offered hand.

Afterward, silence descended upon the group. Everyone wanted to go, but Matt couldn't find the strength to leave Gabriel. Not only did he want to spend an eternity gazing into those mesmerizing eyes, but he also had so many questions to ask about where Gabriel went after saving him this morning.

"I should get going," Gabriel finally spoke. "I'm sure everyone has an early day tomorrow."

Shane complained, "I know I do. I can't call in sick two days in a row."

"Never stopped you before," Dee quipped.

Shane gave Dee a raspberry to which Dee giggled. But the teasing in her eyes quickly turned to horror.

"Shane, what happened to you?"

She pointed at Shane's shirt, which was stained with blood.

"Were you hurt?" Craig asked. His concern was immediate. He quickly crossed over to Shane who stared at the blood in confusion.

"No," he replied lifting up his shirt to reveal an absence of a wound. "Where the hell did that come from? I didn't have it inside. Did I?"

"No," Craig said. "You sat right across from me. I would have seen it."

"Then how?"

Matt suddenly remembered the struggle between Gabriel and Blade. Blade had stabbed Gabriel, but Gabriel tossed the knife aside. Until now, he had forgotten about that part, especially since Matt had intuited the wound to be minor. He had been too swept away by Gabriel and the police's questions he failed to check if Gabriel had been truly injured or not.

"It's from Gabriel. Blade stabbed him," Matt finally said.

They all turned to Gabriel who was zipping up his leather jacket.

"I'm fine."

"I don't think so," Matt said crossing over to him. "That's a lot of blood on Shane's shirt. Let me see."

He gazed down at Matt, a tender smile reflecting in his eyes. "I'm fine," he repeated.

"I'm a nurse. I can help you."

"Your assistance is not required."

"I said let me see," Matt ordered, far more forcefully than he intended. He half expected his exasperated tone to elicit some negative reaction. Instead, Gabriel unzipped his jacket and revealed a bloody stain on the front of his blue shirt.

"Oh my God," Dee exclaimed. "We need to call an ambulance!"

"I'm fine," Gabriel assured her.

How did the police not notice Gabriel was bleeding when they questioned him? Matt wondered as he carefully lifted up the shirt, exposing Gabriel's knife wound along with his chiseled, furry stomach. The laceration looked deep, far too deep for Matt to have so casually dismissed it as a minor injury and certainly far too severe for eagle-eyed officers of the law to have missed so obvious a wound. Was it somehow invisible to them all before now? Matt didn't have the answers. All he knew for sure was that this was the first time Matt's medical intuition had ever let him down, and Matt didn't like the feeling. "You're *not* fine. You've been stabbed. We must get you to a hospital immediately. Check you for internal bleeding."

"I'm not going to the hospital."

"Why not?" Matt asked as he silently cursed his error in judgment.

Gabriel contemplated for a few minutes. "I don't have health insurance."

"I'll pay for it," Matt offered.

"That's kind, but I heal quickly. There's no need to worry."

"I'm the medical professional here. Not you. You'll take my advice."

"I will not," Gabriel replied. His answer was firm and unrelenting.

"Why don't you want to get treatment?" Craig asked. "That's very suspicious to me."

"Craig!" Matt exclaimed. "How can you say that to the man who risked his life for me?"

"Don't be angry with him," Gabriel commented. "He's right. My behavior would be suspicious to a man of the law. But suspicious or not, I will not go to the hospital."

Matt stared up at Gabriel in confusion. "I don't understand. I just want to help."

Gabriel's smile, warm as the sun on a spring day, beamed down at him. "I know you do, but I have my reasons. You will just have to accept that as my answer."

"Fine," Matt said, grabbing Gabriel's hand and leading him toward his car. "But you'll just have to accept my help. I have a medical kit at my apartment. I'll fix you up there myself."

"I'm coming with you," Craig called out. Dee and Shane also announced their intention to follow them to his place.

Matt nodded in response. He knew his friends didn't want to leave him alone with a strange man, but they had no idea that, though they had never met before today, Gabriel didn't feel like a stranger to him at all.

In fact, Matt felt like he had known Gabriel his entire life or at least in a life he knew nothing about.

PART II:
CONNECTIONS

CHAPTER 7

CARLOS CRUZ stared out at the darkening sky. The last time he witnessed clouds gathering so ominously overhead had been exactly one year ago, the day his youngest son was born. It was also the day his wife died.

Although 1985 had been a tough year, he rang in 1986 with high hopes for a better life, for himself and his seven boys. And for the past few weeks, life had improved enough that he no longer thought about the tragedy every single day. He also no longer awoke in the middle of the night, drenched in sweat and reaching out for his departed wife.

But the familiar darkening sky overhead brought the painful memories of last year back to the surface. He felt transported back to his house in Victoria instead of standing on the twenty acres of his country property along Upper Mission Valley, where he had moved his family.

The new house wasn't perfect like the one he left behind. It had only three bedrooms, and with seven boys, private space was a commodity no one enjoyed. The septic system had to be replaced the previous month, the floorboards creaked in the living room, and small rodents often took refuge in their house, hoping to escape the predatory snakes that routinely inspected the area for food.

Some of the bricks on the unattached garage were crumbling, the anorexic windows upstairs didn't let in much daylight, and the lights sometimes flickered, if they turned on at all.

When he purchased this place, his brother Marcos thought he was crazy. Their house in town had more square footage and fewer maintenance problems.

It also had too many memories of Veronica.

It proved too difficult for him and the boys to continue to live there. The oldest, Carlitos, became so grief stricken that he couldn't pass by the master bedroom without crying. Manny and Mando grew belligerent at home and at school, refusing to listen to anyone not their *mama*, while Miguel simply holed up in his room, not talking to anyone. Only a few weeks before his mother's death, Ruben had learned to talk, and he called for his mother in every room, looking under the bed and in closets to find her. Too young to express his sadness, David cried a lot and clung for dear life to whoever held him.

The only one unaffected by his mother's death was Mateo. Not because he didn't miss his mother but because he never knew life with her. His ignorance, more than anything else, made Carlos the saddest.

He had to do something to save his family. Even though he didn't have Veronica with him in body, he had her in spirit. He talked to her every night before bed, seeking her advice. One night, she answered him in a dream.

They had to move.

Changing their environment would pull the family out of their tailspin. It was the only way for them to reconnect as a family, to patch up the hole that Veronica's departure had left in their lives.

At first, the children resented the change. For the first month after they moved in, they complained loudly and often about wanting to go home. Slowly, however, Carlos noticed the healing process begin.

Carlitos's crying fits stopped almost at once. The chips on Manny and Mando's shoulders slipped away, and Miguel rarely stayed in his room. Instead, he and the older boys spent most afternoons playing in the fields. Ruben seldom called for his mother anymore. Instead, he had to know where his *papa* was at all times. Even little David changed his clingy habits; he hated being held, preferring to explore every inch of the new house.

The only one who remained the same was Mateo. Always happy and hardly fussy, he loved to cuddle and snuggle. He was also content with being held or being alone, though he never seemed to be.

Most babies frequently babbled to themselves, but Mateo carried on hours of baby talk conversations with thin air. Carlos often watched him stare at a certain point in the room and giggle. He seemed to focus on a specific spot in his field of vision, and the whole time he cooed and jabbered nonsense as if speaking to someone only he could see.

Carlos always assumed it was Veronica, watching over her baby and her family as their guardian angel. So, whenever he saw Mateo talking to his guardian angel, he made sure he said hello and blew her a kiss.

Even now, the sounds of Mateo chattering with his mother reached him on the front porch. He left Mateo safely protected in his playpen, when the approaching storm drew him outside.

Gathering in angry protest, the clouds approached the house from all sides. The only clear piece of sky reached straight above them. It made him edgy. He felt trapped, something he hadn't felt since the night the stranger in the dark almost killed him.

An internal alarm rang. He knew danger was coming to him in the same way he had known the man tapping on his window one year ago meant him harm.

"The boys," he whispered as he took two giant steps from the porch to the front yard that stretched before him. He needed to find them but he couldn't leave Mateo alone in the house, and he couldn't take him into the approaching storm either.

The only choice he had was to head back to the porch and wait for them to return.

They were all out there, playing together. The older boys had wanted to go out alone with the younger ones. Carlos refused at first, claiming Ruben and Daniel were too young, but they had been persistent.

They wanted to be together, just them. Carlos understood. It was the anniversary of their mother's death, and they felt the need to do something to remember her, as her children, away from their father's prying eyes and before Mateo's birthday party.

He had finally relented after a long debate, but he put his foot down when it came to Mateo. He was too young for their adventures. Ruben and David were just old enough to be entrusted in their older brothers' care. Although he knew his sons would let no harm come to Mateo, he couldn't entrust an infant in the care of boys far too young and boisterous.

Now he wished he hadn't been so understanding. The wind gusted suddenly to about twenty miles per hour and the steady drizzle soon turned into a curtain of rain, which made the yard beyond twenty feet away vanish from sight.

Cracks of thunder rolled in the heavens, and lightning split the sky above. The small patch of clear sky overhead quickly succumbed to the advancing thunderheads until only gray and gloom remained.

"We must leave this place, Mr. Cruz."

Carlos jumped at the sound of a man's voice behind him. He spun around and saw a tall figure standing inside his house with Mateo safely cradled in his arms.

"Get away from my son!" he shouted as he swung open the front screen door and bolted inside. When he saw who it was, all breath left his body.

The man who had saved him, the man who delivered Mateo, had once again appeared just like before—out of nowhere.

HOMER RODGERS wept as the last child's body fell before him. He didn't know the names of the boys he killed, and it didn't really matter. The call had come. He had no choice but to answer it.

Now, the bodies of six young boys lay bloody before him. Gone were six young men who would never grow to adulthood, never know the touch of a woman, and never know how sorry he was.

No amount of shed tears could make up for his actions. He only prayed his wife never learned what he had done to secure her health and to keep her alive.

His contract, though, was incomplete. These boys weren't his target; they were collateral damage, repayment for the loss of a favored minion one year ago today.

The one who would satisfy the terms of his agreement and bring an end to his misery waited in the house across the field. There, he would find the infant who had been marked by the wicked to die.

Homer sighed heavily as he rested the handle of the axe he carried against his right shoulder. The crimson blade, once polished silver, was coated in a bloody sheen. Disgusted with himself, he headed out of the small barn, where he had found the boys playing.

As he crossed the field, the heavens opened up, releasing a torrent of water. He glanced at the axe, hoping to find the blood of the innocent had been washed away. But though his clothes were sodden, the stain of his sins remained emblazoned on the weapon mocking him.

"WHERE did you come from?" Carlos finally muttered, once he found his voice.

"That's not important," his savior said with Mateo still tucked safely in his arms. "We must leave."

"I'm not going anywhere," he told the stranger, who was dressed in blue jeans, a blue shirt, and a leather jacket. "My other sons are out there. I need to get them home."

The stranger refused to meet his eyes. Instead, he stared intently over Carlos's shoulders, looking out the front door and into the storm as if the stranger's vision could pierce the watery veil that enveloped the world.

"We must leave," the man repeated. "Now."

Carlos crossed the room to him, slowly. He owed a great deal of gratitude to this man, but he wasn't about to abandon his children. He also wasn't going to allow the man to hold Mateo for another moment. Danger circulated about them, and he intended for his son to be in his arms when it struck. "I can't go anywhere without my boys," he said calmly, reaching out with nervous hands to take Mateo from the man's well-muscled arms.

The stranger handed Mateo over to him without fuss. The baby, however, voiced his displeasure by whimpering and reaching for the stranger with his tiny, chubby arms.

"Stay with your father, little one." In response to the stranger's musical tone, Mateo curled up in Carlos's arms and fell asleep.

"Who are you?" Carlos asked, while shifting his gaze from his sleeping son to the man he hadn't seen in a year.

The stranger didn't respond. Instead, his sky-blue eyes turned to the open screen door and once again scanned the world outside. The man grew tense. His broad shoulders appeared to double in size as the muscles instinctively flexed like those of a jungle cat preparing for battle.

"Stay inside," he commanded without looking at Carlos. "Whatever you do, don't leave the house."

"Why not?" He asked, embarrassed by the fear in his voice. But fear hadn't only seized his throat; it had spread over him like a slow chill. The hairs on his arms stood at attention, his heartbeat raced frantically in his chest, and an overwhelming sense of dread engulfed the air, making it smell bitter like sulfur.

Something awful was outside in the rain. And his sons were out there with it.

"What's out there?" Carlos asked. His renewed concern for his boys emboldened him. Though he was afraid, he would march out there to save his sons if he had to. "Tell me."

Perhaps sensing the change in Carlos, the stranger looked over his shoulder at him. His eyes were no longer blue. A stormy gray had settled upon them. Though his jaw clenched tightly, his voice remained calm and soothing. "I will take care of it."

"Take care of what?"

"What's in the rain."

"What's *in* the rain?"

"Evil."

The word shut Carlos up. Evil was what he sensed the night Mateo was born. It's what threatened to kill him and prevent his youngest from being born. Now, according to this stranger, that evil was back and it was making its way through the rain.

The man stepped toward the front door and opened it. His gait was sure and confident. Though he was walking toward evil, his body showed no signs of apprehension or fear. Instead, he looked as if this was just another day at the office. When he walked onto the porch, the door closed shut behind him.

"Stay inside," he repeated again. The stranger stared ahead into the rain at whatever was coming their way.

"Who are you?" Carlos asked again. "Please, tell me your name."

"Gabriel," the man replied, pronouncing it as gay-BREE-el. He then stepped off the porch and was swallowed up in the storm.

EVEN before seeing the face of the man walking through the rain, Homer knew who it was. It was the same man who killed the other agent, the one who saved the infant and prolonged his misery and the one he somehow knew was called Gabriel.

Hate he had never before experienced rose from within. It burned hot like magma and threatened to consume his flesh until he was a man of fire instead of flesh and bone.

"You won't be allowed to continue," Gabriel announced. Over forty yards still separated them, but Homer heard his words as if they were standing face to face. Though strong and abrasive, his voice still retained the musical tone of his kind.

Homer had no idea what "his kind" meant. Since he had made the deal to save his wife, his body sometimes wasn't his own. Often, he felt like a spectator, watching the world through his eyes but unable to control his actions.

This was one of those times.

He continued forward, his legs operating on their own steam. The axe's handle now rested firmly in both hands, and his muscles twitched in anticipation of killing one such as Gabriel.

When only ten yards separated them, the veil of rain lifted enough for Homer to see Gabriel clearly. Turbulent, gray eyes glared at him from a finely chiseled face. Gabriel's jaw clenched, and his chest rose and fell like a raging bull's. In his right hand rested a sword made of metal so white he squinted when he looked directly at it.

A good six inches taller than him, Gabriel struck an imposing figure. If Homer truly had control of his body, he would point his feet in the opposite direction and run away. Instead, he met Gabriel's pace until they were a mere swing of a weapon's distance from each other.

"You know how this will end, Barbatos," Gabriel announced rather calmly. "Your power is nothing before mine."

"So brazen. But your kind always is." Homer spoke in a voice he didn't recognize. It sounded gravelly and severe. Ever since he first heard the voice and accepted its terms to kill the infant, he'd often felt out of control. He couldn't help but wonder if that voice, the one Gabriel called Barbatos, now controlled his actions as well as his voice.

"While your kind is cowardly, hiding behind others."

Homer growled in anger at the insult, though he didn't comprehend the offense.

"Let the man be. Face me as you are."

Homer snickered, without a clue as to what was funny. "That's not how this works," he told Gabriel. "You know that better than most anyone."

"Excuses," Gabriel replied in contempt. "I have no wish to harm your host, but I will not hesitate to send both your souls into the fiery abyss. Do not rile me further. Be gone from this man and this place, and I will let you slink back to the shadows that birthed you."

Homer wanted to accept the offer. He thought about throwing the axe aside and seeking penance for what he had done, but the building anger within clouded rational thought. He felt the same way in the barn, so overcome with physical rage that bubbled from within until Homer disappeared and only the fury that was obviously Barbatos remained.

"Never," he replied as he hefted the axe. "My blade will drink of your blood."

Homer swung the axe in a downward arc, but Gabriel's sword easily blocked it.

"Your blade already has the blood of innocents on it. It shall drink no more."

Gabriel slashed his sword diagonally from the right, but the blade whirred within centimeters of Homer's head. With a grace he had never before possessed, Homer ducked and again swung his axe upward to knock Gabriel's sword from his outstretched arm.

They both watched the weapon tumble in the air before disappearing behind the rain that shrouded the land.

"So easily disarmed," Homer snickered.

"I allowed you that small victory in hopes that you will hear the truth of my words. The infant will live. If you cross me further, you will die."

Homer howled in laughter. A pack of coyotes in the distance replied in kind. "I've already killed the boy's brothers. What makes you think I'll stop now?"

"You bastard!" a voice from behind Gabriel called out.

When the form came into view, it was the infant's father carrying a shotgun, aimed directly at Homer.

"Carlos!" Gabriel cried out, but the man didn't hear the warning. Too overcome by grief and anger, Carlos cared only for vengeance. He leveled the barrel of the weapon and fired.

Homer proved faster. Before Carlos could register the movement, Homer was sinking the axe into his back with a wet *thwack*.

It wasn't until Homer looked over his shoulder to gloat that he noticed Gabriel was gone, and after sprinting into the house, he discovered so was the infant.

CHAPTER 8

SO FAR, 2012 had yet to be a banner year for Matt, but it was nothing unusual. Each new year typically started out with promise, but his birthday rounded the corner and then *blam*, instant crap storm.

No matter how positive he tried to be, this year had been the worst in quite some time. Within the past twelve hours he had barely survived two life threatening situations, and the only reason he had was because of the tall, dark, gorgeous stranger he left bleeding in his living room.

If he didn't return quickly with what he needed to tend Gabriel's wound, the man who saved his life might bleed out on his wooden floors.

After a few frenzied moments, Matt located the alcohol under the bathroom sink, tucked the clear plastic bottle under his arm, and then grabbed his emergency medical supplies, which consisted of bandages, latex gloves, medical adhesive tape, and a suture kit.

After collecting everything, he sprinted through the hallway to the living room, where Gabriel still sat on the chair, where he left him, and where Craig, Dee, and Shane still stood like sentries around Gabriel.

"Alright, Flo to the rescue," he said while moving everyone else away from Gabriel, who sat silently watching him. He hadn't said a word since they left the parking lot of the House of Pies. All he seemed capable of doing was following Matt with his magnificently blue eyes.

Being scrutinized made it difficult for Matt to concentrate. Plus, he could tell it was starting to annoy Craig, whose upper lip would not uncurl.

Craig stepped aside as Matt took the latex gloves out of their protective packaging and put them on. "Flo?" he asked.

"It's what they call Matty at the hospital," Dee replied for Matt, who was too engrossed with removing the bandages from the kit and opening them to respond. "Short for Florence Nightingale."

"And here I thought it was short for Florence Henderson," Shane teased.

Matt didn't take the bait. He had a job to do. "Okay, Gabriel," he said while kneeling in front of him. "I'm going to need to remove your clothing."

"Now that's what I'm talking about!" Shane hooted.

Matt glanced sideways at Shane, disapprovingly. Shane was getting on his nerves. "Just his shirt, you perv. I need clear access to the wound."

"This is unnecessary," Gabriel said, finally breaking his silence. "I'm fine."

"You are *not* fine. You've been stabbed, and I need to clean and bandage the wound."

Gabriel placed his sizable hand over Matt's. Even through the gloves, Matt could feel the warmth of his touch. Matt trembled in response. "Believe me, I'm fine."

"What's the big deal?" Craig asked, stepping beside Matt and glaring at Gabriel's hand, which still rested upon Matt's. "You can't be embarrassed to take off your shirt?"

"Why the hell would he be embarrassed?" Shane interjected. "He's hot! If I looked like him, I'd *never* wear clothes."

Matt rolled his eyes. "Shane, you're not helping. Please stop hitting on my patient."

"I hit on *everyone!*"

Matt looked to Dee for support, and the Godsend she was, she jumped right in. "Shane, why don't you take me home? We've both got work tomorrow. Besides, Matt's got Craig and Gabriel here. He'll be fine."

"Oh my God!" Shane complained. "Why does Matt get all the hot ones? I'd like to be in the middle of that hunk sandwich."

"I don't do three ways," Craig replied, more to Matt than to Shane. "I prefer to have my partner's undivided attention."

Matt sighed heavily as he felt the reins he typically used to control his emotions start to slip from his grasp. All he wanted was to repay the kindness Gabriel had shown him by taking care of the injury, an injury that appeared more serious than he had thought, but his efforts were thwarted on all fronts.

Gabriel refused his care. Shane continued to be inappropriate, and now Craig looked pissed off. How did one good deed lead to all this?

"We should go," Dee insisted, noticing the change in Matt's demeanor.

"I think we should *all* go," Craig replied. "To the hospital. That's where Gabriel belongs. Not here."

"I do *not* need to go to the hospital."

"And I would still like to know why," Craig admitted. "Matt might be too kind to press the issue, but you've been stabbed. You failed to inform the police about that when they were on the scene. And now you won't let a registered nurse take care of you." He locked onto Gabriel's eyes. "Would you mind explaining that to me?"

"That's enough!" Matt announced, loudly. He stood up, placing himself directly between Craig and Gabriel. Life was starting to barrel out of control again, and he needed to grab the steering wheel. "This isn't an interrogation, and it certainly isn't a police station. This is my home."

Craig's previously incensed eyes went wide in shock. "I'm aware of my location," he replied icily. By the way he straightened his posture and puffed out his chest, pride, more than anything else, appeared to be the reason for the frosty retort. "But police station or not, I'm a cop. It's my job to protect those I c..." He stopped himself before finishing the sentence.

Matt immediately felt bad for losing his temper. Craig's inability to let the matter drop stemmed from his concern about him. How could he be angry with that? "I appreciate the concern," he told Craig. He made sure to soften his voice, to show Craig he was sorry. "But Gabriel's saved me twice today. That alone tells me he's one of the good guys. So what if he doesn't want to go to the hospital? There are plenty of people who hate going to the hospital. I don't hold it against him or find it suspicious and neither should you."

When he stopped talking, he immediately noticed the confusion apparent in everyone's eyes. Well, everyone except Gabriel.

"Saved you twice?" Shane asked.

"Sweetie, what are you talking about?"

Matt gawked at Dee. "What do you mean?"

"You just said Gabriel's saved you twice. What do *you* mean?"

"Is this the guy you mentioned this morning?" Craig asked. "The one you said carried you off the street?"

"Wait a minute? What guy?" Shane looked at Gabriel then Matt. "You didn't tell us about some guy."

Matt let out a long exhalation. "That's because I didn't think he was real," he finally responded. He turned away from Dee and Shane's concerned eyes before settling on Craig's. "You're the one who told me there was no one else around me. That you saw *me* get out of the way on my own. I figured you were right. That I hit my head much harder than I thought. But now." He turned to look at Gabriel. "Well, now, I know I was right all along."

Craig turned to Gabriel. "You were there this morning? At the parking garage on Kirby?"

Gabriel nodded, reluctantly.

"And you carried Matt off the street like he told me someone did?"

"Yes."

Craig turned to Matt and wrapped his hand around his forearm. "Will you please come with me? We need to talk."

Before Matt could protest, Craig escorted him down the hallway and away from the others.

ONCE Craig had led Matt into the bedroom, he shut the door behind them. From the distressed look in his eyes, it was obvious something Gabriel said worried him, but Matt had no idea what that could be. After all, Gabriel admitted to saving his life not trying to kill him.

"So what's this all about?" he asked while taking off the latex gloves he apparently wasn't going to use.

"You can't be serious?" Craig asked. "That guy's a loon."

"Why? Because he saved my life? Twice?"

Craig ran his fingers through his wavy blond hair. He was obviously exasperated, and Matt didn't appreciate Craig making him feel foolish for not seeing whatever his overly suspicious mind saw.

"Think about it," Craig replied. He put both his hands on Matt's shoulders and stroked them. It was similar to how he comforted Matt at the F Bar a few hours earlier, when Matt admitted feeling responsible for the death of the driver who had almost killed him. Like he did then, Matt wanted to give himself over to the reassuring touch, but he couldn't. For reasons he couldn't explain, Craig's continued distrust of Gabriel infuriated him.

"You don't think I've thought about it? I've almost died today, Craig. Twice."

"That's not what I'm talking about," Craig said. He pulled Matt over to the bed, where they both sat down. "This is a potentially dangerous situation here. One that needs investigating."

"Investigating? Who needs investigating?"

"Gabriel."

Matt couldn't believe his ears. Why in the world would Craig want to investigate a man who had done no wrong? "This makes no sense to me."

"Matt, Gabriel is obviously stalking you."

"You can't be serious?" he asked. From Craig's even stare, he could tell he was. "Why in the world do you say that?"

"He just happens to be at the parking garage *and* the House of Pies?"

"Have you never heard of coincidence? I've run into people in several places on the same day, and no stalking accusations flew about. We just laughed and went on about our business."

"Have you seen the way he looks at you?" Craig asked, deeply troubled. "It's not right. It's like he loves you or something."

Matt felt his cheeks blush. Of course he noticed Gabriel's attentive glances. His eyes seemed magnetically drawn to him, and Matt liked the way it felt. He knew it was wrong, especially considering how much he claimed to have liked Craig just a few short hours before. Still, he felt powerless against the feeling. Every time he tried to fight it, it overpowered him.

"I'll take that as a yes."

"Take what as a yes?"

"You're blushing," Craig answered. He reached out and caressed Matt's warm cheeks, but then withdrew his hand. A profound sadness was visible in his eyes. "It means you've noticed *and* you like it."

"Actually, it means you're embarrassing me," he told Craig, hoping his white lie might spare Craig's feelings. He had no interest in hurting him, but he also didn't feel it necessary to express emotions even he was uncertain of.

"Okay," Craig answered, but Matt could tell he didn't believe him. Apparently, lying to a cop wasn't easy. "But the fact remains you've got a potential stalker on your hands."

"I've got to agree with him, sweetie."

Matt and Craig looked toward the open bedroom door to find Dee standing in the doorway.

"Not you too," he told her.

"Yes, me too," she replied. Her eyes looked equally as worried as Craig's. "You've got to admit, it's pretty damn creepy."

"Well, I think you're both making too much out of this. Gabriel saved my life."

Dee looked at him as if he were a naïve child. He didn't appreciate the look or the way they were ganging up on him. "He's obviously been following you. I have to wonder how long this has been going on."

"Thank you," Craig said. He then crossed over to Dee and kissed her on the cheek. "He doesn't see it."

"Of course he doesn't. Matty's the kindest soul I know. He doesn't see bad in anybody."

Being talked about as if he wasn't in the room was starting to piss Matt off. Besides, both Craig and Dee were overlooking a very important point. "You know, I *coincidentally* ran into Craig two times today, but no one's accused *him* of being a stalker." He stared into Craig's shocked eyes. "By your own logic, I should be just as leery of you."

"Matty!" Dee yelled. "This is different, and you know it. Craig's presence at the accident can be explained. He's a cop for Christ's sake! Gabriel had no reason to be at both places where you were at today. That's just sorta psycho to me."

"And you honestly think Gabriel's psycho? You can say that about a man who's saved your best friend's life twice in one day?"

"I'll be grateful to Gabriel for that," she admitted to Matt. "Always. But that doesn't mean I have to ignore my suspicions. Being careful keeps you alive."

"It seems to me that for the past twelve hours, it's been Gabriel who's been keeping me alive."

"You seem intent on protecting him," Dee observed. "What's going on here?"

Craig nodded in agreement. "That's a good question."

"*Nothing's* going on. At least not what the two of you are implying. I'm just refusing to be as paranoid as you two. Gabriel's done nothing to deserve this."

"Are you listening to yourself?" Dee asked. "I know how stubborn you can be, but I also know how guarded you are. Considering everything you've been through." Dee's comment elicited a look of confusion from Craig. He obviously wanted clarification but decided against it for the time being. "But for some reason. With this guy. You're throwing caution to the wind."

"I'm not throwing anything to the wind," he replied, getting angrier that Dee and Craig refused to let this go. "If I felt threatened, believe me, I would do something about it. But I don't. And the two of you won't convince me otherwise."

"Matty—"

"End of discussion, Dee," he said, cutting her off. "Now, where's Gabriel? Is he in there with Shane?"

Dee nodded. She was obviously upset but willing to let the matter drop.

"I'm going to go bandage his wound, and I don't want to hear another word out of either of you about this." He turned to both of them. "Understand?"

They both nodded.

When Matt walked back into the living room, followed reluctantly by Dee and Craig, they found Shane sitting on the couch watching television. Gabriel was nowhere to be found.

"Where's Gabriel?" he asked Shane.

"He left," Shane replied absently. "He said to tell you thank you but that he would be all right."

"And you just let him go?"

"What did you want me to do?" Shane asked. "Did you not see how big that guy was? If he wanted to leave, I wasn't getting in his way."

"He was wounded, Shane!"

"Yeah, and he's a big boy. If he doesn't want your help, who are you to force it on him?"

Matt wanted to yell at Shane, to accuse him of being a shortsighted fool, who rarely thought about anyone but himself. Instead, he grumbled in frustration.

"What?" Shane asked, clueless as ever.

Matt looked at his closed front door. He wanted to rush out and find Gabriel, not just to take care of his injury but because he wanted to see him again. At this moment, he wanted that more than anything else he had ever wanted in his life.

GABRIEL stood in the shadows of the parking lot across the street, watching Dee, Shane, and Craig exit Matt's apartment complex. Although he didn't want to leave without saying good-bye, he knew he had to. Dee and Craig were suspicious of him.

If he stayed any longer, they might call the police. He had already had to deal with the authorities once, and he didn't want to repeat the experience. He was lucky enough to use his gifts to sidetrack their questions without anyone being the wiser. But inside Matt's apartment, it would be more difficult to pull off unnoticed, especially under Craig's constant scrutiny.

Yet Matt worried him even more than Craig did. Matt held a power over him no one else in creation possessed. If Matt insisted on dressing his wound and looked at him again with those wide, loving, hazel eyes, he doubted he would possess the resolve to continue to deny his request. After all, he would do anything for Matt. Anything at all.

So he had to get out. No one, not even Matt, could see the spot where he was stabbed. It would only make matters worse and add to the already mounting doubt Matt's friends currently carried.

They feared him. They believed he meant to do Matt harm.

They couldn't be more wrong.

His entire purpose revolved around Matt's safety. It was his mission, and he would do whatever was necessary to see it completed. But he couldn't tell them that.

He wasn't meant to interact with Matt or his friends. His orders were to remain in the periphery, to act only when needed and only as a last resort. The only reason he showed himself tonight was because it couldn't have been helped. Had he not intervened, Matt would have been killed, and that was what he had been sent to prevent.

No doubt others already knew of tonight's events, and he anticipated being contacted, most likely by Michael. His brother would remind him to be as invisible as the air.

He understood the rules, but as Michael pointed out earlier, the lines were blurring. Although it wasn't permissible to become actively involved in Matt's everyday world, to take on more than the role he assumed, he found it increasingly difficult to remain in the background.

And as he watched Matt's friends depart in their vehicles, Gabriel faced a choice he had never confronted before—whether or not he wanted to break the rules one more time.

CHAPTER 9

MATT hadn't been this perturbed in a long time. While everyone's suspicions of Gabriel's motives infuriated him, he found himself riled more by Gabriel. His sudden disappearance did nothing to squash the doubts shared by Craig and Dee. When they discovered Gabriel had left, they glanced sideways at each other as if his departure validated their fears.

Since he hadn't the strength for another debate, he told them he was tired, and they left.

Being asked to leave didn't bother Shane. Accustomed to overstaying his welcome, he delivered a peck on Matt's cheek and departed.

Dee and Craig were a different story.

Anger boiled beneath Dee's surface as she gathered her purse to follow Shane out the door. Her full lips stretched pencil thin across her face, and she exited his apartment without a good-bye and without her usual hug and kiss. Matt knew he would pay for his actions later. Big time.

Craig took it the hardest. When Matt announced it was time for them to go, his joyful green eyes became a cheerless pale hue. He asked if he could stay a bit longer and talk, but Matt refused the request. He was tired and didn't want to go another few rounds with him on the subject of Gabriel.

They were going to have to agree to disagree. If Craig didn't want to trust Gabriel, that was his choice. Matt was under no obligation to follow suit. He liked Craig. A lot. They enjoyed a fun evening together, and Matt hoped similar nights would follow in the future.

But now there was Gabriel.

Something about him captivated Matt. Although he logically understood the apprehension Craig and Dee expressed, Gabriel triggered no such internal alarm for him. He felt sheltered, not threatened. Finding Gabriel was like re-discovering the memories of his past and of his parents.

That was why he couldn't believe Gabriel meant him any harm, and no one would be able to convince him otherwise.

Someone lightly rapped at his door.

Matt paused at the coffee table. He had been putting away the medical supplies that were no longer needed, and grumbling rather noisily to himself, so he wasn't certain if someone had really knocked. When the sound repeated, he sighed heavily. He was exhausted. It was likely Craig or Dee, who wanted to revisit the argument one more time before bed.

After stacking the supplies neatly on the table, he marched toward the door. Whoever stood on the other side was about to get an earful. But once he unlocked the door and swung it inward, the irritation caught in his throat.

Gabriel had returned, and Matt's frustration blew away in the warm breeze of Gabriel's smile.

"I wanted to apologize for leaving so abruptly," he told Matt. "And to thank you for wanting to take care of me."

Before he realized what he was doing, Matt grabbed Gabriel by the arm and pulled him inside. "You're not getting away so easily this time," he warned. Matt led him by the arm back to the living room and to the chair he had previously occupied. He motioned for Gabriel to sit and then turned back to his medical supplies.

"I'm not here for that," Gabriel told him. "I just…"

"I'm not asking you," he interrupted. "You've been hurt, and I'm taking care of it. End of discussion." Gabriel opened his mouth to reply, but Matt shushed him. He was surprised when Gabriel complied without further argument. Ordering a man into silence who was almost ten inches taller than him and at least twice as broad was a powerful aphrodisiac. He wondered if he could make Gabriel strip out of his clothes. "Take off your jacket."

Gabriel nodded in obedience. As he took off his jacket, the muscles in his broad, muscular chest fanned outward, and his biceps bulged beneath the fabric of his blue shirt, which was still stained with blood.

Shocked that Gabriel did as instructed, Matt found it difficult to speak. He had to swallow hard to regain his composure, and he had to remind himself to breathe. Never before had he seen a man more beautiful in his life. And never before had such a man been willing to do as he asked. He instinctively knew Gabriel would do anything he said. Anything at all.

"Matt? Are you well?"

Matt nodded and cleared his throat. He had to force the image of Gabriel stripping out of his clothes and taking him in his strong arms, all at Matt's request, from his mind. "I'm fine. Just recalling knife wound protocol." Actually, he was thinking about dead kittens in order to subdue his rapidly rising erection. It would do him or Gabriel little good if he couldn't get his rampant desires in check. He was a nurse after all, and Gabriel was a patient who needed his help. This wasn't some sexual role-playing game. He needed to remain as professional as he would at the hospital.

After a long exhalation, which helped release some of his sexual tension, Matt drew closer to Gabriel. "I need to cut you out of your shirt. The fabric most likely has stuck to the wound, and I need to gently lift it from the damaged tissue."

"It's no longer bleeding," Gabriel told him. "I checked it before I returned. I'm fine. Really."

Matt reached down for the scissors. It helped that Gabriel was a difficult patient. It kept his mind focused on the task instead of the burning desire to rip the clothes from Gabriel's hard body. "Are you a nurse or a medical professional?"

"Not in the strictest sense, no."

"Then my opinion means more than yours right now," he answered. "I'll just cut around the wound, so stay still."

He knelt before Gabriel, but before he had a chance to use the scissors, Gabriel reached down and tugged the shirt free of his body. Matt barely had time to register what had happened. In a typical situation, he would be screaming at the patient, horrified that more damage had been inflicted to the wound.

But staring at Gabriel, who sat bare-chested in front of him, Matt saw only a small cut, no deeper than a cat scratch and no longer bleeding. "I don't understand," he finally managed. His shock chased away his inappropriate sexual cravings. "Where's the knife wound?"

"I told you that I heal quickly."

"Not this quickly. You've healed at a faster-than-normal rate."

"I've always healed quickly, and the knife only scratched me. It looked worse than it really was."

Maybe Gabriel was right. That would explain why he had instinctively felt that the wound had been minor. It also made Matt once again confident in his medical intuition. But as the events replayed in his mind, he shook his head. "I was there. I saw what happened. Blade stabbed you. It was sticking out of your stomach and then you took it out and chucked it across the street."

"It mostly hit the jacket," Gabriel told him.

Matt didn't believe him. He knew what he saw. The knife jutted out of his stomach, not the jacket. "How do you explain all the blood? It even got on Shane, remember?"

Gabriel shrugged. "I can't. But it's not bleeding anymore." He stood and pointed to his midsection. "As you can see."

Eye level with his stomach, Matt fixated on his flawless, uninjured flesh. A soft mat of dark fur covered his rippling abdominal muscles and fanned upward to his broad chest, where the hair swirled over his pectorals and around his perfect nipples. Extending from his trunk were the powerful arms that had twice saved him, and the massive hands he longed to feel caress his body.

When his eyes met Gabriel's, who gazed down at him in worship, he suddenly realized he was still on his knees and had been staring at Gabriel's half naked body in silence for far too long.

So much for professionalism, he thought as he rose to his feet.

The change in perspective allowed his mind to return to the medical conundrum of Gabriel's uninjured abdominal region. If he hadn't seen it with his own eyes, he would never guess Gabriel had been stabbed only a few hours ago.

"Something's just not right, though," he whispered. His education and experience along with his sixth sense in regards to healing overpowered his baser instinct. Everything combined told him that what he now saw was impossible. "I know what I saw."

Gabriel smiled at him, and the warmth of the smile melted away his disbelief. "You were being attacked, and you were afraid. As anyone would've been in your situation. You saw him stab me, and perhaps from your vantage point on the ground, the knife looked to be projecting from my stomach, but I assure you, it wasn't. If it had been, I'd be seriously hurt. Wouldn't you agree?"

He nodded in response. What else could he say? Even though he was certain he saw where Blade stabbed Gabriel, the complete lack of a knife wound proved he had been wrong. Perhaps when he first saw Gabriel's injury after the police left, he saw more than was there. His mind may have made more of the blood than was warranted and imagined more damage than there actually was. That had to be what happened. There simply was no other explanation.

Matt then eyed Gabriel's jacket, which lay draped across the back of the chair. If the knife did penetrate the leather, some of the fabric would be cut or torn. It would prove with absolute certainty that Matt had been wrong.

Gabriel followed Matt's eyes to his jacket. His blue eyes reflected his understanding of Matt's intentions. He turned around to reach for his jacket, and when he did, Matt saw the tattoo that spanned the length of his exposed back.

Strong, majestic wings arched over the curve of his shoulder blades descending to his upper glutes, which peaked over the denim in twin mounds of sculpted perfection. Detailed in exquisite precision, each tattooed feather adjoined to the wings looked three-dimensional, making them a work of art likely crafted in a famous art studio rather than an obscure parlor.

The wings also had a curious quality about them. They shined with a radiance that defied the dark shades and contouring of the design, appearing to draw in all ambient lighting and reflecting it outward. He had to squint to look directly at them like they were a celestial object and not born from the infusing of black hue into skin.

"So beautiful," he whispered and reached out to touch them. When his fingertips traced the progress of the right wing down Gabriel's muscled flesh, he half-expected the inked feathers to ruffle upon contact. They didn't move, but Gabriel shuddered at his touch.

Matt withdrew his hand and was immediately embarrassed. "I apologize. I shouldn't have done that."

Gabriel turned around to look at him. A smile danced on his lips, and his eyes showed no trace of irritation. They only looked at him with adoration, as they had done since this morning. "Don't apologize. It was nice."

Silence stretched out before them, filling the few inches that separated them with heavy, unspoken passion. It rolled over them, dancing across their flesh like hundreds of fingertips. Each feathery stroke stoked the embers of their smoldering desire.

Matt knew he had only seconds to seize control before he leaped into Gabriel's arms.

"How long have you had them?" Matt asked, his voice thick with repressed desire. "The tattooed wings."

"As long as I can remember," Gabriel replied in a soft rasp.

"And how long can you remember?"

Gabriel chuckled. "I have a *very* long memory."

"You're being evasive," he pointed out. "Why?"

"I don't mean to be," Gabriel replied while taking a step toward the couch. He held his blue shirt in his hand. Matt expected him to put the shirt back on and come up with an excuse to leave. Matt had been ogling him like a horny teenager. It would serve him right if Gabriel just up and left. Instead, he draped the shirt over the back of the chair, on top of the leather jacket. "I'm just very private."

"About your tattoo?"

"About most everything."

"Some would call that suspicious behavior."

Gabriel's gaze burrowed into the depths of Matt's soul. "Do you?"

Under normal circumstances, Matt would have responded yes. But Gabriel was more mysterious than anything else. How could Matt doubt a man who saved his life twice?

"No, I don't," he finally responded.

A huge grin extended over Gabriel's dark, rugged features, and his smile, like his tattoo, glowed with an internal incandescence.

The smile illuminated more than just Gabriel's features; it also revealed a truth. Gabriel knew Matt's answer before asking the question. As much as he trusted Gabriel without a doubt, Gabriel had absolute faith in Matt's trust in him.

Matt had trouble understanding how such deep feelings could exist between two people who had never met before today. He heard about love at first sight happening to others. It was something he wanted to find for himself, but he had begun to believe it to be a myth. He was as much of a pragmatist as he was a hopeless romantic.

Still, he wondered: was this love he felt for Gabriel? Had this man won his heart the moment he swept him off his feet and saved him from the oncoming truck this morning? Is that why he trusted Gabriel so implicitly?

"Can I ask you a question?"

Gabriel nodded. His eyes still stared down at him, and he could tell Gabriel had no intention of looking away. Looking at him seemed to be all Gabriel craved.

"Why did you save me? Twice?"

"That's a silly question. You needed saving, so I saved you."

"But twice?"

"Well, you were in danger twice."

"But you were there both times. At just the right moment." Matt looked away. He knew he needed to ask the question, but he couldn't give it voice looking into eyes filled with only adulation. Doing so would weaken his resolve and muddy his thinking. Although he didn't feel threatened by Gabriel, it didn't mean he wasn't curious as to how he had been at both places so coincidentally.

"I won't be angry," Gabriel told him.

"What do you mean?"

"I can tell you want to ask me something, and you're uncertain how to broach the subject. Just ask me. I won't lie to you, and I won't be angry."

"You don't know what I'm even going to ask," he replied. "So you don't know if you'll be angry or not."

"I could never be angry with you," Gabriel responded with absolute confidence.

Matt stood before him, stunned. It wasn't merely the words or the tone that surprised him; it was the fact that Matt believed him, unequivocally.

"Okay then," he replied. "Are you following me like Dee and Craig think you are?"

"No. I'm not following you like Dee and Craig think I am."

"Then how?"

"I like to think it's all part of a grand design. Some things are simply meant to be."

Once again, the answer caught Matt by surprise. Somehow, Gabriel gave voice to feelings Matt had trouble expressing. This whole time he felt something between him and Gabriel, but he had no idea what to call it. Now, he did.

It was simply meant to be.

For some cosmic reason, he and Gabriel were destined to meet. Their paths crossed not because Gabriel was stalking him like his friends believed but because Gabriel was like a gift sent from God not only to save him but to complete him.

Before Matt could stop himself, he crossed the distance still separating him from Gabriel. He stared up into the sky-blue eyes and surrendered himself to the passion that engulfed his entire body. He placed both hands on Gabriel's warm chest. In response, Gabriel wrapped his protective arms around his waist and pulled Matt's body to his.

They rested against each other, fitting together like two pieces of some immense puzzle that, upon contact, slipped into place and set the world right. Matt felt as if he had finally found the home he had been missing, and the whole time that place of comfort and security resided in Gabriel's arms.

He nudged himself into Gabriel's chest, rubbing the soft chest hair against his smooth face. He inhaled deeply, and Gabriel's fragrance filled his lungs. He smelled like the sweet perfume of rain on a spring day. The scent invigorated him, renewing his soul and causing him to blossom like a flower, and like an opening rosebud before a coming storm, Matt turned his head to the expansive sky residing in Gabriel's eyes.

Gabriel craned his neck downward, their lips now only inches apart. The air around them crackled with electricity.

When their lips finally met, the heavens opened up and released their life-giving waters onto the land below.

At first, their kisses were tender and a bit tentative. Although he could sense the burning desire thrumming behind Gabriel's lips, some unspoken hesitancy prevented him from fully giving in to his passion. His lips trembled in both want and fear.

Matt briefly wondered what lay behind the trepidation.

Was Gabriel involved with another man? Maybe even a woman?

No, he knew there was no one else. Of that much, he was certain. Gabriel's conflict stemmed from something other than another relationship. It was a conflict deeply rooted in his soul.

Matt was just about to ask what bothered him when Gabriel's actions stole his voice. Gabriel nibbled and licked his delicate flesh, which brewed an uncontrollable storm that raged across Matt's skin and quickly blew Matt's question from his mind.

Instead, he opened his mouth and drew Gabriel's hungry tongue inside. Powerful and strong, his tongue filled Matt's mouth with the taste of honey, and Matt savored the sweet taste. He wrapped his arms around Gabriel's neck, pulling his mouth further into his own and causing Gabriel's unshaven face to scrape against his smooth skin.

Gabriel moved his hands from his back to his ass, kneading it roughly while also forcing their bodies closer together. His hard cock, still restrained within his jeans, pressed against Matt's stomach, and Gabriel's hardness intensified Matt's already white-hot passion.

Matt braced himself against Gabriel's strong shoulders and wrapped his legs around Gabriel's waist, rubbing the hard shaft against his still-clothed ass.

Gabriel moaned in response. His hands, which now supported Matt's weight in their palms, clutched desperately at him. Matt wanted him to rip the clothes from his body. He longed to feel Gabriel's bare flesh against his own before Gabriel buried himself deep inside.

He licked Gabriel's neck, his tongue scraping against the hard stubble. The moisture that coated his hot flesh wasn't salty like sweat. Instead, it was spicy like cinnamon. The flavor made Matt wild. Matt worked his hands from Gabriel's shoulders to his muscled back, where he grasped and clawed at the bare skin.

When Matt ran his fingers across Gabriel's back and toward the waistband of his jeans, the uncertainty returned. Gabriel's body tensed, and the deluge of kisses subsided to a light drizzle.

"We shouldn't do this," he panted. "*I* shouldn't do this."

Matt leaned back and stared into Gabriel's conflicted eyes. He definitely saw Gabriel's passion, and he still felt his hard dick pressed against him, but the inner tempest blew the lusty winds away.

As much as Gabriel wanted this to happen, there was another part of him that just as equally wanted it *not* to happen.

"I'm sorry." Matt unwrapped his legs from Gabriel's waist, and Gabriel gently lowered him to the floor. Matt felt like an idiot. "I'm so embarrassed."

"Please, don't be," said Gabriel. "I'm the one to blame. I let myself get out of control, and I shouldn't have." He placed his thumb and forefinger under Matt's chin and gently lifted Matt's gaze up to meet his. "I should be stronger than this."

"I don't understand," Matt admitted. "Stronger than what?"

"Than giving into passion."

"There's nothing wrong with giving in if both people want it," he told Gabriel. "And I don't know about you, but I wanted it."

He reached out and took Matt's hands into his. "I've never wanted anything more."

"Then there's no need to stop," he replied while gazing into Gabriel's eyes. "I don't want you to."

Matt then raised Gabriel's hands to his lips and began kissing them. He licked one then two fingers before popping them in his mouth and sucking on them.

"Please, Matt," he begged. "You don't know what you're asking of me."

"I'm asking you to hold me. And as insane as it might sound, I'm asking you to love me."

"I do love you, Matt. More than you can possibly know."

Matt nodded. "I can feel it. It's been there from the moment I first saw you. I don't know how it happened or why. But I'm not going to question it. For the first time in my life, I'm just going to accept it." He placed one arm then the other around Gabriel, and he once again rested within Gabriel's embrace. "I ask that you accept it too."

"But…"

"Please, Gabriel. This doesn't happen to me. I've spent my life searching for something that was always just beyond my grasp. And now it's here. Inexplicably. Its arms are embracing me. Don't ask me to send that away."

Gabriel craned his head downward and kissed his lips tenderly two times before removing his hands from around Matt and stepping away. "It's better this way. For everyone."

"Why do you say that? Do you have a boyfriend or something? Are you married?"

"No."

"Then why?"

"You'll have to take my word on this," Gabriel told him before crossing back to the chair. He pulled his blue shirt back over his body before shrugging back into his leather jacket. He walked back to Matt and stared down at him. Passion and regret still warred within. "Stay safe, Matthew Westlake."

Gabriel then walked past him and out the front door.

CHAPTER 10

SINCE leaving Matt's apartment and meandering through the heart of Houston, Gabriel found it difficult to center himself. The cool night air had always done the trick in the past. It usually revitalized his spirit as the wind currents drove his concerns away. But the oppressive heat stifled the wind, leaving his heart heavy and his soul in turmoil.

He was not accustomed to such spiritual turbulence.

He always prided himself on remaining in control. When his brothers lapsed into emotion that clouded their judgment, Gabriel found comfort within the cold logic of purpose and duty. It gave him strength and direction.

Everything changed in the few short moments alone with Matt. He now felt lost and confused. The emotions he struggled to suppress would no longer be contained, and they were feelings he could not have. Even so, his resolve to keep them contained disappeared once he held Matt in his arms.

Matt wanted Gabriel as more than merely a protector. He wanted Gabriel as a man.

His brother had warned him earlier that he was blurring lines not meant to be crossed. He denied the accusation then. Not because it wasn't true but because he had refused to see the intensity of his feelings.

His years spent protecting Matt and watching him grow into the exceptional man he now was changed him. The beauty of Matt's soul and the tenderness of his heart enraptured him. His jaded perspective saw what true potential resided in the world.

Where others before Matt met the horrors of their past by turning cruel and vindictive, Matt soared above the evil that haunted him. Instead of hurting those less fortunate, he healed them, tapping into the potential that still remained unlocked inside his soul. He saw only the good, even when presented with nothing but tragedy. His heart remained open and accessible, not indifferent and spiteful.

He truly represented the best of what this world had to offer, and though Gabriel couldn't see it before when Michael had visited him, he saw it quite plainly now. Even more than that, he felt the warm glow burn deep within him.

Gabriel had fallen in love with Matt.

But was that possible? Would it even be allowed? Rules existed against such emotions, and for good reason. When the lines had previously been crossed, chaos erupted. Would his feelings for Matt spark such calamity as well?

It was difficult for Gabriel to believe any bad could result from the growing seed of love that took root within his soul. Even now, it spread outward, staking claim to every part of his being, so that all he could think about was Matt's gentle touch and the soft lips that offered kisses like nectar.

In Matt's arms, his singularity of purpose multiplied a thousandfold. His life was no longer his duty or his ultimate function. He became more than what he had been created for. He became the man Matt saw, and in his hazel eyes, he found a different purpose and a new strength.

For the past few decades, Matt had been his duty, his assignment. Matt had become so much more since then. Matt became his reason to live, which he knew would alter his actions and potentially jeopardize his mission.

He had always been willing to do what was necessary to protect Matt. It was his job, and he had done it countless times already. If it cost him his immortal soul, so be it. But now, he was willing to move beyond his job. He was willing to do whatever Matt wanted, even if it required breaking ironclad rules.

And if he hadn't gotten out of Matt's apartment when he did, he would have gladly added his body to his heart, which Matt already possessed.

Though no wind stirred the brown leaves scattered along the sidewalk, Gabriel noticed a slight breeze spring up around him. It turned the air minty cool, and when he heard the faint swoosh of beating wings, he knew his brother had returned.

"Greetings, Michael," Gabriel told the night air. He couldn't detect where his brother would materialize, but the wafting breeze revealed he was near.

"Good evening, brother," Michael replied, suddenly walking by his side.

For a few moments, they strolled in silence. Occasionally, Michael broke the quiet, commenting on the local environment. They had a two-minute conversation on a pigeon, perched on a street lamp. Michael found the green tint of the neck feathers magnificent and an awe-inspiring design. Gabriel then drew his brother's attention to the revealing clothes of those who passed them on the street. Michael, who was far more conservative than Gabriel, dressed in a white button-down shirt and tan pants, remarked on how modesty had all but vanished upon the planet.

They discussed a variety of other topics—the jarring music that blared out of passing cars or the fact that most people avoided making eye contact whenever they passed by.

What they had yet to broach was the unpleasant business that recalled Michael to his side. Neither of them wanted to travel immediately down that path. They had both been there countless times before when they disagreed, and it was rarely constructive. Harsh words were usually exchanged, which typically resulted in battles of epic proportion.

"How are things at Father's?" Gabriel asked, feeling the need to get down to business.

"Pleasant as always. But He is troubled. Deeply troubled." Michael stopped to stare at him. His usually tranquil eyes churned in distress. "We all are."

"There's no need. Everything is under control."

"And what would your definition of control be?"

Gabriel continued his stroll, taking a side path that led to a small park. He figured their conversation needed a more private setting. "Matt is safe," he finally answered when his brother re-joined him at his side.

"And what of the other?"

"I'm charged with protecting no other as you know."

"I do," he replied. "But you also know to what I'm referring. Don't pretend otherwise."

"You know me better than that, Michael. I don't indulge in pretending. I'll leave fantasy to you and Raphael."

Anger registered on his brother's face. His already churning eyes darkened to a soft gray. If emotions weren't brought under control, havoc would ensue. Michael immediately sensed this, and closed his eyes. When they re-opened, calm had been restored, and the turbulent gray returned to the tranquility of blue. "You're walking a most dangerous path. You know this. I sense it. Though we may often be at odds, you and I have always been close. In spite of our differences."

Gabriel didn't respond, for it was true. Though they were as different as night and day, Michael had always been his best friend and his worst enemy. None of his relationships with his other brothers came close to the special bond that connected the two of them. Still, he couldn't bring himself to admit that Michael was right.

"Speak to me, brother. Let us deal with your sins and avoid what must follow."

"And what might that be?" he asked. "Do you plan on wrestling me from this place? On shackling me in chains and bringing me home, bound and gagged like some infidel?"

"Of course not," Michael replied. "But your refusal to voice your sins and accept your part in what has gone wrong could jeopardize everything. You know the gravity of the situation. You know how important Matthew Westlake is to the Grand Design."

"I'm well aware of his importance."

Michael nodded, but his eyes now reflected concern. "Yet he has grown to become more than just the mission. Your purpose has become blunted, and your vision shortsighted."

This time, rage stirred within Gabriel. He resented being spoken to in such a manner, of being accused of falling down on a job he had successfully executed for the entirety of Matt's life. "My purpose is razor-sharp, and my eyes still see the path through the forest of trees. I know my place. I know what I must do."

"Yet you have not only revealed yourself to Matthew and his friends, but you've also engaged in carnal pleasure."

Gabriel sighed. "I had no choice but to reveal myself. Matt would have been killed, and what would have happened to the Grand Design then?" His heart thudded in his chest, and he felt the familiar itch course through the tattoo etched into his skin. If his emotions weren't brought under control, he might reveal his true self to all in the park. That was definitely a rule breaker.

"And the kiss?" Michael asked, his voice low and calm. Like earlier, his brother was trying to defuse Gabriel's temper.

"Was a mistake," he admitted. "And it won't happen again."

"We hope not."

"We?"

Michael nodded. "We are watching you, Gabriel. Becoming emotionally attached with your charge is unacceptable. As you know. It isn't your function to become involved with—" He paused, choosing his words carefully. "—ordinary affairs. If such actions persist, you will be recalled."

Gabriel wanted to lash out. He wanted to strike his brother with all the power housed in his form. Michael was threatening to take him away from Matt, to assign someone else to guard his life, someone who might fail where he had succeeded. He couldn't allow that to happen. So instead of giving over to his fury, he gritted his teeth and swallowed his anger.

"I'll remain in the periphery," he finally said. "And Matt will continue to be safe." It wasn't the response he wanted to give, but it was the only one that would guarantee he remained the one assigned to Matt.

"Then all will be well," his brother replied.

Gabriel could tell Michael remained doubtful. Though his eyes beamed, his lips didn't broaden into their customary smile.

"All will be well," Gabriel repeated.

Michael nodded and turned to walk down the path the two previously traveled together. After a few steps, Michael vanished from view, returning home to deliver his report that he suspected would allay, but not dispel, the fears of those who observed Gabriel's every move from above.

A STRANGE thump woke Matt from a deep sleep. As he surveyed his bedroom trying to locate the noise, he realized his bedroom had changed. The shaker armoire, which usually sat across from his queen-sized bed, was missing. In its place stood a smaller dresser, painted blue. An assortment of toys lined the top—some Hot Wheels cars, a metal Godzilla with arms up and ready to attack, and a few Transformers and G.I. Joe's.

No heavy burgundy curtains hung in front of his arched slider window. Light blue curtains now covered a mulled double-hung window. His walls were painted yellow instead of tan. The art deco prints that framed each side of his bed were missing, and his bed had shrunk from a queen to a twin some time during the night.

Thump. Thump.

Matt turned toward his closed bedroom door, which looked more like walnut wood than the ebony wood it had been prior to falling asleep.

Thump.

The noise was coming from inside, from somewhere downstairs. Except Matt didn't have a downstairs. He lived in an apartment. Could the sound be coming from the neighbors below?

Thump.

Matt pulled back the covers and got out of bed. His feet shuffled across white Berber carpet instead of Pergo flooring.

As he drew closer to the door, the sound grew louder.

Thump. Thump.

They were footsteps, and they were coming up the stairs. They were coming for him.

"Stay away from the door, Matt. Come here with me."

Matt spun around to face the familiar voice. "Gabriel?"

Gabriel stepped out of the shadows, which had engulfed his bedroom. His beautiful blue eyes sparkled like a sun-kissed sky, and as he looked about the room; the shadows retreated underneath the furniture before disappearing completely.

"What's happening? Where am I?"

"Come to me. You'll be safe with me."

Matt nodded and walked across his carpeted bedroom. Gabriel looked down with love as Matt stood before him. The conflict and reservations he had seen reflected within them earlier in the evening had vanished. The glimmer in his eyes told Matt that this time there would be no stopping.

All Matt had to do was reach out and claim what Gabriel now freely offered.

He reached up and caressed Gabriel's cheeks. The ever-present stubble scratched the palm of his hand, and he followed the hard jawline to his strong chin and up to his delicate lips. With his index finger, Matt traced the curves before drawing tiny circles around the soft button at the center of his top lip.

Gabriel blew hot, wet kisses across Matt's fingers. It sent shivers pulsing throughout Matt's body. He then inserted his index finger in Gabriel's mouth, and his tongue darted around Matt's finger while his teeth gently bit down.

With his free hand, Matt trailed down the muscular curves and dips of Gabriel's body, from his strong shoulder cap down to his bulging biceps and over to his broad chest. Gabriel ran his rough hands along Matt's bare back before resting at the waistband of his shorts, where Matt's naked flesh dipped below the fabric.

Gabriel spread his hands across his skin, making Matt weak. He wanted those strong hands to travel below the band and cup his ass, to spread his cheeks in anticipation of Gabriel's hard cock.

Matt turned rock hard at the thought of Gabriel penetrating his flesh, of filling him up with his manhood until he released deep within him and claimed his body with his seed.

Sensing his desire, Gabriel gripped the sides of his shorts and pressed Matt against him, forcing his erection into Matt's stomach. Matt wanted to free Gabriel's throbbing member from its denim prison.

"I want you. I want you so bad," Matt panted. "But I'm scared."

"Of me?"

Matt shook his head. "Of the noise." He turned his head to the bedroom door.

Thump. Thump. Thump.

"It's getting closer. I can hear it," he told Gabriel. What Matt didn't reveal was that he somehow knew that once the door swung open, he would face danger he had never experienced before.

Gabriel hooked his chin and turned Matt toward him once again. "I won't let anything hurt you," he told Matt. "No harm will come to you as long as I'm around."

"You promise?" he asked as Gabriel engulfed him in his protective embrace.

"Always."

Matt burrowed further into the safety he offered. He wrapped his arms around Gabriel, clawing at his back and searching for the handhold that would allow him to stay this way forever.

Gabriel responded by slipping his hands beneath the waistband of Matt's shorts until they slid past his hips and from his body. Matt now stood completely naked in Gabriel's arms, and though he would normally feel vulnerable, he felt only relief.

Matt wanted nothing, not even clothes, to stand between them.

He wrapped his smaller arms around Gabriel's big neck and pulled himself up. Gabriel palmed his ass and supported his weight as Matt found his mark with his hungry lips.

He dove right in, slipping his insistent tongue inside Gabriel's mouth. Their slick tongues danced around each other, slipping and sliding from Matt's mouth back to Gabriel's. In between kisses, they grunted and moaned. Searing hot pants of breath scorched across their already burning flesh, working them into an unstoppable frenzy.

"I love you," Gabriel told him as his index finger drew small, lazy circles around the rim of his hole.

Matt groaned, pushing downward against the big finger. "I love you too," he managed to reply before Gabriel used the sweat collecting at the nape of Matt's ass to slip his finger inside.

Matt whimpered and threw his head back as he rode Gabriel's finger. "Oh yes," he muttered. "Yes."

Gabriel nibbled at his throat and then licked his way up to his chin before once again diving inside his mouth. Matt felt like his body would explode from the sensation of Gabriel's finger pushing in and out of his ass and Gabriel's tongue wedged deep in his mouth.

He bucked down harder, wanting to force more and more of Gabriel inside him, and he practically devoured Gabriel's persistent kisses.

Still, he needed more. This wouldn't be enough. Gabriel's clothes needed to come off.

"I want you naked," he begged. "I need you naked."

Gabriel nodded and then set him gently down on the floor. He moved to take off his shirt, but Matt stopped him. "No," he said. "I want to do it."

Matt lifted the blue shirt from his body, exposing his hairy chest and stomach. He ran his fingers through the dark hair and teased Gabriel's left nipple with the tip of his tongue. Gabriel moaned while Matt worked to pebble the sensitive flesh. Once the left nipple was moist and erect, he repeated the process on the right one until it too stood hard and wet.

As he knelt before Gabriel, Matt ensured his hands never left Gabriel's body. They surfed through the soft, dense fur until they arrived at the denim barrier. He quickly unbuttoned the jeans and undid the zipper. When the pants fell to the floor, Gabriel's enormous erection sprang into view.

The shaft was thick and veiny and ended in a bulbous mushroom head, which leaked steadily. Behind the beautiful cut cock hung two walnut sized testicles surrounded by a dense forest of dark, soft hair.

Matt took the hardness in his hands and jacked the massive meat until it turned so hard it must have hurt. He rested Gabriel's cock on his lips and delivered soft kisses across the swollen head. His tongue darted outward to lap up the sweet juice collecting at the tip, and then he trailed his tongue up the shaft and to the musky base.

Deep within the curly bush, Matt detected a whiff of rain mixed with the odor of man. He inhaled deeply, filling his lungs with the atmosphere Gabriel's body created. Matt rubbed his face in Gabriel's pubic hair, along his cock, determined to keep Gabriel's musk on him forever.

When he couldn't stand it any longer, he opened his mouth and swallowed Gabriel whole. Gabriel moaned and immediately thrust his hips, resting his thick head against the back of Matt's throat before pulling it out until only the tip rested on Matt's tongue. Then, he shoved the length all the way back in.

At first, Matt had difficulty taking Gabriel's fat cock in his mouth. Both the size and the fervor with which Gabriel thrust inside him made Matt gag, but once he relaxed his throat muscles, Gabriel's thickness slid comfortably down his gullet. Matt then wrapped his tongue around the shaft and tickled the head while his cheeks and throat muscles gently massaged the length of Gabriel's tool.

"You feel so good, my love," Gabriel said dreamily. His eyes rolled in the back of his head, as his body seemed to get lost in the intensity of Matt's wet mouth wrapped around him.

Gabriel's breathing became more ragged, and his body tensed. It seemed his cock doubled in hardness. Matt knew it meant Gabriel was close to climax, so he eased up on his suction and released Gabriel from his mouth.

"I want you to finish inside me," he told Gabriel after lying on the bed. He spread his legs and held them open, revealing his eager center. "Here."

Gabriel lowered himself on top of Matt, kissing his neck and his lips. "I'll do whatever you ask," he replied in between kisses.

Matt held Gabriel's face in his hands. "Do you want to?" he asked. "I only want you to do it if that's what you want."

Gabriel smiled broadly and tears pooled at the corners of his eyes. "I've never wanted anything or anyone more."

He then pressed his full body weight against Matt and covered his mouth and face with kisses. Matt went wild, exploring as much of the muscled man lying between his legs as he could. He clawed at Gabriel's back and grabbed his firm ass. He moved up on the bed in order to bite Gabriel's shoulders and lick at his ear, all in anticipation of Gabriel entering him.

Gabriel undulated on top of him, rubbing their hard cocks together and forcing them to slip and slide past each other like copulating snakes. He ground his thick, hard cock into Matt's pelvis, where Gabriel's undulating motions caused its heft to inch further downward from Matt's abdomen, to his groin, until coming to rest between his legs.

Breathlessly, Matt gasped in excitement when Gabriel's hands slid to his knees and brought them forward to rest on Gabriel's shoulders. He guided his manhood to Matt's shuddering center and pressed it at the entrance.

"Are you ready?" Gabriel asked, staring down at him. His eyes mad with passion.

"Just do it," he pleaded.

Gabriel nudged forward, evidently using the copious amounts of precome from his cock to gain entrance, and Matt felt himself open up to accommodate his bulk. They never lost eye contact as Gabriel penetrated Matt. His eyes grew wider and bluer, and his mouth hung open in bliss as Matt now held Gabriel within his protective embrace.

Once he was buried to the hilt within Matt, Gabriel pulled out almost completely and then rammed himself all the way back inside. Lost in pleasure, Matt bit his lip and bucked back against Gabriel, driving the hardness further inside until Gabriel's balls rested against his ass.

Gabriel craned his neck down to Matt, probing the inside of his mouth once again. Matt wrapped his arms around his neck, trying to force more and more of Gabriel inside, and Gabriel did his best to oblige.

He thrust deep, long strokes, and Matt bore down on his cock. The friction they created together seemed capable of powering a small city. They rocked and pushed each other until they were both at the point of no return.

"I'm so close," Gabriel whispered.

"Do it," he panted in reply. "I'm almost there."

After a few more plunges inside Matt's flesh, Gabriel's cock grew even harder before ejecting his hot seed deep inside Matt.

When Matt felt Gabriel's cock pulse within, pumping out its contents inside him, he jacked his cock to its own creamy finish, coating both his and Gabriel's skin in his come.

Though softening, Gabriel stayed within him and set his head on his elbow. "I love you, my sweet man." His eyes looked tired and also sad.

"I love you too," Matt replied. "But what's wrong?"

"I want to give you the world."

"I don't want the world. I want you."

"This is all of me you can have," Gabriel told him. His voice sounded distant, as if it were withdrawing. When Matt blinked, Gabriel was no longer on top of him. He was now dressed and across the room.

"Gabriel, where are you going? What's happening?"

"I want to give you the world," he repeated. "But I can only give you this."

Gabriel's form turned transparent, almost ghostlike. Then, he became only a shimmering outline before disappearing altogether.

MATT sat bolt upright in bed and looked around. Gabriel wasn't there, but he was once again in his room. The burgundy curtains, tan walls, Shaker armoire, and Pergo floors greeted him in the early morning light.

"What the hell? Was that a dream?"

He pulled back the covers, revealing his naked body. Unless he had an overnight guest, he always slept in his black gym shorts. He never slept in the nude, and he recalled putting shorts on before bed.

He remembered it clearly because he had been in the middle of calling himself a dumb ass, for throwing himself at Gabriel, when he took off his clothes and slipped into his black gym shorts.

Did it happen or was it all a sex dream?

Matt ran his hand over his chest and stomach, which were crusty with dried come. His sex dream had also apparently been a wet one. He hadn't had one of those since middle school.

He didn't understand what was happening to him.

Why did strange things happen on his birthday? What brought Gabriel into his life? But more importantly, why did his dream change yet again?

While the dream started out like most others, it quickly changed. He was in his childhood bedroom. He heard Clifford Crouch's footsteps coming up the staircase, but this time Gabriel intervened before he got to the door and before it started disintegrating.

He appeared out of nowhere, and they had sex. Hot, passionate, scorching sex. Never had a sex dream ever taken place in the setting of his childhood nightmare.

He had to figure out why Gabriel was there and what was the connection.

CHAPTER 11

MATT again found himself sitting on the taupe couch in Dr. Owens's waiting room. When there last week, he had just survived the first of two near-death experiences on his birthday and he had believed the man who saved him to be a hallucination created by his concussion.

Since then, he had been proven wrong. Gabriel was real, and he had returned to save him from near-death experience number two later that night. Though he thought they had a special connection, Matt hadn't seen him since he had walked out of his apartment one week ago.

Not unless he counted Gabriel's appearance in his dreams.

Each night, it was the same. After stopping Matt from approaching the disintegrating door that would somehow flood his life with horror if opened, he and Gabriel made love, and each morning when he woke up, he was naked, though he put on his gym shorts before bed nightly.

He had even taken a picture with his camera phone the night before to document that he crawled into bed with gym shorts on. This morning when he woke up, his shorts were off and his body was caked in spunk.

He needed to know what was happening to him, and he hoped Dr. Owens would shed some light on his situation.

"You ready, Matt?" Dr. Owens asked from his open office door.

Matt nodded and proceeded into his office and to the same overstuffed plaid chair. Dr. Owens took his usual spot behind his desk. Matt knew by the end of the session, Dr. Owens would be sitting in the chair to his left, marking the progress of the session with closer proximity.

"You look troubled. Has something more happened since last week?"

"Loads," he replied, smiling to himself at his unintended double entendre.

"You smile, yet I sense no real joy in the expression."

"That's because I'm confused, befuddled, and bewildered."

"Okay, then," he replied while sitting back in his leather chair. "Fill me in."

Matt told Dr. Owens everything that happened the night of his birthday, but he left out the sex dream that started that night and had occurred nightly since. Although his primary reason for coming this week was to discuss those dreams, he couldn't bring himself to admit them.

He wasn't embarrassed. Sex was a part of a normal adult life, and Dr. Owens already knew he was gay. So his homosexuality wasn't the sticking point. He just felt uncomfortable raising the subject with Dr. Owens.

It wasn't that Dr. Owens was incapable of understanding human sexuality. He was a psychiatrist after all. Heck, he assumed even Dr. Owens got lucky on occasion, though it was hard for Matt to imagine anyone having sex with someone who looked like Mr. Bean.

The man wasn't married. He suspected as much from the lack of a wedding band and an absence of pictures featuring an adoring wife and children. The only photo that decorated his office contained a snapshot of his mother.

This man was a professional. He knew that, but he still couldn't bring himself to utter the words he so desperately wanted to speak. He felt the need to keep the information a closely held secret.

"Matt?" Dr. Owens asked. "Are you okay?"

He focused on Dr. Owens's brown eyes, which narrowed in considerable concern. "I'm fine. Why?"

"Well, I've been talking to you for the past few minutes, but you seemed to have zoned out on me."

"My apologies."

Dr. Owens waved the apology away. "There's no need for that, but I would like for you to tell me what caused you to drift away like that. You've never done that before." He pulled out his pad and readied his pen to record the response.

"Can we get to that later? I'd like to discuss the rest of it first."

Dr. Owens put his pen down and nodded. "Of course. We'll follow whatever pace you want."

"Then what do you think? About my almost getting killed again? About Gabriel appearing out of nowhere and saving me twice?"

Before Dr. Owens could speak, Matt unleashed another set of questions. "And what about Craig? Isn't it weird that I met him the same night as Gabriel? And that Dee and Craig instantly distrusted him? Could he have been stalking me?"

Matt stared at Dr. Owens who only blinked in response. "Well?" he asked. "What do you think?"

"Are you finished?"

He nodded. "Sorry. I know that's a lot of ground to cover. And I seem to be rambling uncontrollably, so I'm just going to stop speaking and let you talk now."

Matt pinched his lips closed with his thumb and forefinger.

"I don't think holding your mouth closed will be necessary," Dr. Owens commented. "But I must first point out that you seem to be in a great deal of distress. Does your distress stem from the events of last week or is there more you haven't told me?"

Matt exhaled. "There's more, but I don't want to get to that. Yet."

Dr. Owens set his pad and pen on the desk and laced his fingers together. "You've been through quite the ordeal. Two near-death experiences within twelve hours is a record for someone in the business of saving lives and not endangering his own.

"But from what I can tell, it's mostly coincidental. The two events have no clear connection that I could even begin to fathom. After all, what could an automobile mishap and a drug dealer have in common?"

"Gabriel," Matt replied.

"True. This Gabriel was at both scenes, but even that could be coincidental. I've run into friends at one store only to see them again at a restaurant having dinner. They weren't following me, and I certainly wasn't following them."

"That's what I told my friends."

"However, just because I wasn't following my friend and he wasn't following me doesn't necessarily mean Gabriel wasn't following you."

Matt shoulders slumped. He feared Dr. Owens might say something like this. "So you think he *is* stalking me?"

"I didn't say that either, but I do think Gabriel deserves further scrutiny. And perhaps even a touch of caution. No one knows for sure what Gabriel's motives are except the man himself. So until you know for certain that he means you know harm, I suggest treading lightly."

"That's what my friends think too."

"And do you trust your friends? Do you think they truly have your best interest at heart?"

Matt nodded. He expected nothing less from them and they from him.

"There you go then. You've answered your own question."

"But how do I find out if Gabriel means me harm or not? Because I've got to tell you, Dr. Owens, I trust him. He makes me feel safe."

"Of course he does. The man saved your life twice in one day. What you're feeling is natural."

"That's the thing. I don't know if it's natural or not."

Dr. Owens's eyebrows arched high over his head. They did that whenever Matt said something that threw him off guard. "What do you mean?"

Matt swallowed. It was hard for him to admit, but he knew he had to. The only way to learn the truth was to drag the secret out into the light. That was what Dr. Owens had told him on his first visit three months ago. "I think I'm in love with him."

"Him?"

"Gabriel."

"I see," Dr. Owens replied. He reached for his pen and jotted some notes onto his pad. "And why do you think you're in love with this Gabriel? Do you think it could be how you're reacting to the fact that he saved your life two times in one day?"

"I don't think so."

"Curious. Why not?"

"When I saw him, that first time, he felt familiar. Like I knew him from somewhere. When I saw him later that night, I felt it again. I felt like I had found my home."

"The home you've been searching for? The one you've repressed since the night your parents were murdered?"

"That's the one."

"Interesting," he replied, once again scribbling on his pad. "And you haven't seen him since that night? Or talked to him?"

Matt averted his eyes. He still didn't want to admit it, but he had to. It was the only way. "Yes. And no."

Dr. Owens stopped writing and set his pen down on his desk. "I don't understand. Either you have seen or talked to him since or you haven't."

"I haven't seen or talked to him in the real world," Matt replied.

Dr. Owens's eyebrows arched so high they almost joined his hairline. "What other world is there besides the real world?"

"Relax, Dr. Owens. My psyche isn't creating an alternate reality to cope with my stress. I'm referring to my dreams."

His eyebrows relaxed and returned to normal, resting like fuzzy caterpillars a few centimeters above his eyes. "So you've been *dreaming* about him? Well, that's certainly not abnormal, Matt."

"But I've dreamt about him every night. And they're sex dreams. Pretty intense sex dreams."

He smiled broadly. "Completely normal. Enjoy them."

"Okay, then, here's the kicker, doc. Gabriel appears in the dreams at my house. With the disintegrating door."

Dr. Owens's expression turned dark and serious. "Tell me everything."

When he was done, Dr. Owens sat back and contemplated. He could see the man's internal thought processes turning like cogs in a machine. He was trying to make rational sense out of the dreams, to shed light on the secrets that remained buried in Matt's subconscious.

"I think it's simple really. Gabriel saved you twice. He's become like your guardian angel for lack of a better word. As such, in your dreams, in dreams where you're extremely vulnerable and subject to serious childhood trauma, your subconscious mind projects Gabriel onto the dreamscape. To protect you from the pain. To shield you from the memories that wait on the other side."

"And to have sex with him?"

"Well, sex offers us security. In the arms of someone we love, we feel safe from all harm."

"So I *am* in love with him? After just one day?"

"I can't tell you what you feel, Matt. That's for you to discover. I can only offer opinions as to why Gabriel has appeared in your dreams. No doubt, you share a strong bond with the man. Whatever more exists, if anything, is up to you."

"But I haven't seen him, except in my dreams, since that night."

"I have no answer for that. Perhaps you'll never see him again and some other man will slowly replace him in your dreams. This Craig perhaps."

"You think so?"

"It's a possibility. You told me yourself you found the man attractive and were interested in pursuing something more tangible up until Gabriel re-entered your life."

Matt nodded. "That's true. So where do I go from here?"

"My advice is this: don't wait for a dream. Dreams are manifestations of our desires. They change as we change. Don't focus on one week's worth of dreams and turn them into your life's mission. Continue living day-to-day. Explore a relationship with Craig if you're still willing. Wait and see if Gabriel returns. If he doesn't, then pursuing the matter will be moot. But if you blow Craig off while you wait, you run the risk of letting someone you yourself called a 'good guy' who was 'relationship material' get away. Is that a chance you want to take, on the off chance that this Gabriel will return?"

Matt thought long and hard about his answer. While he felt a strong connection with Gabriel, he had all but vanished, except for in his dreams, and a dream wasn't the foundation of a long-term relationship.

He hadn't stopped living his life before. He saw no need to change that now.

"No," he finally replied. "I won't take that chance."

Dr. Owens smiled and stood up. He rounded his desk and sat next to Matt. It was at that point, Matt knew he had made the right choice and that Dr. Owens agreed with him.

SINCE his appointment with Dr. Owens, Matt felt better about his situation. He had direction and purpose, two things he loved having in life. Though he couldn't shake his strong feelings for Gabriel, he wasn't going to let them dictate his life. He hadn't seen him in a week, and he had no way to contact him.

Like Dr. Owens said, he might never see Gabriel again.

The prospect saddened him. In the few short hours he spent with his mysterious stranger, Gabriel had come to mean a great deal to him. He even finally admitted to himself that he was in love with the man, as insane as that prospect might be. But love alone didn't a relationship make.

There had to be the willingness of both parties for a relationship to flourish, and while he parked his car in the lot at Baba Yega, where he was meeting his grandmother, Dee, and Shane for lunch, he accepted that Gabriel might not be willing to meet him half way.

That made his feelings moot.

He would always be grateful to Gabriel for saving his life, but he wasn't going to place his life on hold simply waiting for Gabriel to return.

Not when Craig was there, willing and ready to walk down that path with him.

Matt didn't want to be with Craig because Gabriel became unavailable. Craig deserved better than that and so did he. Although he still didn't know what would happen with Craig if Gabriel returned, he owed it to their potential to give it a try.

He felt so good about his decision he called Craig on the way to the restaurant. Though they had only spoken once since his birthday, Craig sounded happy to hear from him and agreed to meet him for coffee after his shift at the hospital.

Though he tried not to get his hopes up, they remained pretty high. Craig was just the type of man he had been searching for—kind and strong and smart and funny, not to mention employed, sane, and wicked hot.

Matt entered the front door of the restaurant and told the hostess he was meeting a party that had already been seated. She nodded and he walked by her smiling face to find everyone sitting at a back table against the wall. The location was unusual for Dee and Shane, who preferred to dine where everyone could see their magnificence, but the choice fit his grandmother, the Duchess, perfectly.

While the Duchess wasn't one to shy away from people, she preferred to dine in relative peace. Too many times were her meals interrupted by casual acquaintances trying to schmooze their way into the next social gathering at her house. Though she loved the perks of being a society dame, she abhorred having to be on call twenty-four hours a day. She often referred to herself as Dr. Duchess in those situations.

But today, the Duchess wasn't sitting at the table. It was his grandmother Joanna Westlake, dressed casually in a black blazer, white blouse, and gray pants. Her shoulder-length white hair looked immaculate, and when she saw him, her perfectly manicured hands waved him over.

"My Duchess," he said, giving her a peck on her smooth and flawless cheek. "Don't you look fabulous? As always."

"Oh, please. I look absolutely dreadful. If any of my friends saw how I was dressed, they'd be tweeting about how Joanna looked like a hag!"

"You use Twitter?" Shane asked, surprised. His typically flamboyant attire had been turned down a couple of notches. As always, whenever they dined with the Duchess, Shane dressed far more conservatively. He sported a short-sleeved polo and blue jeans.

"Of course she tweets, silly!" Dee responded. "She's a tech-savvy woman!" She gave his grandmother a wink and flipped a stray black lock from her eyes. Dee, too, wasn't wearing her typically low-cut blouses or offensive graphic t-shirts. She wore a lightweight blue Henley and tan pants.

"I wouldn't say tech-savvy, Deidre. I tweet because I must. Gossip flies too quickly not to be in the know."

"Ah," Matt added. "It's social death by tweet these days among your circle?"

"Sadly, yes. Just last week, Anita Coleman's affair with Bryce Billingsley was re-tweeted at least a dozen times before the poor woman returned home to her husband, who was, unfortunately for her, following someone who tweeted the news."

"That's awful!" Shane exclaimed, pretending not to like the scandal.

"It was terrible. Someone even shared a twit pic of Aaron Coleman kicking her out of the house."

"Good God!" he told his grandmother. "What about Darren and Celia?" He went to school with Darren, and Celia had always been a good friend. He hated to hear about their parents' messed up relationship being tweeted to the greater Houston community.

"The kids have taken it hard, I've heard, but they're almost thirty so they should live."

"Duchess!" he scolded while she feigned being hurt.

"What? I've done nothing wrong. I'm simply sharing public knowledge. Nothing more."

"You're propagating gossip, and you know it."

The waiter came by to take their order, and after Shane flirted shamelessly with the shy teenager, they placed their orders and returned to their conversation.

"So, let's continue the gossip, shall we?" his grandmother asked.

"Who now?"

"You," she said while poking him in the chest.

"Me? What's there to gossip about me?" he asked staring into Dee and Shane's guilty faces. "Or have my two former best friends been speaking out of turn?"

"To anyone else, yes," his grandmother answered. "To me. Never." She smiled at Dee and Shane, letting them know they were under her protection. Their relieved expressions revealed their appreciation. "Now, I had believed I was done berating you about the events of last week, but from what I've learned, I'm far from finished."

"What do you mean?"

"You never spoke of this Gabriel person who saved you. You mentioned that police officer. What was his name again?" she asked, staring over at Dee and Shane.

"Craig," Shane replied while blowing a kiss to Matt, who returned the gesture by sticking out his tongue.

"Yes. Craig," she replied. "Put your tongue back in your mouth, dear. It's not very attractive." When Matt complied with her request, she continued. "Now from what I hear, this Craig is… oh, how did Deidre put it…? Man-tastic. Was that it, dear?"

Dee nodded her head, grinning from ear to ear. His friends knew how worried his grandmother was that he hadn't been in a relationship for quite some time. She wanted him to find a man to settle down with, so they could adopt a whole house full of children that she could spoil as rotten as she did him.

When she first learned about Craig, she was ecstatic, hoping perhaps the police officer might be the one. She had even asked Matt to invite him to dinner at her house. A request he quickly denied. At the time, he wasn't certain of his feelings for Craig and had no intention of subjecting him to her longing for great-grandchildren.

She had been willing to let the matter drop. Until now.

Now that she knew about Gabriel, whom Dee and Shane most likely didn't paint in a positive light, she fully intended to re-double her quest at uniting Matt with Craig.

"Matthew, pay attention to me when I'm speaking to you," she scolded.

"I'm sorry," he replied. "I drifted off there for a bit."

"I could tell. Your mouth was hanging open. I was certain a fly was going to take up residence at any moment. But as I was saying, this Craig seems like quite the catch based on what Shane and Deidre have shared with me, but this Gabriel person, you told me nothing about him. And I want to know why."

Instantly, Matt understood how Dr. Owens felt this morning when he unleashed a barrage of questions at him. He was already exhausted, and he hadn't even been to work yet. Still, his grandmother was all the family he had, and he wouldn't trade her for anyone else in the world. "There's really nothing to tell."

"That's not what my sources say," she announced. "They tell me you're quite taken with him. That you might be considering him as your life partner."

"My life partner?" he asked her while looking at Dee and Shane, who averted their eyes. Though they had all made up since last week, Gabriel was still a bone of contention between them. While he admitted his persistent attraction to Gabriel, he never once intimated he wanted to spend the rest of his life with him. That was something they added to spur his grandmother further on her tirade.

"So it's true then?"

He shook his head. "No, it's not."

"It's not?" Dee asked. Her dark eyes positively beamed with delight.

"Since when?" Shane added, clearly not believing him.

"Since this morning," he told them, with a smug arch to his brow. Although he wasn't telling the complete truth, it was close enough for him to feel smugly justified. But when everyone stared at him, urging him to tell his story, he recounted most of his appointment with Dr. Owens, leaving out the sex dreams, and repeated the advice he had been given.

"Dr. Owens is a smart man," his grandmother chimed. "I'm glad I suggested you see him."

"I do feel better," he told them. That admission wasn't an exaggeration. "I feel more in control. I realize I owe Gabriel my life, but I'm not going to wait around for him. I even have a date with Craig later tonight."

Dee clapped her hands in joy.

"'Bout damn time," Shane commented.

"Shane Vanslooten!" his grandmother reprimanded. "Your language is atrocious."

"I'm sorry, Mrs. Westlake."

"Don't be sorry; just don't curse."

Shane nodded while Matt and Dee snickered. His grandmother was always getting on Shane for his potty mouth, and next to Gabriel, she was the only one who ever got him to apologize.

"Now that your personal life is making some progress, what about the rest?"

Matt knew his grandmother was inquiring about his dreams. When he shared the recurring dreams with her months ago, she recommended he see Dr. Owens not because of the dream itself but because she saw how the dream affected him.

He had difficulty falling asleep, fearful that the door from his dreams would return. He became moody and withdrawn, the same way he acted for about a year after his parents were murdered.

Now, of course, he understood why he reacted that way to the dream. The door in his dream, the one he feared to open, was the door from his childhood bedroom. It was the one that separated him from Clifford Crouch, who wanted to kill him after murdering his parents.

His grandmother didn't know the connection between the door in his dream and the one to his past. The memory proved as painful for her as it was for him. Her only son was murdered that night, and since he realized what the door represented, he didn't want to bring it up.

It would only hurt her, and he had no intention of doing that.

"Dr. Owens and I are making good progress," he told her. "I'm understanding the dream more and more."

"That's great news," said Dee.

"No, not great," his grandmother added. "That's fantastic news."

"How so?"

"If you've made such progress, then I can only assume you've made the connection."

Matt was caught off guard. Did she already know what the door represented? And if she did, how was that possible?

"Oh stop looking at me as if I'm some old fool!"

"You're not an old fool," he told her. "I would never look at you that way."

"Good. Then don't think I'm not smart enough to realize that the door that's been haunting your dreams is the same one…" She paused and swallowed hard. The carefree socialite disappeared. In her place sat a woman who suffered the most awful loss imaginable—the death of a child. After she had collected herself, she continued. "The same one that protected you that night."

Matt couldn't believe his grandmother had it figured out long before he did. His grandmother was one smart cookie, but the accuracy of her perception astounded him. "You've known that? All this time?"

"Of course," she replied, while drying her eyes with her napkin. "Why do you think I sent you to Dr. Owens in the first place? If it were a regular dream, you would've gotten over it rather quickly. When you kept having it, I suspected it was a repressed memory from that night."

"But how could you have possibly known that?"

"The door was the one thing separating you from that awful man. He couldn't get it open. If he would have..." She paused again, this time to blink away her tears. "Well, I don't even want to think about that. That door saved your life, Matthew. It kept you safe. It's no wonder you're having nightmares about that door falling apart."

"That dream makes so much sense to me now," Shane said while Dee nodded in agreement. She was too choked up by his grandmother's emotions to speak. Whenever someone cried, Dee always cried with them.

"I know we don't talk about it, and I understand why. I really do. But can I ask you a question?"

"You can ask me anything, Matthew. I'm your grandmother. It's part of my job to answer your questions."

"And to spoil him beyond rotten," Shane added. Everyone smiled at his attempt to lighten an emotionally heavy situation.

"That too!" His grandmother grinned. She reached across the table and patted Shane's hand as a thank you. "Now, what is this question?"

"Why couldn't he get the door open?" he asked, not needing to clarify the pronoun. They never mentioned Clifford Crouch by name. "Was he on drugs or something?"

"No drugs. They tested him for that. For everything. He was obviously insane by the way he was chattering on when the police arrived. But there were no drugs."

"Chattering on? What was he saying? And what about the door? Why couldn't he open it?"

"It doesn't matter what that crazy man said," she replied, waving aside the question. "As for the door, no one knows. It opened just fine for the police when they arrived."

"That's bizarre."

"Not to me," she said quite confidently.

"What do you mean?"

His grandmother reached out and lovingly cupped his chin before squeezing his right cheek. "You've always been a special boy, Matthew. When your parents found you, it was like a miracle. They had prayed and prayed for a child, but they hit one roadblock after another. I even tried to buy one for them, but not even that worked. Then, you came. So beautiful.

So full of joy. I'd never seen such a ball of life as you. Not even when your father was a baby. We called you our Miracle Matthew."

"You did?" he asked, tears streaming down his face.

"Oh God, yes. When you came into our lives, you brought such happiness. And I watched your parents beam with pure joy every single day. They loved you with all their heart. As you grew up, the three of you were inseparable. I had to beg them to let me steal you away for a night. You know, most parents are thrilled to go a day or a weekend without their child, but your parents couldn't bear to be away from you for one moment. I know you can't remember any of that, but one day you will. And you'll know what true love feels like when you can remember the way your parents loved you."

Matt sniffled and wiped the tears from his eyes. "I still don't understand what any of this has to do with the door."

"Don't you see, Matthew? Love has always been the greatest part of you. It's what makes you a nurse. It's what makes you such a caring man. You've got so much love in your heart that I've always felt you're meant for something special in this world. Something so special that you're protected from all harm. That's why your door wouldn't open. Your special protector, your guardian angel was there preventing that man from getting inside."

"You think I have a guardian angel? After everything that's happened in my life?"

"Most especially so," she nodded. "You've had terrible things happen in your life, Matthew. That's true. But not once have you been hurt. Think about that."

Matt sat in stunned silence. For so long, he looked at his life as if he was a walking tragedy. Not once did he consider himself a walking miracle. But it was true. No matter what happened to him, no matter what crazy event life threw at him, he always walked away, unscathed.

Maybe he did have a guardian angel after all.

And as their lunch arrived, he entertained the thought of Gabriel, his mysterious savior, being his guardian angel. It explained why he was present when he was in danger or how he healed so fast, but when his grandmother asked Shane if he was still dating Karl, his friend's moan of torment and ensuing drama chased the crazy idea from his mind.

CHAPTER 12

EVERY night for a week, Clifford had quietly contemplated the shank he pulled out of the toilet, the one the voice told him would be his key out of jail. He hadn't wanted to use it. He didn't want to kill Kenny. But the desire to do as the voice told him became harder to resist each passing day as Kenny slowly wore on his nerves.

Kenny had always been a chatterbox. From the moment he woke up till he fell asleep, he told some story—about his childhood, about the bitch he loved then killed, or about his father who beat him, the mother who whored around, and the gang he hung with. He knew more about Kenny than he knew about anyone else in this joint.

At first, he enjoyed the stories. Not much of a talker himself, it was nice to have Kenny's voice playing in the background like soft music. It made life here comfortable.

Lately, Kenny's constant babbling turned more grating than usual. It made him jumpy. He wanted to sink the shank deep in his guts and watch as the blood pooled out of the wound and over his hand.

If he did, not only would Kenny finally be quiet but he would also be free of prison.

He could return to life outside these walls and live once again in the sun like the voice promised.

"Man, Clifford, I fuckin' hate when they serve us that Mexican food crap. I'm gonna be fartin' for days. I hope you don't mind smelling beans dipped in shit all week long." Kenny chuckled to himself and let loose a long, wet gas explosion. "Damn, I almost shit myself on that one."

Clifford held his breath and closed his eyes. "Kenny, please stop."

"Hey, I would if I could, man. But you know what they say: wherever you be, let your breeze blow free." He punctuated the saying with a second disgusting fart, which was even wetter than the first.

"Kenny," he warned.

Kenny laughed. "I'm sorry, man. I'll try to hold it in. Just be glad you're on the bottom bunk. It stinks like the inside of a wetback's ass up here."

Clifford reached under his pillow and found the shank. With his fingers, he traced the edges of the cool metal, which extended about four inches above the taped handle. As he played with the rusty point, he studied the mattress above him. Not more than two inches of padding separated him from Kenny, who was flopping about on the mattress above. One forceful lunge from down here would be enough to get the job done, especially if he twisted the handle and broke the blade inside him.

If he stabbed in the right spot, he could sever a major artery. Kenny would be dead in mere moments. No suffering. No pain. Just one swift motion. Quick and easy.

"Oh, man, Clifford. I feel another one coming on."

He gripped the shank's handle tightly. "Don't do it, Kenny."

Kenny responded by farting so loudly it echoed halfway down the cellblock.

In response, Clifford jabbed the shank upward in one swift motion. His actions seemed guided by supernatural forces as he aimed for Kenny's throat. The garbled noises from above told him he hit his mark. He twisted the shank forty-five degrees, breaking it off with one clean snap. When he pulled back on the now bladeless weapon, the bottom of Kenny's mattress soaked through with blood, and the whole bunk shook with Kenny's death throes.

Clifford sat up against the wall, watching the dark red spot bloom across the mattress. He pulled his knees up to his chest and tossed the handle into the toilet, which flushed on its own.

"You'll soon be free," the voice replied from the commode.

He didn't respond, but as he sat there, shivering, a shadowy figure rose from the open bowl and flew straight into him.

AS MATT sat in his car parked outside the Beanery, his stomach fluttered incessantly. He was ten minutes early for his coffee date with Craig, and he wanted to make a better impression than the one he left Craig with last week. Unfortunately, that caused a mounting burden to weigh heavily upon his shoulders.

Work proved to be an easy distraction, though. His two patients, one with a C2 fracture-dislocation and the other with an aortic arch stab wound, kept him focused on his professional duties and not his personal woes. Both patients were already on their way to recovery from some truly serious injuries. Perhaps he had a magical healing touch after all. If he potentially had a guardian angel looking after him, then why *couldn't* he have healing hands too?

That thought kept him focused on only his work, and when he left the hospital, after a long twelve hour shift, both patients were stable and in good spirits.

He wished he could say the same thing. If he truly had a guardian angel watching over him, he should be in a much better mood than he currently was. But his invisible guardian angel couldn't save him from the thoughts that plagued his mind.

That, unfortunately, fell to him to fix.

Although he looked forward to his date with Craig, memories of making love with Gabriel in his dreams crept into his mind all day long. The intense, sky-blue eyes that always seemed to reflect the ambient light in the room, looking down at him as Gabriel thrust deeply inside. His tanned body covered in soft, dark hair and rippling with muscles, straining against his body. Hard, breathy kisses covering Matt's neck, his mouth, his chest. The broad shoulders, the chiseled abs, the firm ass, and the beautiful cock.

Those images had pestered him ever since he left his grandmother, Dee, and Shane at the restaurant that afternoon, and only his work routine kept them at bay. Since he clocked out, the live sex show clocked back in, playing the steamy scenes in a continual loop in his mind.

He thought he had put his obsession with his leather-and-denim clad savior behind him earlier today, but that was before the notion of Gabriel being a guardian angel added even more heat to the fantasy and his desire.

Gabriel's memory, or at least the memory of the dream, fought even more staunchly against being released. What love he inexplicably held in his heart for Gabriel resented potentially being replaced by the possibility Craig represented.

Feeling so conflicted now made him feel guilty. Craig deserved better from him. He wasn't some runner-up, who the audience rooted for but who never received the rose, in one of those stupid reality dating shows. Craig had romantic lead potential.

Their time at the F Bar wasn't forced or awkward. It proved seamless and easy. They laughed without pretense. They flirted without vulgarity.

It was simple, and sweet, and wonderful.

That was why his current vacillating emotions upset him. When he made up his mind about something, he followed through with it. He didn't seesaw back and forth like some adolescent incapable of deciding between his boyfriend or his new crush.

As an adult, he expected better from himself and from those he associated with. How could he go through with the date if he still felt as conflicted as he did now?

A light tap on his driver's side window caught his attention.

He turned and saw Craig standing outside, smiling at him. Dressed in his black Houston P.D. uniform he looked breathtaking and rugged. His wavy, blond hair had been slicked back with gel and parted on the side, which was different from his slightly messy club look from last week. His smooth, square jaw appeared both impervious yet delicate, and his big, beautiful green eyes outshone the creamy radiance of his skin. But what struck Matt as the pinnacle of Craig's beauty was his smile, broad and generous and absent of all guile.

That smile revealed the inner beauty and strength of character that resided in his soul.

"You looked like you were contemplating a quick getaway," Craig commented as Matt exited his car.

He blushed, embarrassed that Craig could read him so easily. "I was actually."

Sadness caused the smile in his eyes to slowly fade. "Well, if you want a rain check or something, I'll understand."

"Not at all," he replied quickly. No matter how at odds he felt internally, he was determined not to hurt this man. "I was wondering if I had time to go home and change out of my scrubs. I didn't think I could carry off a complete pea green ensemble in public."

Craig's grin returned, lighting up his face and his eyes. "On someone else, probably not. On you, it's fabulous."

Warmth quickly spread across his cheeks. Matt knew he was not only blushing, he was probably as red as a strawberry.

"Red and green looks good too," added Craig. "Reminds me of Christmas."

Matt laughed and hid his face. "Stop that," he replied while reaching out to playfully swat at Craig. Instead, Craig caught his hand and held it.

They hadn't held hands since they were at the F Bar. Then, his touch had felt warm and comforting, as if he had been holding Craig's hand his entire life. That sensation still lingered today, but it was even better than before. It told Matt that whatever happened between them that night wasn't a fluke.

It was real. Certainly more real than a dream or the possibility of Gabriel being a guardian angel. And it was a reality he wanted to explore.

"Shall we go inside?" he asked, holding Craig's hand firmly in his own.

Craig squeezed his hand and tugged him toward the front door. "I thought you'd never ask."

CLIFFORD placed his hands behind his head as the two correctional officers standing outside his cell instructed. He then walked over to the wall opposite the cell door and turned around.

As he heard the metal door slide open with a clang, he looked down into the toilet where he threw the shank's handle. It wasn't there. Whoever or whatever flushed the toilet eliminated the evidence for him.

Without a murder weapon, the cops had nothing.

"What the fuck happened to Kenny?" one of the guards asked. He couldn't see the man, but it sounded like the newbie Officer Garcia.

"Don't know," he replied. "I was asleep."

In response, the guard jammed a nightstick into his lower back. The force shoved him forward into the wall, but pain didn't immediately explode through his body. In his almost twenty years in lock up, he had been beaten with those clubs on many occasions, and those damned things hurt.

Except for some reason, this one didn't. It felt more like being struck by rubber than aluminum surrounded by polycarbonate.

"Don't get smart with me, motherfucker!" Officer Garcia bellowed. "I'm not afraid of your crazy ass. Your Devil Dude reputation don't mean shit to me, goddammit! Now tell me what the fuck happened to Kenny!"

"Kenny got shanked."

"No fucking shit," the officer shouted. He spun Clifford around and shoved the nightstick against his throat, while pinning him to the wall. The pressure against his windpipe would normally render breathing difficult. Clifford found he had no trouble drawing air into his body.

Officer Garcia's chubby face turned beet red from anger, and his fat sausage fingers forced the club harder against his throat. He obviously wanted Clifford to pass out from asphyxiation, which would make his job a lot easier.

"Back up, Jerry," Officer Greene replied while inspecting Kenny's dead body. "You're gonna kill him, and that won't look good for anyone."

Clifford wanted to laugh. The fat fuck was named Jerry Garcia. His baby face and round body didn't come close to the rock legend's appearance. He looked more like a boy pretending to be a man. Although right now, he looked more like a man who was about to die.

Officer Jerry Garcia didn't know that though. And neither did Officer Greene.

MATT sipped on his iced latte while Craig enjoyed his cup of steaming black coffee.

He found Craig's choice of beverage refreshing. He didn't order some low fat something or another with a double shot of espresso.

His preference was simple, uncomplicated. It spoke volumes to Matt and made him even more endearing.

"What?" Craig asked. "Do I have something on my face?" He hurriedly wiped his nose with a napkin.

Matt was confused. "What are you talking about?"

"You were staring at me so hard I thought there must be something disgustingly embarrassing hanging from my nose."

He laughed. "There's nothing disgustingly embarrassing *anywhere* that I can see."

Craig arched his eyebrow provocatively. "Well, you haven't seen everything. Yet."

"I guess I haven't," Matt bantered back, pleased that the previous sexual tension from last week had returned with a vengeance. "I'll let you know if my statement still proves true when I do."

"Confident. I like that in a man."

"What else do you like?" he asked. "In a man I mean."

Craig chuckled. "I'm glad you clarified that. Because I could've just embarrassed myself."

"Hmmm. Can I withdraw the amendment to my previous question?"

Craig shook his head. "Too late," he said before taking a sip of his coffee. "Let's see. What do I like in a man? Well, there's confidence. I enjoy a man who knows what he wants and goes for it. But he can't be cocky. I hate that. Beyond confidence though, I treasure honesty the most. Liars have burned me in past relationships. They claim to want one thing but really want something else. I prefer to see the road ahead of me. If you want something from me, say it and hell, you might even get it. But when you lie, when you hide what you really want or who you truly are, well, there's not much I can give that type of person."

Matt held his iced latte up in the air. "Amen."

"What about you?"

"Well, if you really want to know?" he asked to which Craig nodded his reply. "Okay, it's silly and probably a little girly, but I want to be swept off my feet. Don't get me wrong or anything because I'm not a prude, but I'm tired of the endless sexual conquests and games. I miss the romance. Most guys are only interested in the hook up, and as gay men, we've reduced ourselves to the profile pictures on the dating apps like Cyber. That's not romance. That's called shopping, and we so often get caught up in the latest fad that we forget we are people not clothes we can toss away once it's no longer en vogue."

"I couldn't agree more. In fact, I don't even use those dating phone apps anymore. I deleted them about a month ago."

"Me too. Six months Cyber-free. I even got my six month chip at the meeting the other day."

"Congratulations on your success at Cyber Anonymous! You're an inspiration to us all!" Craig said, reaching across the table to hold his hand. When his sturdy yet gentle touch closed over his once again, Matt didn't want Craig to ever let him go.

The simple act felt more like a convergence of two forces than something as mundane as two men holding hands in a coffee shop. It took on a greatness all its own, and Matt basked in the resulting glory.

"This feels nice," he told Craig. "Very nice."

Craig nodded in reply. "When I first touched you that night at F Bar, something happened to me. It's hard to explain, but it was like finding your childhood blanket, if that makes any sense. You know, the one you used to sleep with every night and then one day, for whatever reason, you didn't sleep with it anymore. And then, years later, you find that blanket in a box in some closet. And when you pull it out and you run your fingers through the fibers and you hold it against your skin, you remember exactly how that blanket made you feel and you ask yourself: why did I ever let you go?" Craig blushed and looked away. "Well, that's kind of how touching you feels to me."

Matt was speechless. Words refused to form on his lips. The honesty and sincerity in Craig's admission affected him profoundly. He wanted to respond. No, he needed to respond, but when he opened his mouth, no sound issued forth. So instead, he grabbed both of Craig's hands in his and pulled him over the table separating them. He leaned in half way, and for a few seconds they stared into each other's eyes, gazing deep into each other's souls, both familiar and new.

Craig's right hand caressed Matt's cheek before cupping his chin and tilting his head to the right. He then crossed the remainder of the distance, and their lips met for the first time.

A universe of unlimited possibilities stretched before Matt upon contact. Since their first meeting, he sensed a profound connection. Now that their lips brushed together, first in tentative nibbles and then in open-mouth passion, he understood the rarity of his find.

In Craig existed the potential for not just a relationship but a true partnership. Someone who wanted the same things out of life and love that he did. Charming, romantic, and sensitive yet rugged and strong, Craig Belton might just be the man he had waited his entire life to find.

After what seemed like an eternity, Craig's kisses, which had feverishly filled his mouth with his slick tongue and hot breaths, slowly abated until Craig kissed him one final time and rested his smooth forehead against his. "That was awesome," he told Matt. "You're a great kisser."

"It takes two to tango."

They both resumed their seats in the booth. The flush of their passion reddened their cheeks. "I don't typically make such a public spectacle of myself, especially in uniform, since the brass doesn't really like that, but to hell with them. I couldn't help it."

"That makes two of us," Matt replied while once again lacing their fingers together on the table. "What would you say to perhaps coming back to my place?"

"I'd say hell yes."

Matt and Craig rose from the booth and walked hand in hand out of the coffee shop. As they walked, Matt felt invulnerable for the first time in his life, as if no matter what further tragedy awaited him, he and Craig would defeat it—together.

Perhaps Craig was the only guardian angel he needed.

CLIFFORD snapped Officer Greene's neck with little effort and then let the body slump to the floor. He picked up the dead man's keys and eyed the bloody mess he made of Jerry Garcia's face, when he bit off his nose and gouged out his eyes.

He killed both men with ungodly speed. As he took the life of one and rushed over to the other, the world crawled by around him. They stood perfectly still while he moved in a blur of motion, incapable of being stopped.

Now that both men were dead, the world caught up to him. Prisoners in cells around him were hooting and egging him on. Begging him to let them out. They would help him take out all the guards or so they claimed.

They would definitely be of assistance, but not in the manner in which they believed. They were useful as distractions, nothing more. Beyond that, the lot of them could burn for all he cared, and sooner rather than later, each and every one of them would be ablaze in endless torment.

Sirens blared throughout the cellblock. Somewhere, someone knew what he had done and had set off the alarm that would bring more officers to subdue him. Like the two men dead in his cell quickly learned, Clifford Crouch was no longer so easily subdued.

He sprinted to the cell to his left and unlocked it. He tossed the grateful inmates the jailer's keys and ordered them to free as many as possible. They needed an army, he told them.

The men nodded quietly and set off to complete their task. While they worked busily freeing others, who howled loudly in triumph, Clifford returned to his cell and took the nightsticks from the dead officers.

He tucked Officer Greene's club in the waistband at the small of his back and then palmed the weapon belonging to the fat Jerry Garcia. Its cold, dead weight consumed him, as if transferring the destruction contained within the instrument directly into his form. Fueled by the raw power coursing through his veins, he turned to the approaching stampede of boots on metal, which indicated the arrival of more guards.

"It's show time," he whispered to Kenny's dead body. Although he previously resented killing Kenny, that emotion no longer remained. Whatever affection he carried for the wayward young man disappeared the moment he accepted the voice's offer of freedom. Now, Clifford only concerned himself with his needs.

And his needs required the deaths of everyone contained within these walls.

CHAPTER 13

FOR the past few hours, Matt and Craig reclined on the leather couch in Matt's living room. They told their pasts as well as lounged comfortably in their shared embraces.

Matt learned Craig came from a loving family, who took his coming out of the closet without missing a beat. His parents, both liberal educators, heralded their son's brave announcement by immediately joining Houston's PFLAG chapter. Since the organization boasted itself as an educational advocate for parents, families, and friends of gay men and women, Craig's parents made it their life's mission to help anyone in the gay community who needed them. Apparently, the Beltons were the poster family for PFLAG since their smiling faces could be found on most of the local chapter's literature.

Craig's two older brothers didn't care that their youngest sibling liked men. Though they were shocked in that Craig had been blessed with athletic ability and didn't fit the preset stereotype of an effeminate man, they quickly blew past their initial surprise. Now, his brothers hounded him about when he was going to settle down and raise kids like they had done.

While he admitted he wanted kids, Craig didn't know if his chosen career would allow that to happen. Work kept him extremely busy, and with only three years on the force, more veteran officers reminded him of his rookie status on a daily basis. He felt pushed to prove himself, especially since he was the only out gay cop he knew.

Few people hassled him about it, although one man did his first few months on the force. But after a spirited sparring match, the homophobe learned that this sissy could kick his ass. He hadn't bothered Craig since.

"So, when do you see yourself having kids?" Matt asked nuzzling up in the crook of Craig's neck.

"Maybe in five years or so. I'm trying to get assigned to homicide. Once that happens and I get promoted to detective, I think I'll be able to support my husband and kids quite nicely."

Matt liked hearing the word husband fall from Craig's lips. Most people said boyfriend or life partner. To him, husband was far more accurate, whether or not gay marriage was legal in Texas.

"What if your husband doesn't want to be supported? What if he likes having a job?"

Craig laughed. "Oh, my husband will need to work. Although I'd love to keep him barefoot and pregnant, it's not really practical these days."

Matt smiled but didn't respond. Craig's talk of his future family sounded delightful. It also echoed his own wishes of a loving husband and two point five kids. The fact that they shared similar dreams drew him closer to the man who cradled him protectively in his arms.

"I want to learn about you now," Craig said and kissed the tip of his ear. "Besides your adventures with Dee and Shane."

Matt pressed his face back into Craig's kiss and sighed.

"What's that heavy sigh for?"

"My story's far less happy than yours. In fact, it's quite the downer."

Craig squeezed him tighter until it felt like his back would merge with Craig's chest. "I still want to hear it, if you want to share."

Although Matt didn't relish telling about his past, he didn't mind the idea of opening up to Craig. His story was a sad tale of tragedy and woe, but somehow he believed that by sharing it with him, the crushing pain might lessen to a dull throb.

After the twenty minutes it took to bring Craig up to speed, he sat up and looked into Craig's eyes, which were saucer wide. "Told you it was bad. Do you regret hearing it now that you know what a screwed up life I've had?"

Craig shook his head and drew Matt back into his arms. "Not at all. It's just hard for me to believe that someone as wonderful and positive as you could have gone through so much and still be so well-adjusted."

"I don't know about the well-adjusted part."

"No, it's true," asserted Craig. "I've known people who've suffered only a fraction of what you've been through, and they're now sitting in jail serving ten to twenty."

"Well, I used to look at my life as if I was a walking tragedy. I sat in wait for the next bad thing to happen to me, looking over my shoulder for the next catastrophe. But I've decided I don't want to live that way anymore. Well, at least since this morning," he admitted with a sheepish grin.

"What happened this morning?"

"My grandmother," he told Craig. "She made me realize that I shouldn't see only tragedy. I should see the miracles. No matter what I've been through, I've survived, unharmed. She thinks I have a guardian angel watching over me. And you know what? I kinda like the idea." Mentioning his guardian angel made Matt think about Gabriel, but he banished the thought from his mind. He wanted to focus on Craig. Only Craig. No one else.

"Your grandmother sounds like a wise woman."

"She is," he replied, using Craig's warm touch to turn his focus from Gabriel and toward the man whose arms draped around him. "And she'll tell you as much if you ever meet her."

"I would welcome that. She sounds like someone I would like."

"Like?" he asked. "No one *likes* my grandmother. Everyone *loves* her."

"I'm sure I'll be no different."

Matt placed his head on Craig's chest, still covered in his black uniform, and gazed up into his green eyes. Like two emerald fields, they beckoned him for a stroll, but something prevented him.

There still existed a barrier between them. He saw it reflected in the corner of Craig's eyes. Within him, a doubt remained about Matt, something he needed to ask before their relationship progressed any further along the current path.

"What's the matter?" he finally asked, sitting up. "You look a million miles away."

"I was," Craig admitted, moving from a reclining to a sitting position.

"There's something you want to ask me," Matt announced. "I can see it in your eyes."

Craig nodded.

"Then ask."

He sighed, sitting forward on the couch with his elbows resting on his knees. "Remember how I told you I like honesty in a man?"

"Yes."

"Well, I do need to ask you a question, and I need you to be extremely honest with me. No matter what. Okay?"

Matt agreed. "What's your question?"

"Is there anything going on between you and that Gabriel guy?"

Matt exhaled. It looked like he was going to focus on Gabriel whether he wanted to or not. And Craig's question was tough. He was uncertain how to truthfully answer it. He didn't want to lie, but he didn't understand his lingering feelings for Gabriel any better than he could recall his buried memories of his parents. And the nightly sex dreams? He didn't know *what* those meant or if he should even bring them up.

"I'll take that as a yes," Craig replied, sounding disappointed. "I thought as much from the way he looked at you that night."

"You're jumping the gun," he told Craig. "And you've misread my pause. You asked for honesty, so I'm trying to formulate the truthful answer you deserve."

Craig nodded. "I can accept that. As long as you remain honest."

"I don't lie, Craig. And I don't appreciate your assumption that I do."

"I apologize. I've just been hurt by lies before, so I'm a little gun-shy."

"Okay, then," he began. "Here's the truth. I can't deny my attraction to Gabriel. He's a hot-looking man. And I know I came on a bit overzealous last week when you and Dee were suspicious of him, but I have to tell you that I didn't share your doubts. I can understand why you both had them, but I didn't. And still don't. Unfortunately, our conflicting opinions put us at odds. And we left things rather uncertain between us last week." He reached out and patted Craig's left hand. "I'm hoping we've remedied some of that tonight."

"We have," Craig admitted. "But you haven't really answered my question. You've only retold me what I already know." He paused before repeating himself. "Is there something going on between you and Gabriel?"

"No, there isn't. I haven't seen Gabriel since that night."

"But do you want to see him again? And if you do, how are you going to feel about him?" Craig asked. "I really like you, Matt, but I don't want to get involved with someone who isn't free to get involved with me."

"You're asking me a question that I can't answer. Would I like to see him again? Sure I would. I want to thank him for what he did for me. But you're asking me to predict how I'm going to feel. I can't do that. I suspect I'll feel grateful, and I'll probably still find him attractive. But I can't say with any kind of truth what I *might* feel *if* I ever seen him again."

"I appreciate the truth," Craig replied and then stood from the couch. He surveyed the coffee table, looking for his car keys.

"What about my answer did you not like?"

"I don't like feeling that Gabriel could come between us if he comes back."

"*If?*" he asked. "There are so many ifs in this world, Craig. We can't take each one into account. I know that better than anyone else, considering all the things that have happened to me." He stood and walked over to Craig, grabbing both his hands and holding them tightly against his chest.

"A relationship between two people is *always* a gamble. We never know if we're going to get hurt. That's part of the deal. It comes with the good morning kisses and the hot sex a couple enjoys. When you accept someone, you also accept the power that person has to potentially destroy you. We can only hope that our faith is placed in worthy hands, and that *that* person cherishes the relationship as much as we do."

He raised Craig's hands to his mouth, brushing his lips across them before continuing. "I can't promise you forever right now. It's too soon for both of us. But I can promise to remain honest with you. And there's nothing I want more than to explore these intense feelings I have for you."

Wrapping his arms around Craig's neck, Matt drew himself up the three inches he needed to look Craig in his eyes. "I'm willing to gamble it, Craig. But I need to know if you're willing too."

Craig responded by resting his hands on Matt's waist and pulling him into a kiss. He parted Matt's lips with his tongue and entered his mouth. There, he lolled like a vacationer on a beach. While he dove in and out of Matt's mouth with his hot, wet tongue, Matt undid the buttons of his police shirt.

He parted the fabric, letting it fall to the floor and his long fingers ran up and down Craig's soft skin. Craig unleashed moans of pleasure into his greedy mouth and he moved his hands from Matt's waist to his scrub pants, which he tugged free, along with his blue briefs, from his hips.

Matt's hard cock sprang between them and Craig took it in his hands. He broke the kiss long enough to look down at the seven inches he slowly jacked in his hand. "Nice," he whispered before grabbing the back of Matt's head with his left hand and forcing their mouths into kisses even more passionate than before.

Matt lifted Craig's white muscle shirt, revealing soft tufts of golden hair curling around his nipples and trailing down his stomach, where it disappeared beneath the waistband of his uniform pants. He licked a path from Craig's smooth face to his neck and nibbled there for a few seconds before departing for the sculpted pecs, which begged for attention.

"I love that," Craig cooed when Matt tickled his right nipple erect with his tongue. In response, Craig leaned over Matt and yanked the top of his scrubs up and over his head. He lifted Matt's head back to his mouth and continued to greedily kiss him, enflaming their passion with dueling tongues.

"You need to get out of those pants," Matt muttered in between moist kisses.

"I don't know," Craig said. His hands ran down Matt's smooth back until they reached his ass. After squeezing it, he delved into the crevice and played with the opening in the middle. "I kinda like you naked. At my command."

Matt bit his lip as Craig teased his hole with feathery caresses. "What do you want me to do, Officer? I'll do anything not to get a ticket."

Craig smiled, hungrily. "On your knees," he commanded to which Matt immediately responded. "There's only one way out of that ticket. And you're staring right at it."

"I don't know if I can, sir," he replied, coyly. "It's *huge!*"

"You'll do it or I'll take you to jail. Understand?"

"I don't want to go to jail, Officer. I'll do anything you ask."

He grabbed the back of Matt's head and forced his face against the bulge in his pants. "Do you feel that? Do you feel how hard you've made me?"

"Yes, sir," Matt responded, his voice muffled by the fabric. He opened his mouth and gnawed on the hard cock straining against the black trousers. Even from outside the material, he caught a whiff of Craig's heady, manly scent.

"You like the way that hard cock feels against your face, don't you?" Craig asked, his eyes smoldering in passion.

Matt only groaned in reply as Craig forced his throbbing member harder against his face. He lapped at the fabric, biting down on Craig's prick and longing to be given permission to set it free of its confines.

But the permission didn't come. Craig ground his pelvis into his face, lacing his fingers through Matt's hair to show him who was in charge. Never before had Matt had a lover take such control of him. He prided himself on staying in charge, but now, kneeling before this man, he handed over the reins without a second thought.

"Take that dick out of my pants."

Matt hurriedly undid the belt and zipper. He reached inside the pants and wrapped his fingers around the throbbing prick before tugging it out of his fly. His cock was just as long as Matt's but almost twice as thick. It throbbed angrily in his hands and wept profusely from the slit.

"Don't you suck it yet," Craig ordered. "Jerk it! Get me rock fucking hard!"

Matt did as he was commanded. He moved his hand feverishly up and down over the pulsing piece of meat and watched in amazement as Craig's veiny flesh flushed a deep red. The loose skin relaxed at every upward stroke and grew taut on the downward pull. With each passing moment, more and more precome oozed out from the slit, collecting like milky pearls on the tip.

Matt licked his lips, wanting to run his tongue across the head, but Craig yanked back on his hair. "Don't you dare," he instructed. "I'll let you know when it's time."

Matt whimpered in exasperation, but he dared not disobey. He continued to jack Craig's cock, squeezing more and more liquid from the tip until his hand was slick from the abundant moisture. Throwing his head back in pure bliss, Craig yanked hard on Matt's hair, shoving his face against his steel rod.

"Suck it! Suck it now!"

Wrapping his lips around the head, he suckled the drops of manly sugar from the tip before gliding slowly down the length of the shaft. He swallowed the full seven inches to the hilt, forcing his nose into the blond pubes surrounding the base. While his throat massaged Craig's cock, Matt inhaled the mix of cock sweat and musk deep into his lungs.

The scent proved intoxicating. If he could, he would spend the rest of his life with Craig's cock buried in his throat and the smell of his groin in his nostrils.

Craig had other ideas.

He held Matt's head and started moving in and out of his throat. His thrusts started slow and deep but quickly grew to short, rapid pistons, his cock barely sliding down his throat before its head rested on the tip of his tongue.

The entire time Craig drove in and out of his mouth, more tasty drops of his love juice coated Matt's tongue and the back of his throat.

Matt could tell he was quickly losing control. Looking up along the taut stomach and past the chest covered in golden fur, he watched as Craig's eyes rolled back in his head and his mouth drooped open in ecstasy.

"Oh my God," Craig panted. "Your mouth is so good. I'm so damn close." He chewed on his lower lip, trying to prolong the pleasure. "I don't want to come yet, but you're such a good cocksucker that I want to reward your greedy little mouth."

Since Matt was stuffed full with Craig's amazing cock, he couldn't respond, so he replied in the only manner that would deliver his message. He rested his hands against Craig's hips and helped him jam his hard cock faster and harder inside his mouth.

He increased his suction and danced his tongue along the shaft. He wanted nothing more than for Craig to unleash inside his thirsty mouth.

Craig understood his message. He pounded faster and faster inside Matt's throat, his hands weaving through his hair and making it a tangled mess. Moans of pleasure became groans of anticipated release. His ball sack tightened, drawing his testicles up closer to his body.

Matt knew the moment had arrived. He buried the entire shaft down his throat, lodging the head deep inside him. He constricted his muscles and increased the suction, and Craig let loose with a primal scream.

The hard cock embedded deep in his mouth released hot jets of come down his gullet, pulsing and throbbing violently with each spasm. Matt brought the cock out of his throat in order to coat his tongue with the thick cream before swallowing the final volley.

When he let Craig's cock slip from his lips, the officer collapsed onto the couch.

"Oh my God." He whistled while wiping the sweat from his brow. "That was the most intense orgasm I've ever had. You definitely got yourself out of that ticket."

Matt crawled onto his lap and kissed his lips, softly. "I'm glad. I'd hate to have to attend defensive driving."

A huge grin stretched across Craig's face. He then pulled Matt closer, rubbing his strong hands across his shoulders, down his back, and to his smooth ass. "You feel so good in my arms," he said before licking Matt's lips and inserting his tongue where his hard cock had just been.

From between his legs, Matt felt a formerly spent soldier once again standing at attention. "Officer Belton, your gun seems to be reloading."

Craig smirked. "One thing you should know about my gun is that it's not a single shooter. It's capable of going off multiple times a night."

"In that case, you should know I wasn't wearing my seatbelt. And that I was texting while driving. Wouldn't that be two more tickets I'd need to get out of?"

Craig pushed Matt back onto the couch. "I like the way you think, good citizen."

"Oh, I'm not good at all, Officer," he replied while Craig shucked off his pants and white briefs. "I'm bad. Very, *very* bad."

"Then I'll have to use the full arm of the law on you," Craig replied while staring down at his manhood, now as hard and red as before.

"It's the only thing left to do."

Craig lowered his naked body on top of Matt, burying his face in Matt's neck and swirling his tongue over and inside his ear before snaking a trail along his hairless chin. Matt clawed at his ass and bit his shoulder, delighting in the reckless abandon with which Craig lapped at his neck.

He spread his legs wide, feeling Craig's engorged member slide down his crack and rub against the tiny opening. He bucked hard against it, trying to force it inside him. Craig repositioned his throbbing piece on top of Matt's hardness.

"Not yet," he told Matt. "I'm going to make you beg for it."

He sat up on his knees, between Matt's legs and scooted them both further down the couch. He then rested his full weight upon Matt, and their tongues resumed dancing in their mouths.

While they kissed, Craig traveled down to Matt's right nipple and tweaked it with his right hand. He rolled the sensitive flesh between his thumb and forefinger until it was sore and red. He then flicked it twice and lightly scratched his fingernails along the protruding nub.

"Oh God," Matt moaned when Craig moved to his chest to take the stinging nipple in his mouth. He licked it to life while proceeding to torture the left nipple in the same manner he pleasured the right.

Matt bucked against Craig, forcing their hard dicks to slide against one another and sparking a sexual fire that burned deeply in their loins. His desires had already pushed past their limits during the blowjob he had given Craig; Matt didn't know how much longer he could last without his own release.

But Craig insisted on taking his time.

He worked one nipple with his mouth, while he tugged and pinched on the other. When Matt was certain he could take no more, he switched nipples again.

"Please," Matt begged. "I need you inside me. Now."

Craig shook his head no and then lifted Matt's arms as he dove into Matt's left armpit, which Matt knew contained the sweat of a twelve-hour shift. Obviously enjoying the scent and taste, Craig moaned while he licked lazy trails, matting hair against Matt's salty flesh, which further fanned the flames of Matt's growing lust.

While he lapped up the day's sweat, Craig reached between Matt's legs with his right hand and teased his pulsing hole. He scratched at the opening, forcing it to pucker in want before drawing long radiating circles from the center to along the rim.

Matt shuddered in response, licking at Craig's ear and running his hands along the rippling muscles in his arms. Each time Craig touched him or played with his sensitive areas, he relinquished more control, giving himself over not just to the passion but to the man who fanned its flames.

"Are you ready?" Craig asked.

Matt nodded his head. "Yes, please. Do it. Now."

Craig's lips parted into a smile that looked more like a taunt. "Almost."

He kissed a path from Matt's armpit down his side before lapping his tongue around his belly button. While he darted his tongue inside, he increased the pressure of his fingers at Matt's backdoor. The tip of his index finger entered him for a second before withdrawing and once again circling his outer rim.

Craig nibbled on his lower stomach, biting down toward his cock, which lay in a pool of sweat and precome. He licked at the head and then planted short, breathy kisses along the shaft before lapping at his balls and popping one then the other into his mouth.

Matt arched his back and almost came off the couch, when Craig suddenly inserted two fingers inside him before removing them just as quickly.

Craig's mouth now hovered over his cock. The hot, humid pants buffeted the hard skin and then before he knew it, Craig sucked the entire thing into his mouth. He sucked and licked while jacking on the shaft with his right hand and tugging on his balls with the left.

Matt had been afraid to touch himself for fear of coming too quickly. Now that Craig was feasting on his cock as if it were his last meal, he found it difficult to hold back. He wanted to feel the sweet joy of release as he jettisoned his spunk in spasms of pleasure.

Craig jacked his cock feverishly, working him to the point of climax and then abruptly stopped.

"What? Why did you stop?"

"It's not time for you to come yet," he replied while grabbing Matt by his knees and hoisting them into the air. Craig then dove into the hole he had relentlessly teased and used his powerful tongue, which wouldn't be denied, to probe inside.

Craig parted Matt's flesh and undulated inside him. Matt bucked back against his face, enjoying being fucked by such an expert tongue like Craig's, which wiggled and withdrew, pushed and flattened, and curled and lapped up inside him so vigorously that Matt was certain he would pass out from the sheer bliss. Just when he thought he could take no more, Craig stopped and looked directly into his eyes.

"Guess what?" he asked.

"It's time," Matt replied. "Please tell me it's time."

Craig nodded, and after rolling on the condom he retrieved from his pants, he positioned the head of his rigid cock at his opening. Slick with spit and having been thoroughly worked over by Craig's tongue, his cock easily slid past the first ring.

Matt threw his head back from the mixture of pleasure and pain as inch after inch of Craig's thick dick parted him until Craig was firmly entrenched inside. When Craig's hairy balls rested on the crack of his ass, he opened his eyes.

Craig stared down at him. The teasing glint in his eyes disappeared. In its place, he saw only an ever-deepening affection and the promise of much more. He craned his neck up to taste Craig's sweet kisses, and when their tongues came to life in each other's mouths, Craig slowly moved himself in and out of Matt's ass.

The pleasure was intense. With each full thrust, Craig's thick head rubbed his internal pleasure button, causing his cock to grow harder and leak more liquid onto his stomach. When he withdrew, Matt's muscles grasped onto Craig's withdrawing member, trying to pull it back inside and prevent it from leaving his body.

They kissed and panted into each other's mouths as Craig continued to drive faster and harder inside him. Sweat trailed from his hairline down his face before raining down upon Matt's face and chest. Matt wrapped his arms around Craig's neck, using the leverage to meet Craig's increasingly rapid thrusts with his own.

He met each forceful plunging of Craig's cock with equal force, shoving him further and further inside. Matt and Craig surfed their hands wildly over each other's sweat-slick body, and their lips never once parted as their hips continued to crash together in loud, moist collisions.

After several more minutes of high-intensity lovemaking, Matt felt Craig's hard cock turn to stone. Its increased girth nudged his prostrate constantly, bringing him ever closer to the edge of their shared glory.

"I won't last much longer," Craig warned. "I'm so close."

"Keep going," he urged. "I'm right there with you."

Craig pounded away more furiously, working harder to bring them both home. "Oh, Matt, I'm coming inside you. I can't stop it. Here it comes!"

And with a final push, Craig unleashed another torrent of semen inside Matt. He growled and bucked harder as he came deep inside. Matt fisted his cock, jerking feverishly to bring himself over the edge while Craig filled him from within.

After a few strokes, Matt's toes curled and he let loose a flood of thick, ropy come that shot from his cock all over his and Craig's chests.

When the spasms subsided, Craig lowered himself onto the couch and pulled Matt on top of him. Their bodies cemented together by spit, sweat, and semen. Craig ran his hands up and down Matt's body and kissed his forehead, cheek, and lips.

"You're amazing. You know that?"

"You're not too shabby yourself, Officer."

"I'm not shabby at all, thank you very much!"

Matt traced a slow circle around Craig's right nipple. "Confident," he finally replied. "I like that in a man."

They smiled at each other as drowsiness slowly fell across their eyes. Before they knew it, they were asleep, holding on to not only each other but also to what they found in the other.

FROM the rooftop of the building across the street, Gabriel watched as the lights inside Matt's apartment blinked off, signaling that Matt and Craig were finally going to sleep.

He turned his eyes to the night sky, praying for a cool, refreshing breeze to blow away the heaviness in his heart. No revitalizing wind sprung up around him in miraculous response. Instead, the still night remained unseasonably stifling and humid.

Gabriel wondered if the crushing pain in his heart was penance paid for his trespass. His brother warned him against moving out of the periphery, and he chose not to heed the advice.

He had no one else to blame but himself for his breaking heart.

He succumbed to carnal pleasure, when he kissed Matt, a mistake that almost cost him his assignment. But since then, he secreted himself inside Matt's dreams. It was a place where they could safely enjoy the physical contact they both desired, without getting into trouble.

The late night visitations blurred lines without breaking his promise, but they also proved beneficial in fulfilling his role as Matt's guardian.

Within Matt's recurring nightmare, Gabriel distracted him from opening the door in his dreams and protected Matt from what lay on the other side. Matt believed opening the door would allow him access to the memories of his parents. That was true, but more than memories existed beyond the door. Something far more malevolent waited on the other side.

As long as Gabriel appeared nightly, Matt remained safe.

With Craig now in Matt's bed, Gabriel's visiting his dreams would no longer be appropriate. Matt's progress toward opening the door would continue, and once the door swung open, true evil would flood Matt's reality.

This was something Gabriel couldn't bring himself to allow. Since Matt's infancy, he had taken a far more active role in his life than any other guardian had ever assumed with their charge.

He had swooped in and saved Matt when he needed him the most. Sometimes true success required action, not standing by on the sidelines.

After all, if he hadn't sprung into action all those years ago, Matt wouldn't be here today.

Perhaps he needed to revisit those lessons from the past. If protecting the man he loved meant standing dead center and not remaining in the periphery, then it was something he had to do, no matter what the consequences might be.

PART III:
REVELATIONS

CHAPTER 14

HIGH above the clouds, Gabriel held the young Mateo in his arms as he spirited him away from the residence where he had lived with his father and brothers just moments before. He had only moments to act before the demon inside Homer Rodgers sensed the boy's presence and tracked him down.

He couldn't deliver the boy to his uncle who resided in Victoria or to any of his other five uncles. If he did, the boy would be easily found.

He needed a more permanent solution, one that would safeguard the boy from further harm or at least grant the child the respite he needed to grow into a man capable of fending for himself.

Leaving with Mateo and taking a more active role meant a serious reprimand for Gabriel would be warranted. He had vowed only to stand as vigilant protector, not to help carve out a future that the boy himself was responsible for sculpting.

Yet, he was an innocent baby, incapable of fending off the dangers that swirled wretchedly around him. Someone had to take charge; someone had to act to preserve the glorious future potential Mateo's lineage bestowed upon him.

Gabriel didn't know the extent of the boy's promise. His potential remained shrouded by the veil of time. Still the fact remained, he was given the duty of protecting the boy. After all, Mateo wasn't assigned to any guardian angel. The task was given to Gabriel, an archangel, one of the seven mighty generals of his Father's army, and he would move heaven and earth itself to see the boy delivered from harm.

"Brother, you must stop this mad plan immediately!"

In a blaze of blinding golden light, Michael materialized before him, bedecked in his golden celestial armor and held aloft by his magnificent white wings.

Gabriel held Mateo close, shielding the infant beneath the curve of his left wing. "Why? So he can be murdered as viciously as his father and brothers? I think not, Michael." His heavenly sword appeared in his right hand. "Stand down or fight me! I offer no other options."

"Meddling in human affairs beyond the supernatural is forbidden," Michael replied, drawing his own sword out of thin air. "Father has charged humanity with taking care of itself. He has withdrawn from active involvement with them and has commanded the same of us. Mankind must learn to flourish or falter without divine intervention."

Gabriel gritted his teeth, and he watched as Michael studied the sky. Ever the strategist, his brother searched for an opening from which to strike. "And what of this boy? The one He charged me Himself with protecting? Am I to leave him searching for suckle as the hyenas and vultures encircle him?"

"You are to follow orders, Gabriel. As we all must. Your involvement threatens the course of humanity."

"Demons are already involved, so the course of humanity is already threatened. To be idle is no longer appropriate. Not when my involvement strengthens humanity." The rage in Michael's eyes lessened. His brother was obviously heeding Gabriel's words. "This boy is the seventh son of a seventh son. Such a birth hasn't occurred in untold centuries. You know of the promise he brings to humanity. Why should I not act and guarantee the safety of such a miracle onto those we claim to love and protect?"

"Because if such a promise is to be fulfilled, humanity itself must work to allow that to happen."

Gabriel scoffed at Michael's naïveté. "You obviously still hold your much-vaunted opinion of humanity while I see what man has become. They are incapable of pulling themselves out of the ocean of sin they drown within. They clamor for self-gratification only. They will be too busy with their own selfish needs to take care of a child so important to the Grand Design."

Michael's sword disappeared from his hand, turning into a small cloud that stretched away behind him. A white tunic glimmered into view, replacing his golden armor. Michael's face, which before gazed only in anger, now stared at him with profound sadness. "If you rob them of the chance, how would we ever know?"

Gabriel hated nothing more than staring into his brother's disappointed face. Though they had a long history of conflict, their disagreements never embittered their souls against each other. They were always brothers first, antagonists second.

Gabriel tossed his sword away and watched as a long, arching rainbow formed in its wake. "I don't want to fight you, Michael, but I can't allow harm to come to this boy."

His brother smiled, and flecks of golden radiance reflected off the billowy white clouds. "You don't realize how happy that makes me. Or Father."

"What do you mean?" Gabriel asked. "Is Father not furious?"

"He's not pleased that you've disobeyed Him, but angels have free will. Just as humans do."

"And you're both happy I've used that gift to break the rules?"

"In a way, yes. You've grown over this past year, brother. More than you have in the millennia that trail behind us. No matter what you may think you believe about humanity, your constant requests to bring about judgment with one blow of your horn have stopped. In your care and your love for this boy, you've rediscovered your love for humanity. That in itself is a glorious event."

Gabriel thought long and hard about his brother's statement. He was shocked when he realized it was true. He no longer carried his horn tied to his waist, waiting for the opportunity to bring forth judgment and vengeance on the wicked.

As he looked down at the infant sleeping peacefully in his arms, he realized Mateo was responsible for the change. In the boy, he lost his prejudice and anger. Love and compassion grew in its place.

"What happens now?" he asked Michael. "You won't permit me to proceed. I refuse to return him from whence we came."

"How about a third option?"

Michael waved his hand and the cloud to his left hardened into a block of ice. In it, he saw reflected a couple. The man looked to be in his late thirties, and the youthful spark in his eyes revealed a kind, compassionate soul. Short blond hair framed his handsome face, which broadened into a smile whenever his eyes fell upon his wife.

A heavenly twinkle lit up the woman's brown eyes, when she saw her husband. She reached for him and shivered when her olive flesh pressed against his fair skin. He tucked the long black hair behind her ears before kissing her tenderly on her lips and taking her hand in his.

"Why do you show me this? Who are these people?"

"They are William and Nicole Westlake, and they have been waiting for years to love a child of their own."

"How do I know they are good people? How do I know they will watch over the boy as his parents tried to do?"

"Father himself sent us this vision."

"Father?"

Michael nodded. "He heard your request, and He has seen fit to give you this couple. They are far enough removed from where you just came for the boy's scent to be lost in the wind. But with them he will be returned to the everyday concerns of humanity."

"And what if they find him again? What then?"

"You will still be his guardian angel, brother. It will be your duty to keep him from harm that falls outside of the scope of humanity."

Gabriel wanted to thank his brother, but a sob quickly formed in his throat. It prevented him from speaking. It didn't matter, for Michael saw the gratitude reflected within and nodded in response.

"Take the boy to Houston, and there you will intuit the intermediary who shall deliver the young one to the Westlakes. They will adopt him and care for him."

Without further comment, Gabriel soared past his brother and toward Mateo's home, where his new parents would love and rear him and where he would continue to guard him with his life.

HOMER RODGERS bellowed in anger; the boy's scent had disappeared in the wind. When he opened his mouth a second time, fire spewed forth and quickly engulfed the home, where the infant previously resided.

He had failed, and in his failure, he had doomed not only himself but his wife. Unable to uphold his end of the bargain, the voice called Barbatos that resided within him would demand payment, and their souls would ferry the price.

No other option remained. With one blow of his axe, it would be done. For them both.

"Not just yet," the voice inside hissed. "You may still prove useful."

"But how?" Homer asked. "He's gone. Taken away by the angel who guards him. We have no way to track them through the heavens."

The voice cackled menacingly. "Heaven can't protect the boy forever. There are rules even they must obey. The infant will return to earth. Of that, I do not doubt. And when he does, we will find him. And then, he will die."

Again the voice within him started to laugh. This time, Homer joined in. He still had a shot to make good on his contract. His wife might still live if he managed to kill the boy before the cancer consumed her from within.

Homer would track him to the ends of the earth if he had to. His wife was worth any price—both the boy's life and Homer's soul.

CHAPTER 15

LIKE motherly caresses urging him awake, the streaming sunlight through his bedroom window roused Matt from sleep. He wasn't ready to wake up. Today was his day off, and besides sleeping late, the only other thing he planned on doing was having hot, passionate sex with Craig. And if that meant cancelling his appointment with Dr. Owens, that was fine by him.

Spending time with Craig had become important to them both. They had spent almost every possible moment together the past couple of weeks. Meeting for lunch or spending the night was now part of their routine. Although they had yet to label their relationship, they were well on their way to becoming a bona fide couple.

Matt turned over, eyes still closed, reaching across the bed to find Craig's naked form next to him. He intended to use his hands and his mouth to drive Craig so crazy he had to fuck him again.

Instead of Craig's smooth, muscular back, he found a dresser, which was much closer to him than it should be.

His eyes fluttered open, and the bed he lay upon was a twin, not a queen. Blue sheets with an assortment of balls—basketballs, footballs, and soccer balls—replaced his tan sheets and olive duvet.

Matt sat upright in bed, terrified. He hadn't had this dream for the past two weeks, not since he started sleeping with Craig. When he told Dr. Owens at his last visit that the nightmares had stopped and that he no longer dreamt of having sex with Gabriel, the psychiatrist believed that his burgeoning relationship with Craig was most likely responsible.

Since Matt felt safe in a potentially true romantic partnership, the new hope and longing for that relationship displaced his inner turmoil.

But as he surveyed his childhood room, the small blue dresser with the usual assortment of toys, the light blue curtains, the yellow painted walls, and the white Berber carpet, Matt realized that inner turmoil hadn't moved that far off after all.

Thump. Thump.

Matt turned toward the closed walnut bedroom door. Clifford Crouch was making his way to his room.

Thump.

He was now at the foot of the staircase, with the bloody knife he used to murder his parents in their sleep. The same knife he wanted to use to kill Matt.

Thump.

As always happened on the fourth thump, he pulled back the covers and shuffled forward on unsteady legs toward the door, which was unlocked. He had to reach the door before Clifford. He had to stop him from getting inside the room.

But then he remembered Gabriel. For a whole week, his savior had appeared in his dreams to stop him from approaching the door. They made love all night long on his bed, and Gabriel's arms and kisses kept the door from opening. In his embrace, Matt was safe from the horrors that lay behind the door.

He looked over his shoulder, willing Gabriel to step out of the shadows as he had once done, but he wasn't there. And neither was the sunlight that first woke him. Night had since descended, carpeting his room in long, inky shadows that crawled toward him.

In the distance, thunder rumbled. A storm was on its way.

Thump, thump, thump, thump.

Matt spun back toward the door as the footsteps ran up the staircase. They had never done that before. It had always been an unhurried progression up the stairs, like in a scary movie, where the slow movement of the deranged killer drew out the scene's intensity.

Now, his parents' murderer bounded toward his door in a mad frenzy, wanting nothing more than to slit his throat.

He sprinted for the door just as the doorknob turned, and he threw his weight against it. In response, whatever waited on the other side snickered in derision. The noise didn't sound completely human; he also heard the bleating of a goat. The realization made him shiver uncontrollably.

Whatever existed on the other side, which he no longer believed to be Clifford Crouch, slammed with tremendous fury against the door. The impact was sharp, like hoof and horn meeting wood and not the thud of flesh and bone.

The door rattled in place and opened six inches before Matt managed to force it back closed.

"Come out, come out," the voice bleated. "Don't you want to play?"

"Go away!" Matt yelled, embarrassed by the fear apparent in his voice.

Again, the thing on the other side slammed into the door, harder. Hooves and horns scraped deep into wood. The door opened halfway before he forced it shut again.

The creature, for Matt was certain that it couldn't be human, whinnied in anger and set upon the door in an angry barrage. Thunderous assaults of hoof, horn, and body slammed into the door, repeatedly. Matt braced his shoulder against the wood, but it splintered and popped beneath him.

Incessantly, the being punched and kicked, slamming against the wood until every blow sounded like gunfire. Each collision shoved the door further open, inch by inch, and Matt glimpsed a furry leg try to gain entrance to the room before he slammed the door shut once more.

Then, without warning, the attack stopped. The creature still stood opposite the door. Matt could hear it panting, out of breath before it unleashed another volley of maniacal laughter.

"You can't stop this," the voice bleated. "You can't hide forever."

Over and over, it repeated the same statement. "The Gifted One must die. The Gifted One must die."

Matt pressed his palms against his ears, trying to block out its crazed voice, but it didn't help. The words resonated within him, vibrating against his lungs and rattling his bones until his entire body hummed with the prophetic words.

In horror, the door he leaned against turned to paper. Holes magically carved themselves out of the material and along their perimeter; burning embers appeared that quickly spread across the surface. Smoke billowed around the door, venting heat so intense he had to back away in order to avoid being burned.

Then the door transformed to fire and smoke, suspended magically before him. Fiery tendrils of flame reached out to the bedroom and singed whatever they touched. The thick gray smoke turned his yellow walls black with soot.

Sulfur hung heavy in the air. Matt choked and coughed, covering his mouth and nose in vain. The stench crept through his fingers and snaked down his lungs until his insides burned with a fire reminiscent of the blazing door, which wavered before him like a smoldering mirage.

The fire suddenly snuffed out as if someone turned off a switch, and the door no longer existed. A dense, tangible darkness stretched out beyond.

Matt tensed his body, waiting for the thing on the other side to pounce and take his life, but nothing happened. Nothing stirred within the darkness, and no sounds emanated from within the shadowy folds.

Matt stood up from where he crouched against the wall opposite the door. He took a step toward the darkness. Though his mind warned him to run back to the safety of his bed, his feet shuffled forward.

He had to know what was in the darkness. If he learned what waited on the other side, he might be able to overcome his fears and regain the memories of his parents.

As he stood at the threshold of the black void, he looked down to where the shadows on the floor met the light of his bedroom. At the juncture, a thin golden line of light prevented the two from touching. He followed the trail and realized it encircled the entire perimeter of the door. The blackness flowed like liquid on the other side, reaching toward the golden radiance before quickly withdrawing.

The darkness parted and a long hallway stretched out continuously before him. Its sudden appearance caused Matt to move away until his back rested against the opposite wall. As he stood there, the hallway continued to elongate like some room in a funhouse until it abruptly stopped at about a hundred yards away.

A figure, small and colorful, appeared on the other end. Its face, caked with clown-white makeup, stared back at him. Although he couldn't see the eyes clearly, they looked coal black and deadly like a hungry shark's.

As if loaded on a spring, the figure bounded toward him. It leaped through the air at least five yards per jump, and though it drew nearer with each superhuman bounce, the figure remained tiny, no bigger than a two-year-old baby.

Closer it hopped, ricocheting off the wall, the ceiling, and the floor, a mad red smile stretched across its pale white face. Heat, even more intense than the burning door, preceded the bounding figure, which laughed and twirled and jumped ever closer, heading straight for him.

He had to move. He had to get out of the way. If it touched him, Matt knew he would die. But he couldn't move. His feet were glued to the carpet, and his arms were heavy and useless. All he could do was scream, as the bouncing devilish baby clown got ever closer to him.

Its smile grew wider, and drops of crimson liquid fell from its cherry-red lips.

That was when Matt knew what it wanted. It didn't just want to kill him. It wanted to devour him, body and soul.

Matt screamed at the top of his lungs, calling for someone, anyone, to help him.

A pair of strong hands grasped at his shoulders and spun him around.

"Gabriel?" he called out before the world went dark.

HOMER stood on his porch, gazing out on the back forty of his property. It was his morning ritual, surveying the land while drinking his cup of coffee. It brought him the peace he needed before he began his heartbreaking daily tasks.

He didn't seek escape from the duties of owning a working farm. Feeding the livestock, repairing the fences, or supervising the ranch hands weren't the root of his discontent. Those duties gave him purpose and reminded him of the simple life he had taken for granted almost twenty years ago.

Back then, when he was ordinary Homer Rodgers, the man who loved the land and his wife Lily, he promised to do anything required to keep his loves with him, forever. He had sacrificed a great deal to ensure that happened.

Today, he wished he had had the wisdom and maturity he now possessed back then. He would kick the shit out of his younger self, make him realize that what he wanted was selfish and wrong. He had deceived himself into believing that what he did was for his wife, to spare her the pain of the cancer that ate away at her body.

His true motive proved far less selfless. He did it so he wouldn't be alone.

Fear of loneliness had called the shots twenty years ago. It drove him to make a promise he never should have made, and because he did, his wife still lived, if anyone could call it living.

Cancer still riddled her body, and her waking moments, which were few and far between, were filled with humiliation and pain. She crapped herself, ate mush, and could no longer speak or see. She took a variety of medication to dull the agony, but none of them worked, and though doctors believed she should have been dead decades ago, her body persisted to function.

It wasn't that his beautiful Lily didn't want to die. She had begged God to take her out of this world and end her torment.

Her body simply refused to comply.

Twelve years ago, Lily asked him to help her commit suicide. She couldn't go on anymore, and she needed his help to end it. Finally, he relented. He gave her an overdose of pain medication, and she fell into a deep sleep. He sat beside her until she finally stopped breathing. And though the pain he felt at losing her was immense, it was nothing compared to the pain they continued to endure since she gasped for air five minutes later.

When her eyes sprung open, she looked around, angry that God rebuked her. She didn't understand why He closed the gates of heaven to her, committing her to living in writhing pain.

She had no idea that God wasn't responsible. He was.

Had he simply decided not to go through with killing that infant, his soul might have been damned, but his wife would have been set free from this life. Since he attempted and failed, he activated a hidden clause. Now, her cancer continued to grow, but her body would no longer die.

He tested the theory several times. He mixed rat poison in the mush she consumed. She vomited blood for a week but continued to live. She survived electrocution in the bathtub, the severing of an artery, and even a .22 fired point blank.

Nothing brought an end to their shared hell.

Where once he would do anything to save his wife's life, now he would do anything to give her the peace of death.

"Anything?"

Homer jumped at the sound of the voice. He turned around toward the closed back door. No one stood behind him.

"Have you forgotten me already?" the voice asked. It sounded off-key, like a misplayed note on a guitar. This wasn't the same voice from before. The one that Gabriel had called Barbatos. He had spoken with a hiss.

"I don't know you," he told the open air. "Don't pretend that I do."

Laughter filled the covered porch, destroying his peaceful morning in its cacophony. "You're right," the voice admitted. "I'm not Barbatos. I'm different from him. Better. More suited to the task at hand."

"What task?"

"The one you failed."

Homer's coffee cup slipped from his hand and crashed onto the wooden slats below. He hadn't been contacted since the day he killed that family, since he failed to kill the infant.

"What do you want from me now?" he asked. "Haven't you taken enough from me already?"

"You've lost nothing. You still have your wife."

"She might as well be dead," he railed. "She *should* be dead. What she's doing isn't living!"

"That's your fault. Not mine," the voice accused. "The boy lives as does your wife."

"Then where is he? Tell me where he is and I'll kill him. If that's what it takes to let her soul move on, I'll do it. I'll do anything." He knew how desperate he sounded, and he hated it. He didn't want to travel this road again, but he had no choice. Lily had suffered enough. And so had he.

"That's the deal I now offer. Kill the boy and your wife will die."

"No scams this time," he told the voice. His eyes darted to every shadow searching for where it hid. "I don't want any fucking tricks. I don't want her to die, but her soul to linger on. I don't want her to be some fucking ghost haunting me for the rest of my life. I want her to die and for her soul to move on."

"No tricks. Kill the boy, and your wife's soul shall be released. Never to return." The voice paused. A cardinal chirped in the distance, filling the silence left by the discordant voice with its melody. "Do we have a deal?" it finally asked. Its harsh notes frightened the bird away.

Homer thought about the terms. This time, the voice promised exactly what he wanted. Lily needed to die. With her death, they would both receive the peace they deserved. If that peace cost the life of someone already destined to die, then it was a price he would gladly pay.

He already had the blood of seven innocents staining his soul. One more would hardly make any difference.

"Deal," he said with conviction.

Like smoke, a shadow wafted up from beneath the wooden slats of the porch. Shadowy wings stretched the breadth of the porch before the hidden figure entered his nose and his mouth, filling his already empty shell with its corrosive presence. When it was done, when he felt the evil as much a part of him as the air in his lungs, Homer smiled.

The time had come to end what he began long ago. He was headed for Houston, where the boy who was now a man resided.

THE hot coffee splashed around inside the rim of the cup. Even after being shaken awake by Craig fifteen minutes earlier, Matt's body had yet to stop trembling. He still saw the bounding figure hurtling toward him.

Never before had he felt such evil or been so afraid. Matt doubted he would ever sleep again.

"Still not doing any better I see," Craig commented while joining him at the small circular breakfast table. "And still a full cup of coffee too."

"My hands won't stop trembling," he replied while rubbing his hands for warmth. "And I'm freezing."

Craig cupped Matt's hands in his and lifted them to his mouth, where he blew five hot puffs of air into his shivering, ice-cold hands. Craig's touch and his hot breath, which always aroused him, caused his body to slowly relax. Each exhalation somehow had the power to blow away his fears and ground him in the here and now.

"Much better already." Craig kissed his hands before letting them go. "Now drink your coffee."

Matt nodded and brought the hot cup to his lips. Its warm liquid melted away the remaining chill Craig's kisses couldn't disperse. After a few sips, he felt more like an adult instead of a frightened child. "Thanks," he told Craig. He hoped his words expressed the depths of the gratitude he felt.

If Craig hadn't awoken him when he did, before that maniacal clown baby reached him, he couldn't guess what might have happened.

"I'm glad I could help," Craig commented. "I'm just sorry I wasn't what you wanted."

Craig's sudden cattiness confused him. He knew the recurring dream was the repressed memory of his parents' deaths. Since the dreams stopped after he and Craig took their relationship to the next level, they joked about Craig being the solution to his nightmares. Craig couldn't really be upset because they returned, with a vengeance, and blame him? Could he?

But Matt clearly saw anger and a hint of disappointment as he stared into Craig's forlorn countenance. Something definitely troubled him. "I don't know what's going on here. Would you mind filling me in?"

He knew Craig would tell him the truth, regardless of the answer. One of the things they established at the beginning was the importance of honesty. They both heralded it as the cornerstone of a relationship, and they promised to always tell the truth when asked, no matter how unpleasant the truth might be.

"You asked for Gabriel," Craig replied with a sigh.

Matt still had no clue what he was referring to.

"When you were dreaming, you were calling for Gabriel. Not me."

"I was?" And then he remembered how his dream ended. The hands that suddenly grasped him and shook him awake. He thought it was Gabriel because Gabriel had been in the dream the last few times he had them.

"Oh, Craig," Matt said, rising from his seat. He took Craig's head and held it to his stomach. "I remember now. I'm sorry. I truly am, but you're reading more into it than there is."

"How can that be? You were calling for him *not* me. How can I *not* read into that?" Craig gently pulled himself out of Matt's embrace and rose from the table. He walked over to the kitchen bar and leaned against it. More than physical distance grew between them.

"You are. I promise."

"Explain it to me then. Make me feel better. I really want you to."

Matt filled him in on the dreams prior to Craig, the ones where Gabriel stopped him from approaching the door by having sex with him.

"See the only reason I called for him was because he was there the last time."

"I see," Craig replied. No look of comfort replaced the sadness. Instead, his face turned hard. "So you dreamt about Gabriel. Sexually? For an entire week?"

"Yes, but it was just a dream. It's not like we *actually* had sex or anything."

"But when I asked you if there was anything going on between you two, you told me no."

Matt nodded. "And there was nothing. Craig, it was a dream. You understand that, right?"

"I do. All too well." Craig walked into the kitchen and turned on the faucet. He vigorously washed his cup in the sink.

"Then I don't understand why you're still so upset. Nothing happened."

"Not because you didn't want it to but because he never came back after that night." He dried the cup and placed it on the counter. "Tell me. What would have happened if he did? Where would you and I be right now if Gabriel showed back up? I asked you that once, but you made me believe it wouldn't matter if he did. Right now, I'm not so sure."

"You're asking me 'if' questions again that I can't answer. I don't know what would have happened. I can't predict how something might have changed or even tell you if nothing would have changed at all."

"Actually, those questions aren't that difficult to answer. When you know what the answer is."

"What does that mean?"

"You know my past with Tony," he told Matt.

He nodded. They had discussed Craig's most recent ex-boyfriend at length one night in bed. The two dated for over a year, and Craig had fallen completely in love with him. Since Tony worked in business, he was often out of town, but when he was in Houston, they spent every waking moment together.

He even pseudo moved in with Craig since most of his travel clothes gravitated to his place. Craig believed that meant their relationship was progressing toward something more permanent, and that Tony would be soon telling everyone who Craig was and what they meant to each other.

That illusion shattered when he overheard a phone conversation one evening between Tony and his wife.

It was then that he learned Tony was married with two children. He promised Craig he would leave his wife for him, but after six months of waiting, Craig had enough and ended the relationship.

It had taken Craig a few months to get over Tony, but he had. Bringing up their past now confused Matt.

"What does Tony have to do with this?"

"Ask me what would have happened if Tony came back into my life after we met. If he had divorced his wife, come out to the world, and wanted me back. Ask me what would have happened."

Matt didn't need to. He understood where Craig was going with this. "But that's a completely different situation. Tony hurt you. You fell out of love with him. Gabriel's never hurt me."

Craig arched his eyebrow. "And what? You're in love with Gabriel?"

"What? How did you get to that conclusion from what I said?"

"You said they were two different situations. Number one, Tony hurt me, and I don't love him anymore. Number two, Gabriel never hurt you and…"

"And nothing," he replied, even though he knew there was some truth to Craig's accusation. His feelings for Gabriel had never disappeared. Matt had only suppressed them. "You're being ridiculous and blowing this out of proportion."

"Maybe," Craig admitted. "But maybe not."

Craig walked over to Matt and placed his hands on his shoulders, rubbing them gently to comfort him like he'd done since the first night they met, and it worked. His anxiety subsided. "But I'm beginning to think that there's more to your feelings for Gabriel than you're letting on. Why else would you be calling out for him and not me, the man who's sleeping by your side?"

"Because in my dream, he protected me. Just like he did when he saved my life. Twice."

"And since then, I've been here every day. I jumped into that fight at The House of Pies, or at least I tried to. Until you stopped me. I would've saved you from the truck heading for you too if I'd been faster."

"But you're asking me to explain a dream. I *can't*."

"I'm not asking you to explain the dream. I'm asking you to look at it for what it might be. Your dreams are strong emotional attachments to your past. To memories you're desperately trying to recover. To emotions even *you* don't understand. And Gabriel's in those dreams. He's the one saving you. Not me."

Matt could see where Craig was coming from. Truth be told, if the situation were reversed, he would feel just as apprehensive as Craig. He wished he knew what to do or say to make things better. All he could think to do was wrap his arms around Craig and hold him tight.

"I need to ask you something. And I want you to be honest," Craig announced.

"Okay," he agreed, feeling uncertain about the question forming on Craig's lips.

"You haven't seen Gabriel since that night, right?"

"Right."

"But do you think about him? Do you still find yourself attracted to him?"

Matt wanted to lie. He didn't want to admit that sometimes late at night, before he fell asleep, his thoughts drifted to Gabriel and what he was doing. He wondered where he lived and if he would ever see him again.

He thought about his insanely blue eyes, which hung like twin skies set inside his handsomely rugged face. The dark hair, the tanned flesh, the angel wing tattoo on his back.

Remembering the details of their sex in his dreams sometimes caused his heart to flutter and the breath to catch in his throat. His flesh trembled when he recalled the way Gabriel held him close as he penetrated him or how his body tensed as it rocked inside him.

Though his time with Craig had been great over the past two weeks, Gabriel had not been banished from his mind.

"Yes," he finally responded. He looked up into Craig's eyes and saw that he already suspected the truth. "I don't want to hurt you, but I don't want to lie to you either."

"I know you don't. Whatever's going on inside you isn't intentional and has nothing to do with me," Craig told him with a kiss to his head. "But you need to work those things out. You need to understand where Gabriel fits into your life. Until then…" He paused, inhaling sharply.

"Until then, what?"

"Until then, I think we need to take a break."

"What? Why?"

"Because I can't enter into another relationship with a hint of uncertainty. I did that already with Tony. I can't do that again. It hurt too much the last time."

"But we can work this out. Together."

Craig shook his head. "No, we can't. This is something I can't help you with. This is something you need to work out on your own."

He craned his neck down and kissed Matt on the lips before walking away. "I'm going to get my stuff. You need space. We both need it and some time to think. When you think you have it all figured out, call me. No matter what the answer may be." Craig smiled, and it hung on his lips without expressing any joy. It simply sat there. "I always handle honesty the best. No matter what it might be."

"Please, Craig," he called out. "Don't do this to us."

"I'm doing this *for* us. Not *to* us," Craig replied before turning around and heading for the bedroom. When he reached the door, he looked back over his shoulder. "One day, I hope you'll be able to see that as clearly as I do."

When Craig left the room, Matt fought the urge to chase after him, to plead for him not to leave, but he didn't. He sat back down at the kitchen table because he knew Craig was right. He deserved better, more absolute answers than Matt seemed capable of giving.

He owed it to both of them to finally solve his inexplicable feelings for Gabriel once and for all.

CHAPTER 16

MATT looked down at his watch. It was a quarter after 11:00, which meant Dr. Owens was late. While the doctor had been late for appointments before, the majority of the times had been extended sessions from patients prior to Matt's scheduled time. That wasn't the case today. According to the secretary who left for lunch, Dr. Owens had called in to cancel all his morning appointments. Except for Matt's.

That bit of information intrigued him. Either Dr. Owens enjoyed the progress they were making or Matt was so screwed up Dr. Owens didn't think he could go one week without their usual appointment. Matt secretly wished it was the former, but after the latest turn of events in his life, he would have to go with the latter.

After all, he just let a potentially wonderful relationship slip through his fingers because of his obsession with Gabriel. If that wasn't screwed up, he didn't know what was. He certainly had issues he needed to work out today, and Dr. Owens had always been good about helping with that.

If he bothered to show up to the appointment at all.

The outside door to the office opened with a flourish, and Dr. Owens scrambled inside. He looked pale and sickly, as if he hadn't seen the light of day in weeks. The tufts of hair remaining on his head were a disheveled mess, and his wrinkled clothes made him look homeless.

Matt wondered what had happened since last week, when he looked to be the picture of good health and presented himself in a far more professional manner.

"My apologies for my tardiness," he coughed without covering his face. Matt grimaced at the surprising lack of etiquette. Most people coughed into the crook of their arms these days to prevent transmission of germs. Well, everyone except Dr. Owens who now rubbed his right palm vigorously over his nose before reaching for the doorknob. "My allergies are killing me."

"No worries," Matt replied. He tentatively followed Dr. Owens into his inner office and took extra precaution to avoid contact with the snot-covered handle.

Mountain cedar had been high the last couple of days, and many people in the area were coming down with sinus and upper respiratory infections as a result. Matt's gut instinct pegged something else as the true cause.

Though the man looked physically haggard, he appeared ill more from severe emotional distress than from physical ailment. His experience with families of patients, whose loved ones were gravely ill or dying, told him the pale skin and runny nose stemmed from long, emotional nights in a hospital, not an excessive amount of pollen.

Something had happened in Dr. Owens's personal life, some family tragedy, perhaps involving his mother. Since hers was the only picture to grace his office, Matt assumed she was the only person Dr. Owens truly loved or the only one he had in his life.

He wanted to reach out to the man and offer some measure of comfort. It was something he constantly did while at work. He chose to engage in polite conversation instead.

"Have you seen a doctor? Sometimes a steroid shot does the trick."

"I hate doctors," he announced. Brusque and unfriendly, his tone caused Matt to rethink the merits of keeping the appointment, no matter how badly he needed to hash things out. "I've seen too much of them lately. They don't know a damn thing about anything."

His comment redoubled Matt's conviction. The man's mother was most likely *very* sick. He wanted to help, to offer the man some solace, but that would be overstepping the doctor-patient relationship they shared. Instead, he hoped humor would lighten the situation. "Aren't you a doctor?"

Dr. Owens laughed. "I suppose I am. But unlike them, I know I'm not a quack." He unceremoniously tossed his briefcase onto the carpeted floor and plopped himself behind his desk. Dr. Owens's inner turmoil waged a battle on his face, but he tried his best to squash the emotional rebellion. After closing his eyes to perhaps center his mind, he asked. "So, shall we begin?"

"I don't know, Dr. Owens. You're under the weather. Perhaps we should postpone until you're feeling better."

"Nonsense," he replied while kicking his feet onto his desk and reclining backward. He sniffled and brought up a huge glob of phlegm, which he promptly swallowed. Matt's stomach turned. "I came in just for you, so let's make use of the time. Tell me, what's been going on in your world."

Matt didn't know where to begin. The man's behavior disgusted him so much he had trouble believing the person sitting in the chair opposite him was Dr. Owens at all.

"Come on," he urged Matt while clearing his throat. "Out with it. I can tell it's a doozy."

"Okay, well, things with Craig have sort of... faltered."

"In what way?"

"In the way that he told me we should take a break and that I shouldn't call him till I've worked out my issues."

"Interesting," he sniffled. "What issues?"

"Gabriel."

This got Dr. Owens's attention. He sat upright in his chair. "Gabriel's returned?" His voice became serious and unfamiliar.

Matt shook his head, and Dr. Owens exhaled in relief. "Why did my answer make you happy?"

He stared at Matt, pondering his answer while quietly mumbling to himself. "I was pleased for *you*," he finally answered as if settling on the appropriate response. "Gabriel's re-entrance into your life would... complicate matters."

"Well, it's complicated. With or without his actual presence."

"Explain," Dr. Owens replied while once again kicking back in his chair.

"Craig thinks I have unresolved feelings for Gabriel. He won't continue in our relationship until I work past my feelings for him."

"And if you can't, then your relationship with Craig is over?"

"In Craig's eyes, yes."

"What about in yours?"

Matt considered his answer. Now that Dr. Owens had stopped hacking and sniffling and had resumed his previous insightful questions, he felt more at ease, more capable of discovering the truth he desperately needed to find. He just wished the man would sit in his chair like he typically did. Lounging back in his seat didn't fill Matt with confidence.

"Honestly, I just don't know. Craig's a fantastic guy. Given time, I think we could carve out a happy life together. I could certainly do worse. But Gabriel... there's just something about him. Something I'm drawn to. I can't stop thinking about him. No matter what I feel for Craig, my feelings for Gabriel seem to take center stage. I tried doing like you suggested. Focusing on what I have in front of me and not what doesn't exist, but it became impossible. Eventually, when I had my dream again, I called for him, even though Craig was in bed next to me."

Dr. Owens tilted his head to the side in curiosity. "Which dream would that be?"

He immediately grew resentful toward Dr. Owens, as if the man was intentionally being dense. "If you *really* have to ask which dream…"

"I ask for clarification only. I don't want to put words in your mouth."

Matt sighed. He didn't mean to snap, but he felt edgy like an animal searching for a place to hide from an approaching storm. To make matters worse, the office grew chilly, and he half expected the thumping from his dreams to commence here in the safety of Dr. Owens's office.

"Matt? What's wrong?"

"I don't know," he answered, surveying his surroundings. "I feel like I'm being watched."

"Interesting," Dr. Owens offered for the third time. That was when Matt noticed Dr. Owens hadn't been writing on his pad. Whenever the man said the word interesting, he jotted notes to himself. Today, his usual instruments seemed forgotten.

"I wish I found it as interesting as you do," Matt replied.

"Dismiss the feeling for now," he told Matt with a wave of his hand. The man had never told him to dismiss anything in the three months he had been coming to see him. They pored over every emotion and every event with a fine psychoanalytical comb. The psychiatrist was obviously not up to snuff today. "Tell me about the dream and Gabriel's presence in it."

Although he still felt unseen eyes observing his every move, he recounted his dream for Dr. Owens. He told him about the door fully dissolving and the devilish clown baby who bounded toward him. And how when he asked for someone to help him, it was Gabriel's name he shouted.

"*Very* interesting," he replied. The pad and paper still sat untouched on his desk.

"You have anything more than that?" Matt asked. His feet tapped nervously on the carpet. They wanted to sprint from the office, and Matt had to force his body to behave. His need for flight perplexed him. He had never been this uneasy in his life. At least not when he wasn't dreaming.

"First, I must say I find it peculiar that Gabriel remains a dominant emotional force even though you haven't seen him in weeks. That is correct, right?" When Matt nodded his response, Dr. Owens continued. "You have an unhealthy attachment to Gabriel, which seems to be intruding on your life. And your emotions. We need to get to the bottom of that."

"Any suggestions?"

"I've actually been giving this a lot of thought. I think instead of continuing to probe the dream, we should focus on the memory."

"What do you mean? I thought the dream *was* the memory?"

"It is, but the dream keeps changing, becoming more fluid like a river of thought."

"I don't understand."

"Think of your dream like this: its events originated in memory much like run off from mountains creates rivers. But as the river flows, it becomes bigger as other tributaries feed into it. Your fears and anxieties, whatever emotional stresses you're currently under now or were under in the past, are adding to that dream, changing it and making it more than what it originally was. We need to filter out all the accumulated emotional detritus and return to the memory from which the dream began."

"Okay, I guess I can understand that. But how do we get back to the memory?"

"How do you feel about hypnosis?"

Matt always thought hypnosis to be more of a gimmick than a reliable psychiatric tool. It relied too heavily on the power of suggestion, and the individual's ability to surrender. And since he wasn't one to willingly concede control, he seriously doubted the effectiveness of the parlor trick.

Still, the idea intrigued and terrified him at the same time. Traveling beneath the subconscious waters of his mind to the root of the dream held promise, if he could relinquish control to Dr. Owens, a man whom he had come to trust. After all, he helped Matt progress this far with his dream and his problems, yet some hesitancy to agree remained.

More than just his distaste for hypnotism gave him pause. The man was obviously going through some traumatic event, and though he didn't want to hold it against him, he also didn't know if today was the right day to embark on such a venture.

Dr. Owens still looked sick, though not as awful as when he first entered the office. His color had yet to return, but the coughing and sneezing fits had ceased. He looked to be trying real hard to maintain his professionalism and act normally, so Matt didn't see why he couldn't meet him half way.

"Let's do it," he finally said.

"Great," Dr. Owens responded while rising from his chair and taking the seat next to him. He seemed more like the man he knew last week, as if the internal tug of war momentarily halted unexpectedly.

"What should I do? I've never done this before."

"I want you to close your eyes," Dr. Owens replied in a calm voice. "Imagine a peaceful place, somewhere you feel safe. Like a beach or a meadow."

Matt complied. He pictured his grandmother's house on Lake Travis, where they spent many months during the summer. He had often lain out by the water's edge, lulled to sleep by the breeze tugging on the water and pulling it onto the shore.

"Can you see it?"

He replied with a nod.

"Let your feet relax, and your legs relax. Feel your hips releasing their tension. Your waist is relaxing. And now your chest. With each breath out, your body gets more and more relaxed. Now your shoulders. Your neck. And your head. Your entire body is relaxing."

In response to Dr. Owens's low, soothing voice, Matt's entire body grew heavy as the words spoken released all tension from his body.

"Your body feels heavy," he continued. "That heaviness is descending all over you. And as I continue to talk, that relaxed feeling will get stronger and stronger. And as you fall into a deeper sleep, you will hear my voice but you will no longer be sitting in my office. We will be in the past. On your tenth birthday. You will see everything as you saw it then. But you will only observe it. Like a movie. Nothing there can hurt you.

"Now you're resting comfortably. You are asleep but also awake. Going deeper and deeper in both sleep and time, where you will remain until I bring you back.

"Slowly, I want you to open your eyes and tell me what you see."

WHEN Matt opened his eyes, he looked around his room. He clutched his blue sheets under his chin, and he was trembling. His eyes swept from one yellow wall to another, searching for someone he couldn't see but someone he knew to be there.

"Can you see your room?" Dr. Owens's voice asked.

"Yes," Matt replied. He pulled the sheets over his head. Something was wrong. He wasn't supposed to be afraid, but he was. He had never been this scared before, not even in his dreams.

"What's happening?"

"I'm afraid," he replied, panting heavily. He found it increasingly difficult to catch his breath. "Something's happening. It's bad. I know it's bad."

"Nothing can harm you. You're safe," he reminded Matt. "You're only observing. Take deep breaths."

"I don't want to," he protested. "It smells bad in here." He gagged and covered his nose. If the smell persisted, he was going to throw up.

"What does your room smell like?"

He shook his head and held his breath.

"You'll be fine. Just breathe normally. Tell me what it smells like."

Matt took a tentative whiff before covering his nose with his hand and sheets. "Rotten eggs."

"You don't smell the rotten eggs anymore. It's gone. Take a deep breath and smell for yourself."

Matt sniffed, and the smell disappeared. He inhaled deeper. Still nothing. Then, he pulled the sheets from over his head and looked around. Everything he saw, he reported back to Dr. Owens. The room from his memory matched the one in his dreams, from the toys on the dresser across the room to the bed, the drapes, and the color of the walls.

Seeing it again, in memory as opposed to dream, caused missing puzzle pieces to slip into place.

He remembered picking out the yellow paint for the walls. A man with blond hair and blue eyes stood at his side. The man's face broke into laughter, and his big hand ruffled his hair before hoisting him into the air and over his shoulder.

Then, a woman's face magically appeared. Her dark brown eyes lit up when she saw him, and she pulled Matt from the man into her warm embrace. He nestled his face into her hair and inhaled deeply. She smelled like fresh gardenias.

"Mom? Dad?"

"Do you see your parents? Are they there?"

"No. I remember them. What they look like. Not from photos. But from a memory. One different from this one." Tears streamed down his face as he recalled the trip to Home Depot, where they purchased the new paint. His previous dark blue room with an animal border made him feel like a kid. When he told his parents, they agreed to repaint the room in time for his big tenth birthday.

As his eyes flew across the room, he recalled that the three of them painted the room together. They had such a good time. They listened to classic rock, his father's favorite on the radio. They sang and played air guitar, whenever a Queen or Led Zeppelin song played.

"Don't get lost in that memory," Dr. Owens told him. "Focus on the door."

"What? Why? I want to remember them. That's why I'm here."

"But all your memories are on the other side of the door. If you want them all, go to the door."

Matt stared across the room at the door. He knew he should stay away from it. Something bad was on the other side. "No," he replied. "I'm not going to the door."

"You have to. The answers are there."

Matt shook his head. He refused to listen to what Dr. Owens said. He wouldn't cross his room, and he wouldn't approach the door. He was to remain where he was, curled up in his bed, and safe. As long as he stayed where he was, nothing would hurt him.

Then, he heard a thump. "He's here. Clifford Crouch is here."

"Is he in your room?"

"No. But he's coming."

"Get to the door," Dr. Owens urged. "Get to it before he does."

"I told you I'm not going to the door," he shouted. "He told me to stay here!"

"He?" Dr. Owens asked. "Who?"

Matt heard two more thumps as he tried to remember who spoke those words to him. It wasn't his parents. They were nowhere near his room, but he felt someone else, someone very close by.

The revelation didn't frighten him. He felt safe.

"Who told you that, Matt? Who's in the room with you?"

"I don't know," he replied. More thumps resonated in the hallway outside. In response, he scooted up toward the wall, pressing his head against the cool, yellow paint. "But he's here. I can feel it. He's close by."

"Clifford Crouch?"

"No," he responded. "The voice. The one that speaks to me. The one that sounds like music."

More noises echoed outside, but they were no longer thumps. They were footsteps, walking slowly across the wooden floor. "He's getting closer."

"Who? The voice?"

"No, Clifford. He's standing outside my room. I can see his shadow underneath the door."

Matt watched as the doorknob started to slowly turn, but as it swung inward an unseen force pushed it close. From the other side, someone yelled in fury. Though it sounded more animal than man, he knew it was Clifford Crouch.

He would be safe. He would always be safe. Even though he didn't know how he knew that, he accepted it with unquestioning certainty.

The doorknob turned, and the door rattled. Clifford banged against the door in unbridled anger. "The Gifted One must die," he shouted. "He must die!"

"The Gifted One?" Dr. Owens asked. "Is that what you said, Matt?"

Matt nodded. "That's what Clifford is screaming outside my door."

"Is he trying to get in still?"

"Yes," he replied. "But he can't. The door won't open. No matter how much he pushes on it or beats on it. It won't budge."

"Why not? What's keeping it closed?"

"I don't know."

"Did you prop anything against the door?"

Matt shook his head.

"Stare at the door, Matt. Stare at it hard. Will yourself to see whatever you're not seeing. You can do it," Dr. Owens announced. "This is what you've wanted."

He focused on the door, trying to pierce through the wood to the other side. He saw nothing. Only the door as it continued to shake and rattle in protest to the murderer's insistent attempts. No matter what he tried, though, the door didn't budge.

"I see nothing."

"Keep looking. Tell me what you see."

"I see the door. Nothing else."

"Are you certain?" Dr. Owens's voice grew darker again, more intense. "You must be sure."

"Why?"

"Because this moment can reveal *everything*. But you must want to see it."

"I do," he replied.

"Then look again."

Matt focused even harder, squinting. His body shook as he focused all his willpower on revealing what prevented his parents' murderer from reaching him.

A form shimmered into view, like the one he sometimes glimpsed in the mirror as he got dressed in the morning. An outline glimmering with sparkles of crystal light. It faded in and out of existence before the shape became less transparent and more opaque. The ethereal edges slowly became solid, as if some unseen artist leisurely sketched the person into existence.

Color gradually filled in the empty space of air. Blue spread from the floor up, revealing two legs dressed in denim. From there, the blue fanned into black leather before revealing strong, tanned arms resting against the door.

When the face became flesh instead of translucent light, Matt gasped and opened his eyes. Dr. Owens, sitting in the chair next to him, stared at him in surprise.

"What happened?" he asked. "Who did you see?"

"Gabriel," he mumbled in disbelief. "I saw Gabriel."

GABRIEL stood on the top level of the parking garage across from Dr. Owens's office building. Matt was at his weekly session with his psychiatrist, and like he did whenever Matt visited Dr. Owens, he stayed out of the room to give his charge some privacy.

Although it had been difficult to remain in the periphery for the past two weeks, he managed to keep his promise to his brother. He longed to hold Matt once again in his arms and feel his soft flesh against his own. He restrained himself from entering his dreams, especially since Craig sometimes occupied his bed, but now that Matt and Craig appeared to be over, he entertained the possibility of returning to him at night.

He shook his head and gazed into the heavens above. The bright blue dome helped refocus his thoughts, and he convinced himself taking the more active role he wanted would be wrong.

He couldn't be selfish. Matt's life was his own, and he obviously cared for Craig. The fact that he might have been the unintentional cause of their break up worried him. His brief involvement in Matt's life might have altered a path meant to be maintained.

Although angels, and most assuredly archangels, were powerful beings capable of changing the course of a mighty river, the chartered waters of destiny lay beyond even the seraphim.

Only the All Father held sway over providence.

Gabriel's only choice was to continue to play the role assigned to him. Guarding Matt from the demons that wished him dead needed to be his focus, not inserting himself within ordinary affairs. To dive any further into waters he had previously dipped into could prove disastrous.

While he might not like it, playing an active role in Matt's life went against divine mandate he was honor bound to obey.

Still, no matter how much he tried to convince himself to stay away, the love in his angelic heart threatened to force him from the sidelines and into the arms of the man he loved.

Together, he knew they could weather both hellish assault and heavenly consequences.

The air around him suddenly changed. The refreshing breeze ceased, and an oppressive humidity clung to the air. In the distance, black clouds roiled across the sky, advancing like mountainous soldiers from all sides of creation.

The tattoo across his back itched like mad.

Evil was close.

Gabriel scanned the area, his eyes sweeping past the buildings and around the numerous vehicles that both sped by and sat idle. If any threat approached the building, his keen vision would ferret it out. When it did, he would stop the enemy cold.

But he found nothing.

Only pedestrians walked the concrete paths. Drivers zoomed by going about their business. No hint of evil present in any of them.

Still, Gabriel sensed it near. It was much too close, and he didn't understand how it resisted his scrutiny.

Pain he had never before experienced shot through his celestial form. Gabriel fell to his knees, clutching at his heart, which felt cut in two. Agony exploded again within, and on his back he fell, clawing at the air, searching for the invisible demon that snuck up on him and struck him down.

His eyes registered no assailant, but his body continued to writhe in pain as unseen weapons pierced him and threatened to gut his corporeal form. They bit his flesh and twisted his insides. Blow after blow struck him—his head, his chest, but most insistently his heart.

Huge claws reached inside and tore at it, dragging poisonous nails across the throbbing organ before squeezing it tightly in an unbreakable grip.

Lashing out with his massive fists, Gabriel struggled to find a form to grab onto, to use his heavenly might to end the torment as quickly as it had begun, but his hands flailed against empty air.

His nemesis remained either too fast or too strong, something Gabriel was not accustomed to facing. This meant that hellish forces more powerful than ever, ones that had not only been banished long ago but had also the power to destroy him, again walked the earthly plane.

And they were here for Matt.

The man he loved was in more danger than he feared.

"Matt," he whispered through gritted teeth as he dragged his body across the asphalt covering the parking garage. Gabriel had to get to him no matter what the cost.

If this unseen evil had been unleashed on him, he could only imagine what lurked in wait for Matt inside Dr. Owens's office.

CHAPTER 17

AN ANGRY storm assaulted the world outside Dr. Owens's office. Thunderclaps exploded, echoing in the distance like artillery rounds fired in some celestial battle. Howling winds slammed the rain against the window like bullets, and lightning lit up the office with the glow of suppressive fire.

Matt wondered if World War III had somehow started while he had been hypnotized. In the span of a few minutes, the weather had turned cataclysmic.

As he surveyed his surroundings, he realized more than just the weather had changed. Even the office appeared different. Typically comfortably lit with the warm glow of lamplight instead of harsh overhead fluorescent lights, the room grew darker. Long shadows stretched from the corners of the room, reaching out with obsidian fingers to pluck all traces of light from existence. The air turned chilly in response.

He rubbed his hands together for warmth as the shadows marched forward, clawing their way toward the area he and Dr. Owens occupied. Outside, the storm continued its loud rampage.

Matt glanced in Dr. Owens's direction, wondering if he too noticed the change.

But when he looked into the eyes of his psychiatrist, the man who had been integral to recovering the memories of his past, only cold detachment greeted him. His brown eyes hardened, looking almost black in the shadow-enshrouded office, and the smile that extended across his face carried no warmth. It made his features dark and menacing.

The awkward Mr. Bean doppelganger disappeared. In his place sat an intimidating stranger.

"Are you okay?" Matt asked with a slight tremor to his voice.

"I will be," Dr. Owens replied. "Quite shortly. Thanks to you."

The unsettling response took him by surprise. More than just the man's physical features had been altered. His soothing, congenial personality withdrew and a harsher persona stepped forward. "What does that mean?"

"I wish I could explain it all in detail," he answered. Dr. Owens rose from the chair beside him and crossed over to his desk. He lifted his previously discarded briefcase off the carpet and placed it on the wooden top. "But I'm afraid there isn't time."

"Sure," Matt told him. The man obviously wanted to leave, and Matt was more than happy to end the session early. Besides, Matt felt the need to get out of there. Fast. "You've got stuff going on that you need to take care of. I understand." He stood up, ready to depart from the approaching madness that swirled around him.

"We're not done here."

"I think we are," he announced. "The world outside's gone crazy."

Leaving his briefcase standing open, Dr. Owens nodded and walked back around his desk. "You've just had a breakthrough. We need to discuss what that means."

He wanted to explore what he remembered. He didn't understand how Gabriel could have been the one preventing Clifford from killing him. From what he saw while hypnotized, Gabriel looked the same in his memory as he did two weeks ago. That wasn't possible. His tenth birthday occurred almost twenty years ago.

The memory must be flawed, warped by his secret desires. That was the only reason that made sense. Any other explanation promised to be far too surreal.

"We can discuss it next time," Matt replied, though he had no intention of returning. Dr. Owens's sharp change in character effectively ended their professional relationship.

"There won't be a next time," the man replied. "You and I both know that."

Matt stared at Dr. Owens, whose smiling face continued to make him uneasy. To make matters worse, his eyes grew darker and rounder with each passing second. "Excuse me?"

"You've remembered Gabriel in your past, which means you are what's been suspected."

Matt couldn't respond. His throat muscles tensed, preventing any sound from escaping.

"I had to be certain. I couldn't just do what the voice asked. Not even for her." Dr. Owens strolled back toward his desk and lovingly ran his fingers down the glass picture frame containing his mother's photo. "If I was going to do this, it would be a sacrifice worth making. I couldn't just assume you were the right one. That wouldn't have been the wisest thing to do, right?"

He backed away from Dr. Owens, slowly. Although the man spoke to him, he looked only at his mother's face in the picture. He could use the distraction to reach the door and run for the elevator.

"I mean, really, making such a pact without proof is just plain stupid," Dr. Owens continued, unmindful of Matt's progress to the door. "And I'm anything but stupid. In fact, when the voice first came, I didn't buy it at all. I even thought I was going crazy. Especially when it promised me it would cure Mother, make her Alzheimer's better. Make her remember me."

Dr. Owens looked up and shook his finger at him. Matt stopped, only six feet from the door, in response to the small warning. His psychiatrist made no effort to close the gap between them. Instead, he sat on the edge of his desk, hugging his mother's photo to his chest. "But it showed me things it could do. One day, she was back to normal, and I was so happy that I forgot about the voice. Until it returned the next day, and Mother was even worse off than before. All I had to do was give the voice one thing. One little thing and everything would be all right. Do you want to know what that one thing was?"

Matt shook his head. He knew whatever words Dr. Owens next spoke would haunt him forever.

"You," the man finally said with a small laugh. "That's all it wanted. You in exchange for my mother's health."

"What the hell does that mean?" Matt asked before he could help himself.

In a blur of movement, Dr. Owens stood at his side. The man's arm wrapped around his neck, choking him with strength far exceeding his short stature.

"You're about to find out," he whispered.

TOSSED like a feather in a tornado, Gabriel flew across the parking garage, slamming into the wall. Chips of concrete exploded outward from the impact as his body slid down to the wet pavement.

Though dazed from the attack, Gabriel refused to let his guard down for a second. Too much depended upon him. But more importantly, Matt's safety rested on his shoulders.

He wasn't going to fail Matt or his mission, so his eyes scanned the parked cars and the top floor of the parking garage, searching for his unseen foe. The rain, which now ceaselessly hammered the area, would obscure the vision of an ordinary creature. For him, it was hardly a deterrent. His gaze cut through the watery curtain as if no rain fell.

Still, he saw nothing.

Another blow, this one from the right, sent him careening into an SUV. The car's hood crumpled inward like paper. Before he could catch his breath, something grabbed his feet and slammed him downward three times until he, as well as the vehicle's engine, crashed to the ground.

Blood freely spilled from his head, nose, and mouth. The unfamiliar taste was bitter on his tongue. It had been more centuries than Gabriel remembered since he faced an enemy capable of inflicting such damage upon him.

He had to end this quickly. He had to get to Matt.

Invisible hands again wrapped around his throat and yanked him upward. Gabriel dangled helplessly seven feet off the ground and at the mercy of his hidden adversary. The strong, massive hands grew ever tighter, promising to choke the heavenly air from his lungs.

But his foe made an egregious error. By the sheer size of his grasp, Gabriel's suspicions about whom he battled were confirmed. This was no ordinary hell spawn or even one of his fallen brothers. His unseen enemy was a Nephilim, the race of giants born unto mortal women and the angelic hosts who raped them.

With that knowledge, he knew what he had to do. Though he couldn't pry himself free, since heavenly blood coursed through the aberration's body and made his foe mighty, a strategic assault might release him.

Gabriel's sword appeared in his hand, and he thrust forward. Metal forged by the heavens pierced invisible flesh, and the creature bellowed in response before flinging him to the side.

He tumbled across the pavement, finally colliding to a stop against the door of a red Corvette, which shredded to pieces on impact.

"You're wounded, Nephilim," Gabriel announced to the empty air. "Show yourself and let's finish this."

"So you know you battle family, my uncle?" The disembodied voice asked. Its speed and movement prevented Gabriel from discerning its location.

"I know you are an abomination. Nothing more."

An angry howl filled the air before an unseen force slammed into him from the right. The collision chased the air from his lungs, and the repeated blows of the massive fists to his head kept him off balance. "You call me an abomination, yet you're in love with a mortal," he shouted between blows. "How far the mighty have fallen!"

"How dare you proclaim to know the feelings of one such as me!" Gabriel landed a mighty punch onto the invisible form that sent it flying backward. The vehicle the giant landed on flattened upon impact, and the top level of the garage began to crack from the stress of their battle.

"The angelic host suspects your sins, Gabriel, but the legions of hell know the truth. You visit your charge in his sleep. You engage in carnal pleasure, and you keep him from us on the other side. You proclaim to enter his dream and his body to protect him. But it's a lie. You do it for your pleasure. No one else's. And you call me an abomination. Your love for a mortal male is the abomination!"

The giant leaped upon him, using his enormous legs as pile drivers to squash Gabriel into the ground. He kicked and punched, using his massive size to pin Gabriel down. All were attempts at keeping him defenseless, but his words, more than his actions, paralyzed Gabriel.

Was he being selfish? Was he lying to himself? Was he no better than his fallen brothers?

"You deserve to die for your sins, Archangel. Just as my brothers and all our sires were punished. And your lover will follow you into the pits of hell!"

The mention of Matt pulled Gabriel out of his self-doubt, and he refused to listen to the taunts. The words of a being created out of angelic lust held no power over him. It didn't make him feel guilty for the love that filled his heart when he thought of Matt. His fallen brothers, the ones who sired the giant Nephilim, abandoned their God for the sake of carnal pleasure. They came unto women without being invited and forced themselves onto the innocent.

As a result, they created wicked offspring, who terrorized Father's children. They burned down civilizations created by the faithful. They needed to be wiped out, their memories erased from existence, and it was they who were responsible for the great flood.

He would not be compared to their wickedness. While his feelings broke the rules, love, not lust, for Matt ruled his heart.

Gabriel lashed out with his sword, slicing through skin and sending a spray of blood across the ground. "You know nothing of love," he spat as his sword again hit its mark. "Your kind is capable of only hate, born from lust and deception and rape." He swung downward again, sending more blood into the rain-drenched air.

"You murdered my brethren!" the voice complained in misery. Gabriel watched as a trail of blood trotted from him and behind a row of automobiles. The giant blinked into view before disappearing again. Whatever dark magic it used to hide itself was failing. "Without mercy. Without prejudice, you hunted us down and sent my kind to hell."

"Your kind was never meant to stride across this earth, but you were allowed to flourish even though most in heaven had their doubts. In His kindness, Father let you live, and you repaid that kindness with treachery. You murdered and wreaked havoc upon creation until mankind was nothing but twisted facsimiles of Father's original intentions. You and your kind brought destruction upon your own heads!"

"And now I bring destruction upon the man you love," the giant replied while leaping through the air toward him. "Your failure will be on your head."

Although he didn't want to do it, Gabriel had no choice. The pathetic creature wasn't responsible for its birth, but its wretchedness couldn't be denied. It chose to walk with the damned, and as a result, it had to be returned to whence it came.

Gabriel flung his sword at the descending giant, impaling him in the chest in midair. He then kicked upward to meet the falling creature and knocked the sword clean through its body. He fell backward and landed with a thud, a gaping hole in his chest.

Gabriel stood over the dying Nephilim, who fixed its cold eyes upon him one final time before they closed in death.

Gabriel waved his hand and tongues of white holy fire sprung up, quickly consuming the corpse. As the body turned to ash, he wept tears for the aberration, which was a first for him.

Tears usually only fell from his brother's face at such needless loss. After all, Gabriel was the Angel of Vengeance, and the Nephilim required vengeance far more than Michael's mercy. But as he watched the body surrender to the power of his flame, he realized the tragedy of the situation.

This creature never knew love in its life. Only anger and hate. It never appreciated the chance it was given to become more than the horror that created it. It wallowed in wickedness and fear. Had it chosen a different path, the collective fate of its kind might have been different.

As the fire slowly died and the giant's body was no more, Gabriel wiped his tears from his cheeks and turned his attention back to the building across the street.

The time for grief had passed. He had more serious matters to attend to. Matt's fate still rested in the balance, and it was up to him to make the difference.

MATT struggled against Dr. Owens's viselike grip. He kicked at the man's legs and clawed at his skin, hoping the assault would buy his freedom. Nothing he did, not jabbing his elbow in his sternum nor clawing at his eyes, caused the death grip to loosen.

Instead, the man unleashed a hideously insane laugh that sounded more like the braying of a jackass, and his breath burned the back of Matt's neck. It reminded him of when he sat too close to the fireplace in winter. The waves of heat gnawing on his skin caused his flesh to blister. The pain became unbearable, and just when Matt thought his flesh would bubble in response to the heat, Dr. Owens flung him into the chair he had previously occupied.

Both he and the chair toppled over.

The force of the collision knocked the air from his body, but still he struggled to his feet. He needed something, anything, to defend himself. On the doctor's desk sat a letter opener. If he could reach it, he might be able to do some damage of his own.

He lunged for the desk, but before he could reach the weapon, Dr. Owens descended upon him again.

"Nice try," Dr. Owens announced. He pressed his right hand against Matt's neck, constricting his windpipe and slapping him across the face twice with his left. "But not good enough." He pushed harder against Matt's neck, and Matt gasped for air that would not come. "You will die, and you will suffer. For all the times you escaped death before this. For all the minions who died because of you, your death will be long and tortuous."

Dr. Owens fell into another laughing fit, and while he trumpeted in victory, the man's physical features began to change.

Coarse, black hair inexplicably grew on his head, spreading from the top down to his forehead before covering the entirety of his face. From the top of his head extended long hairy flaps covered in the same dark fur that coated his body. To Matt, they resembled horse ears, and as Matt watched his Mr. Bean eyebrows turned dark and merged with the new coat of ever-extending fur, while his eyes stretched further apart until they resided on both sides of a snout that bulged outward from where his mouth once resided.

As impossible as it might seem, Dr. Owens had grown a donkey's head.

"What the hell?" Matt mumbled.

The thing that used to be Dr. Owens brayed. Its giant horse teeth snapped viciously together just inches from Matt's face. "That's correct," it snuffed before dropping Matt to the floor.

Matt crawled away from the creature, pressing his back against the far wall. The sight of the monster paralyzed him with fear. He knew he had to get away. He had no time to be afraid, but the monstrosity that Dr. Owens had somehow become crippled his strength and his will.

Trembling was all he could manage.

"I do enjoy cowering mortals," the creature announced while casually crossing the distance. "And I think I shall enjoy it much more if you saw me in my complete and true form. Therefore, before you die, I shall grant you the privilege of knowing who has ended your existence. Before I snuff the light of your potential out of this world, I'll send you screaming into madness before reaching into your throat and turning you inside out."

As he drew closer, Dr. Owens's thin arms grew twice their normal size, shredding his button down shirt in the process. He kicked free the brown loafers, revealing two hooves, and when it ripped the pants from its body, he saw thick equine thighs covered in long black fur.

It neighed in delight at Matt's revulsion. Then, to his surprise, a thick plume of black and gray peacock feathers fanned outward from its rear. Nestled inside the feathers were eyes. Not the traditional bluish-green eyes found in ordinary peacock plumage. These eyes were black with angry red irises, and each crazed orb looked around the office before setting their sights upon him.

"Oh my God," Matt whispered as he tried to claw through the plaster for protection.

The creature fell into another laughing fit, and as it hee-hawed uncontrollably, its tongue darted out between its thick teeth, leaving gobs of spit dangling from its muzzle. "Guess again."

Fear held Matt firm as it dawned upon him where this creature came from.

No God created it. No benevolent being would sculpt such a blasphemous mockery of a donkey and peacock. A hybrid such as this could only be birthed from the bowels of hell.

"Now, it's time for you to die at last."

A huge explosion shook the room, and Matt cried out in surprise.

"Back away, Adramelech," a musical voice commanded from his right.

When Matt turned his head, Gabriel stood at the doorway with remnants of the door scattered about the room in dozens of broken splinters. His face looked granite hard, and his fists clenched at his side.

He was ready to battle the monster and save Matt's life for the fourth time.

"Gabriel!" The creature called Adramelech howled in anger before trotting between them. "I'll not allow you to interfere. The mortal will die!"

Before Matt had time to wonder how the thing that was Dr. Owens knew Gabriel, Gabriel charged into the monster, knocking it backward and away from Matt.

They struggled, exchanging blows that shook the foundation of the building.

Impossibly strong, Gabriel held Adramelech's head down, while unleashing a blurry barrage of punches to his trunk. Each blow caused the thing to howl in pain. But a deadly fire burned in the eyes adorning its feathery plume. The peacock feathers lunged forward, slicing Gabriel's shirt to ribbons before biting into his tattooed back. Streams of blood ran down his skin.

As he watched, Matt saw the angel wing design flutter across his flesh.

"Get out of here," Gabriel called out to him. His sky-blue eyes locked briefly onto his. "Now!"

But Matt couldn't move. The sight of the tattoo pulsing across his body prevented any action. All he could do was stare at Gabriel's back, unsure if he imagined the movement or if the tattoo actually fluttered like a leaf in the wind.

The divided attention gave Adramelech an advantage. It bit into Gabriel's arm before kicking him off and sending Gabriel flying across the room. He crashed into Dr. Owens's bookshelf, packed full of books, which fell on top of him and trapped him underneath.

With Gabriel incapacitated, the creature sprinted for Matt, spittle flying from its open muzzle.

Matt found his feet and jumped out of the way as Adramelech crashed into the wall, where he had previously sat. The creature whinnied angrily before charging toward him again.

Sprinting across the room, Matt headed straight for the desk, where the letter opener waited. If he reached it, he might be able to defend himself instead of relying solely upon Gabriel.

He closed his hand around the letter opener, the cool handle feeling like salvation in his grasp, but Adramelech grabbed him by the shoulder and spun him around. Matt flew across the desk and fell off the other side. Adramelech followed him over the desk. Before it could land on him, he stabbed upward and punctured its right eye.

It bellowed in agony, blood pouring from its punctured eyeball, but that didn't halt its attack. Its peacock tail wrapped around Matt. The prehensile feathers grasped him tightly before turning sharp and hard. Dozens of tiny needles pierced his skin, and liquid fire spread through his body. Matt screamed in pain.

"Enough!" Gabriel yelled from the far side of the room.

From his cocoon of feathers, Matt saw Gabriel emerge from under the bookshelf. Even though Matt's vision turned blurry, he watched as Gabriel's blue eyes turned a stormy gray. "It's time to end your madness!"

"It's too late," replied Adramelech. "My poison courses through his veins. Your charge is already dead, and all of hell will celebrate my victory."

"Your celebration is premature," Gabriel announced as a bright coppery light filled the room. Through the haze that settled upon his vision, Matt saw a copper aura cascade over Gabriel. Beautiful white wings sprouted from his back and spanned the width of the room. "The victory will be mine."

Gabriel launched himself across the distance, his beating wings churning up a rush of wind that buffeted them from all sides. He slammed into Adramelech while magically pulling a shining sword from the air. He swung the blade in a wide arc, clipping the feathers that bound Matt to Adramelech.

Before Matt could fall to the floor, Gabriel caught him with his left hand while tucking him beneath the protection of his left wing. "No harm shall come to you while I'm around," Gabriel said, whispering the same words Gabriel had spoken to him in his dreams.

Immediately, Matt felt safe. Although he still didn't understand what was happening, how Dr. Owens became that monstrosity, or how Gabriel's tattoo suddenly became wings, he knew the words were more than a promise. They were a guarantee.

"You believe yourself capable of too much, Gabriel," Adramelech pronounced. He rose from the spot where Gabriel had shoved him. The fan of dark feathers on his left drooped to the ground. Some of the eyes within glared angrily. Others, like the ones decorating the floor, were closed in death. "You don't face a lowly demon. You face the King of Hell itself."

"I see no king. I see only a mockery of life."

"You see the future, Gabriel. The future that will come to pass when the boy in your wings breathes his last." The creature's eyes on his head and the ones in his feathers locked onto Matt. "The Gifted One *will* die!"

"What do you know of his promise, you wicked creature? You can't possibly fathom the boy's importance to the Grand Design, and in your ignorance shall rest your defeat."

Adramelech brayed in laughter. "*My* ignorance, oh mighty Hero of God?" His words dripped with sarcasm and disdain. "You can ask such a question when not even your Father has seen fit to explain to you the boy's life purpose? But I know of his promise. I know what his presence foretells as do even the lowly denizens of hell. We will rise up in vast numbers, and our combined strength will prove victorious."

"Even an army of ants can be crushed by the heel of a single angel."

Adramelech's peacock tail tensed and spread out. The eyes set within burned in anger. He barreled toward Gabriel, fire leeching from his open maw and as it spewed flames outward, Gabriel waved his hand erecting a wall of white flame. When the forces collided, a huge explosion rocked the building, shattering the windows of the office outward.

"Your hellfire is nothing compared to the purity of the embers stoked from the hearth of heaven."

Gabriel pointed at Adramelech and tentacles of flame stretched out from the white wall of fire, which protected them. They wrapped around the creature, and its flesh began to bubble and burn.

It howled in protest as its fur caught fire. The angry eyes set into the feathers burst into flame before exploding outward from the heat. "You can't protect him forever," Adramelech cried out in agony.

"I can and I will," replied Gabriel. "With body, heart, and soul."

Completely engulfed in fire, Adramelech sputtered forward for a few steps in a vain attempt at one final assault. But the flames finally claimed dominion.

The donkey-peacock creature turned to ash, and in its place, Dr. Owens fell to the floor dead.

Gabriel stretched out his wings, releasing Matt from his protective grasp and set him back onto the floor.

Matt had a million questions churning through his mind, all of them wanting to be asked at once. But as he tried to give voice to them, his strength left his body. Whatever poison Adramelech injected him with made his world go black.

The last image Matt saw was Gabriel calling out to him and reaching for him with his strong, loving hands.

CHAPTER 18

THE tumultuous sky in the distance grew calm. Dark, angry clouds slowly broke apart, and the lightning, which had previously crackled through the horizon, fell dim. The rolling thunder faded away. A far more deafening silence than the furious storm remained.

Streaks of sunshine penetrated the clouds, banishing them from the city ahead. Light streamed downward in arrows of golden radiance, as they reclaimed the land from the darkness that had staked a temporary claim.

From the rolled down windows of the eighteen-wheeler, which barreled down the highway, spring-perfumed air wafted in on the breeze. Its scent promised renewal and hope.

Clifford found the stench disgusting. It turned his stomach and made bile rise like magma in his throat.

He understood what the quickly departing storm meant. Another attempt on the Gifted One had failed. The notion pissed him off. He didn't understand how one puny boy kept on living.

Still, the retreating storm made him hopeful.

Another failure meant he still had a chance to fulfill his contract. Clifford wanted to be the one who finally killed him. If he was successful, then everything the voice promised would be given to him, and Clifford would not lose the promised wealth and power. Not to mention the never-ending parade of skanks he would pork nightly.

"Sho' glad thet sto'ms passed," the man driving the rig commented. "Ah hate drivin' through nasty weather. Most idiots on th' road don't know how t'drive when it's dry. When th' road's slick them dumbasses git even mo'e reckless."

"I suppose," he halfheartedly responded to the trucker who had offered him a ride into Houston. When he spied the man in the men's room at the rest stop ninety miles back, Clifford had wanted to kill him and steal the rig for himself.

He could make good time with his own set of wheels, and after murdering a whole building full of prisoners and guards in Huntsville, one more death wouldn't amount to much in his opinion.

Deciding he could use the company, he had instead asked the man for a ride, and Bubba happily agreed. Bubba seemed nice enough, but his constant babbling made Clifford rethink not breaking the man's neck. For some reason, Bubba felt the need to provide the life story of every artist who played on the radio.

Right now, he rambled about the rock band Kiss, who sang "Detroit Rock City." Clifford didn't give a flying fuck about Kiss or rock. He preferred rappers like 2Pac and Notorious B.I.G, who knew what the fuck they were talking about.

Those rock and rollers were nothing more than faggots dressed up in skintight unitards and high heels. They weren't real men, and they had no idea what life was like for those who had to fight every day to stay alive.

The fact that Bubba liked rock only made Clifford want to kill him more. He imagined ripping open Bubba's throat with his teeth the way Ozzy Osbourne used to bite the heads off bats on stage, but the voice stopped him.

It was too soon for more violence, the voice told him. He had to bide his time.

Even though he hated restraining himself, he did.

No one knew Clifford Crouch was still alive. Even the media believed everyone in the Huntsville prison had perished in the blaze he set, so no outstanding reports on escaped prisoners circulated through police departments, which meant no manhunt for him existed.

If he killed Bubba, some do-gooder would find the body, and an official homicide case would open. And if he slipped up, if he left one piece of evidence behind, they would know he survived, and his secret would be out.

After over a week of hiding out in an abandoned warehouse, waiting for the ruckus to die down from the fire, he couldn't chance exposure. Not now.

For the time being, Clifford Crouch was dead and off the radar. At least until he found Matthew Westlake in Houston. Then, all bets were off.

IN THE distance, beyond the veil of darkness that descended upon Matt, someone sang to him. The sweet melody and soothing voice staved off the fear that would have normally seized a hold of him.

Matt didn't like the dark. He had had far too many encounters with darkness already. Within it, something terrible always lay in wait. He never saw it, but he could feel it, slinking about the shadows like a predator stalking its prey.

It made him feel vulnerable and alone.

But the honeyed voice told him he had nothing to fear. All would be well, and when he opened his eyes, light would return to his world.

So Matt tried.

He focused all his willpower on forcing his eyes open, on banishing the darkness that swirled around in the empty void.

A pinprick of light glowed in the distance. It set fire to the darkness and burned it away. The tiny glimmer grew until a dozen points of light sparkled into view and chased away the ebony folds, which withdrew from its gleaming touch.

The dozen lights became hundreds and then doubled in number. Before long, the rays of light outnumbered the gloom until it howled in defeat and retreated beyond the warm reach of the light.

When Matt opened his eyes, he saw Gabriel, staring down at him. Gabriel's blue eyes sparkled like the open sky, and in them reflected the boundless joy that Matt had awoken.

"I feel so weak," he mumbled.

"Side effects of the poison," Gabriel told him.

"And you...?" he didn't know how to finish the question.

"Cured it," Gabriel answered. "Yes."

In reply, Matt snuggled deeper into Gabriel's protective embrace. Cradled in arms both strong and tender, Gabriel's touch communicated a promise of keeping Matt safe. No harm would come to him as long as Gabriel was around. Those were the words Gabriel spoke in his dream and before he defeated the thing Dr. Owens had become. Earlier, the words alone carried the weight of his conviction, but in his arms, Matt felt invulnerable, as if nothing on this planet would be allowed within striking distance.

He looked over Gabriel's shoulder at the dead body of Dr. Owens, the man who had helped so much over the past few months and the man who had tried to kill him. Seeing his lifeless body filled Matt with sadness and relief, which made him feel guilty.

While he didn't know what had happened to his psychiatrist or why, he understood that if it hadn't been for Gabriel, again, he would be dead right now.

"I'm sorry."

Matt switched his focus from Dr. Owens, with the letter opener still jammed in his eye socket, to Gabriel. His sky blue eyes clouded over in disappointment. "What are you apologizing for?"

"For letting him get close enough to hurt you. If I had been quicker, if I hadn't been delayed, he never would have touched you."

The regret and self-loathing in his voice stirred within Matt the need to make Gabriel feel better. Reaching out with his left hand, he caressed Gabriel's face, running his smooth skin across Gabriel's scratchy stubble. "I'm fine," he whispered. "Because of you."

Gabriel shook his head. "I should have known better. I never should have left you alone."

"You can't be everywhere at once."

"I don't need to be everywhere. I just need to be with you."

Gabriel held him closer, pulling Matt's body against his bare chest. His hands grasped at Matt's thighs as if he were trying to hang onto him in fear of losing something too precious to be misplaced.

As Matt lay there in Gabriel's arms and looked up into eyes that stared at him with adulation, Matt felt a type of love he'd never truly before experienced seize control of his body. His pulse accelerated, and his face flushed. He felt heavy and light at the same time, as if his body couldn't decide to collapse in relief or jump up and down in excitement.

At that moment, Matt knew he loved Gabriel. No, it was more than that. He was *in love* with Gabriel. It was a truth he had tried to deny since their first meeting. While he admitted that he might be in love with Gabriel two weeks ago, he never fully embraced the emotion. He kept it at arm's length, not willing to surrender himself to the feeling, out of fear that Gabriel had permanently exited his life.

But that hadn't been true. Gabriel was here and had always been here, waiting in the wings to protect him, and those same intense emotions, the ones that reminded him of home, welled up inside Matt once again.

If this wasn't true love, he didn't know what else to call it, and love such as theirs proved too rare to do anything less but welcome it without reservation. Now that Gabriel was back, and held him, he vowed not to waste a single moment more in denial.

"I love you," Matt whispered, speaking the words Gabriel voiced when they were last together. In response, Gabriel pulled Matt to him and leaned closer, crossing the distance that separated them.

When their lips brushed, time ground to a halt. Nothing mattered more than the shameless exploration of each other's mouths or the delicious sweet taste of their love. Matt had waited far too long for the man of his dreams to find him. Now that he'd found him, Matt would never let him go.

"I love you too," Gabriel replied, breathlessly. He withdrew his lips from Matt's and rested his forehead against Matt's cheek. "But we are something that can never be."

The admission took Matt by surprise. "What? Why not?"

"Look at me, Matt. *Really* look at me. See me for what I am."

"I do see you. I see the man I've always loved. The one I've waited for."

Reluctantly, Gabriel lowered him to the ground and took a step back. He flexed his wings and they stretched out to touch both walls on opposite ends of the room. "You still think me a man? Someone like you who is free to follow his heart?"

"I'm not an idiot. You're no ordinary man. You're my guardian angel. The one my grandmother told me protected me from harm." He crossed the distance Gabriel had placed between them though Gabriel's eyes begged him not to. Being so close without touching obviously pained him as much as it did Matt. "But guardian angel or not. I love you. And you love me. That means something. Doesn't it?"

"Of course it does. To us. But it breaks too many rules. And to break those rules brings about consequences neither of us wish to face."

Matt placed his hands on Gabriel's hairy pecs. The warmth of his chest increased Matt's longing to again lie within his embrace. "I'll face Heaven itself to be with you."

With his right hand, Gabriel gingerly caressed Matt's cheek. "I'd not wish that fate upon you."

"What if I wish it upon myself?"

Gabriel shook his head. "Only because you know not of what you wish."

Matt opened his mouth to argue, but Gabriel covered it with his large hand. He tilted his head to the right, and worry descended upon his features. "They're coming," he whispered. Immediately, his wings fluttered like a hummingbird's, and with each flap, they grew progressively smaller until they flitted into his skin and reverted to their tattoo form.

"Who's coming?" Matt asked, looking around. He feared the attack of another hellish creature.

"The police," Gabriel answered.

His tense body relaxed. "Isn't that a good thing?"

"No, it is not. They cannot know what has happened here, and they can never know the truth. I must remove all traces of heavenly battle, and I don't have much time."

Gabriel waved his hand, and Matt watched as the office repaired itself. The scorch marks that burned the carpet disappeared, replaced by fabric that magically rewove itself. Shards of glass from the broken window danced in the air and gathered like jigsaw pieces suspended within the pane. When the puzzle was complete, the shattered edges merged, making the glass appear brand new.

Matt stared in silent astonishment until his gaze once again fell upon his dead psychiatrist. "How are you going to fix Dr. Owens?"

"That is beyond my power. We will have to cover our tracks with the police."

"You mean lie?"

Gabriel nodded.

"Angels lie?" The concept seemed too unlikely to be true. Angels were protectors of the innocent, heralds of God's light. They couldn't possess the ability to lie.

"Only to protect the Grand Design."

Apparently, he was wrong. It seemed everyone, even heavenly beings, were capable of using deception to cover their own behinds. If that were the case, he would do his part. "Leave some signs of a struggle," Matt told him. "I'll handle the rest."

"Are you certain?" Gabriel asked.

"He did attack me. What happened was self-defense. And with our corroborating stories, the police won't have anything suspicious to follow up on."

The door to the waiting area outside the office opened, and urgent male voices filled the room only a few feet from them. "It's show time," he told Gabriel. "Follow my lead, and we'll be fine."

"Over here," one of the men said. "This has to be the place."

Matt recognized the voice immediately, and his previous confidence vanished. Craig was on the other side of the door, and no amount of lies, no matter how well crafted, would convince him that nothing more than a random act of violence had occurred.

Craig already distrusted Gabriel, given Gabriel's connection to Matt's previous life-threatening situations. Adding another to the mix would only make matters worse.

A CLEAR blue, cloudless sky hung over the highway that stretched before Homer as he sped down US 59 in his Chevy Silverado truck. A few minutes earlier, a storm had darkened the horizon, but those clouds had long since dissipated, had been ripped to shreds by the never-ending sunshine.

For the moment, the battle in Houston was over, and the Gifted One had been spared yet again. The victory would prove short-lived.

Within the hour, he would arrive and begin the hunt, and this time, he was prepared. While Homer might look as he did the last time he almost killed the Gifted One, he now housed a more formidable enemy.

The damned archangel would face a threat far greater than Barbatos could ever hope to be, and Gabriel would be unable to prevent him from fulfilling the contract. With information gleaned from his new companion, Homer knew Gabriel's enemies were numerous and consisted of more than just the demons that sought to kill the boy. Events were already in motion that would negate Gabriel's interference, and they were obstacles the foolish angel placed in his own path.

By his own actions, Gabriel doomed the boy he rescued by falling in love with the man he became. The delicious irony of it all made Homer laugh. His companion had been there long ago, in love with a mortal, and when he committed the same sin that now tainted Gabriel's soul, their Father had harshly punished him and his brothers for their trespasses.

Soon, the mighty archangel would join the ranks of the Fallen Ones.

MATT answered the last of the officer's questions, while the coroner's office removed Dr. Owens's corpse in a black body bag. The harsh zip of the closing bag made his hair stand on end. It added a finality to the horrifying situation, and for reasons he couldn't explain, he felt guilty for Dr. Owens's mad transformation.

"And that's it?" the officer asked. His badge identified him as Vasquez. "You have nothing else to add."

He thought about the question. There was a lot he could add to his statement, none of which he was free to share. He couldn't tell anyone that Gabriel was an angel or that Dr. Owens became some half donkey, half peacock hybrid that tried to kill him. Doing so meant a one-way ticket to an insane asylum for him, and Lord only knew what the truth would mean for Gabriel.

No, it was better to avoid the truth and stick to the story he had concocted and which Gabriel corroborated: Dr. Owens became agitated and attacked him, mad with grief at his mother's terminal illness. Gabriel heard the commotion from the other room and came in to save him. During the struggle, he stabbed Dr. Owens with the letter opener.

"Nothing," Matt responded. "That pretty much sums it up."

"You're not having a very good month, are you?"

Matt turned to face Craig, who now stood beside him in his black officer's uniform. For most of his and Gabriel's interrogation, Craig had stood with the CSI team as they gathered evidence for their report. He refused to meet Matt's stare but constantly glared in Gabriel's direction.

Gabriel either didn't notice or chose to ignore the looks. Instead, he answered whatever question was asked of him with his arms crossed over his bare chest. He had been handed a shirt by one of the lab geeks. Apparently, Gabriel's well-sculpted physique made the men feel inferior, but the offered shirt proved too small for his muscular build. They were all forced to question him and work around him as he stood half-naked in their midst.

No one was pleased, especially not Craig. He fumed in quiet protest, but now that Vasquez's questions were over, it appeared the silent treatment had come to an end. "No, I'm not," he told Craig.

"I don't know many people who escape death three times within two weeks."

"I guess I'm just lucky," Matt offered. He saw the hurt in Craig's eyes, and more than anything else at the moment, he wanted to provide Craig the solace he needed. Though they didn't have a long tenure as a couple, he had come to learn what comforted Craig. A gentle touch or a long, passionate kiss usually made Craig forget whatever troubled him.

That bag of tricks wouldn't work today, especially since he had caused the sting that twisted Craig's handsome features. As such, he was powerless to do anything about it.

Realizing no reassuring touch or soothing words would be offered, Craig blinked the hurt away. Cool curiosity took its place. "And Gabriel has been at every one of those scenes," he added with a nod at Gabriel, who now chatted a few feet away with Officer Vasquez.

Matt nodded. He didn't know what else to say.

"I find the whole thing far too coincidental."

"Meaning what exactly?" he asked. Although he felt bad about hurting Craig, he didn't appreciate the unspoken accusation. "That Gabriel is somehow responsible for *any* of it?"

Craig shook his head. "Responsible? No. I no longer believe that."

"Then what?"

"He's *connected* to it all somehow."

Matt couldn't stop his eyes from widening in shock. Craig's deductive skills never ceased to amaze him. He had an uncanny ability to spot patterns or motives that few saw. It was one of the reasons he was being considered for a place in homicide. "Connected? How?"

"I'm not certain," Craig said, studying him with his perceptive gaze. "But I'm beginning to think you do."

"Me?" he asked, hoping he sounded incredulous instead of guilty.

"Yes. You."

"What makes you think that?"

Craig swallowed hard before answering. "Because it's better than the alternative."

"What does that mean?"

"I'd rather think there's something suspicious going on here. Some hidden agenda or motive that's causing you to cover up whatever Gabriel or you and Gabriel are involved in. Because if there's no hidden agenda, if there's not some *reason* all this is happening, then that means you're not the man I thought you were. It means you're some player who played me until he got what he wanted." His eyes once again shifted to Gabriel.

When Craig looked back at him, his gaze turned hard. But beneath the steel veneer, Matt glimpsed the truth. Behind Craig's rough exterior hid the hope that Matt was everything he wanted him to be.

That realization tore Matt apart. Craig's suspicions were warranted, but Craig didn't know he was right on both accounts. There *was* more to their story and to his feelings for Gabriel. Craig had asked him to be truthful about Gabriel, but Matt had never been. Instead, Matt had deceived him. He'd not done it intentionally, but he had lied nevertheless.

What he hadn't lied about was his feelings for Craig. That had been genuine. Matt had seen a potential future with him. They shared similar interests and perspectives on life. They were a good match. A forever together definitely fit within the realm of possibility.

But Gabriel came back, bringing with him the same emotions and desires Matt had tried to replace with Craig. When he compared the feelings, there was no contest.

It had been Gabriel from the moment he first saw him.

"So which is it?" Craig asked. His eyes wavered in hope.

"There's nothing suspicious going on."

Craig shook his head in disappointment. "Oh, but there is. I see the truth in your eyes, Matt. We both know you're not a good liar."

It was true. His face read like an open book. Never before had he wished for Shane's ability to lie his way out of sticky situations. "What truth do you see?"

Craig scoffed. He was evidently becoming irate. "I won't give you truth. I'll give you evidence. This morning, we woke up in the same bed together. With you calling out to Gabriel for help. I tell you to call me when you've got your feelings for Gabriel figured out, and I come here, to your doctor's office because of a report of a disturbance, and find you and Gabriel together. Where he's saved you from yet another attack. And he's not even wearing a *fucking* shirt!"

Everyone in Dr. Owens's office stopped to stare, including Gabriel whose arched eyebrow expressed his displeasure at the cuss word.

"I already explained why he's not wearing a shirt."

"Yes, I know. Because Dr. Owens' ripped it off him during the struggle. But why was he here, Matt? You claimed not to have seen or heard from Gabriel this morning, yet here he is."

His eyes demanded the truth, and there was only one truth Matt could give that would prevent Craig from investigating further. Unfortunately, it was what Matt didn't want to admit.

"I asked him to come." Matt found the lie easy to tell. It was for a greater purpose, even if it destroyed a man who didn't deserve it.

"You asked him? Why?"

"So Dr. Owens could help me sort out my feelings. It's what you wanted."

"And? What did you discover?"

Matt gulped. It was now or never. "You were right," he finally admitted. "I have unresolved feelings for Gabriel. Feelings I want to explore."

Craig's eyes mirrored his broken heart. They grew narrow, and the hope that once illuminated within instantly blew out.

Craig nodded, clearly unable to speak. He faked a smile and turned around, walking toward the splintered door Gabriel had broken to save Matt. Craig stopped at the threshold, his hand gripping the doorjamb tightly. He turned his head to the right, using his peripheral vision to stare back at Matt. Craig opened his mouth as if to speak, but no words came out.

Craig faced forward again. Then proceeded through the outer office and exited the front door.

CHAPTER 19

AFTER a few additional hours of interrogation at the police department, Matt exited the station. Gabriel, who now wore a Houston P.D. T-shirt given to him by the obese desk sergeant, stood at his side. Matt lifted his face to the unseasonably bright February sun, and the warmth chased away the chill of the interrogation room. In its place, a soothing heat spread throughout him, reinvigorating his exhausted body, tired from both his ordeal with Dr. Owens and the countless questions asked by inquisitive law officials.

The questions had been grueling, and their stories had been quadruple checked. Luckily, they managed to pull off the ruse and keep Gabriel's identity and the true events within Dr. Owens's office a secret. Some of which they owed to Gabriel's heavenly abilities.

His psychiatrist's death was on its way to being labeled self-defense, and no charges were being brought against either of them at the moment. Matt had been grateful when the detective in charge gave him the news, but his appreciation was short lived when he spied Craig sitting at a far desk.

Craig stared off into space like a man set adrift on a lifeboat after the capsizing of his vessel. Lonely eyes gazed at nothing, and though Matt believed Craig saw him leave the detective's office, Craig made no gesture of acknowledgement. He continued staring into the nothingness that filled his vision.

Guilt again crept across him, its icy fingers tugging at the part of him that still felt very deeply for Craig. Even so, Matt did what had to be done.

They couldn't know Gabriel was an angel. The information defied belief. Matt knew that all too well and had his own difficulties wrapping his mind around the notion that angels were real. He had so many questions waiting to be asked, but he didn't know where or how to begin.

"Are you well?"

Gabriel's question pulled Matt out of his thoughts. He looked into the smiling radiant face of the angel who loved and protected him, and his internal struggles retreated from the forefront of his mind.

"I'm fine. Just thinking."

"About Craig?"

"Yeah."

Gabriel made no reply as they strolled away from the police station and down the street. Since the police had driven them to the station, they had no ride back to the parking garage where Matt left his car. They either had to walk, which wasn't ideal, or call someone to pick them up. Matt didn't dare call Dee or Shane since his best friends were likely to berate him for being with Gabriel, when just yesterday he had been with Craig.

Matt decided the five-mile walk back to Kirby Street to be the best option.

"I'm sorry for his pain," Gabriel said after a few minutes of silence. "I don't enjoy watching anyone hurting."

"Neither do I. Especially not Craig. He doesn't deserve what I did to him."

"He's a good man. I can sense that." Gabriel paused as if he was uncertain whether to say what hung on his lips. After a deep exhalation, he continued. "He loves you. I think it only fair for you to know that."

Matt nodded. He hadn't been blind to Craig's feelings for him. Craig had fallen for him quickly, almost as quickly as Matt had fallen for Gabriel. Admitting that didn't ease his guilt.

"I apologize for hurting you with such a frank admission, but I felt it important that you knew."

"I understand, but it makes me feel worse than I already do."

Gabriel stopped. He turned to face Matt, reaching out to hold his hands for all to see. Matt trembled when Gabriel's hands enveloped his. "Nothing's stopping you from going to him, Matt. He's a good man, and the two of you would be great together. Please don't let me stand in the way of your happiness."

"You're my happiness," Matt replied. "I've made my choice, and it's you."

"But I'm not an option. I've told you that already. There are…"

"Rules against this. Yes, I remember. But damn the rules, Gabriel. I love you, and I'm not letting anything, not even all the powers of Heaven stand in our way."

Gabriel frowned at his use of the word damn, but he allowed the trespass to go unmentioned. "There's so much you don't understand. So much I want to tell you to make you understand."

"So tell me," Matt pleaded. Gabriel's tortured face told him that the truth was unpleasant and the rules absolute. "I can handle anything. As long as it's the truth."

The irony that he now spoke words that Craig once said to him didn't escape Matt's attention.

Gabriel looked around, surveying the street around them and the sky above. He seemed to be searching for someone, perhaps other angels, who would, at this moment, descend and prevent him from divulging top-secret information.

"We can handle anything together," he told Gabriel.

"Fine," the angel replied. He grabbed Matt by the hand and led him off the main street and down an alley. Dumpsters and numerous piles of discarded trash obstructed the view from the street. Here amidst the stench of decay, they were safe from prying eyes.

"How romantic," Matt commented as a mouse skittered from beneath a pile of garbage.

"We're not going to talk here, silly man." Gabriel said as he once again scanned to his left and his right. He pointed to the sky, his muscled arm looking comically tiny compared to the huge shirt he wore. "We're going up there."

"What?" Matt asked, suddenly feeling apprehensive. "It's broad daylight."

"Do you trust me?" Gabriel's blue eyes looked down at him. They melted away all doubt.

"Of course I do."

Gabriel took a deep breath, and his wings exploded outward, ripping the oversized shirt to shreds. They flapped three times, stirring up a slight breeze, before once again tucking under in rest.

"Are you crazy?" Matt asked, looking around while simultaneously attempting to shield Gabriel from passersby. "Someone's going to see you."

"I thought you trusted me."

"I do, but that doesn't mean you have to show the world you're an angel. I thought we lied to the police and Craig to prevent just that."

Gabriel smiled at him as if he were being ridiculous. "I can control who sees me in this form."

"You can?"

"Of course. It's one of the many things of which an angel is capable."

Matt contemplated Gabriel's words. "Then, that means you let me see you defeat Dr. Owens instead of making me see something else. Like when you saved me from the oncoming truck or from Blade."

"Blade was a drug dealer. There was no need to assume my true form for him."

"What did that make the man who drove the truck?"

A shadow swept across Gabriel's eyes. "Something far worse than a mortal choosing a life of sin."

"Something like Dr. Owens?"

Gabriel nodded. "What I fought ceased being Dr. Owens the moment Adramelech took possession of his body."

"You called Dr. Owens that name. Who is Adramelech?"

"A demon," Gabriel replied matter-of-factly.

The revelation took Matt by surprise, even though he had already guessed the answer. There was no other explanation for the donkey-peacock creature Gabriel battled. Still, the information added to the questions he now had. If Dr. Owens, no, Adramelech, was a demon sent to kill him, then it begged the question as to why it had been sent for him in the first place.

But before Matt could voice his concerns, Gabriel lifted him off the ground, cradling him in his arms. He leaped into the air, and his wings carried them into the sky. Below them, the city drew further away as they headed for the clouds above, and the magnificent view of Houston stole Matt's breath, preventing him from giving voice to the fear that gripped him as tightly as the man he loved.

MICHAEL hovered, unseen, above the city, staring at his brother who flew across the sky with his charge in his arms. Although Gabriel had erected the heavenly veil that shielded him from human eyes, his actions bespoke impending calamity.

Gabriel had appeared in angelic form before Matt, a move that had been expressly forbidden. Although angels had revealed themselves to man in the past, such days existed in humanity's long forgotten memory.

The lives of angels and men no longer intersected. They lived parallel to each other. The blind faith of humanity boosted the powers of Heaven, and in return, the angelic hosts protected their charges from above and ushered them through Heaven's gates upon death.

Not since the time before Noah had angel and man intersected in the manner with which Gabriel now clung to Matt. Their love, for Michael knew it for what it was, had the potential to decimate the heavens as it once did. When his lustful brothers fell to the sins of the flesh, they gave birth to the giant Nephilim, who tormented humanity until the great flood.

Such an occurrence could not be repeated.

And if Michael had to bring down all the archangels to prevent history from repeating itself, then it was something he would do, even if it cost him the life of a brother he loved most dearly.

MATT clung onto Gabriel for dear life, his hands wrapped around the angel's neck so tightly he feared he might be cutting off Gabriel's airway. That was if angels even needed to breathe. The possibility of Gabriel not requiring oxygen distracted him from his fear of heights for a few seconds until Gabriel ascended at a steep incline.

The change in velocity and gradient caused Matt's stomach to lurch backward. Closing his eyes, he hid his face in the crook of Gabriel's neck. The calm rhythmic beat of the angel's heart reminded him of a lullaby, which quieted his panic. But being so close to Gabriel, inhaling his scent, which reminded him of a warm, spring day, caused a stirring of a different kind.

His previously calm heartbeat spiked, and Matt's cock grew hard in his jeans. It made him self-conscious, especially now that he knew what Gabriel was. He wasn't supposed to be lusting after an angel, one of God's most sacred creations. But here he was, his erection growing in his pants and straining against the unforgiving denim.

"You should open your eyes," Gabriel commented. "The view is spectacular."

Not as spectacular as the way you smell, Matt thought. He fought the urge to lick Gabriel's neck and taste the spring rain that emanated from his pores. Instead, Matt lifted his head from the delicious warmth of Gabriel's neck and looked around. Their steep incline had ceased, and they now flew level across the sky, hundreds of feet from the ground. They dashed in and out of clouds, which coated their skin with a fine mist that instantly dried from the warm sun above.

Matt found his previous fear quickly fade away, released into the atmosphere as easily as he exhaled. Being in Gabriel's arms made him secure, and he knew nothing bad would happen to him as long as Gabriel was there to protect him.

But Gabriel's embrace also somehow made Matt more confident in himself, as if the angel's presence sparked something to life that lay dormant within. While he understood that Gabriel would protect Matt with his life, Matt realized there was within him a strength he had never known existed.

After all, he managed to fight Dr. Owens after Adramelech took possession of his body. While he had been terrified, he fought back and stood his ground.

He'd been scared of his dreams for so long it felt good to know he could take care of himself when he needed to.

The only place he'd ever felt that confident was at work. There, he never questioned what to do. He just knew to do it. His life had always been different, more out of his control. But now that he'd taken action, instead of just waiting for someone else to step in and save the day, Matt felt the certainty with which he approached his profession spill over into the rest of his life.

He'd no longer stand by like a spectator, waiting for the next curveball that life would throw at him. He stood ready at the plate with a bat in hand. When life threw its next insane pitch, he planned on knocking it out of the ballpark.

Matt's new faith made him smile, and the view that greeted him from up here in the arms of the man he loved filled him with joy like no other.

Below, Houston pulsed with life. Miniature cars traveled down toy roads, and the high-rise buildings of downtown looked to be made of glass blocks that a child could move about with ease.

Life seemed deceptively simple from this vantage, but Matt knew better.

A demon named Adramelech tried to kill him by possessing someone he knew and trusted. Based on what Gabriel insinuated, this hadn't been the first time something like this happened. The man who almost ran him over on his birthday had been a demon as well.

It was time to find out *why* these things were occurring.

"Why do these awful events always happen on my birthday?"

Gabriel slowed the flap of his wings. Their speed dropped quickly, and they now leisurely soared through the sky. The angel looked at him sideways, evidently deciding if he should answer the question.

"I don't understand your hesitation. I thought you brought me up here to give me answers. No one's around, so unless you're planning on telling me there are invisible flying demons in pursuit, you might as well just spill it."

After a few moments, Gabriel relented, "It's because of how special you are. On the anniversary of your birth, your potential resonates the strongest throughout creation, like a solar flare bursting from the sun. Unfortunately, that light serves as a beacon that draws those to you who would do you harm. On your birthday, you're the most vulnerable, and it's my job to keep you safe."

"But it's not my birthday anymore," he reminded Gabriel, to which the angel nodded in agreement.

"No, it's not," Gabriel answered. "But every year brings you closer to your perceived destiny, and every year, the light within you grows."

"So this means I'm getting closer to my destiny, then?"

Gabriel nodded.

"But what does that mean?"

"You shouldn't worry yourself about that," Gabriel told him. His soothing blue eyes stared deeply into Matt's. He could feel the power of the angel's gaze filling him from the inside, urging him to accept the words Gabriel spoke. "I'm here. That's all you need to know."

Matt shook his head to clear his fuzzy thoughts. Gabriel's melodic voice soothed his troubled soul, making him want to forego his questions and abandon them to the sweet symphony that played in his ears.

More than anything, he wanted to release his worries to Gabriel, cast the burden onto his broad shoulders and live carefree. Doing so, however, would be a disservice to his new self-confidence. While Gabriel might be charged with taking care of him, this was Matt's life. *His* destiny. "You're wrong," Matt replied. "That's *not* all I need to know. Demons are trying to kill me, and I'd like to know why."

"I don't know why the demons are after you," Gabriel finally admitted. "Father hasn't shared His knowledge with me, and one doesn't push Father."

"But you suspect the truth? You think you know why."

Gabriel nodded in reply. The fear that clouded his eyes told Matt the truth might be worse than being ignorant.

"I want to know. It's my life, Gabriel. I have the right to know what's going on."

"Not when it concerns matters beyond the scope of man."

"This isn't beyond the scope of man. I'm a man, and this is happening to me. I'd say this is well within my scope."

"But the answers you seek are not for one such as me to divulge. There is a Grand Design to life, Matt. What you see is only but a thread, and you think that increased perspective gives you great power, but it doesn't. You're blind to the other threads that entwine around yours. Providing you with more knowledge before it's time can cause more damage than good. If you're meant to know the answers to your questions, you will learn. On your own. Without my assistance."

Matt hated how logical Gabriel was, but he couldn't fault the argument. Knowledge had been disastrous in humanity's past, especially when he thought about Adam and Eve. They suffered for gaining wisdom, when it wasn't time for it to be imparted. If he traveled down that path, the same thing might happen to him.

"I guess you're right," Matt finally admitted. "I just don't like being in the dark. For too long, I've had so many questions about my past. Who were my biological parents? What happened to them? Why did they give me up for adoption? And now that I remember my adoptive parents, I want to know why they died. I want to know why Clifford Crouch killed them, and I…" He stopped. His words stuck in his throat.

Suddenly, answers to questions he hadn't thought to ask filled his mind.

Sensing Matt's anxiety, Gabriel stopped their flight and hovered in midair. "Matt, what's wrong?"

"Clifford was possessed just like Dr. Owens. That's why my parents died. They died because he was supposed to kill me, but he couldn't." From his position within Gabriel's arms, Matt looked up into the angel's eyes. Gabriel's even stare told him his assumptions were correct. "My dream. The one where the door falls apart, and there's something evil beyond the door. That was Clifford, wasn't it? That's my childhood memory of knowing something evil waited for me on the other side. Right?"

Gabriel nodded.

"But you were there," Matt added. "Not just in my dream but in the memory. You've been protecting me this whole time."

"I'll protect you for as long as your heart continues to beat."

"How long have you been protecting me?"

"I think you already know the answer."

Matt nodded. It made sense now why he felt so instantly connected to Gabriel from the moment he met him. He wasn't a stranger; Matt had known Gabriel his entire life, and in some strange way, he had loved him for just as long as well. "You've been protecting me since the day I was born. That's why I felt like I found home when you saved me on the street. I've known you my whole life."

"I've always been at your side, and I always will be."

"You know who my biological parents are. Don't you?"

Gabriel looked away, a profound sadness settled into his vision. "I do."

"But they're dead," Matt announced. He didn't need Gabriel to respond to know it was the truth. "Just like my adoptive parents. Dead because of me." A chill spread throughout his body. Too many people he loved or who had loved him died because of him. They were innocent people caught between him and the evil that wanted to claim him. He felt just as guilty as if he had murdered them himself, and that realization caused the smoldering flames of his newly found confidence to flicker. "I'm not worth it."

"Not worth what?"

"All this death. Good people have suffered because of me, and I don't even know why."

Gabriel shifted Matt in his arms. No longer cradled in Gabriel's embrace, he now hung from around the angel's neck, while his arms wrapped around Matt's waist. Gabriel held him to his body, tightly.

His bare chest pressed against Matt, allowing him to feel Gabriel's rapidly accelerating heart. Matt knew what that meant. Being this close drove Gabriel as crazy as it did Matt, and right now, he longed for Gabriel to remove the rest of the boundaries that kept them apart, not just their clothes but the heavenly rules Gabriel struggled to follow.

"I won't say the deaths of those close to you aren't tragic. Because they are. But you are worth so much more than you realize. Your parents sacrificed themselves to save you. That tells you how much they loved you. How much you're worth. And if that doesn't convince you, then know this: I would lay down my life if it meant allowing you but one more moment of breath on this earth."

Staring into Gabriel's blue eyes, which welled with tears, convinced Matt that he was worth any sacrifice. The dying embers of his confidence roared to life once again.

"I'm just a man, flawed and imperfect," he told Gabriel.

"Your flaws and imperfections make you beautiful." A tear ran down Gabriel's cheek, and Matt wiped it away with his right hand. Gabriel leaned into his touch and sighed, obviously grateful for the sensation of his flesh. "I only wish you could see yourself through my eyes. Then you would know how beautiful you are. How special you are, not just to me but to everyone around you."

Gabriel released his left hand from around Matt's waist, holding him aloft with only his right arm while his wings beat a steady rhythm that kept them suspended. With his free hand, he caressed Matt's smooth skin. His fingers danced around Matt's cheekbone before sliding down to his chin. "I've never fallen in love with anyone in all the years of my existence, Matt. But I have fallen in love with you. Your presence in my life has changed me. It's made me a better angel than I was before you entered my life." His fingers skated a slow path to Matt's lips, where his big finger followed the outline of the sensitive skin. "To me, that makes you very special indeed."

Matt wanted to respond. No, he needed to respond, to somehow give voice to the emotions that filled his heart beyond capacity, but he found words couldn't express the depths of his feelings. What he felt for Gabriel sprung up from the depths of his soul and multiplied through every cell until he felt filled with nothing else besides the love he and Gabriel shared.

That was why words were insufficient. Only action could truly express his emotions.

Matt tightened his grip around Gabriel's neck, bringing their faces closer together. Only inches apart, Gabriel's warm breath brushed against his face, fanning the flames of a desire he wanted to burn even hotter. The angel's perfectly blue eyes, which once reflected Gabriel's internal struggle with his own desires, blazed with a longing that defied the rules.

Everything that once kept them apart vanished instantly, and they crossed the remainder of the distance to each other.

When their lips met, their passion raged like a sudden storm, and like a storm, only the ensuing deluge would satisfy the atmosphere they churned in each other's embrace.

CHAPTER 20

AFTER a speedy flight back to Matt's apartment, he and Gabriel stood within his bedroom staring at each other. Though they were only six inches apart, the distance measured more like miles, and Matt feared the hesitancy Gabriel had once expressed about consummating their relationship might resurface.

But when he gazed deeply within Gabriel's eyes, he saw love and desire had filled in the space previously occupied by fear and uncertainty. Gabriel wanted to be intimate with Matt as much as he did. Seeing his own passion reflected in Gabriel's eyes made him yearn to devour Gabriel on the spot.

Instead, he took two slow steps toward Gabriel, who didn't move. He remained in place, looking at Matt with eyes narrowed by longing. A few steps before Gabriel, Matt stopped. Although he wished to get naked immediately, it needed to be special. After all, it was Gabriel's first time.

He didn't want this moment to rocket by on the launch pad of desire. Gabriel deserved a leisurely stroll along the path of sexuality where he could stop and explore each new sight, smell, and taste until his senses were overloaded and he couldn't stop the inevitable, shuddering conclusion.

He took a step toward Matt, but Matt told him to stop.

"What's wrong?" Gabriel asked, concerned. "Have you changed your mind?" A wave of misery washed over his face, as if Matt had stabbed him in the heart and thoughtlessly plucked it from his chest.

"Of course not," he whispered in response. Gabriel sighed in reply. "I love you, and I want there to be no doubt about that. Do you believe me?"

Gabriel nodded like a child, who was being asked if he wanted to go to Disney World by his parents. His gaze and demeanor were eager yet tentative at the same time as if he were uncertain if the promised event would happen or not.

When Gabriel's passion flickered to life again and a drop of perspiration beaded from his temple and slid slowly down his cheek, Matt knew it was time to begin.

He undid the buttons on his shirt, one at a time, stretching the material open further with each new button undone. Before he moved onto the next one, he ran his fingers leisurely across his smooth flesh, encircling his nipples that hardened at his touch.

Two additional beads of sweat broke upon Gabriel's flesh and slid after the first, snaking lazy trails down his skin. When Matt finally unclasped all the buttons and tugged the fabric free of his chest, Gabriel bit down on his lower lip.

"I must touch you," Gabriel said, stepping forward.

Matt stepped back. "Uh-uh," he reprimanded. "Good boys who wait will be well rewarded."

Gabriel continued forward. "I've been good enough."

Matt laughed. He found it amusing that an angel who spent the last twenty plus years patiently watching over him had become so impatient. "Stop right there," he commanded to which Gabriel quickly obeyed. "You must follow my lead. I promise you it'll be worth it."

"But it's so hard."

Matt arched his eyebrow in response and glanced down at the bulge in Gabriel's denim. "I can see that."

Gabriel's cheeks lost their tan as they blushed a deep scarlet. He self-consciously dropped his hands in front of his crotch.

"You don't need to be embarrassed," Matt told him. "You're having the same effect on me." Matt unbuttoned his jeans and pushed them past his thighs until they fell to the floor, where he stepped out of them. Before Gabriel, he stood only in his blue Andrew Christian boxer briefs, which tented outward revealing his own obvious excitement.

Gabriel's gaze shifted down to the protruding fabric, and his mouth stretched into a seductive grin. "So beautiful."

"No, you are."

Gabriel shook his head in response and then pointed back to Matt. He mouthed the words, "No. You."

Matt slipped his fingers beneath the waistband of his underwear, tugging downward. His erection flopped out of its confines and pointed directly at Gabriel. "See," he replied staring down at his hardness. "He even agrees it's you too."

"I'd be pointing back at you if you'd let me."

"Not just yet. But pretty soon you won't just be pointing at me. You'll be pointing in me."

A low, desperate moan rose from Gabriel's throat.

Matt crossed the few remaining inches separating him from Gabriel. Though Gabriel tried to reach out to touch him, Matt swatted the angel's hands away. It wasn't time for Gabriel to take charge. For now, Matt was in control. He planned on bringing Gabriel to the edge before they tumbled down the other side together, in one sweaty, sticky mess.

He reached up and lightly danced his fingers across Gabriel's heaving chest. When Matt's fingers brushed against his left nipple, his eyes rolled in their sockets and he looked like he would pass out.

"Are you okay?"

Gabriel opened his eyes and stared down at him with the same intensity he always did, full of unwavering love and affection. "Better than okay. I've never felt so alive."

"I'm just getting started," he announced before moving his body to a mere inch from Gabriel. The heat of their passion blistered their flesh.

Matt kissed Gabriel's chest, causing Gabriel to inhale sharply. Darting his tongue around the left nipple, he caused the flesh to constrict until it stood at attention, wet from Matt's saliva. Gabriel's breath turned ragged, and when he tried to wrap his arms around Matt's naked body, he gently placed Gabriel's arms at his side, which elicited a groan of frustration.

With his tongue, Matt flickered a feathery trail across Gabriel's chest, through the soft black hair that tasted of rain, before finally arriving at the right nipple, which he treated to the same light suckling as the left. This time, his teeth bit gently down on the sensitive skin. Gabriel shivered in response.

"Please, Matt," he begged. "I must touch you now."

Matt shook his head no as he alternately licked and nibbled on his nipple. "No," he finally answered, forcing his hot breath across Gabriel's broad chest, but his raging erection, which stood rock hard from his dark brown bush, told a different story. Matt wanted Gabriel to take him immediately.

But it still wasn't time.

When Gabriel's nipple turned red from the torture of being lightly gnawed upon, Matt lifted Gabriel's arm and proceeded to lap up the skin between his chest and the thick patch of hair that sprouted from his armpit.

Gabriel moaned as Matt covered the abundant fur with his spit. As he inhaled the sweet, musky aroma, Matt moved his hands around to Gabriel's back. Matt surfed his hands along Gabriel's deltoid muscles, which instinctively flexed in response to Matt's touch, before he followed the curve of his body to where Gabriel's bare skin ended and his jeans began.

Matt dove his hands beneath the fabric and grabbed hold of Gabriel's ass. "Oh, yes," Gabriel muttered as Matt eagerly massaged his ass before withdrawing his hands from beneath the fabric.

"Please, don't stop," he pleaded. His blue eyes scorched red from passion.

"I'm not stopping," Matt replied. He glided his fingers from Gabriel's back around to his stomach. He then pushed them up and through the dense hair that covered his trunk. "I'm moving on."

"Okay," said Gabriel, almost out of breath. "But I don't know how much longer I can *not* touch you."

Matt only smiled in response. He didn't know how much longer he would last either. His cock was so hard it hurt, and a thread of silky precome dangled from the swollen head of his member.

He couldn't give in. Not yet. He had to take his time, so he exhaled sharply and continued his exploration of Gabriel's body.

Out of the forest of chest hair, his hands reached up to Gabriel's face. He lingered in the rough facial stubble on Gabriel's chin with his right hand while he traveled through the close-cut dark hair on his head with his left.

Gabriel closed his eyes in dreamy pleasure. "I could do this forever."

"As far as I'm concerned, we can."

Matt then traveled downward, sliding past his cheeks and along his rugged jawline. Passing his throat and through the tangle of chest hair, he surfed further downward, skimming the abdominal muscles that rippled under his touch, until he came to the button of Gabriel's jeans. Matt slipped each finger quickly below the waistband and tickled the sensitive flesh above the groin, before sliding back out.

"You're driving me crazy," Gabriel panted.

Matt smirked in reply before pulling on the waistband and forcing Gabriel's body against his. When their bare chests touched, Matt almost gave himself over to Gabriel, whose arms immediately wrapped around his shoulders, grasping at his bare flesh before moving down to cup his ass.

Gabriel forced their hard cocks, still separated by Gabriel's jeans, together.

The thick hardness that strained against the fabric elicited a moan from Matt. He wanted to rip the jeans off and impale himself on Gabriel's fat pole, but he regained control quickly. He stepped out of Gabriel's embrace and waved his finger at him as if he were a naughty child. "You don't want me to stop, do you?"

"Heavens, no!" Gabriel exclaimed.

"Then no more grabbing."

Gabriel let out a long breath before he nodded in agreement.

Satisfied that Gabriel wouldn't break his promise, Matt again drew closer. He wanted this to last as long as possible, which was why Gabriel couldn't touch him. Whenever Gabriel did, Matt lost all control, and he didn't want that to happen. If he did, their uncontrollable passion would sweep them away. Matt wanted them to lounge in each other's flesh, to prolong the passion as much as possible, and he was intent on achieving his goal.

Matt rested his naked body against Gabriel's, pressing his hard cock into Gabriel's throbbing hardness. Gabriel's eyes blazed with passion, but he gnawed on his lower lip to maintain control.

Nodding with approval, Matt awarded Gabriel's efforts. He traced his fingers along the hard shaft nestled within Gabriel's jeans. When he found the tip, he squeezed it lightly before traveling back down to trace an outline around his balls, which had gathered close to Gabriel's body.

"That feels so good," Gabriel purred.

"It's about to get even better."

Matt worked both hands up Gabriel's crotch, massaging his balls and his hard cock, until arriving at the button, which he finally unfastened. As he unzipped the jeans, he looked up into Gabriel's longing eyes, which silently asked if this was it.

"Almost," he replied.

When Matt gazed down at the open jeans, a light coat of pubic hair peeked from the unzipped area. The sight made Matt want to fall on his knees in worship. Instead, he pushed the jeans off Gabriel's muscled thighs until his thick rod popped out and the jeans fell away.

Naked, together, for the first time in real life and not in a dream, all Matt could do was stare at the sight before him. Gabriel's hard, muscled body shivered in waves of passion that rolled just beneath the surface. His broad chest, dark body hair, sculpted muscles, gorgeous cock, and the most fascinating blue eyes set into the most handsome face he had ever seen were almost too much for Matt.

"So beautiful," Matt told Gabriel.

"No. You are," he replied.

Matt grinned as he mimicked Gabriel's earlier gesture. He pointed at Gabriel and mouthed the words, "No. You."

When Gabriel smiled in reply, Matt felt his heart jump from his chest. It fluttered uncontrollably, as if it were trying to escape and find its mate within Gabriel.

That was when Matt knew it was time.

He grabbed Gabriel's hands in his and placed them on his waist as he slipped inside Gabriel's warm, protective arms.

"Is it time?" asked Gabriel. The hope in his voice was unmistakable.

Matt nodded.

Gabriel swept Matt off the floor and into his arms. He pulled his naked body against him and leaned in for the kiss that would add the final spark needed to turn their passion into a blazing pyre.

Their lips met, and Gabriel's tongue darted inside. Matt welcomed the slippery intrusion by wrapping his own tongue around Gabriel's. Opening his mouth wider, he tried to consume as much of Gabriel as possible, for he felt nothing short of actually eating this man would be enough to satiate the hunger that ravaged him on the inside.

Gabriel walked Matt over to the bed. He gently placed him down before lowering himself on top and resting between Matt's parted legs. The weight of his body against Matt caused Matt to buck his hips upward to which Gabriel responded by grinding against him.

Their hard cocks nudged together, and Matt grasped at Gabriel's shoulders, pushing himself harder against Gabriel's body, hoping their flesh would give way and meld them into one.

Gabriel lapped at Matt's neck before licking his own trail to Matt's chest, where he proceeded to lick and nibble on Matt's nipples in the same manner Matt had previously chewed on Gabriel's.

Matt squirmed in delight. He forced Gabriel's head harder against his chest while wrapping his legs around Gabriel's waist. As Gabriel feasted in delight on Matt's smooth skin, his stubble scraping across his flesh, Matt used his legs in conjunction with his hips to increase the pressure of their cocks as they slipped in the sweat that now coated their bodies.

He went wild, his hands traveling down Gabriel's back to his ass, which he massaged. Sliding his fingers down Gabriel's crack, Matt lightly caressed his center. In response, Gabriel grabbed Matt's hands and held them secure at his side.

Restrained and at the mercy of Gabriel's sexual craving, Matt whimpered as Gabriel's tongue charted a path past his silky chest and over his belly button before he slobbered at the base of his cock.

Gabriel sniffed at the base and growled in appreciation of the musky scent before his lips closed around the head of Matt's dick. Greedily, he sucked the plump head into his mouth, and the hot, wet sensation of Gabriel's mouth almost caused Matt to black out.

Bobbing up and down, Gabriel coated Matt's shaft with abundant amounts of spit, which caused the hard cock to easily glide past Gabriel's lips before resting in the back of his throat. His tongue tickled the shaft and darted into the slit, lapping up the liquid, which poured out.

"So sweet," Gabriel commented before slurping the whole member into his throat once again.

Matt strained against Gabriel's arms, trying to free himself, but he couldn't. He was too dangerously close to blowing his load, and it was too soon for that. "Slow down," he begged. "I'm too close."

Gabriel pulled off his cock with a grin. "Now, who's doing the pleading?"

"I am."

"Good," he replied before grabbing Matt's knees and pushing them forward. "Because now *I'm* just getting started."

He dove between Matt's parted cheeks and heartily ate at his opening.

Matt squealed in response as his flesh threatened to crawl off his body. Gabriel's tongue traced crazy circles around his center before he felt the wetness probe past the opening and into his body.

"Oh, Gabriel," Matt cried out as Gabriel's tongue pushed further inside him before withdrawing. When it had withdrawn completely, Gabriel again outlined the perimeter before shoving inside a second time.

"I need you inside me. Now."

"Begging again?" Gabriel asked. His eyes danced in play mocking. "What happened to you?"

"You did," replied Matt. His voice was nothing more than a whisper.

"Do I just…?" Gabriel seemed unsure how to finish the question.

"Get on your back," he replied. "I'll get you as slippery as you've made me."

Gabriel rolled off Matt and onto his back. Matt straddled him, running his fingers through the chest hair before he slid downward and took Gabriel in his mouth. When his lips closed around Gabriel's hardness, Gabriel's body tensed and he grabbed the back of Matt's head, forcing his cock further down Matt's throat.

"That feels wonderful," he commented while he thrust himself deeper inside.

Matt slobbered all over Gabriel's thickness, making sure to lube up the shaft with enough spit to make insertion possible and not quite as painful. He sucked on the head, flicking his tongue along the shaft as he slurped. He then slid down to the base until his nose rested against Gabriel's dark bush. The heady aroma of his sex filled Matt's lungs.

Matt could wait no longer.

He climbed back on top of Gabriel, grabbing his cock and pointing it at his center. The hard member wildly pulsed in his grasp as he sat back. Gabriel's head nudged against his opening. Rubbing the head around the hole, Matt applied the excess spit to him as additional lube before bearing down.

When the head slid past the opening and popped inside, Matt and Gabriel sharply exhaled in unison. After what seemed like forever, there were no more boundaries separating them. They had finally become one. It wasn't until Matt slid further down Gabriel's shaft and he rested against Gabriel's pelvis that they both remembered to breathe.

"You feel so good. So warm," Gabriel told him.

Matt slowly began to ride Gabriel's stiff cock. "You can stay inside me forever."

"Okay," he told Matt as he thrust upward meeting Matt's downward motion.

Clawing at Gabriel's flesh, Matt bucked downward harder and faster. Gabriel held onto Matt's hips, using his arms to time their motions. With each thrust, he pummeled inside Matt with increasing force.

Matt howled in passion. Each time Gabriel rammed his cock inside his ass, Gabriel stimulated his button. Pleasure rippled across his flesh, and sweat poured down his skin, collecting in small pools upon Gabriel's bronze body.

"More," Matt commanded. "Faster."

Gabriel complied. He bucked upward as Matt rose and fell on his thick pole, slamming Gabriel deeper inside him with each downward motion. Matt's cock leaked copious amounts of clear fluid, which splattered across Gabriel's muscled abdomen.

Faster and harder, Gabriel pounded inside him until Matt knew he could wait no longer. "I have to come," he announced to Gabriel who nodded in consent.

Matt furiously tugged on his cock while he bucked wildly against Gabriel. He felt his balls churning the load, ready to eject it from his swollen, red cock. His left hand pulled on Gabriel's thighs, forcing him inside harder and faster until it pushed him over the edge.

Within three more pulls on his rigid member, Matt cried out as thick, ropy jets of come blasted from his cock. They landed in white pools across Gabriel's body as his muscles spasmed around Gabriel's still hard dick.

Spent, Matt collapsed in Gabriel's arms, his face resting on the soft mat of fur on Gabriel's chest.

"That was awesome," Matt said, between short, ragged breaths.

"Yes, it was," replied Gabriel as he kissed the top of Matt's head.

"Now, it's your turn."

"Is it time for that now?"

"Most definitely."

Gabriel rolled Matt over onto his back, being extra careful not to cause his still hard cock to exit the snug place where it resided. Once Matt held his knees to his chest, Gabriel resumed his previous thrusts.

His hard cock withdrew almost completely from Matt before Gabriel slammed it back inside. With each thrust, Gabriel grunted as the friction edged him closer and closer to his own release.

Matt bore down against the cock, clenching his muscles tight in order to increase the friction that would ultimately milk the pleasure from Gabriel's body. "Whatever you're doing feels wonderful," Gabriel commented as his body continued to piston in and out of Matt.

Though he had just come, Matt's cock grew hard again. Gabriel's relentless thrusts inside him aroused his passion.

Gabriel covered Matt's face with kisses as perspiration dripped from his brow. Their tongues, mad with passion, swirled in and out of each other's open mouths, leaving the salty sweet taste of their lovemaking lingering on their lips.

Matt skated his hands down Gabriel's sweat-slick back. When they reached his ass, Matt used the leverage to force Gabriel further inside.

"I'm getting close," Gabriel told him.

Matt whimpered. He felt his own impending release return. "Come inside me," he demanded. "Fill me with your love."

Spurred on by his words, Gabriel slammed harder inside Matt. The bed shook violently with each thrust, causing the headboard to chip the paint with each strike of wood upon plaster.

"Oh, Gabriel," he moaned. "I'm coming again."

Matt's cocked pulsed to life a second time, ejecting its second load in a matter of minutes onto his chest and Gabriel's stomach. The resulting spasms caused his ass to clench even tighter around Gabriel's thrusting cock.

"I can't hold back anymore," grunted Gabriel, and with a final thrust, his heavenly rod pulsed inside Matt, unleashing a torrent of spunk inside. As he came, Gabriel's wings sprouted from his back, beating wildly within the room. They knocked over Matt's bed stand and caused the curtains to fall from the windows.

When it was over, Gabriel collapsed on top of Matt, his wings slowing to a flutter before drooping to the side in exhaustion.

"Stay inside me," Matt said. "I don't want you to ever leave."

Gabriel looked down at him. His blue eyes were even brighter than before. "I won't ever leave you."

"You promise?"

"I will be with you until the last breath leaves my body."

Satisfied, Matt wrapped his arms and legs around Gabriel. More than just their sweat and body fluids cemented them together. The love in their hearts and souls bound them for eternity.

CHAPTER 21

SOARING through lavender and pink painted clouds that surrounded his home, Michael took no pleasure from the majestic beauty that infinitely sprawled before him. The pastel-colored clouds glowed a sparkling yellow or a radiant white, depending on how the perennially sunlit sky glinted off the billowy tops.

Usually, whenever he detected the first hint of rosy pink in the clouds that signaled his proximity to Heaven, Michael's heart filled with both joy and relief. To once again be in the house Father built was all he ever craved.

But, today, sadness replaced joy. Worry trumped relief.

His return didn't herald cheerful tidings, and those who waited behind the golden walls that rose before him, demanded reckoning.

Michael passed through a sun-kissed archway that stretched higher than his eyes could see, and on the other side, the sparkling city of Heaven spread out for miles in every direction until disappearing at the horizon. Enormous spires rose from the temples, absorbing the light until each needle appeared to have been sliced from the sun itself.

Below him, the Saved Ones lived out their afterlives with their families, rejoicing in each other and in Father's love. They knew nothing of the heaviness that weighted down his heart, and as he returned their waves and smiles with his own, all he could think about was the fate that now awaited his brother.

Michael adjusted his flight path toward the Throne Room, which sat at the city's center.

Held aloft by clouds whiter than snow, the circular structure overlooked Heaven from its alabaster walls. From the clouds that supported its base, all of creation was clearly visible. Here, Father watched over His children, delighting in their accomplishments and fretting over their stumbles along the path home.

It was here Michael would meet with his brothers and fellow archangels to discuss their brother's trespass.

On the marble steps outside, leading up to the Throne Room, Michael spied five figures attired in their angelic armor, weapons already in hand. All apparently dressed for a fight while he arrived in only his tunic.

His choice of clothing would no doubt raise questions, and as he drew nearer, descending toward them on his fluttering wings, heated words reached his ears.

"We must act now!" Raguel told the assembled brothers. "There's no time to wait."

"We promised Michael we would await his arrival."

"To what end?" Raguel asked Uriel. "So he can attempt to fool us with false promises forced from our brother's dishonest lips?"

"Your words sting," Michael spoke while landing between Raphael and Jophiel. "I have never spoken with dishonesty in all the time since Father breathed me to life."

Raguel, always impatient and gruff just like Gabriel used to be before he became involved with a man, crossed his arms at his chest. His red gauntlets clanged against his silver breastplate, and a violent storm brewed in his deep black eyes. "Don't pretend the fool, Michael. You know of whom I speak."

"Can you not even say his name? The name of a brother we have loved for all our lives?"

"Raguel means no disrespect," Raphael intervened. Always the healer and peacemaker, Raphael's long brown hair cascaded over his bronze armor. Raphael always looked silly when dressed for battle, considering his inherently pacifist nature. "You know how he is about the rules. Being the Angel of Justice and all."

"I don't need anyone to apologize for me. Much less you," Raguel snapped. "Gabriel has broken our laws and made me thirst for justice. For that, he must pay."

"I'm aware of Gabriel's actions as much as you are," Michael told his brothers. "But rash actions will get us nowhere."

"Rash?" Raguel fumed. "We've sat idly by while you handled the situation. A situation you promised you could keep under check." Raguel crossed over to Michael and pointed his finger into his chest. "You've handled nothing. You used words to keep Gabriel under sway, but Gabriel's not an angel of words, he's the Angel of Vengeance, the vaunted strength of our Father. He understands only action. Not the endless prattling of Mercy." He scowled at Raphael. "Or Healing."

"And would Justice blindly condemn without all the facts, dear brother?" Jophiel asked, stepping forward in his pearl-white armor. Michael was glad to have Jophiel, ever the voice of reason, on his side.

"Thank you," Michael told him.

"Do not thank me, Michael," Jophiel warned. "I support neither you nor Raguel. I value only the information we collect, and from that wisdom, will my decision be made. While Raguel sees justice in only black and white, you, Michael, see the world with far too much gray. Your kind soul too keenly offers clemency when wisdom would impart otherwise." His silver eyes scanned the others, before he spoke again. "In the middle lies the balance."

"Jophiel's words are wise as ever," Uriel said. His hand found Jophiel's shoulder and squeezed it once before letting go. Uriel's armor, topaz blue, reflected the serenity of the sky. "While our dear brother has most certainly broken heavenly rules, he hasn't done so out of malice. His sins are not that of the Watchers."

"They are close enough," Raguel accused. "He has been tempted by the flesh and given in to carnal urges. Do we need more monstrosities born unto man before we act? Must another flood occur to once again wash the wickedness away?"

"Matthew Westlake is a male," Michael reminded them. "Incapable of conception."

"And that somehow absolves Gabriel of his sin?" Raguel asked, looking to Jophiel. "Tell me, Angel of Wisdom, does the fact that Gabriel has lain with a man over a woman somehow serve as a loophole to the rules by which we are all bound?"

Jophiel pondered in silence. His silver eyes cast downward as he weighed the arguments in his mind. "No," he finally spoke. "Carnal lust is the broken rule. The same rule our brethren broke in the days before Noah."

"Yet you overlook the most basic of facts," Chamuel announced. Not one to engage in heated debate, Chamuel usually deferred to the will of the majority. But today, his green eyes were set ablaze with a truth only he saw. "Gabriel hasn't fallen prey to lust like those of us who once watched over mankind."

"And what would you call it, Chamuel?" Raguel asked.

"Something neither Justice, Mercy, nor Wisdom can see," he replied. "But something the Angel of Love knows all too well."

"Love?" Uriel asked, astonished. "Can that be possible? Has Gabriel fallen in love?"

"We are all creations of our Father," said Chamuel. "We are capable of feeling love just as man. Why else do we watch over and protect Father's flock, if love were not our guiding force?"

"That's a different kind of love and you know it. Like Michael, you make excuses."

"I do no such thing," Chamuel replied calmly to Raguel's accusation. "Love is love. It is the greatest force in the universe. It allows for mercy, it heals pain, it ushers peace, it motivates justice, and it inspires wisdom." As always, when Chamuel spoke with his heart, his red hair set ablaze. "Love can happen to us all, even angels."

"If what Chamuel says is true," Jophiel interjected. "Then, this changes everything."

"It changes nothing," Raguel announced. His white wings lifted him from the marble step, and he hovered in the air. "I will go to Gabriel and bring him home to face his crime. With or without the consent of the majority."

With blinding speed, Michael dashed to Raguel. His blue eyes stormed in fury. "You'll do no such thing." He grabbed Raguel by the arm and flung him back onto the steps, where he sprawled onto his back.

"You dare!" Raguel bellowed as he rose to his feet.

"No," Michael howled back. "You dare to act on your own, without the majority and without directive from Father. We are His messengers. We do nothing without approval."

"I'll not stand idly by while Gabriel brings destruction not only upon mankind, but upon the Gifted One. His actions threaten the very life of the one he has sworn to protect."

"Brothers, please," Uriel begged, standing between them. "Let this not divide us."

Michael and Raguel looked around at the others, who stood shoulder to shoulder with Uriel. Their demeanor communicated they would brook no further dissension or violence, and no matter how powerful each was individually, in unified numbers, archangels were a force few could overcome.

"I apologize," Michael said, offering his hand to Raguel. Wisely, Raguel embraced the sign of peace. "You are motivated by love of Father as much as I am, Raguel. No matter how much we disagree, I should never hold that against you."

"Nor I," Raguel replied with an embrace.

"If that unpleasantness is over, let's go see Father."

Michael nodded at Chamuel's suggestion and followed his brothers up the steps to his Father's Throne Room, where Gabriel's fate would ultimately be decided.

MATT couldn't help passing out after his sexual encounter with Gabriel. He wanted to stay awake and bask in the warmth that still spread through his body, but his eyes became too heavy to resist the call of slumber. Gabriel begged him to rest and promised he would be there when he woke up, so Matt curled up on the soft down of fur on Gabriel's chest and fell asleep.

When he opened his eyes thirty minutes later, he half expected to see the bedroom of his childhood and find himself transported to his recurring nightmare. The tan walls of his apartment greeted him instead, and rather than the eerie thump of Clifford Crouch's footsteps on the staircase, Gabriel's even breathing filled the silence.

"Awake already?"

Matt nodded and stretched, his legs and butt sore from their sexual workout. Though his muscles hurt and his ass felt numb, he wasn't complaining. He enjoyed every ache and pain, and they were all well worth it. "You didn't sleep?"

"I don't need to sleep," Gabriel told him.

"Angels don't sleep? At all?"

"We don't require rest like mortal men." He ran his big right hand through Matt's messy head of brown hair. "Besides, how could I sleep when I have you in my arms?"

"Is that a line?" he asked as he crawled on top of Gabriel's still naked body. His skin smelled like sex and rain, and Matt felt a familiar stirring down below.

"A line of what?"

Matt laughed before softly kissing Gabriel on the lips, which still tasted sweet like honey.

"What's so funny?" Gabriel asked as he rested his hands on Matt's butt. "Are you mocking my ignorance of common vernacular?"

"Maybe," he replied while gnawing on Gabriel's lower lip. "What are you going to do about it?"

What looked like a shit-eating grin stretched across Gabriel's face, before Gabriel rolled over on top of him, bearing the full weight of his strong body on top. Matt felt Gabriel's thick cock come to life and grow across his stomach.

"Looks like someone else doesn't need to rest either," Matt commented while shoving his hand between their bodies and taking Gabriel's erection in hand.

Gabriel pressed his lips against Matt's and his tongue slipped into his mouth. The hardness in his hand throbbed in need. "I've never felt this way before," he told Matt. His blue eyes burned with reignited passion. "All I want is to feel your body against mine. To be one with you always."

Matt wrapped his legs around Gabriel's waist and used his hand to guide Gabriel back to where he belonged. "I could live with that," he said as he helped Gabriel slide inside him, his ass still moist from their previous lovemaking.

When Gabriel once again rested snugly within, the angel's eyes rolled back in his head, and Matt's breath caught in his throat. Never before had Matt felt this alive, this connected to another being, than when Gabriel was inside him, slowly moving his hard cock in and out of his body. He didn't want these moments to ever end.

Before long, Gabriel increased the pace of his thrusts. His cock worked like a jackhammer, spreading Matt's insides so that the path he created within Matt belonged to him and him alone.

"I love you," Matt mumbled as his tongue fought inside Gabriel's mouth.

Gabriel held his face in his hands. Their bodies continued to rock in syncopated rhythms. "And I love you," Gabriel panted. "More than I can possibly express."

Matt pulled Gabriel's head to his neck as his thrusts became more animalistic, communicating his primal need for the flesh Matt so eagerly offered. His hot breath blew across Matt's neck, setting off a blistering fire across his damp flesh. The heady aroma of musk and sweat filled the room, and Matt inhaled the intoxicating scent until he felt drunk and dizzy.

"Hold on to me," Gabriel told him.

Without asking why, Matt wrapped his arms around Gabriel's neck as his wings sprouted in a loud whoosh from the tattoo imprinted on his skin. They flapped in controlled motions and lifted them both six inches off the bed.

Suspended in the middle of the room, with Gabriel's wings beating to the same time as his undulating hips, Matt completely surrendered to the passion that consumed him from within. He bucked upward against Gabriel, trying to shove as much of the man he loved inside him as possible. He didn't want a single inch of Gabriel's hard cock to be denied entrance. Everything Matt was and everything he could be now belonged entirely to him.

Gabriel fluttered his wings to change their position. They were now hanging vertically, perpendicular to his bed. Matt grasped at Gabriel's shoulders using them for leverage while Gabriel's hands both supported and guided his ass even harder onto his crotch.

In the mirror, Matt glimpsed the miracle of their lovemaking. Gabriel's darker flesh pressed fervently against his lighter-toned skin. The muscles in Gabriel's body tense and impatient, he appeared to want only the sensation of being within Matt. Sweat drenched their bodies in winding rivers, while Gabriel's mighty white wings kept them from crashing to the floor below.

Gabriel's breathing turned to quick pants, and his body became even more rigid. Matt knew Gabriel was about to deposit his second load deep within him. The prospect of being filled with another dose brought Matt to the edge as well.

He craved another helping of Gabriel inside him. It meant that even after they physically parted a piece of Gabriel would remain, held away in the most secret part of his frame, the part that Gabriel now owned.

"Are you ready?" Gabriel panted in his ear.

Matt replied by bearing down on the hardness within him until Gabriel wailed in passion and unleashed another torrent of come deep inside. Gabriel's swelling, pulsing cock massaged Matt's prostate at just the right angle, which caused Matt to erupt again for the third time that day. His spunk landed on Gabriel's dark chest hair, matting it to his tan flesh.

Gabriel's wings fluttered again, this time angling them back toward the bed, where they came to rest, with Gabriel still inside and on top of Matt. Then the wings beat like a hummingbird's before shrinking in size and withdrawing into the tattoo.

"That was awesome," Matt said in between short breaths. "Sex while suspended in midair. All I can say is wow."

Gabriel blushed. "I'm glad you enjoyed it."

"As long as I'm with you, you never have to worry about that."

Gabriel looked away for half a second before resting his gaze upon Matt. In that time, a sense of dread crossed his eyes before Gabriel managed to blink it away. "What's wrong?" Matt asked as Gabriel's softening cock slowly withdrew.

"It's nothing to worry about." He positioned himself so that he lay next to Matt and was able to draw Matt's head to his chest.

Matt played with the sweat- and come-matted fur, rolling the strands between his thumb and forefinger. The look in Gabriel's eyes worried him. Although it lasted less than a second, the effect it had on Gabriel was profound.

His previously relaxed body grew tense, and Matt knew if he looked up into Gabriel's eyes, he would again see that look of foreboding. Even though he didn't want to ruin the moment, Matt did it anyway. He rose up on his left arm and stared at Gabriel. Gabriel's handsome face was darkened with worry, and his blue eyes had lost some of their prior luster.

"Please tell me."

"You know I can't lie to you," Gabriel sighed. "Please don't make me speak what's on my mind."

"But how else am I going to know what's bothering you? How else can we fix it if we don't communicate? That's what couples do."

Gabriel sat against the headboard and sighed heavily. His gaze shifted down to his hands, which fiddled nervously in his naked lap. "I fear my actions will yield disastrous results," Gabriel finally replied. "The couple you want us to be will be an impossibility."

"Why do you say that?" Matt's heart caught in his throat, and he found it difficult to voice his next question. "Do you not love me?"

Gabriel wrapped his arm around Matt, drawing him close. "That's a foolish question. Of course I love you. I wouldn't have broken heavenly rules if I didn't."

"Then, I don't understand. If we love each other, why can't we be together?"

"Physical relationships between heaven and earth are forbidden. I have crossed the line and set events in motion that may have dire consequences."

"Like what?" Matt asked sitting up in the bed. For the first time, he was afraid. Gabriel had mentioned there were rules against a relationship like the one they both pursued, but he never once thought that anything bad could come out of their love. He expected God and the heavens to be able to empathize with an emotion it touted as the strongest weapon in all of creation. Gabriel's current demeanor told him he had been wrong.

"I can be recalled and another would take my place."

"I don't want another. I want you."

"That's no longer up to us."

"Why not? We love each other. What's wrong with that?"

"Because physical love between angels and man once led to chaos and treachery."

Matt was confused. He knew the Bible. His grandmother had taken him to church every Sunday, and he didn't recall any chapters that discussed, much less forbade, angels from falling in love with those they protected. "What are you talking about?"

When Gabriel again spoke, he told Matt the tale of the Watchers and how the Nephilim came to be.

PART IV: DIVERGENCE

CHAPTER 22

THE sun bore harshly down upon the land of Sumer, where the Watchers resided after their fall from grace. Here, Samyaza and those who followed him down from Heaven made new lives for themselves that no longer centered on the needs of Father. Now, more private desires held sway over their hearts and their actions, and Samyaza knew the sun that now scorched his land served as punishment for what he had dared to do.

Whereas they had once watched over Father's flock of men, keeping them safe from treachery, he and his brothers had decided instead to live among them, to take the women they coveted and claim them for their own. In doing so, they abandoned their divine duty and sullied their once pure souls with sin.

At least that was the way Father saw it.

Father didn't understand how Samyaza's flesh or the flesh of his brothers longed for the loving that could only be found within the embrace of another. Father had removed Himself too much from humanity, and in doing so had grown distant and ignorant of the needs of His children, both man *and* angel.

After all, Father had made Man in His own image, and the daughters of man were fairer than any creature that strode the land. Samyaza had been previously content with merely remaining on the periphery of those he watched, but as time passed, he couldn't fight the urges the daughters stirred within his heavenly frame.

With all his angelic might, he battled the yearning. Then, he set eyes on Istahar.

Her olive skin and sand-colored eyes entranced him. He could watch no other but her, and he spent many days simply gazing down at her beauty until he could control himself no more.

It wasn't fair that man had the right to choose a mate, while angels were forever denied the same comfort. Why were beings such as he forbidden from enjoying the loving embrace of the same daughters? Were angels somehow less deserving than man?

So when Samyaza gathered his brothers, he found he was not alone. They too longed to sample the delicate flesh of a woman, and he, and two hundred of his kind, each decided to take a daughter and claim her as his own, whether she wished for it or not.

That night, he came unbidden unto Istahar and filled her with his presence. Shortly thereafter, all his brothers were wed, and their wives carried their children, who walked the land as giants among men.

Instead of trying to understand the desires that raged in their flesh, Father grew distant, cutting them off from home and abandoning them to the paths they had chosen. He offered no favor to angels, who once did His bidding without question. Their millennia of service afforded them no special treatment, so Samyaza and his brethren carved out a living on their own.

For that, Father resented them. For not remaining dependent upon Him. For not tucking tail and running home. He despised that His so-called Fallen Ones had not fallen at all. They *thrived* without His assistance and without glorious praise to His name.

Samyaza and his brothers introduced charms and enchantments to man in order to procure a livelihood for their families and newly created community. They unlocked the mysteries of the plants, animals, and the land. Their children, the mighty Nephilim, proved stronger and fared better upon the earth than those Father had created in the Garden of Eden.

Because Samyaza and his followers dared all this, because he had proven himself to be a better provider than Father, the community Samyaza helped create and the land they lived on suffered from Father's wounded pride.

Fields, once a dazzling green, turned brown and barren. Dirt hung in the air on stifling winds that further parched the land. It had been years since the last blessed drop of rain saw fit to fall from the heavens, and all felt its absence.

Beasts of burden died as quickly as they were born unto their mothers, who snorted indifferently at their fallen offspring. Their deaths meant food already scarce would no longer be shared, and their corpses were abandoned to the circling vultures above.

Families, which once thrived in both life and wealth, broke apart. Mothers wandered the roads, calling for children taken by death or misfortune. For comfort, they painted their faces and sought the arms of men who were not their husbands. Marriages splintered, and mortal existence became a burden rather than a gift.

Samyaza worked to build a paradise on earth, a great civilization to rival the home his Father built in the heavens above. It had been his goal to prove that his treachery had *not* been for naught.

Now, that thriving civilization crumbled around Samyaza, leaving behind only a desiccated husk of a once glorious people.

It made him mad. His Father was punishing his people, and if all of Heaven turned its back upon him, then he vowed to repay it in kind.

"Anak," he called out for his son. Within moments, the ground shook as his precious boy bounded to his father's side. Taller than most of the children sired with the daughters of man, Anak stood higher than four grown men stacked upon each other's shoulders. "Fetch the Prefects, and bring them to me."

Anak replied with a nod and dashed off to do as his father commanded.

Though he was their chief, Samyaza needed the Prefects to side with his plan. They advised his rule in Sumer. The Prefects were the voice of his brothers, who had grown discontent in the years since they descended to the mortal plane.

Many expressed a desire to leave Sumer, to travel to adjoining lands and resettle in areas more bountiful than Sumer now was. Samyaza had foolishly refused that request. He had still clung to hope that Father would forgive them. That He would shine His favor upon what they had built. Instead, He turned His back upon them and relegated them to misery.

Now, the time had come to sow those seeds of discontent and bring forth a harvest born of blood. If Father would not give unto them, then they would take from His most favored children, and when they were done, man would be but a memory.

GABRIEL flew into the Throne Room, incensed at the evil his fallen brothers spread throughout Sumer. His wings beat in furious flutters carrying him to his assembled brothers, who, in armor, gathered like him to await Father's arrival.

He grew tired of waiting; action was now required.

For four generations they had watched as Samyaza and his ilk descended like locusts upon their unsuspecting, peaceful neighbors either destroying them or corrupting them with their presence. The gifts bestowed upon mankind became tainted, and the flock needed to be thinned.

That was the only way to purge the land of its festering disease.

"It is time," Gabriel announced.

His brothers lifted their sad eyes from the portal set into the floor. Below, the Nephilim, the children of their brethren, extended their rampage into Elam to the east of Sumer. No longer content within the boundaries of the many-citied nation they now governed with violence and treachery, they declared war on all surrounding life, whether beast or man.

"How much longer will we stand idly by and watch as Samyaza desecrates all we hold dear?"

"Gabriel speaks true," Raguel agreed, seething in anger. "Justice must be visited upon the Watchers and the Nephilim."

"Perhaps we can still achieve peace," Uriel pleaded. "Hope cannot be lost to war."

Gabriel snorted. "War has already been declared. While we wait, Samyaza grows fat with power digested from sin and treachery. It was you who urged us to forgive his sins when the Watchers fell from grace, Uriel." Gabriel's sword appeared in his hand, flashing with the fire of his rage. "Against my better judgment, I relented to the majority. I allowed myself to embrace the prospect that Samyaza's brood bred from rape would somehow benefit mankind. They have destroyed humanity instead."

"The fault lies not with Uriel," Michael replied. He crossed over and placed a reassuring hand on Uriel, whose guilt weighed heavily in his eyes. "Do not cast blame where it does not belong."

"I do not blame Uriel. His way is peace. It is his nature, and I embrace him freely. But the time for peace has passed. Vengeance is at hand."

"But is such a move wise?" Jophiel asked. "You speak of war of cataclysmic proportions, dear Gabriel. Man might never recover once angel battles angel upon the land."

"Man has become lost," Chamuel uttered. His voice trembled in anger, not fear. Of them all, he took the fall of the Watchers the hardest. Their defiling of women and the abominations they birthed bore insult to what the Angel of Love stood for. More than any other, he wanted Samyaza and the others to have paid for their trespasses long ago. Now, as he bore witness to the devastation that now rampaged across the land, the anger, which before only simmered, raged, setting his red mane of hair aflame. "The Nephilim corrupt everything with their presence. Even love. For that, I will not stand."

"That's three," Gabriel announced. "Who will join us for the majority?"

"I stand with you," Raphael said, crossing over to Gabriel, Raguel, and Chamuel.

"Raphael?" Uriel asked, surprised.

As the Angel of Healing, Raphael, like Uriel, preferred peaceful resolutions to conflict. But within the angel's brown eyes blazed anger never before seen upon his countenance. His open and eager face became hard and unrelenting.

"Do not mistake my passivity for meekness, Uriel," Raphael commented. "I am an archangel, more than ready to battle any evil that threatens the good Father has created."

"But peace brings healing," Uriel reminded him. "It's what you've always believed."

Raphael's hard stare softened for a moment before again turning to stone. "I still believe in peace, brother. And I will always embrace it. But my first priority will forever be toward healing. And sometimes in order to heal, the infected limb must be severed." His brown staff, which he always carried, shifted into a sword. "Samyaza and his corruptive influence must be cut free if the entire body of mankind is to recover."

"Argue no more, My children."

The voice of their Father suddenly filled the space of the Throne Room. Immediately, they supplicated on bended knee.

"Rise. We have much work to do."

In unison, the seven archangels rose as they waited for Him to take form.

First to shimmer into view were the seraphim, the most powerful of all the angels. They followed wherever Father appeared, singing His praise and regulating all of Heaven from His side. Six wings, made of red and golden fire, sprouted from the back of each, and when the Throne began to form, those wings spread in exultation.

Floating into view came the cherubim, their tiny peacock wings beating furiously as they charioted the Throne into existence. Within the seat sat a young boy, no more than twelve, dressed in a dirty brown tunic and dusty sandals.

Father had arrived.

"I have heard your words, and I agree with the majority. The wickedness of man on earth is great. In his heart, evil lives continually."

From beneath the Throne, the cherubim wept. Their tears fell through the portal, sending a storm across the land. It spread over Sumer and the lands in every direction.

The young boy changed into a woman, with skin as black as the night. From Her ears dangled big hoops, and a long, flowing gown fluttered at Her ankles.

"I have watched as the wickedness has spread, originating from where the Fallen Ones took root. It has grieved Me that My creations have chosen the path of destruction, turning their backs on all that I have given.

I will, therefore, destroy all that I have created. From creeping creature to denizens of the air. All shall be erased, including man. I shall cause a great flood, and wash away all corruption."

Father's form changed again. This time, He appeared in only a loincloth with a feathered headdress draped across His brow. He stood from His Throne and walked on air toward the gathered archangels.

"But there is one who has found My favor. His name is Noah. As he walks with Me, so shall I walk with him."

He turned and spoke to Uriel, who bowed in reverence. "Go to Noah. Tell him what is to come and instruct him to build an ark upon which he will carry his family and a pair of every animal in creation. The beasts will march two by two to him, and he, his family, and the animals in his care shall be spared My judgment."

Uriel nodded before flying out of the Throne Room to complete his task.

Now in the form of an elderly woman, wrapped in a pink kimono, Father stared at Gabriel and Michael. To Gabriel, He ordered, "Go to the children of lust and sin and destroy them. The wickedness has corrupted them. Let them destroy themselves with that wickedness. Send brother against brother until they destroy themselves in battle."

Father then spoke to Michael. "Bind Samyaza and those who have taken up his cause, defiling themselves and the daughters they have claimed from My flock. And after they have witnessed their sons spill each other's blood and the destruction of all they hold dear, bind them in the earth and toss them into the abyss, where they will be confined forever."

Once again a young boy, Father returned to His Throne, which slowly faded from view.

"Let My will be done," He spoke once more before disappearing. In response, the cherubim and the seraphim blinked out of existence.

"We have our orders," Michael said, staring solemnly at Jophiel.

"Indeed," replied Gabriel. His sword flashed in his grasp. "Samyaza and his kind will pay the price of defying our Father's law."

TEARS no longer fell from Samyaza's eyes. Although grief deeper than the pit of hell opened in his heart, wrath quickly filled in the void once occupied by the love of his wife.

Istahar now lay dead before him, slain by one slice of Chamuel's sword. For what seemed like hours, he begged for Raphael to heal her, to call her soul back to her body. Raphael ignored him, choosing to aid the other archangels in striking down the brides of all the Watchers, while each fallen angel was bound helpless in chains, held by Michael who hovered above.

Since Istahar breathed her last, he had watched as all of Sumer burned, the revitalized crops, the trade routes, the industries they had established, and the empire he had built. All reduced to ash. The golden light of enterprise they had inspired through domination now burned a fiery red in the distance.

But what hurt Samyaza the most was when Gabriel descended, calling upon their children, whom he urged toward war. Vengeance was theirs, he told them. There could only be one Nephilim, to rule the land which they sought to conquer, and the last giant standing would claim the prize.

And with those words, Samyaza watched helplessly as his child Anak, and the cousins with which he was raised, set upon each other in bloody battle. One by one, the Watcher's children fell, and with each death, the cries of a grief-stricken father filled the sky as giant bodies, impaled by spears, lay sprawled along the blood-soaked earth. When massive heads, separated from their corpses, fell to the ground, more wails of torment rocked the heavens, begging for forgiveness from a deity who demanded the blood of the child for the crimes of the father.

Even as he watched Anak gutted by his best friend, Samyaza refused to ask for forgiveness. His embittered soul demanded vengeance of his own.

He was a Watcher, a special class of angel created by Father, imbued with powers to rival Michael and his ilk, and he refused to remain bound one moment longer.

With a howl of fury, Samyaza ripped to pieces the golden chains that wrapped around his neck and limbs. He flung his body into the air, and the wings that had not sprouted from his back since coming into Istahar burst forth from his skin. No longer white, wings as black as a raven hurtled him toward Michael, whom he knocked across the sky with one mighty punch.

His brothers shackled below heralded his name as he grasped the chains and shook his brethren free. Each one leaped into the air, the same sleek black wings emerging from their backs, as they took to the sky in revolt.

"Kill the archangels," Samyaza called to his approaching army. "Show them what vengeance truly means."

They responded in one mindless, deafening shriek. "Kill!"

As Samyaza turned, Gabriel slammed into him, knocking him toward the ground. "You defile the angelic host further with wings as black as sin." Gabriel followed him as he plummeted to the ground below. "Being confined to the pits of hell is too good for you, Samyaza. With one plunge of my sword, I shall erase you from existence."

"I have powers at my command that you can't even fathom," he replied as Gabriel descended toward him. Samyaza raised his hands and the earth parted; shadowy tentacles shot out from the crack and wrapped themselves around Gabriel's neck and arms. "Since my banishment from Heaven, I embraced the occult. Called upon the Dark One through blood sacrifices and offerings, and he heard my pleas."

Up above, Gabriel struggled. For every tentacle he severed, another grew in its place, until he was completely bound in their shadowy grasp. The obsidian limbs then pulled him downward, toward Samyaza and the split within the earth.

"The ground will now devour you, Gabriel. As it will consume your brothers and then the sky above. Heaven's reign is at its end, and the Dark Lord shall claim dominion."

"You're a fool," replied Gabriel. He no longer struggled. He simply stared at Samyaza with pity and defiance. "Neither you nor the Dark One has the power to overcome Father."

"As blind as always," Samyaza spat. "Look around, Gabriel. See what my brothers have done to your archangels."

Raguel and Jophiel fell to the horde of fallen angels. Raphael's attempts to heal the wounded Uriel proved to be in vain. Half a dozen enemies befell him and took him down. Surprisingly, Chamuel lasted the longest, striking down at least two dozen Watchers before finally succumbing to the advancing horde.

"It is done," Samyaza reported as the shadowy tentacles held Gabriel above the split in the ground. "You will be but the first to fall before our might. Soon, we will march upon Heaven, decimating the angelic hosts on our way to the Throne Room, where we will slit Father's throat."

"You have truly become corrupted," responded Gabriel. "Evil so great resides within you that the angel I once called my friend has simply ceased to be."

"Friend?" Samyaza scoffed. "You've hunted us down. Killed our wives and children. If this is what friendship means in Heaven, I'm glad to have embraced the other side."

"As always, you choose incorrectly."

"I beg to differ. Since I stand before you in victory."

"You stand before me, yes," Gabriel replied. "But your victory is hollow."

Samyaza laughed, and his laughter mocked the heavens. "Why is that? Because I haven't killed you yet?"

"Because this has been a test."

Samyaza's eyes narrowed. For the first time, doubt slowly crept into his darkened soul.

"Father wanted to give you one last chance to repent, to see the evil your actions have caused. Instead of seeking forgiveness, you embraced evil in its purest form and tainted your once heavenly soul with poison so vile, you are unrecognizable."

"And what are you going to do about it? You're powerless in my grasp."

A knowing smile stretched across Gabriel's face. "With faith comes power," he reminded Samyaza. "Something you have apparently forgotten."

A coppery aura enveloped Gabriel, tearing through the black limbs, which strained to hold him captive. The shadowy arms resisted the light at first, attempting to snuff out its radiance with the darkness within, but the copper glow proved too strong.

Eventually, the tentacles retreated into the void that created them, and the cracked ground closed shut.

"No!" Samyaza yelled. "Don't forsake me!" He fell to his knees, clawing at the earth in attempts at ripping it open.

"It is you who has forsaken Father."

Samyaza looked up, and the seven archangels hovered above him, each aglow with a heavenly light he could no longer stare at. Throwing his hands in front of his face, Samyaza looked around as his two hundred brothers lay beaten and bloody. Chains once again bound them to Michael.

"I only wanted to feel love," Samyaza wept. "How could that have been so wrong?"

"You perverted love," Chamuel accused. "Lust prompted you to rape the woman named Istahar. You think she married you of her own free will? What other choice did she have once her chastity was stolen by one sent to watch over and protect her?"

"That's not true," he wailed. "She loved me!"

"Wisdom imparts otherwise," replied Jophiel. "Did she ever look upon you save with fear? When she birthed your child, did she suckle it without the look of horror etched to her face? Why else would she have turned into the foul creature she became? A woman with only hate and fear in her heart."

"We freed your wives from their misery," Michael added. "It was the only merciful thing left to do."

Raphael nodded. "In death, they have the chance to heal. Their souls may yet reach Heaven once they have been cleansed."

"And with the Nephilim and your kind wiped from the land, peace will once again reign supreme." Uriel looked upon him, a profound sadness weighing heavily in his eyes.

"Do not look upon me with pity," Samyaza shouted. "I'm not some errant child who deserves your punishment. I was an angel. I was one of you."

"You were," Raguel agreed. "But justice recalls the title and relegates you and your brothers to never-ending imprisonment

"I will escape," he told the assembled seven. "And when I do, I will tear your limbs from your body."

"Still you resist," Gabriel told him, the anger in his voice sharper than a blade. "You've learned nothing."

The archangels looked at each other and nodded.

"The decision has been made," Gabriel announced. "And vengeance is at hand."

The seven pointed downward in judgment, and the earth again split beneath Samyaza's feet. For a moment, he hung suspended over the black hole. Within it writhed many indistinguishable forms.

"Farewell, dear brother. For the fate that awaits you is one of your own choosing."

Gabriel then hurled his sword at Samyaza, impaling him with its heavenly metal. He fell backward into the hole, and thousands of hands reached out and grasped onto his form. As they rent him limb from limb, his hate continued to grow, and he vowed to one day return to seek his revenge upon Father, upon creation, and upon Gabriel, who had cast him down into hell.

CHAPTER 23

FOR a few moments, Matt sat in stunned silence. He found it difficult to comprehend the tale, which Gabriel just shared.

He recalled the story of David and Goliath, but for some reason, he never took the word giant literally. Like many, he believed that the characters and tales in the Bible were allegorical. They were lessons designed to teach the faithful how to become better people through acceptance, love, and faith.

For Matt, Goliath was a symbol of oppressive government or society that wanted to squash the little people, those like David, with their brute strength. But when David stood up to the giant and slew him, he proved that even the smallest individual, with courage, could conquer the most insurmountable of obstacles.

Apparently, he had it all wrong.

Goliath had not only been a real giant but a descendent of the surviving Nephilim from the civil war Gabriel started in Sumer.

Giants were real. Just like angels, and demons, and God.

Although he believed in them, it had been on faith. A leap of faith was no longer required. They existed, plain and simple. Well, maybe not that simple.

It was a bit much to take it all in at once.

"Matt, are you well?"

He nodded at Gabriel, whose blue eyes gazed at him in concern from where he still sat naked against the headboard. "It's a lot to process," he replied. "And I'm shocked more isn't written about it."

"A great deal of scripture has been lost, hidden, or translated incorrectly. What you know from the commonly called Old and New Testament contains a great deal of misinformation."

"Misinformation? How is that possible? Isn't it the word of God?"

"As translated by man," Gabriel told him. "There were bound to be errors. Some minor. Others intentional."

"Intentional? Who would do that?" But before Gabriel had a chance to respond, he answered his own question. "Those in power."

Gabriel nodded. Irritation drifted across his blue eyes. "The Bible has been used far too often to subjugate instead of enlighten. The hate and intolerance that infects your society now has been based on those errors. Father loves all. Even those your religions claim He hates. There are no conditions to His love. He doesn't discriminate against groups of individuals the way man seems to. He also doesn't keep attendance at church or punish you for your sins. Mankind torments each other enough for their transgressions that anything further is unnecessary."

As he spoke of God, Matt felt the power of Gabriel's love emanate from him like light from the sun. Its warmth quickly filled up the room and Matt.

"That's what makes Father's love so perfect and absolute. Those who know Father's true message already embrace that. Those who twist His words will eventually learn how wrong they are."

A huge weight lifted off Matt's shoulders. He had always suspected this truth. That God didn't advocate hate. To have it confirmed by an archangel no less made his spirit soar. It told him that as long as he lived a good life and loved with his full heart, he didn't have to worry about being gay or any other "moral" wrong that religious wing nuts focused on.

The specter of damnation that seemed to hover around those shunned by society didn't exist.

But when his mind returned to the story of the Nephilim and the Watchers, his new calm drifted away on the turbulent waves they called forth. The wickedness of their actions reminded Matt that just as true goodness existed in the world, so did its darker counterpart.

And that darkness, for whatever reason, kept coming for him.

"You told me about the thing you fought outside Dr. Owens's office, when he was possessed by Adramelech. That was a Nephilim, right?"

Gabriel nodded. He told Matt that the Nephilim who survived the great flood reproduced. His vile children, Goliath being one, spread throughout the land, but without the support of the Watchers, humanity managed to contain their inherent treachery until all but one existed. With that one now gone thanks to Gabriel, the Nephilim were no more.

"But what about the Watchers? Are they dead?"

"Imprisoned," Gabriel clarified. "Deep within the earth."

"Except Samyaza? Who was cast into hell?"

Gabriel didn't answer. Instead, his eyes looked downward again, the guilt apparent in his eyes. Matt understood that Gabriel felt as if he now traveled the same path Samyaza had. The one that ended with him cast out of Heaven, living a life of evil, and then being sentenced to hell. Although Matt understood why he felt that way, their situations had nothing in common.

"You do see the difference between our story and the Watchers, don't you?"

"I see only sin," he replied. "I was there, and I should know better. Yet, I traveled the same path as Samyaza and his followers." Gabriel lifted his gaze, and when he stared at Matt, the light in his eyes returned. "And to make matters worse, I would do it all over again."

Matt grinned in reply. He wanted Gabriel to take him in his arms. No, he longed for it, but that would have to wait.

"Samyaza and the others raped those women. You did no such thing. I love you, Gabriel. I willingly gave you my body and my heart."

Shaking his head, Gabriel replied. "I sullied the purity of my soul with knowledge of the flesh. While the circumstances may be slightly different, I have committed the same error."

"Are angels always this stubborn?" he asked. Gabriel's handsome face twisted into a frown. "I thought that sexuality wasn't an inherently evil action. Any more than eating or drinking. It's when you cross over to lechery or gluttony that there's a problem. Or am I wrong?"

"You're oversimplifying a matter divine in nature, Matt."

"Maybe," he replied. He got off the bed and held his hand out to Gabriel. Gabriel took it and stood with Matt next to the bed. Matt pressed his naked body against Gabriel's bare flesh. Instinctively, the angel's strong arms wrapped protectively around him. Matt not only felt safe and loved, but he felt complete. "What I feel for you in my heart is not bad. It's not tainted by only lust. It's pure and good. I can feel it." He placed his hands on Gabriel's chest, directly over his beating heart. "It's as natural to me as a heartbeat. Could the wives of the Watchers say the same thing?"

"No, they could not."

"Then have faith. Heaven will see the differences, despite the similarities. They're motivated by love after all. Right?"

Gabriel nodded in agreement. The hope that swelled in his heart reflected through his eyes and his ceaseless smile. "There's no one else like you, Matthew Westlake."

His statement brought Matt back to his previous concerns. "Is that why demons want to kill me?"

The light in Gabriel's eyes died immediately. "No one will kill you. I promise you that."

"And I believe you. But I still need to know why. I know you don't want to tell me. For your own reasons. And I accept that. But that doesn't mean I'm satisfied with not knowing. It scares me to death, and if I have to, I'll find answers myself."

"What does that mean?"

As before when Matt was soaring through the sky in Gabriel's arms, he felt refortified by the strength that now welled up from some eternal spring within. Just because Gabriel couldn't give him the answers didn't mean he would remain ignorant. "You've been protecting me since I was born. That means the reason for all this might lie in my past. In who I was before my parents adopted me. If I find out who I was, I just might learn the truth."

Gabriel grasped Matt's shoulders. His eyes darkened with worry. "Matt, your past is best left in the past. To stir it up will only invite more heartache. And danger. You need to leave it alone."

"Then you tell me," he told Gabriel. "You know where I was born and who my parents were. Give me the information I need."

"I can't. You know that."

"I do," he smiled. He stood on his tiptoes and planted a kiss on Gabriel's lips. He crossed the room to where his clothes lay in a heap. "Which is why I'll find out myself."

"Matt, please," Gabriel pleaded. "Listen to me."

Someone knocked on the front door.

"Coming," Matt called out. He turned back to Gabriel as he pulled his pants back on. Although Matt knew Gabriel wouldn't approve of him finding answers on his own, Gabriel wasn't giving Matt much of a choice. He needed to learn why demons wanted him dead. In those answers rested the solution that would keep him and those he loved safe. Besides, Matt knew knowledge was power. Without it, he was helpless, and it wasn't a feeling he enjoyed.

It would be far easier for Gabriel to simply tell him, but he and Gabriel had broken enough rules. He didn't want to push their luck. Whether Gabriel approved or not, Matt's decision had been made, and no matter how much Matt loved Gabriel, he wouldn't compromise on this.

"If I have to accept that you know and won't tell me," he told Gabriel. "You'll just have to accept that I'm going to search for answers until I find them."

"Hold your horses," Matt shouted to the person who continued to pound on the front door. "I'm getting dressed."

In a blur of motion, Gabriel suddenly appeared before him, still naked. "Nothing good can come of your search."

"Do you know that for certain?" Matt asked, knowing full well Gabriel couldn't lie to him.

Gabriel sighed. "I do not."

Matt arched his eyebrow, signifying that he had won the argument, but Gabriel continued trying to convince him anyway. "That doesn't mean I'm not right. I know the past you seek. It's best left behind you."

He sidestepped Gabriel and continued forward. "And here I thought angels knew everything."

"I'm not Father," he replied. "I know only what He allows me to know. I cannot see the future, unless that is His will. I'm powerful but not omniscient or omnipresent."

"Well then, I guess we'll find out together," Matt told him as his hand rested on the front door. "Or rather you'll be there when I find out. And I will." He admired Gabriel's naked body for a few more moments before speaking. "Now, as much as I love seeing you naked, you need to put on some clothes. I don't want the world to know you as I do." He blew Gabriel a kiss. "What you got there is for my entertainment only."

Gabriel held his hands up in exasperation. "Fine, but this conversation is not over."

"Oh, yes it is," sung Matt as Gabriel disappeared into the bedroom to fetch his clothes. When the bedroom door shut, he swung the front door open.

Matt's breath caught in his throat, when he saw who waited on the other side.

A man, with golden hair and eyes just as blue as Gabriel's, gazed down at him.

"Hello, Matthew," the man spoke. "I'd like to speak to my brother."

Although he had never seen this man before, Matt instinctively recognized him. The glow in his eyes and the smile on his face were all too familiar. The fairer skin and blond hair seemed to be the only difference. When Matt tried to answer, his mouth refused to obey. All he managed was to mutter a one-word question. "Brother?"

"Gabriel," he responded. "Would you tell him Michael is here to see him?"

CRAIG refused to take being dumped lying down, especially since nothing about this situation felt right to him. Something was off. He had no proof, only a hunch. It gnawed away at the back of his mind the same way a curious smell piqued the interest of a bloodhound. It was only a gut instinct, but his intuition had gotten him this far in his career. He wasn't about to start ignoring it now.

Gabriel's presence in Matt's life demanded investigation. Although he no longer believed Gabriel to be the cause of Matt's problems, he suspected there was more to his involvement than was already known. Matt might know some of the truth, but he doubted Gabriel had provided all the facts.

And those facts might be the difference between life and death. Craig couldn't live with himself if he allowed his broken heart to interfere with Matt's safety, even if Matt chose Gabriel over him.

Matt's decision didn't affect how Craig felt. He loved Matt, and love meant doing what was best for the other person. Whether that person wanted it or not. And while it might not be in the cards for him and Matt to have a future together, doing this might give Craig the closure he needed to move on.

Craig crossed the homicide department, where he had been temporarily assigned, and approached the desk of Detective Ybarra. He had been the detective in charge of the Dr. Owens case and had conducted most of the interviews with Gabriel and Matt. Since both had been cleared and the case closed, Craig anticipated a buttload of questions on why some rookie wanted to look over the files of a seasoned detective.

If he didn't play his cards right, he might piss off someone and ruin his homicide career before it even began.

"Ybarra," he spoke as he approached the man's desk.

Ybarra peered over his thick-rimmed glasses at him. Like most veteran detectives, his physique, though still intimidating at over six feet and about two hundred pounds, looked worn down. The stress of this profession wreaked havoc on one's body and soul. Most of the men and women who chose homicide worked themselves to near death and exhaustion as there was always another dead body found and another criminal to be brought to justice. As he looked into Ybarra's tired, brown eyes, he realized how much he admired men like Ybarra, who dedicated themselves to helping others instead of themselves.

"What is it, Belton?" he asked. "You're looking at me like you wanna get in my pants or something."

"Sorry," Craig apologized as he felt his cheeks flush with the familiar burn of embarrassment. He didn't realize he had been staring as long as he had obviously been. "I was just wondering if I could take a look at the Owens file."

The man took off his glasses and eyed him suspiciously. "Why's that? Case has been closed. I was just about to send it down to the file room."

"Just a hunch, sir," he replied, hoping the detective sensed eagerness instead of criticism.

"A hunch? About what? It was self-defense."

"Something's just not sitting right."

Detective Ybarra opened up the file, which sat in his outbox and peered through it. "You think one of these two guys is hiding something?" When he gazed back at Craig, he looked at him with the probing eyes of an investigator.

"Not Westlake, sir," he replied, hoping he didn't sound like a lovesick schoolboy. "The other one. His presence at three scenes involving Ma—I mean, Westlake seems curious."

"Curious?" Detective Ybarra asked with a snort. "It's more than curious. It's damn well suspicious if you ask me. But there's nothing to go on. CSI reports corroborate their stories." He stared at Craig in silence, obviously expecting something enlightening to come out of Craig's mouth.

"I understand, but I just thought I'd take a look. If you don't mind."

The man stared at him with eyes that sensed the truth hidden behind Craig's suspicion. "I understand hunches. It's our bread and butter, but I've gotta warn you, Belton. Don't let your personal life cloud your professional judgment. That's a one-way ticket out of homicide. Especially for you."

Craig nodded. "I understand, sir. But I think there's something there that we might be missing."

Before the detective could answer, the phone on his desk rang. "Ybarra," he answered while he continued staring at Craig. The concern in the man's eyes changed to battle-hardened gloom as he wrote down some information on his notepad. "Call the coroner's office and have them meet us there," he said before hanging up the phone.

"Your personal vendetta will have to wait," he said as he stood. "Double homicide at a truck stop on the Katy Freeway. Grab your shit and let's go."

Craig nodded and headed back for his desk, picking up his keys and cell phone, and as he followed Detective Ybarra out of the department and toward the elevator, a strange feeling overpowered him.

He couldn't shake the idea that somehow the dead bodies at the truck stop were connected to Matt.

MATT motioned Michael into the apartment and shut the door behind him. His constricted throat continued to prevent words from escaping. The shock of finding another archangel on his doorstep had yet to subside. He had just grown accustomed to the presence of one heavenly being. Now that two were present under his roof, he wondered whom he might find on the other side of his front door the next time he opened it.

For some reason, the idea terrified him.

"Don't be alarmed, Matthew," Michael spoke in a lyrical tone similar to Gabriel's as he strode into the living room. Dressed in khaki pants and a long-sleeve white button-down shirt, he looked more like a professor than the Angel of Mercy. His blue eyes, however, the same sky blue as Gabriel's, revealed not only his purity of being but the power hidden within. Inside Michael resided the potential fury of a natural disaster, but when he spoke, his words took on a soothing quality, like a lullaby. "I mean you no harm."

Matt nodded in response. His throat still closed shut.

"Should I get Gabriel or will you?" Michael asked. His gaze settled on the closed bedroom door. "I assume he's still in your bedchamber."

Michael took a step toward the door before Matt found his voice. "I'll get him," he told Michael.

The angel nodded and retreated to the couch, when Gabriel's voice came from the other room. "Who is it?" he asked. "Is it safe to come out? I still don't have a shirt. None of yours will fit me."

"Just come out," Matt called back. "It's for you."

"For me?" He heard the confusion in Gabriel's voice.

When Gabriel exited the bedroom and saw Michael sitting on the couch, his wings sprouted from his back, knocking over a side table and some books. He then positioned himself between his brother and Matt.

"What's the meaning of this?"

"Stand down, Gabriel," Michael replied, while placing his hands in his lap. "I'm not here to fight."

"Then answer my question." His wings were still spread wide, shielding Matt from a suspected salvo of celestial fury.

"I'm here to talk. Obviously. Now tuck back your wings."

Gabriel eyed Michael suspiciously before glancing over his shoulder at Matt. It was evident from the concern in Gabriel's eyes that he wasn't sure if he should believe his brother's story.

"It'll be fine," Matt reassured him. "He's an angel. Just like you. His word means just as much as yours does. Right?"

Nodding, Gabriel inhaled, and his wings fluttered back to their tattoo form.

"Does my word no longer mean anything to you?" Michael asked Gabriel. "Must a mortal now speak toward my character?"

Matt walked to Gabriel's side, hoping the move expressed the solidarity he wanted to demonstrate. "I'm sure Gabriel meant no offense," he said. "He's likely just as shocked as I am that you're here."

"I don't know why. Considering what has occurred."

Michael's words needed no further clarification. Apparently, Heaven knew that he and Gabriel had had sex.

"Is that why you're here? To chide me?"

Michael shook his head at his brother. "As Raguel pointed out, you're not an angel of words, dear brother. You're the Angel of Vengeance. Action communicates more than spoken argument."

Gabriel's muscles tensed, and the tattoo on his back fluttered. "So, you are here to fight?"

"Action isn't solely defined through a brawl. If you wish to spar, I won't deny you the pleasure, but as you know our battles are capable of devastating cities." His eyes locked onto Gabriel's. No anger raged; his face was as calm as an ocean breeze. "Is that what you want?"

Shaking his head, Gabriel sighed and relaxed. "I do not."

"Then, sit," said Michael with a wave of his hand. "We have much to discuss."

Matt sat down in the love seat, adjacent to the couch, where Michael rested. Gabriel positioned himself next to Matt, making sure to keep himself between Michael and Matt at all times. While Matt appreciated Gabriel's protective nature, his actions worried Matt a great deal. They told him that demons weren't the only ones they had to contend with. Based on the rules they had broken, Heaven might no longer be an ally.

"I'm surprised to find you here," Gabriel at last spoke. "I can usually sense your presence."

Michael nodded. "And you did not?"

"No. Which is why I suspected an attack. A sly angel is a deadly angel."

"Quite true," he agreed with Gabriel. "But I wasn't masking my presence. You simply failed to detect my approach."

Concern dimmed the light in Gabriel's eyes. "Impossible. We always sense one another."

"Yet you failed to sense me," Michael pointed out. "What does that tell you?"

Gabriel stood, looking around. "That you're lying." His eyes scoured the room, searching for more unseen threats. "Who else is with you? Raguel? Chamuel?"

Michael looked inconsolable. His eyes drooped with profound sadness. "No one else is with us," he assured. "That is my solemn vow."

Reaching up to take Gabriel's hand, Matt pulled him back onto the couch. His body remained tense, and his eyes continued to search the room. "I think he's telling the truth. Why don't you believe him?"

"Because I should have sensed him. There's no other explanation for his presence catching me off guard."

"Yes, there is," Michael chimed in. "And you know it."

Matt shifted his gaze from Michael's face shrouded in misery to the look of panic that seized Gabriel's tanned features. "What's going on?"

"My brother's heavenly powers are waning. A result of the most recent actions undertaken."

Michael's response made Matt angry. He couldn't believe that Gabriel was being penalized for being in love, for expressing with his body what his heart and soul longed to communicate. According to what he learned from the Bible and from Gabriel, Heaven was better than that. Perhaps they needed a reminder.

"I can't believe you're hurting Gabriel this way," Matt voiced through gritted teeth. He found it difficult to contain the anger that spewed forth. "We love each other. How we choose to express that love is up to us. Or is Heaven now in the business of limiting free will?"

"Matt," Gabriel pleaded. "Impertinence isn't wise."

"Impertinence?" he asked. "This is my house. And I choose to greet my guests as they choose to greet me."

"Are you claiming I'm being disrespectful?"

Matt nodded to Michael's question.

"You're a brave man," Michael asserted. "But from you I would expect no less. However, you're wrong to accuse me of impertinence. No one is punishing my brother. His inability to sense me is symptomatic of the problem. The one I was sent here to demonstrate."

"That's what you referred to then?" Gabriel asked. "When you said actions would prove far more useful."

Michael nodded.

"I still don't understand what's going on."

"It's quite simple," Michael replied to Matt. "By embracing carnal pleasure, Gabriel has dulled his abilities, the very gifts from Father that he so expertly used to protect you from harm. This puts you in grave danger."

Matt turned to Gabriel, who had difficulty meeting his gaze. "I don't understand how that's possible. You're still the same man you were before."

"But that's the problem," replied Gabriel. "I'm not a man."

"Precisely," Michael agreed. "Angelic and mortal flesh weren't meant to be joined. In the past, it led to great evil. A repeat of that won't be allowed."

"I wasn't raped. I gave myself willingly to Gabriel. If you've been playing Peeping Toms in Heaven, then you know that."

"We do."

"Then, you must also realize I'm incapable of getting pregnant. Of giving birth to a brand-new race of giants."

"The merging of angel and man comes with consequences other than wretched offspring," Michael told him. "An angel is a pure being, whose power derives from that purity. It's what keeps us close to Father. It allows us to use the gifts He bestowed upon us when He breathed us to life. When the purity is sullied, our connection to Father and those gifts diminishes."

"Are you saying that if we continue to be together, Gabriel will fall from grace? Like the Watchers?"

Michael nodded.

"But that's not fair. Love is meant to be kind. It doesn't envy or boast. It doesn't get angry or dishonor those in love." Matt couldn't recall the verse from Corinthians verbatim, but he was certain his paraphrase came close. He hoped it would remind Michael and heaven above what love was designed to be.

"You're correct, Matthew," Michael conceded. "The love you two have found has never been experienced before in all of creation. It originates not out of lust but out of a spiritual connection formed between the two of you."

"Then stop this," he pleaded. "Surely Heaven is capable of that."

"Heaven is capable of a great deal, but it cannot stop what is meant to be. That is part of the free will Father's creations have been given. Choices exist, but for every choice, consequences are found. This is one such consequence. As Father cannot stop someone from choosing evil, He cannot and will not come between the two of you. Yet if you choose this path, if you decide to embrace the pleasures of the flesh, Gabriel's power will fade away, and he will be the Angel of Vengeance no more."

"What will that make me?" Gabriel asked.

"It will make you a man, and it will place both your mission and the man you love in jeopardy." Michael settled his gaze upon them both. "Is that a chance you're willing to take?"

Before either could answer, someone banged upon the front door. The violence of the pounding fist startled both Gabriel and Matt, who stood up. Michael, however, remained calm and still.

"Open up, bitches, we know you're home," Shane called from the other side.

"Damn straight," shouted Dee. "We also know what's going on. We've talked to Craig. Now open up, so we can give you both a piece of our minds."

Matt sighed, heavily. He had enough to contend with based on what Michael had revealed. He didn't need to add Dee and Shane's insanity to the mix, but by the way they continued to hammer on the door, Matt knew the only way to get rid of them was to deal with their collective chaos.

Then, he and Gabriel would be able to work through the problem, together.

Because no matter what Michael told them, Matt knew that he and Gabriel could take on anything, from heaven above to hell below. They just needed the opportunity to show what their love was capable of overcoming.

CHAPTER 24

SHORTLY after Matt opened the door to let Dee and Shane in, his friends blew past him like a tornado sweeping across the heartland.

"How could you?" Dee asked. Anger, like lightning, crashed across her dark face. "Craig was a nice guy. The best guy you've ever met, and you just up and dump him."

Before Matt could respond, Shane chimed in. His voice thundered in disappointment. "Not only that but you don't even tell us what the hell is going on." He crossed his arms and jutted out his right hip, his standard irritated pose. "What the hell's the matter with you?"

"A lot's happened," he told them. "And I would have gotten around to calling you both."

"Gotten around?" Shane rolled his eyes and gawked at Dee. Their dueling storm fronts of fury threatened to unleash a massive deluge of bitchiness. "Can you believe him?"

Dee shook her head and wagged her finger at him as the first drops of nastiness came crashing down. "Oh hell no. We're your best friends, not something you check off a list."

"If you'd just calm down."

"Don't tell me to calm down, honey," Dee warned. "I've a right to be pissed off at you."

"Perhaps if you'd allow Matt to speak, he could explain," offered Gabriel, who walked up behind Dee and Shane unaware of the storm headed for him.

When the two of them turned around, their clouds of rage released their full volley.

"Do you ever wear a damn shirt?" Dee asked. "Or do you walk around half naked just so you can steal guys away from their boyfriends?"

"Dee!" Matt shouted as Gabriel's face flushed. The cattiness of her attack caught Gabriel completely off guard. "What's the matter with you?"

"What's the matter with me?" she asked Matt. "What's the matter with *you*!" She waved her hands in Gabriel's direction. "Every time this guy shows up, he's half-naked and turns you stupid."

"I'm not a fan of the stupid," Shane added. His eyes danced lecherously across Gabriel's muscular torso. "But I kinda like the half-naked part."

Dee smacked Shane on the shoulder. "Really, horn dog? I don't need you eye fucking Gabriel too."

"I don't like cursing," Gabriel told her. His previous stunned silence vanished. His grimace and hard eyes communicated his displeasure as he stared straight into the pair's coalescing storm.

"Yeah, well, I don't like you," Dee blurted. She crossed over to him, and though she was about ten inches shorter than Gabriel, she attempted to get in his face. If the atmosphere weren't so tense, Matt would find the image comical instead of verging on the absurd. "Home wreckers are lower than dirt in my eyes."

"That's enough!" Matt boomed. The rage in his voice caught all of them by surprise. Never before had Matt been so upset at his friends than he was at this moment. He understood their anger stemmed from worry about his well-being. They were trying to piece together what was going on with Matt since he hadn't spoken to them about his break up with Craig, but he wasn't about to let them run over him like a trailer park in the path of a tornado. He had enough to deal with, and if they couldn't be supportive or at least cordial, then they could just leave.

Dee's eyes became narrow slits. "Who do you think you're yelling at?"

"You," Matt told Dee. "The same person who's come into my apartment screaming like a banshee." She opened her mouth to speak, but Matt cut her off, dispelling her tempest with his own. "I'm sorry for not telling you what's been going on, but that doesn't give you the right to come in here and scream at me, much less the man I love."

"Love?" Shane asked, staring at Dee, who shrugged her shoulders in reply.

"That's right. Love. I'm sorry if you don't like it, but who I love isn't up for approval by committee. If you can't be nice and accept that's the way I feel, then just go. I don't need your shit right now."

As usual, Shane folded first, his storm abating as quickly as it had come on. "I'm sorry, man," he said before crossing to give Matt a hug. When he spoke, his tone became contrite. "We're just worried about you. You haven't been yourself these past few days. Isn't that right, Dee?"

Dee glared at Matt, her expression frozen in embarrassment masking as outrage. Whenever she realized she was wrong or jumped the gun, it always took her a few moments to retract the claws and make nice. Bullheaded to the end, she simply snorted in reply.

"That's as good as it's gonna get right now," Shane commented. "You know that as well as I do."

Matt nodded and flashed a smile at Dee in hopes of calling a cease-fire. She averted her eyes in feigned pissiness, but the raging storm slowly grew calm. Her thinly stretched lips relaxed as proof.

"And I'm sorry for throwing a bitch fit," Shane told Gabriel. He extended his hand toward Gabriel, who welcomed the truce with a shake.

"Thank you," Gabriel replied. "I know your anger was born from concern, but I do wish you would stop cursing."

Shane laughed. "You really hate that shit, don't you?"

"You have no idea how much."

"Fine," he told Gabriel. "I'll try to control my potty mouth, but cursing is like breathing to me. It just comes naturally."

"Are you going to tell us what's been going on with you or not?" Dee asked. She wrung her hands together, which was her way of apologizing without having to admit she was wrong.

Matt nodded. "Let's go sit first."

When they entered the living room, Michael still sat on the couch, his hands resting comfortably in his lap. He greeted Dee and Shane with a friendly smile. "Is the fighting all done?"

"Who the hell are you?" Shane asked.

"Shane!" Gabriel yelled.

Sighing in response to Gabriel's frustration, he repeated his question, "Who the heck are you?" Shane glanced at Gabriel who nodded approvingly.

"I'm Michael," he announced, rising to shake Shane's hand before delivering a soft peck to Dee's cheek. "Gabriel's brother." Afterward, he returned to his seat.

"Brother?" Shane asked giving Michael the once over. He immediately dashed over to him. "I see being hot is a family trait."

Matt glanced uncomfortably at Gabriel and then back to Michael. He didn't want either of them to strike down his friend for coming on to the archangel. While Gabriel appeared aghast, Michael looked only amused. "Shane, please don't," Matt pleaded.

"What?" he complained in response. "You know I prefer blonds."

Dee walked over to slap Shane across the back of his head. "Cool it or I'll turn the hose on you."

"I never get to have fun."

"You have *too* much fun," Dee told him as she took the seat next to Michael. "That's the problem."

Shane attempted to scoot Dee over, so he could sit next to Michael, but she wouldn't budge. Defeated, and grumbling rather loudly, he occupied the seat across from the couch while Matt and Gabriel sat on the love seat.

"So, tell us what's going on," Dee told Matt.

Matt filled in his friends about the events at Dr. Owens' office, omitting the demonic possession and the heavenly assistance Gabriel provided. Even though they were his best friends, his story had to remain consistent with the police reports.

Shane spoke first. "I can't believe Dr. Owens tried to kill you!"

"I can't believe you almost died again!" Dee added, incredulously.

"And I would be dead too, but Gabriel saved me. Again."

Dee shifted her attention to Gabriel. The previous storm in her eyes disappeared completely. "Thank you for keeping Matt safe. You're like his guardian angel or something."

Michael laughed.

"What's so funny?"

"Nothing," he told Dee. "My brother just has a knack for rescuing persons in distress."

"Well thank God," Dee exclaimed.

"That would be correct."

Dee stared crossways at Michael, unsure how to take his response.

"But you're okay?" Shane asked. "You weren't hurt?"

Matt nodded, grateful for Shane's interruption. "I'm fine."

For a few moments, they sat in silence. Dee and Shane mulled over the information while Michael's eyes found Gabriel's. The two exchanged unspoken communication that revealed to Matt that Michael hadn't finished his business with his brother.

"I'm going to go see the Duchess," Matt announced. Even though he didn't want to leave Gabriel's side, he somehow knew that the rest of Michael's message was meant for Gabriel's ears only. Going to visit his grandmother would give them the opportunity to be alone, and it would also be where he would start the search into his past. "I need to tell her what's happened, and if she doesn't see me in person, she'll only worry."

"You've got that right," Dee agreed.

"I'll come with you," Gabriel told him. "After what happened, I don't want you to be alone."

"He'll be fine," Michael commented. "I'd appreciate some time alone with you. To finish our discussion."

"Out of the question," argued Gabriel. Hardened determination turned his eyes cold. "I'm not about to leave Matt's side for one second. You know that better than anyone."

Michael met his unwavering gaze with an unflappable smile. "I'm sure there's some other guardian angel out there who'll look after him while we chat. After all, I've come all this way."

"We'll go with him," Shane said while rising from the couch. "I was gonna call in sick today anyway."

"Again?" Dee asked. "Boy, you're gonna get yourself fired!"

"Let them fire me," he replied. "The Gap's not the only store in town, you know."

"Then it's settled," Michael replied. "Dee and Shane will go with Matt. You'll stay here with me."

Before Gabriel could protest again, Matt grabbed his hands and held them. "I'll be fine. I'm just going to my grandmother's to let her know I'm okay. She wouldn't be pleased with me if I didn't."

"It's too dangerous," Gabriel whispered. "If I had difficulty sensing Michael, I might not…" He stopped, unable to admit that he might not be able to detect Matt's distress or make it to Matt in time.

Matt kissed Gabriel and ran his fingers over Gabriel's shoulders.

"You need to hear out your brother," Matt told him. "What he has to say might be more important."

"Nothing's more important to me than you."

"And nothing's more important to me than you. That's why you need to hear him out. What if he has information you need to know about your affected abilities? Wouldn't it be better for you to find out now rather than later?"

Gabriel looked over Matt's shoulder at his brother, whom he eyed suspiciously.

"Are you boys done whispering sweet nothings in each other's ears?" Shane asked.

Matt turned to see Shane and Dee waiting for him across the room. "Maybe for now," he told them while looking at Michael. "But just for now."

Michael nodded in understanding.

"I'll be back soon," Matt told Gabriel after a parting kiss. He hoped the gesture communicated to Michael the sincerity of his feelings for his brother. Their love was nothing to hide or be embarrassed about. He wanted it to be out in the open for all to see.

After grabbing his keys from the coffee table, Matt crossed over to where Dee and Shane stood.

"I love you, Matt."

He turned around. Gabriel's eyes looked uncharacteristically forlorn. Being apart obviously distressed Gabriel more than anything else. "I love you too," Matt told him. "And I won't be gone long. I promise."

Gabriel nodded in reply, and Matt followed Dee and Shane out of his apartment. As he closed the door behind him, Matt suddenly feared never seeing Gabriel again, but he dismissed the idea. After all, Michael told them that Heaven wouldn't come between them. If they decided to pursue a relationship, it would be their choice.

An archangel wouldn't tell such a bold-faced lie.

CLIFFORD parked the stolen Ford Mustang in a lot directly across from an upscale apartment complex. According to the voice, his prey lived on the sixth floor, and although eager to complete his assignment and collect his stash, it wasn't the right time.

Not one but two angels protected the Gifted One. The thing within him could sense their presence.

Clifford had to wait. Fighting one angel proved difficult enough. Against two, he had no chance of winning.

He only hoped the opportunity to take out his target occurred before police discovered the bodies of Bubba and the previous owner of the car he now drove. It would do him no good for police to learn that he had survived the fire in Huntsville.

The element of surprise fit his needs perfectly, and he couldn't abandon the advantage it provided.

"Then you shouldn't have killed them," the voice inside reprimanded. "I told you to wait."

"Aw, shut the fuck up," he cursed back. Since the fire, he felt bolder, more confident about his abilities. He didn't need some voice telling him what to do. It might have helped him get out of jail, but it also got him there in the first place. As far as Clifford was concerned, this was his show, and the voice provided only the muscle. It could keep its advice to itself. "Just sit back and let me do my job. I don't need your blabbering in my ear. I killed Kenny for that, remember?"

Clifford sneered at his reflection in the rearview mirror. Although he could only glimpse himself, he knew the voice could see him. He hoped it understood how he mocked it.

"With the blade I provided," the voice reminded him. "Without me, you would be the pathetic loser you were before."

"Fuck you," Clifford told his reflection. "I ain't no fucking loser, you goddamned fucktard."

The voice chuckled. "Of course not. Your vocabulary proves how great you are."

"Yeah, well you can suck my motherfucking dick."

"All muscle. No brain."

"Ya think so?" he asked his mirror image. "Then how come I fucking know that the only reason those angels in there haven't sensed you is because I'm still in control of my own fucking body. You think you're so fucking bad, well, then take me over. Come on. Don't be some pussy chickenshit afraid of those angels." He stared hard at his reflection, daring the voice to take him over as it did when he had killed the Westlakes over twenty years earlier. "Come on. Do it!"

Clifford felt no sudden change come over him. The last time, his flesh had boiled as it took over, and the blood in his veins turned to fire. It had been excruciatingly painful. But as he sat there staring at himself, he felt nothing. He knew he had the damn voice by its invisible balls.

"Didn't fucking think so," he said, flipping himself off in the mirror.

Even more than before, he felt unstoppable. Thanks to the voice, who now had to listen to him, he had the power to do what needed to be done, and once he killed Matthew Westlake, riches and power beyond imagining were his.

So what if he had to kill Bubba and that young kid?

They were means to an end. Bubba got him to Houston. Once he was here, he didn't need that old fart anymore, so he killed him with one blow of a tire iron to the back of his skull. It had given him the rig to drive and some peace and quiet, but the eighteen-wheeler was too obvious. He needed something subtler, so when he pulled into a truck stop, where that young kid was cruising the toilets, he twisted his neck after the guy had sucked him off.

Now, he had a car and a freshly milked cock. What more could he ask for?

The front door to the apartment building opened, and Clifford smiled.

Matt pranced out of the complex and the only people with him were a mighty fine-looking sister with enough junk in her trunk for a family of five and another limp-wristed pansy boy. No angel accompanied them.

When they piled into the black Jeep Wrangler, Clifford started the Mustang's engine and followed them down the street.

DURING the entire drive down the Katy Freeway toward the truck stop off Studemont Street, Craig couldn't shake the hunch that the dead bodies found by a rig operator on the property were somehow linked to Matt.

The idea terrified him, causing him to remain quiet for much of the car trip. Ybarra didn't mind the silence. Craig had worked with the man for the past two weeks and knew that the detective preferred to remain focused while approaching a crime scene rather than chitchatting about non-case related topics.

Craig hoped the fear that suddenly gripped him back at the station would subside by the time they arrived, but as their destination came into view and their squad car screeched to a halt, his heart sank even lower.

The truck stop called Merle's, according to the sign, looked like something out of a horror movie. Broken asphalt with weeds sprouting between the cracks branched out in every direction, and huge oil stains, which resembled pools of blood, spotted the parking lot.

Toward the rear of the structure sat two eighteen-wheelers parked outside of the men's room, which truckers commonly used to shower and sometimes fuck. In front of the two rigs stood a police officer talking to a man dressed in jeans and a button-down long sleeve. As they chatted, the flashing lights atop the officer's squad car cast red and blue reflections onto the building and surrounding empty lot.

It made the area look deserted and ominous.

As they exited the vehicle and walked toward the officer and the man he spoke with, Craig scanned the lot for the dead bodies. He didn't want to admit it, but he half expected to see Matt's Jeep somewhere in the general vicinity.

When he didn't, he felt a bit better. But not much.

"What you got?" Ybarra asked the young officer, whose name was Walters. His clean-shaven face and boyish looks made him look like a teenager.

"Two dead bodies, sir," he responded. "This gentleman arrived on scene approximately thirty minutes ago and found the first dead body in the men's room. The victim's driver's license identifies him as Joseph Baldwin. Only twenty-three years old."

The news eased Craig's troubled soul. His intuition that Gabriel the stalker had kidnapped Matt, dragged him to this truck stop, and murdered him disappeared upon hearing the first man's identity. If the first victim wasn't Matt, it was easier to convince himself that the second body wasn't Matt either.

"And the second?"

"That one's in the rig on the right. His name was Robert Brody, and his age was fifty-five."

Craig wanted to shout out in joy, but he managed to restrain himself. Thankfully, Ybarra was too occupied with writing in his tiny notepad to notice the look of relief on his face.

"Who found Mr. Brody?" Craig asked as the CSI cars arrived. He cleared his throat and schooled his face. It would do Craig no good to walk around with a smile at a crime scene.

"I did," Officer Walters replied. "I thought Baldwin might have been the rig operator, but when I opened up the truck, I found Brody's body in the back."

"Okay everyone," Ybarra announced to the small crowd of police officers gathered around him. "You know the drill. Dust for fingerprints and scour for clues. Make sure the entire area is cordoned off."

Everyone headed out to perform their assigned tasks while Craig followed Ybarra toward the eighteen-wheeler. They pulled on their latex gloves to avoid contaminating the crime scene and stepped up into the rig.

In the back, like Walters had described, lay Robert Brody. His head caved in from a blow to the back of the skull.

"What do you see?" Ybarra asked him.

Craig looked around, wanting to examine the scene carefully before he spoke. This was Ybarra's way of testing him, and now that he knew none of the bodies would be Matt, Craig felt better able to focus on his job and prove to Detective Ybarra that he belonged on homicide full-time. "Blood spatter indicates the victim was in the driver's seat when he was struck from behind. From the blood trail, I'd say he was pulled into the back of the cab, and the assailant began operating the vehicle."

The detective nodded. "Nicely done," he commented as he crawled out of the vehicle. "Now let's check out the other one."

As they walked toward the men's room, the fear that had previously almost immobilized Craig returned. It crawled along his spine like a thousand spiders, and he didn't understand why. None of the victims were Matt. There was no possible way this could be connected to him, but when they entered the men's room and found the young man's body on the floor, the emotion grew stronger.

"Broken neck," Ybarra announced as he stepped carefully around the body and the CSI who worked around the dead man.

Craig nodded, still unable to speak. He looked around for more evidence, something that would somehow tie this to Matt. All he found were graffiti-stained walls advertising cocksuckers and their phone numbers, yellow stained urinals, and toilets he would never in his life sit down on to use.

"We have body fluids," one of the lab guys announced.

The detective and Craig crossed back to the body.

"It looks to be semen. We'll run it through the database and see if we have any matches."

Detective Ybarra nodded at the crime scene investigator as he rubbed the five o'clock shadow that grew across his chin. "So our victim gives the killer a blow job and when the perp comes, he breaks the guy's neck? That's not much of a thanks."

"No, it's not," Craig agreed.

"But why kill him?" Detective Ybarra asked. "The young guy was no obvious threat. He looks no more than 120 pounds soaking wet. Why kill this guy and the rig operator? What's the motive?"

"I'd say Mr. Brody was killed first," Craig speculated. "And the killer drove here for some reason and then ran across Mr. Baldwin in the bathroom."

"Yeah, I got that much," barked Ybarra. "Tell me something I haven't figured out. This guy wasn't killed because he was a bad cocksucker."

Craig hated himself for stating the obvious. Since the driver of the rig was killed in the vehicle and placed in the back, the murderer had obviously arrived here after killing Mr. Brody, not before. It would make no sense for him to kill the man in the rig, move his body into the backseat, and then exit a good getaway vehicle.

That was when the answer hit him hard. "For his car," Craig whispered. "Both victims still have their wallets and their money. There was no other car in the lot except the two rigs."

"Which means our perp has taken off with Mr. Baldwin's car," Detective Ybarra added. "We put out an APB for that car, and with any luck, we'll get our killer."

"I'll call it in," Craig said as he turned around to head for their police car. Though he found no evidence to justify his hunch that this involved Matt and had helped deduce what could potentially lead to this murderer's capture, he felt no joy, only unease.

He needed to find out who the assailant was and fast because somehow he knew Matt's life depended on it.

FROM inside his truck, Homer stared out at the bricked exterior of the Tudor-style estate. It sat behind an automated iron fence, and at least five hundred feet of lush green lawn separated the main house from the road. The closest neighbor looked to be at least two hundred feet away to the east.

He couldn't have asked for a better place to reacquaint himself with the now fully-grown infant he had failed to murder.

All he had to do was gain access, which should prove easy enough. The lie he and the voice concocted was plausible and timely. The thing he carried around inside him knew Matt yearned to understand the tragedies that had befallen him as a child.

It seemed only right that someone with connections to his past finally came looking for him.

CHAPTER 25

AFTER Matt left with Dee and Shane for his grandmother's house, Gabriel silently stared at the closed door. An overwhelming need to be by Matt's side, to protect him from approaching harm, filled him with desperate urgency. He almost chased after Matt, despite Michael's insistent desire to speak with him in private.

Matt remained his primary duty. Listening to further chastisement his brother preferred to dish out one-to-one paled in comparison to his role as Matt's guardian angel, a role Father had assigned to him. But when he closed his eyes and concentrated, he sensed no immediate danger. No demons lay in wait to strike. For the time being, Matt appeared to be safe.

That was if his senses could be trusted.

Michael had already proven that his gifts had been compromised by his knowledge of fleshly desire. If they had not been, he would have sensed his brother's arrival and not have been surprised to find Michael standing in Matt's apartment.

"I already told you he would be safe," Michael repeated. He still sat on the couch with his hands placed calmly on his lap. "I sense no demon afoot."

Michael's demeanor worried him. His brother looked too calm, as if he were only pretending to be composed, but when he gazed deep into Michael's blue eyes, they appeared serene, not turbulent.

"Say your piece, then," Gabriel told him. "So I can return to where I belong."

"And where would that be?"

"You speak your question with hidden meaning. Why not simply give voice to what is really on your mind?"

Michael, who had been staring straight ahead and avoiding eye contact, shifted his gaze to Gabriel. Stray thunderclouds drifted across the calm skies reflected within. "Direct and to the point as always, I see?"

"Why should being in love alter the angel I've always been? I remain the brother you've known since the dawn of creation. That has not changed."

Michael shook his head in disagreement. "You fail to see the obvious, brother. The blinders which you now wear are cause for great concern."

The conversation was going nowhere. Michael seemed only intent on provoking a fight; a goal Gabriel wouldn't indulge. "If you only asked me to stay behind to ruffle my feathers, I see no point in remaining here." He turned and crossed to the door. "I have far more pressing duties."

"And what duty are you referring to?"

Gabriel turned to face his brother. Michael's persistent passive-aggressive questioning quickly became frustrating. As he had mentioned before, Gabriel was an angel of action not words. If his brother had something to say, he had better well say it instead of pussyfooting around the issue. "I beg you to speak your mind," he insisted. "You waste my time as well as your own."

"Agreed," Michael nodded. He rose from the couch and paced. "Let's start with my first question: where do you think you belong?"

"At Matt's side. He is my charge. I'm to protect him with my life if need be."

"And you believe this to be your greatest duty?"

"What could be greater than protecting the Gifted One from the evil that amasses around him?"

"So Matt is your greatest duty then?" Michael reiterated as he stopped at a photo of Matt, Dee, and Shane, which sat on the sofa table.

"It's the duty I've been given," Gabriel replied. "By Father."

"Yes, yes," he said with a wave of his hand. He picked up the frame and examined the picture more closely. "We're all well aware that Father assigned you the task, but the assignment didn't include falling in love with the one you were sent to protect, much less falling into sin."

His last comment rang with an irate timbre.

Before Matt, Gabriel would have lashed out at being spoken to as if he were a child. While he still preferred action to words, he now understood the importance of patience, a virtue he had never truly possessed. So in an effort to keep things civil, he inhaled deeply and calmed the inner swell of anger. Now that he knew love in both spiritual and physical form, it had changed him. Matt's love centered his being and anchored him to what was really important.

Arguing with his brother fell short of that.

"I have no wish to engage in debate about the love Matt and I share," he finally replied once he had wrangled in his hostility. Letting go of the aggression and embracing the tranquility he found with Matt made him proud.

He truly was better for knowing and loving Matt.

"There's nothing to debate," Michael commented. "Your answers themselves prove how far you have fallen."

"Fallen?" The accusation churned his serene waters into a turbulent pool. "Choose your words carefully, Michael. I won't take being compared to Samyaza."

"You deny the similarities then?"

"No, but you fail to see the differences. Differences already made apparent to you."

"I fail to see nothing," Michael replied. He placed Matt's photograph back on the table and stood rigid before Gabriel. "Your priorities have skewed, and your sense of duty has shifted from the righteous path."

"How so?"

"While you think I don't see the differences, I do. I sense the love in your heart for Matthew as well as the love he holds for you."

"Then you make my point for me," Gabriel replied with a grin.

"No," Michael pointed out. "You make my point for *me*. We are archangels, Gabriel. Our hearts and our souls belong to Father. We are to have no earthly wants or desires. To have them clouds our divine duties. Collectively, we are agents of mercy, justice, love, healing, wisdom, peace—" He paused, staring at Gabriel before continuing. "—and vengeance. How are we to fulfill our place in creation if we cease performing in the manner with which we are expected? What happens to the Grand Design when we embrace carnal pleasures that blur the lines between heaven and earth?"

"I would never place the Grand Design in jeopardy."

"Yet you do," Michael accused. "By embracing earthly pleasure you abandon your ultimate duty as the Angel of Vengeance."

"I abandon nothing. I embrace it freely as I always have."

"Yet your abilities are waning. I've already proven this. And the longer you deviate from your true path, the more unbalanced the Grand Design becomes. Did we not already learn this with Samyaza and the Watchers? They left Heaven to dally with women. Those couplings unleashed evil never meant to walk the land."

"And I helped right that wrong. I stood by my brothers as Father commanded, and enacted the warranted vengeance. My union with Matt cannot produce Nephilim or anything of its kind."

Michael agreed. "It cannot. But just because it might not produce another race of giants doesn't mean it won't lead to similar, if not greater, evil."

"The evil Samyaza and his followers created grew from lust, not love. Chamuel himself should know this."

"He does," Michael admitted. "We've discussed this already."

Although he wasn't surprised, the news worried Gabriel. The archangels had gathered to discuss his actions in the Throne Room. This meant that a decision about Gabriel's future had been made. If he had known this earlier, he never would have let Matt out of his sight. "And what did Chamuel say of it?"

"I spoke from my heart, brother. As I always have and will forever do."

To Gabriel's right, Chamuel materialized. Dressed in white shorts and a green tank top, his red hair ablaze in the sunlight.

"It's good to see you again," said Chamuel. "You've been away for far too long."

Gabriel nodded, his eyes searching for the remainder of his brothers.

"What's the matter?" Michael asked, though he knew the answer. "Did Chamuel's presence also catch you by surprise?"

"You claimed you were alone," Gabriel told Michael as the tattoo across his back fluttered. "You lied."

"I did no such thing. We were alone. When you asked the question."

"And now?"

Michael sighed as the remaining archangels blinked into view.

Normally, seeing his brothers assembled triggered unbridled joy. In their presence, he felt complete and at peace, even when they quarreled. After all, they were all connected, pieces of the same fabric that held the universe together.

No such connection existed at the moment. Gabriel felt detached as if the threads that once bound them together had frayed, allowing only the most tenuous of bonds.

"You look surprised, Gabriel," Uriel spoke as he walked around, inspecting Matt's apartment. Like Michael, whenever Uriel appeared, he wore more formal attire. This time clothed in a tan sports coat, button down, and olive pants.

"His abilities have been compromised," Raguel announced from within his black motorcycle jacket and torn denim. "A fact you well know."

"A minor setback," Gabriel told his brothers. His angel wing tattoo itched like mad.

"We certainly hope so," Raphael added. "It wouldn't be home without you."

"I take it then I will be allowed to return?"

"That is why we are here," Michael told him. "To decide just that."

Gabriel stared back into the eyes of his brothers, which reflected the uncertainty that raged inside their warring souls. They wanted him to ascend back to Heaven, to again take his place at their side, but each feared that would not be the case.

They worried that Gabriel would choose Matt and a life as a man over his role as the Angel of Vengeance, and if he made that choice, each one remained unsure as to what their actions or the ramifications of such a decision would be.

In truth, Gabriel wondered exactly what would happen to him and Matt after his brothers were through with him.

THE iron gate separating his grandmother's property from the road swung open and once Matt had driven through, it closed immediately behind. As he pulled into the parking area of the Tudor-style estate in River Oaks, Matt's previously troubled heart began to calm.

Ever since he had left Gabriel with Michael, he had fought the irresistible urge to turn the car around and head back to his apartment. The sad, lost look in Gabriel's eyes when he closed the front door had been out of character. He had only known Gabriel to look out into the world with confidence and strength.

But the angel he left looked troubled, as if some hidden threat waited for Gabriel once Matt left his side.

Matt tried chalking up the expression to Gabriel's dread of rehashing what they had done with his brother, but the more he thought about it and the more distance that separated them, the greater was the weight of concern that pressed against his chest.

Dee and Shane must have sensed his unease because they chatted nonstop the entire drive over from his apartment. Whenever one of them appeared uneasy, they always resorted to discussing upcoming events or gossiping about the latest men in their lives. Dee had a date for next weekend, and Shane's ex, Karl, had been begging Shane to take him back. Matt contributed to the conversation with the occasional follow up question or nod of his head, but he wasn't interested in their standard methods of distraction.

He had been on the verge of turning the car around when his grandmother's expansive twelve-thousand-square-foot house came into view. For many, the six-bedroom and five-bath residence might seem cold and impersonal. To him, it was home.

Here, he felt safe and loved. Nothing existed in the outside world capable of harming him once he set foot on the concrete driveway or walked onto the marbled foyer with the iron banister of the spiral staircase unwrapping itself to the left of the front door.

Being home chased away his troubles and made him think logically.

Gabriel was with Michael, who was not only his brother but an archangel. Matt had nothing to fear from him.

"Whose truck is that?" Dee asked. She hopped out of the Jeep and walked over to inspect the Chevy Silverado. It had been parked next to the Duchess' BMW.

"Never seen it before," he replied as he headed toward the front door. "Probably someone connected to the Duchess' latest society event, I'm sure."

"Or a booty call," Shane teased. "Some young cowboy stud wearing jeans three sizes too small."

"You're disgusting," Matt announced with a grimace.

"Oh, come on, Matt. Even your grandmother needs to hop back in the saddle once in a while."

Preferring to ignore Shane's inappropriate comments, Matt walked up the front steps and used his key to unlock the door.

"Duchess!" he called out, scanning the tan interior of the sitting room that sat to the right of the foyer. Whenever his grandmother had visitors, this was the room she typically used to entertain. The room, however, was empty.

"Maybe we should come back later," Dee said at his side. "She might be otherwise occupied."

Matt rolled his eyes. "Not you too, Dee."

"Hey, I'm not judging, but I don't think any of us want to walk in on something we weren't meant to see."

He turned around and gave them both the stink eye. "My grandmother isn't doing what either of you think she's doing."

"And what do I stand accused of doing?"

The Duchess walked down the arched golden hallway that connected the sitting room to the back of the house. She wore a black long-sleeve shirt and tan pants, immaculately pressed. She was a vision of perfection, as always, and as she drew closer, Matt noticed that her face beamed with excitement that stemmed from more than just seeing her grandson. She only looked this pleased with herself when she had some surprise ready to spring on him.

"Nothing," he told his grandmother as he walked into her open arms. "You know how Dee and Shane are."

After hugging Matt, she eyed his friends suspiciously. "I do," she announced. "And you should both be ashamed of yourselves."

"Sorry, Mrs. Westlake," they apologized in unison, like two children caught being naughty by their favorite teacher.

"I never entertain such guests while it's still light out," she added after hugging first Dee then Shane.

Both broke into hysterical laughter while Matt's face turned four shades of red. "Duchess!"

"Oh, hush," she replied. "I may be your grandmother, but I'm also a woman."

"I'm not hearing this," he replied. To show how serious he was, he plugged his index fingers into his ears.

She rolled her eyes in response while Dee and Shane almost wet themselves.

"Are you finished?" he asked, tentatively removing his fingers.

"Yes," his grandmother replied. "Now, come with me to the kitchen. I've got a surprise for you."

Matt wasn't shocked to learn he was right. He could always read his grandmother like a book, but he didn't want to spoil her surprise. Her news might sound better after he dropped his latest bombshell on her. "I've got something I have to tell you first."

Her excitement disappeared, and the Duchess' face grew serious. "What is it?"

Matt filled her in on Dr. Owens, Gabriel, and Craig.

For a few moments, the Duchess stood in silence. Though she appeared visibly shaken, she did her best to maintain her composure. She blinked until her emotions were under control and cleared her throat of any tear that might cause her voice to waver. She wasn't a cold woman, but she preferred to keep her feelings private. Rarely, if ever, did she break down in public. He had only seen her do it once—at his parents' funeral.

"I'm okay," he finally told her. "As you can see. Thanks to Gabriel."

"For that I'm thankful," she replied. A thin smile stretched across her youthful face. But beneath her smile hid boundless worry.

"But?"

"But this is too much. You seem to be in danger far too often, Matthew. Every time I see you, there's a new tragedy. I'm seriously entertaining the idea of insisting you move in here with me. I can hire bodyguards to patrol the grounds and to follow you to and from work and wherever else you may go."

"I don't think that will be necessary, Duchess. I've got Gabriel. He's better than *any* bodyguard."

She wasn't convinced. Her even stare told him as much. "I've never met this Gabriel," she told him. "And while I appreciate him, he can't be everywhere at once. I can hire men who will be."

Not as effectively as Gabriel, he thought. But he couldn't share that information with anyone. With Gabriel at his side, he didn't need, much less want, a bodyguard. Having a relationship with an angel was difficult enough. Having to hide it from ever-present muscle heads would likely prove impossible. "No bodyguards," he finally told her.

She didn't look amused. Her lips once again stretched thin, and her eyes became narrow slits. If he knew his grandmother, and he did, she was formulating a counterargument that would guarantee she got her way.

"What if I promise to have Gabriel take me to work and pick me up?"

"We can help too," Dee chimed in. As always, she knew what he wanted and came to his rescue. Matt appreciated her intuition and her assistance.

"Yeah, it wouldn't be any trouble," Shane added.

The Duchess shifted her gaze from Shane to Dee before settling her reproachful stare upon her grandson. "I suppose I'm outnumbered," she admitted.

Matt gave her a peck on the cheek. "But I appreciate the sentiment. As always."

"I just don't like this," she told him. "You're the most precious person to me in the world, and I don't want *anything* to happen to you."

"Nothing will."

"You can't promise me that."

"I can," he reassured her. "I've got people who love me. Who'll watch over me."

"And one of these people is Gabriel?" she asked. From her unblinking eyes, Matt could tell she remained skeptical.

"Yes," he told her. "And I would like for you to meet him."

She nodded. "I would like that. This way, I can decide for myself if he is worthy of you."

"He is."

"And what about Craig? We all just had lunch the other day, and he got my seal of approval. I'm still not quite sure I understand what happened between you two."

"Join the crowd," Dee announced.

Matt shot her his shut-up look. In response, Dee grinned broadly, flashing her full set of pearl white teeth. It was how she said fuck you without having to say it.

The Duchess chose to ignore their exchange. Instead, she locked onto his eyes, as she used to when he was a child, demanding to know the truth. And as he shifted his gaze to Dee and Shane, he saw a similar request.

They all wanted to know *why* he would break up with Craig to be with someone he didn't even know.

They thought he was crazy. That was obvious enough, but he wasn't sure he could make them understand without divulging Gabriel's secret.

How could he tell them that he and Gabriel clicked from the moment Matt laid eyes on him? That they had a connection born out of almost thirty years of knowing each other?

Though Gabriel existed in the periphery of his life for most of that time, Matt knew him almost as well as he knew himself. Their souls had bonded over the years, and with Gabriel, he found a sanctuary like no other.

He was the man of his dreams made manifest.

How could he explain any of that without sounding as if he had lost his mind?

Matt then remembered the stories his grandmother told him about how his parents met and fell in love. His father had begrudgingly attended a society ball, where he first set eyes on his mother, who wasn't a guest. She ran the catering business that provided the appetizers and meal. His father bumped into her while she carried a full tray of lobster bisque, which she dropped, and their eyes never once noticed the mess they made.

They saw only each other and the future that stretched out before them.

"It was love at first sight," he finally answered. "Like mom and dad, I guess."

"Really?" the Duchess asked, her face awash in hope.

Matt nodded.

She took him into her arms and squeezed him tight. "I've wanted that for you for so long," she told him. "That's how your father fell in love with your mother. It's how I fell in love with your grandfather." She kissed his forehead. "Love at first sight is the Westlake way."

"I guess I'm in good company then."

"Damn straight," she replied.

"Duchess!" Matt called out. Never before had he heard his grandmother curse. Even Dee and Shane stared at her in shock.

"I curse and have sex," she told them. "Grow up."

In response, they all laughed.

"Mrs. Westlake?" a man's voice called out from the kitchen. "Is everything okay?"

"Oh my," she whispered. "I completely forgot about my surprise."

"Who is that?" Matt asked.

"You'll see." She crossed to the hallway that led to the kitchen. "Why don't you join us in the sitting room?" she asked the anonymous visitor. "I think we'd be more comfortable in here."

"Whatever you say, Mrs. Westlake," the voice called back.

From the sound of the heavy footsteps that echoed off the marbled hallway floor, his surprise was evidently someone of massive size, and when the man entered the living room, Matt took a step back.

He had never seen someone with such awkward physical proportions as the man who now stood next to his grandmother.

While not as tall as Gabriel, at just over six feet, he still managed to look twice Gabriel's size. The button-down cowboy shirt, which appeared two sizes too small, labored to confine the huge, barrel chest shoved inside. His biceps, which looked bigger than Matt's thighs, bulged beneath the fabric, and thick sausage fingers extended from hands larger than a catcher's mitt.

Though he was intimidating physically, he smiled warmly when he set his eyes upon Matt.

"This must be him," the man stated.

"It is," his grandmother nodded.

"The resemblance is uncanny."

"I thought so too," the Duchess replied. "If you hadn't shown me that picture, I don't think I would have believed it."

"What are you talking about?" Matt asked. "Resemblance to who?"

"Your mother," the man replied.

Matt had no clue what was going on. Although he shared his mother's eye color, their resemblances ended there. "I appreciate the compliment," he told the stranger. "But Nicole Westlake adopted me. I couldn't look as much like her as you seem to suggest."

"Please forgive me. I was referring to your biological mother."

"My who?" he asked, staring at his grandmother, whose face lit up.

"This is my surprise," she told him. "This man is your uncle."

"My uncle?"

The man extended his massive hand outward to Matt as he walked to him. "Yes," he answered. "I'm Homer Rodgers, and it's a pleasure to meet you. Again."

When the man's hand engulfed his, a chill traveled down the length of Matt's spine.

CHAPTER 26

WHILE Craig waited for the lab report identifying the person whose semen was left inside the victim at Merle's truck stop, he surfed the National Crime Information Center. Right now, the database was searching its computerized index of criminal records on the federal, state, and local level for any mention of Gabriel St. John.

Since he had time on his hands after notifying the victims' next of kin and the call from the lab, Ybarra gave him permission to resume his investigation into Gabriel's past. His suspicions about Gabriel still ate away at him, but when he added the bizarre sensation that somehow the murders at the truck stop tied to Matt, his intuition threatened to devour him from inside.

A connection existed somewhere. He just had to find it.

His previous inquiry into the Department of Public Safety dug up nothing, except that Gabriel had no driver's license. While that wasn't a crime, for Houston, it was certainly uncommon. Gabriel didn't strike Craig as someone who used public transportation to get around.

He either drove illegally or somehow possessed enough wealth to have a driver service.

Further scrutiny in Social Security records would provide him with exactly what kind of career Gabriel had besides stalking Matt.

His computer beeped. The NCIC search came back with hits for criminal records for three men named Gabriel St. John in Seattle, Detroit, and New York City, but none of their descriptions matched the Gabriel he searched for. Two of them were in their fifties, and the third was only eighteen.

"Damn," he cursed under his breath.

Although he knew it was a long shot, he secretly hoped to find some hidden criminal record that would validate his intuition.

Craig opened up another computer screen to search the Social Security database and see what information he could find there. After entering the social security number Gabriel had provided into the database, on another web page, he performed a Google search on Gabriel.

Ten pages of social media sites, news reports, and blogs downloaded onto his screen. After clicking on all the links, he found nothing.

Apparently, Gabriel didn't use Facebook or Twitter. In fact, he had no presence on the Internet. While still not a crime, it made Craig more suspicious.

In the digital age, most people had at least one hit in a Google search. To find nothing suggested that Gabriel had something to hide, and he was more determined than ever to find what that was.

Although it would serve Gabriel right to be hurt for being the cause of his broken heart, he wanted more than justice. He wanted payback.

Craig ran his fingers through his hair and sighed audibly. "This isn't like you," he whispered to himself.

He had never before in his life felt so overcome with the need for retribution as he did right now. It had overpowered him and begun to take on a life all its own. It even scared him a little.

Being fair-minded and impartial had always been his motivation. He had become a police officer so he could help bring about justice for those who were wronged by others. More than anything else, he wanted to protect and serve.

But he saw himself changing.

Serving and protecting seemed somehow insufficient. Delivering retribution had taken center stage, and it wasn't just with Gabriel.

When he thought about the men murdered at Merle's, Joseph Baldwin and Robert Brody, he didn't want to just bring their murderer in to face the music. He wanted payback for their deaths; anything less seemed unthinkable.

Not even the pain he had gone through with his ex-boyfriend Tony had affected him this way. It seemed he loved Matt more than he realized, and losing him so suddenly turned him into someone he didn't recognize, someone who sought vengeance over justice.

Trying to get his mind off his pain, Craig returned to the screen where the search through the Social Security site revealed one match, a Gabriel St. John who had died over fifty years ago.

A grin worked its way across Craig's face. Gabriel provided false information during an official police investigation. Not only was that grounds for dragging Gabriel's ass back into the station, but it corroborated his gut feeling.

Gabriel wasn't who he claimed to be, and that information might be enough to not only blow a hole in his relationship with Matt but satiate Craig's unquenchable need for revenge.

"Why do you look like the cat that ate the canary?"

Craig looked up to find Detective Ybarra standing in front of his desk. The man's shrewd-looking eyes revealed he already knew the answer.

"I've got him," he told the detective, to which the man replied with a nod.

"I figured as much. Only a man with information in hand to crush a rival grins like you are right now."

Even though he was correct, Craig let the comment go without response. Relishing in his victory seemed prideful, and he wasn't one of those guys. He still felt enough like himself to avoid becoming cocky. "Just glad to know my hunch was right."

The detective winked at Craig. Not a fan of boasting officers, Ybarra appreciated the humility. "What did you find?"

"It seems the social security number Gabriel gave you is fake. Belongs to some guy, of the same name, who died in 1962."

Ybarra whistled. "Only someone with something to hide does that."

"Precisely."

"You gonna call him in?"

Craig shook his head. "Not yet. I want to find what he's hiding first."

"Good idea."

"Any suggestions on where to look?"

The detective thought about the question. His brown eyes scanned the room as he internally processed the request. "Since St. John seems pretty good at covering his tracks, I'd delve into Westlake's life more. If he's been stalking Westlake like you've suspected, chances are he might turn up somewhere in Westlake's social orbit."

"I like it," he told the detective as he turned back to his screen.

As he typed Matt's name into the database and the detective walked away, Craig felt as if he was on the right track. Matt's past had been well documented over the years on social media sites and with the many friends who knew him. He might just turn over a rock and find Gabriel hiding underneath.

More pages than he cared to pore through loaded onto his computer after he googled Matthew Westlake. As he scanned the links, he found nothing interesting, but buried on the seventh page, Craig discovered an old news report covering the murder of his parents.

He recalled the painful details Matt had, one night in bed, shared with him about how a man named Clifford Crouch murdered his parents and almost killed him as well. If his door hadn't been stuck, Matt would have died.

When Matt had finished the story, Craig drew Matt into his arms and held him all night. They had made love again, and when he remembered how Matt's smooth body felt pressed against his flesh, the memory shattered his broken heart into even more pieces.

It made him angry that he lost Matt, that Gabriel now slept in Matt's bed, and that Matt had been, and still was, in danger. The need for retribution filled him more strongly than ever.

He clicked on the link, which downloaded the news excerpt and pictures of Matt and his grandmother being led to a police car on the morning after his parents were murdered. Instead of the confident, strong man he knew, Craig saw the face of a lost and hurt little boy, clutching onto the only remaining family member he had.

Matt's hazel eyes were wide with terror and pain.

But in the background of the picture, standing behind the police car, stood a man wearing sunglasses, dressed in a black leather jacket. His face was turned sideways, as if trying to avoid the cameras flashing in the foreground.

When he zoomed in on the picture, the breath caught in Craig's throat.

It was Gabriel. He had been there the day Matt's parents were murdered, and even though almost seventeen years had passed, Gabriel looked no older now than he did then.

"How is that possible?" he asked the picture. He had no idea how the man in the photo could be Gabriel, but the undeniable proof was displayed on his screen.

"Belton!" Ybarra called after hanging up his phone.

"I've found something," he told the detective. "And you're not going to believe it."

"Forget it," the man told him. "The lab just called, and they've identified the perp. DNA and fingerprints left at the scene match a Clifford Crouch, who was sitting out a life sentence at Huntsville Penitentiary."

Craig's eyes shot toward the detective. "Did you say Clifford Crouch?"

"Yes," Ybarra said as he stood up. "He was convicted of…"

"Murder," Craig replied, finishing his sentence. "He was the man who murdered Matthew Westlake's parents."

The detective stepped away from his desk and rushed to the elevator; Craig darted after him.

Craig remembered that when the Huntsville prison burned, Matt had been happy. Clifford Crouch had finally been erased from his life, and he believed that was one of the reasons his nightmares had stopped.

But the man was alive, and if he was in Houston, then that meant he probably was scouring the city for Matt, most likely trying to finish what he started all those years ago.

Craig wasn't about to let Clifford Crouch anywhere near Matt, and he was also determined to learn Gabriel's connection to Matt and the man who murdered his parents.

THE shifting shadows of dusk descended, and Clifford took advantage of the approaching darkness. He exited the Mustang, which he parked down the street from the house the Gifted One and his friends entered, and made his way to the iron gate.

He needed to get inside, but attempting to climb the eighteen-foot blockade would only get him caught by some nosey neighbor, who would then call the police. He needed to be less conspicuous, so he walked by the gate, and surveyed the property line.

It extended at least two hundred feet before jutting up to the nearest neighbor's brick-wall fence. In between the gate and the wall, huge evergreen shrubs lined up like soldiers. Their full, wide limbs looked promising enough to climb over the fence, and the shadows cast by the shrubs along with the ever-darkening night sky might be just what he needed to get inside.

After a quick survey up and down the street, Clifford dashed into the bushes. The branches fought back, biting into his skin and ripping his shirt, but he paid those minor annoyances no attention. He had a job to do.

He quickly climbed up the branches while resting most of his weight upon the wall behind him to avoid breaking the limbs. He managed to half-crawl, half-climb up the shrubs. Once at the top, he peered through the foliage to make sure no one was coming or that no one was outside watering their lawn.

The street was quiet and empty except for the sounds of children playing in a backyard somewhere.

He positioned himself so that he was able to grab the shrub's trunk as he threw his leg over the top of the wall. He used that leg to gain balance before hoisting the rest of himself up and over the wall, where he fell a good twelve feet to the ground.

"That could've been smoother," the voice cackled from within.

"Shut up, bitch," he uttered once the breath returned to his lungs. "I did it, didn't I? Without your help too."

"If you'd have let me take over, I could have bent the shadows around us and leaped across the wall without damaging your fragile body."

"My body's not fragile. I'm not some fucking sissy who can't take a lick or two. I've survived fucking jail motherfucker."

"You must be so proud," mocked the voice.

"Damn straight. Now shut the fuck up."

"No one else can hear me but you, dumbass. You're the one sitting there talking to yourself."

Clifford felt stupid, and he hated being made to feel that way. Too many people in his life tried to make him feel stupid, and he wasn't going to have some voice calling him names. "Call me that again, and you'll regret it," he warned.

The voice laughed. "What will *you* do to *me*?"

"I won't kill the Gifted One," he replied.

"That will hurt you more than me."

"I don't think so. I think you were punished for your failure, and you're trying to make up for it by taking out Matt Westlake now. And I bet that if I refuse, you'll be in a world of hurt more than I would be."

The voice made no reply, but he could feel it silently seethe within him.

"Now shut your face hole. I've got work to do."

Clifford sprinted across the property, using the shadows for cover. Faster than he thought possible, he made it to the side of the house and peered around the corner to the front door, where a Jeep, BMW, and pickup truck sat.

The truck bothered him. It was out of place. It didn't belong in this neighborhood. Hard, caked dirt clung to the axles and the bed. It looked hard used, not a high-end truck society types sometimes drove around while they pretended to be rough and rugged.

"We've got company," he told the voice.

"Who is it?"

"Do I look like I can see through fucking walls?"

"But you can," the voice responded. "Through a window."

"No shit," Clifford replied as he crawled around the perimeter, searching for the right room. After peering into a few darkened rooms, the sound of voices caught his attention. He headed straight to the window, where the voices came from, and slyly peeked inside.

A man about twice his size sat on the couch opposite of the Gifted One and his friends. Though booming, his voice echoed friendliness, but beneath the hum, Clifford sensed something sinister.

"Do you know him?" Clifford asked the voice.

"I do," it hissed in reply.

"Who is it?"

"Someone we can't allow to kill the Gifted One. I won't lose to the likes of him."

"I won't lose to anyone," he told the voice. "You can guarantee that."

Clifford ducked down from the window and crawled around to the other side of the house. Whether he had competition or not, he played to win. Clifford had been through too much already to lose, especially when he was this close to getting everything he wanted.

CHAPTER 27

HIS brothers stood before him, scattered about Matt's apartment, waiting for an answer. Gabriel longed to tell them what they wanted to hear, but he couldn't lie. No matter how far they feared he had fallen, he refused to stoop to deception.

Lying was something Samyaza would do, and in a way, he had. He had deceived himself. Samyaza made himself believe that what he had done, defiling the woman named Istahar, had been born out of love. Everyone, including Samyaza himself, knew lust had been the primary motive, nothing more.

Now under the assembled gaze of his brother archangels, Gabriel questioned his motives again. Had he given into lust? Had he deceived himself into believing that he loved Matt and that Matt loved him? Was he no better than Samyaza and therefore guilty of the same crimes?

No matter which way he scrutinized the situation, he arrived at the same conclusion each time: he had fallen in love with Matt, but more importantly, Matt had fallen in love with him.

"Yes," he finally replied. "I would sacrifice everything, even my life, to be with the man I love."

His answer caused a stir among his brothers.

Raguel fumed, knocking over Matt's sofa table with one swat of his hand. The pictures of Matt and his loved ones that had smiled out into the room now lay in broken fragments upon the floor. Jophiel turned away from Gabriel, looking out the window and most likely searching the clouds for the peace that eluded him. Raphael and Uriel whispered silently to each other while Chamuel stared at him in silence. His green eyes bored through Gabriel, trying to discern some unspoken truth.

But the reaction that hurt him the most came from Michael, the brother who was the dearest to him of all. Michael's blue eyes turned cold, as if he gazed not upon someone he loved but at a stranger whom he couldn't identify. It made Gabriel feel detached and alone for the first time in the millennia of his life.

"Would you rather I lied?" he finally asked. "Does speaking the truth to my brothers cost me the love they once held in their hearts for me?"

"Lying would have gotten you nowhere," Jophiel replied. His back still faced Gabriel. "You know that better than any angel. Just as you know that our love for you remains unchanged."

"Yet your actions demonstrate hostility for the truth as it is. Whether each of you likes it or not, I am in love with Matthew Westlake, and I would gladly sacrifice all that I am to spend one more moment in his arms."

"You disgust me," Raguel spat out. It was obvious that Gabriel's answer had riled his brother's sense of justice, and in Raguel's eyes made him someone who needed to pay for his crimes. "You drape over your sin with a profession of love, but love such as you speak is beyond the likes of us. It is carnal pleasure. Plain and simple."

"The fact that you think any of this is plain or simple shows how little you know about this situation or of me, brother."

"You're right," Raguel agreed. "I thought I knew you, Gabriel, but I do not. I also know nothing about carnal pleasure because I have never once blurred the line between Heaven and earth. My role as the Angel of Justice keeps me tethered to my duties. I do not cast it off upon a whim. It's an honor and one that I shall carry out for eternity."

"Yet you think me as one to shirk my duties? When in all of existence have I done so?"

Raguel crossed over to Gabriel, standing mere inches from him. "You do so right now," he challenged. "By telling us you would sacrifice all that you are for this man, you tell us you would abandon your role as the Angel of Vengeance."

Gabriel fought the urge to shove Raguel backward. He hated when anyone, besides Matt, invaded his space. But if he were to act rashly, he would start a war of epic proportions, and though his ire had been raised, he wouldn't lash out against a brother he still loved.

"I don't wish to denounce my role as the Angel of Vengeance. I would gladly carry the mantle from now until the end of time. Just because I love Matt and care for his safety more than my own doesn't mean I'm ready to relinquish my part in the Grand Design."

"You can't be both man *and* angel," Raguel told him. "You *must* choose."

"Calm yourself," Uriel said from behind Raguel. He placed his hand upon Raguel's shoulder and gently moved him aside. "Your emotions cloud your judgment."

"My emotions cloud nothing!" he shouted. "I see this situation for what it is. It's the rest of you who remain blind. You refuse to recognize that Gabriel has become no better than Samyaza, and what makes Gabriel's treachery all the worse is that Gabriel was there when the Watchers fell. He saw what happened to mankind as a result, yet he would still place all of creation in danger in pursuit of the flesh."

"You make hasty leaps in logic, Raguel," said Chamuel as he crossed to stand beside Gabriel. He placed his hand reassuringly on his brother's shoulder. "I above all of you know love, and what I see inside our brother's heart, in fact, within his very soul, is not lust. It is love unlike any ever experienced before. It transcends the boundaries dividing Heaven and earth. That makes him nothing like Samyaza."

Gabriel wanted to take Chamuel in his arms and spin his brother around. He feared Chamuel, more than anyone else, would be unwilling to remain objective, preferring to be blinded by the fact that a brother archangel enjoyed carnal pleasure. Chamuel proved to him that not only did he see the truth, but that his feelings for Matt were love, not lust.

"Thank you, brother."

"Do not thank me," Chamuel replied. "While I won't allow Raguel to toss around unfounded claims, I do share in his apprehension about your actions."

"But you labeled my feelings as love. Not lust. That means you embrace the happiness I have found."

"You place words upon my tongue that I have not spoken, Gabriel. I do not embrace your relationship with Matthew Westlake. Though based in love, it doesn't erase the claim that you have fallen into sin." Chamuel turned to walk across the room, standing next to Michael. "Our souls are among the purest in creation, and by knowing the flesh, you have tainted the very purity that makes you what you are. In doing so, you threaten the very fabric of the Grand Design."

"The tear in that fabric must be healed," Raphael added. "To allow it to unravel further threatens everything we hold dear. We cannot allow that to happen."

Gabriel felt trapped. His brothers obviously refused to accept his relationship, and no words would persuade them otherwise. He stood separated from angels whose bond once meant everything to him, and though it saddened him, it made his union with Matt all the sweeter.

In him, Gabriel had a connection that surpassed everything he had once known, and it made Gabriel see that the only bond, beyond the one connecting him to Father, he was committed to maintaining was the one he shared with Matt.

The unwavering acceptance of that love provided him the knowledge, which he now voiced.

"You speak of the Grand Design as if it were some unalterable garment, rigid in both construction and plan. We all know differently. It is a living, breathing entity, and it changes as circumstances warrant. Man's expulsion from Eden, Cain's murder of Abel, and the great flood are all examples of how the Grand Design evolved to deal with the path free will had trekked across heavenly intentions. Father never wanted knowledge to tempt mankind as it had, but it did, so He knitted a new pattern, one that eventually included murder and great evil. Those were never part of His design either, but as He gave man and angel free will, He also embraced the fact that what He wanted and intended for His creations sometimes bore no fruit. He never held that against His children. Like a good Father, He simply worked their flaws into His hopes for His children's ultimate outcome. Why do you assume that He refuses to do the same for someone who loves Him as much as I do?"

For the first time, Jophiel turned to look at him. His silver eyes sparkled with enlightenment. "You speak with great wisdom, Gabriel. With far more insight and reflection than I've ever seen you demonstrate."

"Loving Matthew Westlake has changed me," he told Jophiel as he took a few steps forward. Too much space, both physical and emotional, separated him from the others. He needed to rectify that. Failure to do so would be his and Matt's undoing. "I know you only see the sin of my actions, but what I have done has made me a better angel than I was before."

He turned to stare into Michael's eyes, which still looked cold and removed. "You yourself told me how I changed. I was no longer waiting to sound my horn that would bring about the final judgment. Where before, I saw only the vile creatures that mankind had become and how far they had fallen, I now see the beauty in their imperfection. Their flaws cause true greatness to rise. Without the blemishes, humanity would never have occasion to reflect the love of Father. Their faults give them something to aspire to. They become greater as individuals and as a society when they overcome the limitations of their lives."

Michael nodded. "You're right. I saw those differences in you, my brother. And at first, I embraced them. When I saw how fervently you protected the Gifted One in his youth and how you had rediscovered your love for mankind, I was pleased. As was Father. Your discontent had vanished, and you once again welcomed the potential man had to become."

"You speak as if those changes no longer please you."

"Because they do not," Michael replied. "You have swung too far in the other direction. Heaven and earth were meant to be separate. You no longer possess the objectivity our purposes require."

Gabriel didn't understand Michael's point. His indifferent objectivity had been problematic before. How many times in the past had Michael challenged him to open his heart to humanity and see the good and the potential hidden beneath the defects? Now that he could, Michael condemned him for the changes he once pleaded Gabriel to make. "You speak out of both sides of your mouth," he told Michael. "Now that I see what you once begged me to see, you punish me for it."

"You still refuse to see the truth," Michael sighed. "So I will make it simple for you."

"Please do."

"Sound your horn," he told Gabriel. "The Day of Judgment is at hand."

Gabriel stepped back. His eyes searched his brothers' faces, but their blank stares revealed nothing. They stood silently before him, shoulder to shoulder awaiting him to fulfill his primary role, calling the worthy up to Heaven and putting an end to the wicked that remained below.

MATT had been unable to speak for a few minutes. Instead, he sat back on the couch in his grandmother's sitting room as the large stranger in front of him had claimed to be his uncle. To say the news caught him by surprise would be an understatement.

For years, he wondered who his biological parents were and what kind of family he came from. Out of respect for his dead parents, he never pursued the matter. His grandmother had not been against the idea. In fact, she encouraged him to look for them, even providing him with the name of the woman who arranged the adoption, but he could never bring himself to follow through.

Not only did he feel as if he would somehow be showing contempt for the love of his adopted family, but something inside him told him he was better not knowing.

He never understood why until he learned who Gabriel was.

Gabriel advised him against searching for his past. He had been there, and he knew firsthand the horror Matt managed to survive. To dredge up the past might bring even more danger, and though Matt accepted the warning, he somehow knew he had to find out more about his past.

In that past lay the knowledge about why demons had been trying to kill him since the day he was born. If he could learn why and meet that challenge head on, then he and Gabriel might have a chance at spending the rest of their lives together.

But now that someone from his past sat in the same room with him, the only emotion Matt felt was apprehension.

"Are you okay?" his grandmother asked. She sat in the Queen Anne chesterfield next to the stranger. Her eyes were filled with worry.

"I'm fine," he stammered. "Just shocked."

"Shocked?" Shane asked. "I feel like my nipples were just hooked up to a car battery and fried clean off!"

"Shane, please!" Dee chided.

"It's okay," said Matt. "I feel pretty much the same way."

Shane stuck his tongue out at Dee, who shook her head in exasperation.

"I'm sorry if I've upset you, son," the man named Homer said. "Perhaps I should leave."

Matt wanted to say yes, but his mouth refused to obey. He simply gazed, open-mouthed at the man.

"How did you find Matty, Mr. Rodgers?" Dee asked. "And why now?"

"It's a long story," he replied. "But one I'd be glad to tell if you would like to hear it."

Homer addressed the question to Matt, and though Matt no longer had any desire to hear the story, his grandmother answered for him. "Please do," she replied. "I'm curious as to how you found us."

Homer nodded and told his story.

"I was married to your aunt Lily. She was your mother's sister, which makes me only family by marriage, I reckon, but family nonetheless. Your mother's name was Veronica, a lovely woman. My Lily and your mother were more than sisters. They were best friends, and when your mother told Lily she was expecting you, Lily couldn't wait to meet you."

The man stared down at the carpet. A profound sadness drifted into his eyes, but Matt saw something else as well. Beneath the sadness hid a shadow, one that he had seen before in Dr. Owens's office.

"Unfortunately, your mother died the night you were born. There was this huge storm, and your dad's car didn't make it to the hospital. She gave birth to you in the car and passed away afterward, but before she went, she named you Mateo."

"Mateo?" Matt asked. The name struck an unusual chord with him, causing him to momentarily put aside the need to protect himself and his loved ones.

Homer nodded in reply. "And you're now Matt. Pretty similar, huh?"

Matt smiled in response and nodded for Homer to finish his story. His guard remained up, so he planned on using Homer's story to buy him the time he needed to formulate a plan.

"Well, your father, his name was Carlos, raised you and your brothers all by himself."

"My brothers?" he asked. He never entertained the idea that he had siblings. Since he was given up for adoption, Matt always assumed he had been an only child, perhaps born to two horny teenagers who had suffered the consequences of a night of unprotected sex. He never imagined that his parents were married to each other and had children of their own. "How many brothers?"

"Six."

"Oh my," his grandmother replied. "Where are those boys now? Do they know you've found Matthew?"

Homer looked away. "I'm afraid they're dead. As is your father."

Matt's breath left his body as the words slammed into his gut like a sucker punch.

Not only did he have two dead adopted parents, but now he had six brothers and two biological parents who were also dead. Were they murdered too? And if they were, how many people who loved him would have to die before the demons stopped coming after him?

He opened his mouth to ask how it happened, but no sound came out. Luckily, Dee rode to Matt's rescue.

"What happened to them?" she asked as she reached over and took Matt's hand in hers.

"It's an awful story," Homer replied. "And I've wondered how to tell you this. I'm afraid I'm just going to botch it all up."

"Do it like a Band-Aid," Shane commented. "It's always better that way."

Homer nodded and sighed. "They were murdered."

"What?" the Duchess asked as she rose from her chair. "That's awful. Too awful!" She crossed quickly to Matt and wedged herself on the couch between Dee and her grandson. She wrapped her arms around his shoulders and held him tight. "I think that's enough for today," she said.

"I'm fine," he told her. Matt squeezed her tightly to him and then released himself from her embrace. He needed to hear the rest. Whether it brought him more danger or not, he needed to know the truth. Then, he would deal with Homer Rodgers. "Go on," he told Homer. "Please."

After a deep breath, the man continued. "Not much is known beyond that, I'm afraid. On the day that they were, well, killed, you disappeared, and the person who committed the crime was never found. The police searched for both you and clues to the identity of the murderer, but nothing ever came of it. I'm afraid that the rest of the family, myself included, came to believe that you had died too. But your Aunt Lily never believed it. She knew you were alive, and she never gave up hope."

"Where is she now?" Matt asked.

"She recently passed from cancer," he replied, and in his eyes reflected grief that wasn't deep enough to reflect a wife's passing.

Matt could tell that part of the story was true, but he couldn't help but feel that the man was lying. Homer was only telling him half of the story.

"Before she died, she made me promise to look for you," his alleged uncle continued. "To bring you home to meet your cousins and the rest of the family. So I did. And here I am."

"I still don't understand how," Matt replied.

"Remember Earline Groll?" his grandmother asked.

"Isn't that the woman who arranged my adoption?"

"Yes. She's the one who helped Mr. Rodgers locate us."

Matt gazed at Homer, who still sat across from them. The man's expression beamed with satisfaction, but Matt couldn't help but feel as if the gratification stemmed from something other than finding Matt for his supposedly dead wife. "How did you and Ms. Groll get into contact with each other?"

"It wasn't easy," Homer replied. "I called every adoption agency in Victoria and the surrounding counties but didn't have much luck. So I expanded my search to the bigger cities in Texas, San Antonio, Austin, Corpus Christi, and here in Houston. When I called one of the agencies here, I was routed to Ms. Groll, and I asked about one-year old infants brought by on or about January 17, 1986, the day you disappeared. When she told me there had been one boy brought by on that date, I told her why I was looking for you and faxed over a picture. It was a match of the photo of you she had on file."

"And she just gave you our contact information? Just like that?"

"No. I told her I only wanted to bring you home to meet your family, and when she realized how you might have been kidnapped, she gave me your grandmother's address. It wasn't a closed adoption, and since your grandmother had approved contact from the biological family, it was okay for her to give me the information I needed to find you."

"I don't remember doing that," his grandmother spoke. "But the woman might have been confused. I only told her that Matt had my permission to search for his biological family. That woman was always a bit flighty though, so she might have misunderstood." She rose from her place next to Matt.

"Where are you going?"

"To contact Ms. Groll," she told Matt. "I hope you don't mind, Mr. Rodgers, but I would feel better if I verified the story."

"No trouble at all," Homer replied. The darkness in his eyes became more profound as his grandmother left the room to make her call.

"So what now?" Matt asked.

"I want to bring you home. To see where you came from and to embrace your past."

Thunder crashed outside. Matt turned to look out the window and saw dark storm clouds gathering in the distance.

THE gathering thunderclouds told Clifford time was running out. Demonic presence had been detected, triggering nature's warning system—the sudden storm. Like an annoying car alarm, a tempest raged as long as hell set foot on earth. The peals of thunder and the crash of lightning blared out its cry for help to the heavens above, and when the alarm had been triggered, some heavenly fool descended to end the threat.

"We must work fast," hissed the voice inside.

"No shit," he replied. Since he still remained in control of his body, the coming storm told him the creature inside the man with the Gifted One had begun to rise. If he wanted to claim the victory, he had to beat his competition to the kill.

With his fist wrapped in his shirt, Clifford struck the paned-window of the French door, silently shattering the glass. He quickly unlocked it and stepped into what appeared to be the master suite, which overlooked the rear of the property and the rose garden beyond.

Clifford made his way out of the master suite and down the hall.

CHAPTER 28

A FEW years earlier, Gabriel would have reached for his horn and brought about the End of Days, but that was before he had fallen in love with Matt. He couldn't call for his horn and end the life of the man he loved. It wasn't right, and he refused to go through with it, no matter what Michael told him.

"He hesitates," Raguel stated. "Just as we anticipated."

"Only Father pronounces final judgment upon mankind. Not the Angel of Mercy."

"You're correct," Michael told Gabriel. "Yet you pause not because I'm the one who spoke the words but because of your reluctance to end the earthly existence of Matthew Westlake."

"Is that so wrong?" he asked them. "To not want to casually wipe out creation?"

"Of course not, but that wasn't the true motive. And you know it."

It rankled Gabriel that Jophiel saw through him, but he should have known better than to try and get any sort of deception past the Angel of Wisdom. Jophiel's eyes saw the truth of every action.

"He doesn't deny it," Uriel pointed out. "The Angel of Vengeance embraces only love and welcomes peace before retribution."

"Does that offend you?" Gabriel asked.

"No. My hand ever remains open in peace, not in vengeance. Then again, I'm the Angel of Peace. It's not my duty you fail to fulfill. It's your own."

"Do you now see it, Gabriel?" Michael told him. "We all have a part to play in the grand design. Our presence, our influence, creates order out of chaos. Without love, hate would reign supreme. Without mercy, there would be only cruelty. Ignorance, disease, war, and injustice would abound without wisdom, healing, peace, and justice. As the embodiment of vengeance, you are integral to the balance."

"That's easy for you to say," Gabriel announced. "You represent the positive aspects of life while I symbolize the negative. What pleasure does vengeance bring? What laughter echoes forth from a soul embittered by the misery of retribution?"

"Is that truly how you see yourself?" Raphael asked. His brown eyes mirrored his empathy for Gabriel's pain.

"My ultimate function is the destruction of all we hold dear, the end of all the emotions each one of you embodies. My ears hear the cries for revenge and those seeking reprisal. I settle scores brought about through treachery and wickedness. Yes, I am the strength of our Father but only because it takes great strength to carry such a burden."

"Brother," said Michael as he crossed the room toward him for the first time. His voice and his demeanor had calmed. The cold indifference vanished. "You fail to see the good vengeance brings to the world. Vengeance is more than revenge or an eye for an eye. To pursue recourse so adamantly takes willpower. It motivates mankind like a hammer strike upon the thumb. It provides vigor in times of distress and succor in times of unease. It becomes a guiding light out of grief and a means by which to overcome inflicted misery. Vengeance isn't evil; it's human, and you, brother, have proven to be the most human of us all."

Michael's words caused tears to well in Gabriel's eyes. For too long, he had shouldered the burden of his role in the grand design, thinking his sole purpose to be death and destruction, but Michael was right. Vengeance proved more than he thought it to be.

He had seen the need for retaliation change the downtrodden and give them strength to overcome their tormentors. Throughout time, hard-fought victories had been born from such struggles. Every oppressive government, dictator, or regime had been brought to its knees once the masses gathered in righteous retribution.

His presence inspired such action.

"So you see, Gabriel. Without you, mankind will lose its resolve to overcome adversity."

"Michael's right," Jophiel chimed in. "There must be an Angel of Vengeance."

Gabriel understood his brother's words. As always, they were sage and sound. But the words conflicted with his heart. His place in the Grand Design was important, but being with Matt had become so much more than his duty.

Their souls entwined around each other.

"I now understand what you speak."

"Hallelujah!" Raguel exclaimed. He dashed over to Gabriel's side and embraced him, hard. Tears streamed down his cheeks. "You've eased my troubled soul!"

His brothers echoed Raguel's sentiment. All except Chamuel. He remained distant because he knew the truth that still lived within Gabriel's heart.

"Celebrate with us, Chamuel," Michael shouted. "Our brother returns to the fold, where he belongs."

"You rejoice prematurely, Michael."

"How so?"

"Gabriel has yet to retract his prior statement. He has only voiced his understanding of our concerns. Renouncing the love of the man that prevents him from fulfilling his duties has not occurred, and that is what we seek, is it not?"

"But he understands," Michael replied. He and the rest of the archangels stared at Gabriel, waiting for him to do what Chamuel knew he could not. "He will withdraw from the Gifted One, and a new guardian angel shall be assigned. There is no other option."

"But there is," Gabriel replied.

The light in Michael's eyes grew dim. "And what would that be?"

"To remain by his side as I have been since his birth. To protect him with my body and my soul. To grow in his love and become even greater than I am now."

Michael stepped backward as if Gabriel had punched him. "But you said you understood."

"And I did not lie. But my understanding in no way invalidates the truth that yet resides in my heart. I love him, and renouncing that love and retreating to Heaven is not and will *never* be an option."

"He's mad!" Raguel shouted. His wings shot out of his back, stretching wide across the room. His previous welcoming embrace turned into his battle stance, hands at the ready and eyes fixed and locked on his target.

The remaining archangels followed suit. Their wings sprouted from their backs, and their celestial armor shimmered across their bodies. In response, Gabriel slowly unfolded his wings in preparation for a battle he didn't want to have.

"Then it's war?" Michael asked. "You'd rather turn your back on not only your duty but your brothers and your Father."

"You wound me," he told them. A peace he had never before experienced settled upon him. His previous anger melted away. In its place rested a profound sadness for his brothers' inability to celebrate in the love he had found. "I love Father and all my brothers. I do not turn my back upon you. It is you who turn your back to me. I ask for understanding and celebration for the love that fills me with joy, but instead you greet me with armor and drawn sword. Is there not room in the Grand Design or in all of Heaven for me to open my heart to another?"

A blazing trail of white fire encircled Gabriel in response to a wave of Michael's hand. The move saddened him, for his brothers had turned against him.

"Do you think it necessary to bind me with holy fire?"

"To prevent you from raising arms against us?" Raguel asked. "Yes. A battle would decimate this building and all within it."

"And you think I would cross swords with you? That I'd willingly risk the lives of innocent men, women, and children? Do you hold me in such little regard?"

"Our hearts remain as open to you as always, Gabriel. But Father has called us all home. He wishes to speak with you," Uriel announced.

"I would come without being dragged back in chains," Gabriel told his brothers.

"Not once did you sense the approaching danger," Uriel said with a shake of his head.

Gabriel was confused. No immediate threat existed. But as he focused his attention, clearing his mind of the turmoil that momentarily blocked him, he saw the threats that lay in wait for Matt. Even now, they circled about him, preparing to strike.

"No!" he bellowed. His wings tore out of his back. He leaped into the air, but his flapping wings failed to launch him skyward. The white fire grounded him. Angry, he glared at his brothers. "You sensed the threat to the Gifted One, and you did nothing about it?"

"That was your job," Raphael replied. "Not ours."

"So you would stand by and watch as the promise of Matt's future was snuffed out?"

"Father's will be done," prayed Michael.

"Father ordered this? But why?" Gabriel charged into the fire, but the flames refused to let him pass. Instead, they scorched his heavenly flesh and sapped him of his strength. He was going nowhere as long as the fire remained, for it was impossible to escape a prison erected by an archangel. Besides Father and the higher orders of angels, his brothers were the only ones capable of not only binding him but erasing him from existence.

"That will be for Him to tell you," Michael replied. "Now, come. He awaits us in the Throne Room."

"Please," he begged. "Let me save Matt, and I will head to Heaven after he is safe. That is all I ask of you. Don't let my actions allow harm to come to the Gifted One."

His brothers gave no response as they soared into the heavens, trailing Gabriel behind them in his prison of fire. All he could do as he zipped across the sky was look down upon the land that threatened to swallow the man he loved in treachery and blood.

SLOWLY and quietly, Clifford cut a path through the master suite.

As he passed through the living room, he heard a woman's voice on the phone in the room adjacent to where he now stood. Her tone and manner of speech told him it was the old lady, not the hot-to-trot sister he planned on enjoying after he fulfilled his contract.

He appreciated when those he planned to kill separated themselves from the pack. It made his job that much easier. But he needed to make sure no one else was in the room with her. He didn't want an unwelcome surprise that would draw the attention of the house.

The buzz of conversation still echoed down the hall from the front of the house, where the Gifted One waited, but that didn't mean the old bitch was alone. Clifford inched his way along the wall, listening to the woman's conversation.

"Ms. Groll, this is Joanna Westlake. I don't know if you remember me but…"

When the woman stopped midquestion, Clifford assumed this Ms. Groll hadn't forgotten Joanna Westlake, who now asked how the woman had been since the last time they spoke.

Clifford was grateful for the small talk. It allowed him extra time to sneak up on her and take her out.

When he reached the doorway, he saw a refrigerator and a stove opposite him. She was in the kitchen, which was perfect. Anything in that room could be used to kill her quickly and quietly as long as he took her by surprise.

"We've been good as well," she said. "But I was wondering if I might ask you a question?"

Clifford peeked around the corner and found the woman sitting at the table across the room. Her back faced him as she looked out the window and talked on the phone. As quietly as possible, he moved into the kitchen once he realized Joanna Westlake was alone.

"Tell me some more about the man who came to you inquiring about my Matthew."

Halfway into the kitchen, Clifford spotted a block of knives on the counter on the far side of the room. If he crossed in that direction, she would spot him at once. He didn't need the old bitch to start screaming. A quick scan of the kitchen revealed nothing lying out in the open for him to use to take her out. Everything had been put away in its proper place.

He contemplated searching the drawers for a knife or removing one of the pans from the iron frame hanging from the ceiling, but that proved too risky. One rattle of a utensil or an upset pot would catch her attention.

Luckily, he still had his bare hands, which had always served him well in the past.

"I'm confused," she spoke into the phone. "Didn't you refer a Mr. Homer Rodgers to us and give him my address?"

Clifford drew closer. He flexed his hands open and closed, preparing to choke the life out of the woman.

"You didn't?" she asked. She sounded shaken and confused.

He thought that was funny since she was about to be throttled and dead.

"Thank you, Ms. Groll, but I've got to go. I need to call the police."

She hung up the phone and turned around. Shock washed across her face when she saw him standing behind her. Clifford punched her square in the face, hard, and before the woman's unconscious body could fall and cause a ruckus, he caught her and laid her down on the table.

Although he would have preferred to kill her, the voice inside argued against it: he couldn't risk the sounds of a struggle. Her body would convulse automatically and knock shit everywhere, which would draw attention as well. For now, subduing her was the best choice. He could come back and finish her off once he had finished killing the others.

CRAIG leaped out of the squad car before Ybarra brought it to a full stop in front of Matt's apartment building. He had no time to waste, so he ran at top speed into the building.

Clifford Crouch was alive and most likely on his way to Matt. Getting to him before Clifford did was his only concern. His bizarre findings on Gabriel took a back seat. Once Matt was safe, he would get the answers he sought about spotting Gabriel in a news clipping almost twenty years old.

Matt deserved his full attention. Nothing less would suffice, especially since Craig had been unable to contact him.

He called Matt's cell phone on the way there, but it had been turned off. He didn't know if that was a good sign or not. Craig just hoped it meant Matt was busy and hadn't already crossed paths with the man who killed his parents.

"Wait for the elevator!" Ybarra called out as Craig shot into the stairwell.

"No time," Craig yelled back as he bounded up the steps. The elevator in Matt's building took forever. During the two weeks they dated, he complained about it. He wanted to take the stairs every time, but Matt liked making out once the elevator closed. He couldn't argue with that logic.

But now he wished he had forced Matt to lodge an official complaint. A slow elevator might make a difference between life and—. He couldn't finish the thought. He would make it in time. He just had to.

On the sixth floor, Craig flung open the stairwell door and shot down the hallway toward Matt's apartment. He pounded on the door as the elevator rang down the hall and Ybarra stepped out of the open doors.

"Any answer?" Ybarra asked, slightly winded.

"Matt!" he shouted at the door. "It's Craig. Open up, please!"

He didn't care if Gabriel and Matt were in there fucking. In fact, he hoped they were. Then that would mean that Matt was safe and that he had gotten here in time. As he pounded on the door, however, Craig realized he wanted to do more than protect Matt.

Retribution needed to be delivered to Clifford Crouch, and he wanted to be the one to carry out the sentence. He no longer cared about simply arresting the man and bringing him to justice. His wickedness had been allowed to walk this earth for far too long already.

He deserved only a one-way ticket to hell.

"Houston PD," Ybarra shouted at the door. "Open up. Now!"

No answer came. Craig looked sideways at Ybarra who shook his head.

"We have no right to bust in there, Belton."

"Didn't you hear something? I know I did."

Craig waited for the man to accept his lie. If they heard sounds of distress, they were well within their rights as protectors of the people to enter without a warrant. When Ybarra finally nodded in agreement, he slammed his shoulder hard against the door, which flew open with one strike.

Both men entered the apartment with their weapons drawn, scanning every corner with the barrel of their guns.

"Matt!" he cried out again. "It's Craig. Are you here?"

Detective Ybarra nodded for Craig to take point, and he moved down the hallway and into the living room. On the floor, the sofa table rested on its side. Shattered fragments of glass spotted the wooden floor. A burn mark in the shape of a perfect circle scorched the area beside the couch.

"What the fuck is that?"

Craig didn't answer the detective. He didn't know what it was either, but he understood what it meant. Matt was in trouble. "I'll check the bedroom," he told Ybarra.

The man nodded in reply as Craig kicked open the closed bedroom door to peer inside.

"No one's in the kitchen," Ybarra called out from the other room.

"Nothing here either."

"Where could they be?"

"I don't know," Craig replied while fishing his phone out of his pocket. "But I'm going to call some people who might. Contact the station and call this in."

Although he didn't have the authority to order around Detective Ybarra, the man carried out his instructions as if Craig's words were to be obeyed at all cost. He found it interesting that the seasoned detective followed his lead so quickly, but he chalked up Ybarra's quick compliance to sympathy. Ybarra knew Craig loved Matt, and all signs indicated a struggle had taken place in this apartment.

Ybarra understood how close to home this hit.

Dee's cell phone rang a few times before it disconnected. The call didn't even go to voicemail. Craig didn't like that. His fingers quickly dialed Shane's phone, and when the same thing happened, he accepted the fact that not only was Matt in danger but so were Dee and Shane.

Those two never turned their phones off. Too much gossip might escape their notice, which made them slaves to phone calls and text messages. Wherever Matt was, they were with him.

"Station's sending over a lab crew to scour this place. They'll hopefully be able to give us some answers."

"We don't have time to wait. Something bad is going down, and it's going down now."

"How do you know that?" Detective Ybarra stared at him, not with the suspicion of a veteran but with the awe of a rookie. Craig was beginning to wonder what the hell was going on with Ybarra. The man suddenly looked to him for advice and orders as if Craig were his superior officer.

"I just do," he replied. "And I've a hunch where we need to go next."

"Where's that?"

Instead of responding, Craig ran out of the apartment and back toward the stairs. He didn't have time to explain his foresight to Ybarra. Too much depended on his reaching Matt in time. While he couldn't explain his hunch or the feeling that overcame him, Craig somehow understood that more than Matt's safety hinged upon his actions.

He served something far greater than either himself or Matt now.

CHAPTER 29

SHIVERING uncontrollably, Matt observed the bluish black storm clouds spreading across the sky like irritated bruises upon gangrenous flesh. Flashes of lightning lit up the belly of the heavens in bursts of yellow as thunder exploded around them like artillery shells.

He normally found only beauty and tranquility in storms. The rumble of thunder and patter of rain often eased his troubles, relaxing him enough to drift off to sleep. The storm that made its way toward him now served to agitate, not soothe, his soul.

Danger lurked about him like a pride of lionesses hidden among the tall grass of the African plains. Although he couldn't see them, Matt knew they were out there, waiting, and they were close.

The last time he felt this terrified, aside from his dream, happened right before Dr. Owens attacked him and changed to Adramelech. A strangely powerful storm hit just before Dr. Owens went crazy, and if these suddenly violent storms continued to be signs of demons at work, then Matt wasn't going to ignore it.

He had to prepare himself and prove his worthiness of Gabriel to the heavens above.

"Something's coming."

"Who is it?" Shane asked, standing beside Matt to look out the window. "I don't see anyone."

"I didn't say someone's coming," Matt clarified. "I said some*thing's* coming."

"What the hell does that mean?"

"It must be the storm," Homer answered from where he still sat across from the window.

The soft light of the room's interior caught the man's reflection on the window through which Matt watched the approaching storm. Homer studied Matt with a strange intensity. Matt immediately intuited that the threat didn't lie in wait outside but sat in the room with him.

Matt turned to face Homer, who greeted him with a big smile. Though it looked pleasant, it appeared far from genuine. Some other agenda lay hidden underneath.

"Looks like quite the storm, doesn't it?" Homer asked.

The time for playing coy had passed. A more direct approach was required. "Can I be honest, Mr. Rodgers?"

"Of course, Matt. We're family."

Matt shook his head. "See, I just don't believe that. There's something fishy about your story. It just doesn't add up. I believe some of what you've told me, but not all of it. My gut tells me you've only told me part of it, and I would guess that the real truth is in what you've chosen to omit. How you've claimed to have found me after all these years, it's too pat. Too coincidental."

"Matty! What's gotten into you?"

He paid no attention to Dee. He saw only Homer Rodgers, who sat back in the chair, grinning.

"You're very good, Matt. Apparently, your time with Gabriel has increased your perception." He rose from the chair and cracked his knuckles. "Which is quite a shame, really."

"Get behind me," Matt told Dee and Shane as he stood between them and the huge man.

"What's going on?" Dee asked, a tremble forming in her voice.

"Something quite beyond your understanding," Homer answered. "Had Matt only come with me, you and everyone in this house would have been spared. I have no quarrel with anyone else besides him. But no, he had to suddenly grow a pair and challenge me outright. Now, all of you will have to pay for his trespass."

"Is it you, Adramelech?" Matt asked as he slowly backed away from Homer, making sure that Dee and Shane remained behind him. If he had to, he would sacrifice himself for his friends and his grandmother.

The man laughed, but his laughter contained no music. Instead it sounded off-key and dissonant like the keyboard of a piano played by a madman. "Adramelech burns in torment for his failure," Homer told him. "You face something far worse than that fool."

Homer's skin turned pale white until he looked more like a corpse than a man. Bubbling as if some giant fire had been lit underneath, his flesh became fluid and elastic. Before their eyes, Homer's features underwent a metamorphosis as long dark hair sprouted from his head.

"What the fuck is going on?" Shane asked in horror from behind him. He sounded on the verge of hysteria. "And who the fuck is Adramelech?"

Matt couldn't find the words to answer. Instead, he continued to watch Homer's transformation. Black chains popped out of his muscular shoulders, neck, and arms, hitting the floor with a heavy metallic clank.

The man's hands became talons, covered with black feathers, which began to spread down his groin and thighs.

As they watched in horror, the thing that had been Homer Rodgers snickered when large black wings sprouted from his back and extended across the width of the room.

"Good God!" Dee exclaimed.

"Wrong direction, sweetheart," the black-winged corpse replied. "But I think you get the general idea."

Matt knew exactly who now stood before him. The black wings gave his identity away. This was one of the fallen angels from Gabriel's story, the leader of the Watchers and the reason for the great biblical flood.

"Samyaza," Matt announced in a voice both calm and confident. When Dr. Owens revealed himself to be the demon Adramelech, Matt cowered. This time, he did no such thing. While he was definitely afraid, Matt placed his faith not only in himself but in the heavens above. Those two acts filled him with strength that rivaled his terror.

The fallen angel applauded. His cold, black eyes pierced through Matt like a spear. He, too, obviously sensed Matt's resolve. "I see you've been brought up to date on my past. Is Gabriel not only dallying with a human but also telling tales out of school? I see archangels are becoming just like us Watchers."

"Matty!" Dee cried out, clutching onto his back. "What's going on? What's he talking about?" Her voice told Matt that she was on the verge of madness.

"Close your eyes," he told her. "It's best not to watch."

"Oh, but what daughter of man could not help but look upon me in my physical perfection? My late wife, the one Gabriel and his brothers murdered in cold blood, couldn't resist me. What makes you think your friend would fare any better?"

Matt didn't appreciate the twinkle in Samyaza's eyes as he glared lecherously at Dee. "Touch her and I'll kill you!"

Samyaza found hilarity in the threat. "And what would one such as you do to one such as me?"

"I'm the Gifted One, aren't I?"

This time, Samyaza couldn't hold back his amusement. He broke into such a fit of laughter that his body shook and his wings spasmed uncontrollably, creating a wind tunnel in the room. "You obviously have no clue what that means," he finally spoke between hysterics. "Being the Gifted One grants you no power over me. You're merely the seventh son of a seventh son, a birth that hasn't occurred in many generations."

Matt knew the legend of the seventh son, and Samyaza downplayed its importance. A seventh son had the potential to be a great healer and effect powerful change in the world, and for Matt, it finally explained how he seemed to always know what his patients needed to recover. After all, literature itself abounded with examples of characters that were granted special abilities, such as foresight, based on an unbroken lineage of male births. These characters often lived lives heaped in tragedy, like he had lived, and how they dealt with those disasters affected their contributions.

If the misfortunes were overcome positively, the seventh son proved a powerful force for good. If the seventh son embraced the darker side, the devastation they wreaked made them an equally destructive force of evil.

This had been what the catastrophes in his life had been about. Demons had been attempting to either kill him and remove his positive influence or force him down the path of evil through the constant torment. Gabriel had been by his side to protect him and keep him on the path of the just.

Ultimately, though, the choice would be his.

It explained why Gabriel had been unable to tell him why the demons were after him. The knowledge made the choice of good or evil less of an option, which meant a loss of free will, the one thing God promised mankind.

Demons didn't care about free will. They wanted victory, no matter what the cost.

"If I'm merely a seventh son, then I pose no threat whatsoever."

"You do not," Samyaza agreed.

"Then let us go. Choose the good and honorable path once again, Samyaza. Be the angel you once were, not what you became."

"Angel?" Shane asked. "That fucker's an angel!"

Both Matt and Samyaza ignored Dee and Shane, who trembled together against the far wall. Matt was glad he distracted Samyaza from their presence, but he wanted his friends to run, to get out of there before things went from bad to worse. The hallway to their right led to the kitchen and the side yard. If they escaped, then they could find his grandmother and get her and themselves out of there and to safety, but his friends were both paralyzed by fear.

"Will you do it?" he asked Samyaza. "Will you let us go?"

"No," the fallen one replied.

Samyaza charged at Matt, grabbing him by the throat and lifting him upward. Dee and Shane shrieked in surprise. "Your soul appears far too pure to be led astray, so my orders are to kill you." His talons scratched a bloody trail down Matt's neck. "But I choose to ignore them. I'm going to force you down the path of wickedness, take all your potential and corrupt it, so that not only do I steal the Gifted One from the Father who betrayed me, but I rob my brother Gabriel of the man he loves. Just like he took my Istahar from me!"

"Back off, you black-winged fucker!"

When Samyaza turned to face the voice behind him, Matt's eyes widened in terror at the person who now stood in his grandmother's living room. It was Clifford Crouch, the man who murdered his parents and the man who was supposed to be dead.

STILL surrounded by the holy fire that kept him imprisoned, Gabriel stood in the Throne Room, awaiting Father's arrival. His brothers took their places, silently staring at him. In their eyes reflected a combination of heartbreak and anger.

Since their arrival, no one had spoken to him, no matter how many times he pleaded with them to set him free or to at least travel back to earth and help Matt face the evil, which even now threatened to destroy him.

They simply refused to intervene.

Gabriel found it difficult to believe that Father would abandon the Gifted One now that heavenly protection was needed the most. It had been his duty to keep Matthew Westlake from being taken by the evil, which clamored to either kill him or capture his soul. As a seventh son, Matt held the potential to be either a powerful agent of good or evil, and the denizens of hell had tried their best to sway him to their side for years.

They first sought to murder him and erase his potential from existence. When that failed, they taunted him with the nightmares that plagued his existence. They sought to turn him to evil, to make him one of their own, but Matt continued to shun the evil and embrace the path of a healer.

His commitment to love and family proved to the heavens that Matt would fulfill the greater good for mankind, when providence finally opened the door for his true destiny.

But now all those efforts seemed for naught.

Matt stood alone against the forces of evil, and Gabriel felt responsible.

His failure, his love for Matt, placed Matt in jeopardy. If he hadn't crossed the lines separating Heaven and earth, he would be at Matt's side, protecting him from harm. But now, he sat helplessly in the heavens, awaiting his fate and abandoning the love of his life to almost certain death.

"Brothers, I implore you one final time. Go to Matt's side. Aid him now when he needs us the most. I won't fight my fate any longer. If I'm to be tossed into the pits of hell, I accept that as punishment for my sins, but don't let my trespasses lead to ruin for the Gifted One."

"What happens now is beyond us," Michael replied. "Do not mistake our inaction for indifference. We want nothing more than for the Gifted One to fulfill his destiny, but the Grand Design lies tattered by your actions. You have removed vengeance from the tapestry, and in order for creation to move forward, the fabric must be rewoven and once again made whole."

"I beg forgiveness," he told his brothers. "What I did I did out of love. Is love now a punishable offense?"

"Of course not," Father's voice echoed all around them. Immediately, Gabriel and the archangels fell upon their knees. "If I speak in the tongues of men or of angels, but do not have love, I am only a resounding gong or a clanging cymbal."

The seraphim materialized, lifting their voices higher than their fiery wings, which spread in anticipation of Father's arrival.

"If I have the gift of prophecy and can fathom all mysteries and all knowledge, and if I have a faith that can move mountains, but do not have love, I am nothing."

Shimmering into view came the cherubim, carrying forth the throne upon which Father would appear. Their brightly colored wings danced in joy.

"If I give all I possess to the poor and give over my body to hardship that I may boast but do not have love, I gain nothing."

Upon the throne, taking on the form of a young man wearing shorts and a T-shirt, Father materialized. "And these three remain: faith, hope, and love," He continued. "And the greatest of these is love."

For a few moments, Father sat in silence, and in those moments Gabriel's misery multiplied a thousandfold. He sensed how disappointed Father was in him and his actions. Gabriel had let Him down and must now face the consequences for breaking His law.

"Leave us," Father ordered the archangels.

Without a word, Michael and the others flew out of the Throne Room. But before exiting, each one looked back at Gabriel one final time before abandoning him to his fate.

"Rise, my child," Father spoke as He stood.

Gabriel immediately obeyed, taking precaution not to touch the blinding-white fire that still encircled him.

With a wave of His hand, Father made the fire disappear. "We'll have no need of that," He commented absently as He crossed over to stand in front of Gabriel.

"I'll not attempt escape," Gabriel replied. "I accept Your judgment, whatever it may be."

"While your brothers are powerful and wise, they are wrong about you," Father said while smiling. "You're nothing like Samyaza."

"But I've sinned. I've broken Your laws and made impure my soul. I've quarreled with my brothers and made a mess of the Grand Design. I am no longer worthy to be what You have made me to be."

"You have caused quite a stir in the heavens, Gabriel. Your actions definitely warranted your brothers' responses. There was great potential for treachery in what you did, but I find no such wickedness in you."

"You don't?" Gabriel asked, unable to believe his ears. "But Michael and the others said my soul had been stained by my actions."

"That much is true," Father agreed. "But stains can be washed away by absolution. Seeking forgiveness makes it temporary. Compounding the blemish with further treachery, as Samyaza and the Watchers did, made the corruption everlasting."

Gabriel understood absolution. In order for it to be bestowed, the penitent not only had to be sorry for his sin but to promise never to commit the sin again. He regretted breaking the rules and upsetting the balance, but he couldn't seek absolution for falling in love. If love truly was the greatest force, he saw no need for such an act to be considered a transgression. "I want forgiveness for the things that I have done, but at the risk of sounding impertinent, I can't apologize for falling in love."

Father shifted forms, appearing now as an elderly woman, garbed in a sweater made from alpaca wool and brown pants. The style of clothing marked Her from Ecuador.

"True love isn't something you can apologize for," He told Gabriel. "But your love has blinded you and allowed you to unwittingly interfere with the Grand Design."

"Does that make it wrong? I didn't ask for the feelings, Father. They came upon me as when the sunshine parts the cloudy sky and falls upon the land. The land doesn't seek the sun, yet the light falls upon it. Are either the light or the land to blame for what naturally occurs?"

"No, but the light and the land must face the consequences of their union, whether good or bad."

"What do you mean?"

"When light falls upon the land, the land responds in many ways. In some areas, the light invigorates, calling forth seeds from their slumber and giving birth to plants, which thrive and prosper within the warm embrace. Then, there are the times when the light scorches the earth, burning away all seeds and making life scarce with its oppressive heat. And what would happen if light were to be introduced to places where it was never meant to shine? What if light penetrated the earth? What would happen to the blind mole? What if light fell upon the darkest parts of the ocean? Would the marine life which thrived in the darkness now perish because of the light?"

"Are you saying the light of the love Matt and I share was never meant to be?"

"That's precisely what I'm saying," Father replied as He once again shifted forms. The elderly Ecuadorian woman became a blond haired, blue-eyed man. He sported a mohawk, tattoos, muscle shirt, and ripped jeans. "Consider what you know. Who do you think was meant to be with Matthew Westlake all along?"

Gabriel didn't have to think too hard about Father's question. Matt met him the night of his birthday, and it was the same man, who had been trying to protect Matt from the danger he perceived Gabriel to be—Craig Belton.

"It was Craig? Wasn't it?"

When Father nodded, guilt once again descended upon Gabriel. He never once contemplated that his actions changed the destiny of another. He had been so focused on his love for Matt and what they could accomplish together that he never considered the devastating ripple effect their love had on others—not on his brothers, not on the Grand Design, and most certainly not on Craig.

Bitterly disappointed in himself, Gabriel fell to his knees and wept at the mess he made of so many lives. He wanted to right the wrongs he had unsuspectingly caused, but he didn't know how.

CHAPTER 30

SAMYAZA tossed Matt aside, sending him flying into the wall. A cloud of white dust exploded outward upon impact as the plaster caved before he fell to the carpet below. Dazed, Matt tried to clear his head. He needed to focus if he wanted to stay alive and protect his friends from the new danger that now threatened them.

As impossible as it was to believe, Clifford Crouch was not only alive but here in his grandmother's house, challenging Samyaza for the right to kill him, a task he had failed at many years ago.

"The Gifted One is mine," Clifford shouted. "I claim the right to spill his blood."

Samyaza laughed, heartily. The arrogance of the challenge amused him. "You have no claim here. I snatched this host from Barbatos, to complete a task neither he nor you were capable of accomplishing. This one is mine for the taking for all the wrongs I've suffered at the hands of those who I once called Father and brother."

"Your petty grievances mean nothing to me," Clifford spouted. The flesh across his body boiled and shredded like paper as the man howled in agony. Matt knew what was happening. The demon inside had taken control and was asserting its physical form. "I've pursued this one for far too long to hand him over to an outcast of the heavens."

A long snake like tail uncoiled from Clifford's ass. Its green scales slick with slime oozed a black trail across the carpet as it moved closer to Samyaza. His limbs grew thick with brown fur, which extended to powerful paws that elongated until Clifford walked on all fours, and then the small, insane eyes that looked upon the world with only anger, grew. They became huge black saucers, surrounded by brown and white feathers, and Clifford's nose and mouth extended to a razor sharp beak.

Clifford Crouch no longer existed. In his place stood an abomination with a snake tail, a canine body, and the head of an owl, a monstrosity far worse than Adramelech's donkey-peacock form.

"You'll not take this victory from me, Amon," Samyaza told the owl-headed creature, as his black wings extended across the room, barring Amon from Matt. "I'll rip you in two first."

In response, Amon lunged at Samyaza, digging his claws into the fallen angel's pale skin. The owl beak viciously tore at his neck while the snake tail wrapped around Samyaza's trunk.

"Gabriel, where are you?" Matt whispered to himself. He looked out the window, expecting to see the man he loved flying toward the house to protect him. He saw instead rain drenching the earth and a flash of lightning as thunder boomed all around them.

Gabriel wasn't coming. Matt was on his own.

The fears he had earlier about never seeing Gabriel again seemed a forgone conclusion. They were both being punished for their sins, and now his friends and his grandmother shared the burden of his guilt.

If he and his friends were to survive, it was up to him. Once he got them all out of this, he would find a way to bring Gabriel back to his side. He would accept nothing else.

"We have to get out of here," Matt said as he ran to Dee and Shane, who remained paralyzed in fear. "Where's the Duchess?" As he asked his question, Samyaza withdrew a black sword from Amon's chest. The creature hissed in pain.

"We'll find her," Shane said while he helped Dee to her feet. "We need to go. Now!"

The three of them ran down the hall and toward the kitchen, without giving the side door, and their chance for safety, a second glance. They couldn't leave, not without finding the Duchess first.

When they entered the kitchen, Dee ran to the island in the center. She pulled a butcher knife out of the drawer. She obviously intended to be prepared for a confrontation. Shane made a beeline for the computer desk to the right of the butler's pantry, where they all knew the Duchess kept her secret weapon. Within the bottom drawer, Matt's grandmother hid her handgun, a Colt Python revolver. The weapon looked odd in Shane's dainty hands, but his friend's grip told him he knew how to handle the firearm.

As his friends prepared to defend themselves, Matt could only wonder about Gabriel. Had Gabriel been bound in chains and thrown into prison like Samyaza had once been? Had their love been such an abomination that the angels and God above demanded retribution?

"Gabriel!" he screamed at the top of his lungs. "Gabriel, can you hear me?"

"What's gotten into you?" Dee asked. "Have you lost your mind?"

Before he could respond, Matt detected movement out of the corner of his eye. Someone stirred from on top of the kitchen table, and it took him a few moments to realize it was his grandmother. All thoughts of Gabriel vanished as he dashed to her side.

"Clifford's here," she mumbled while straining to sit up.

Her nose was swollen red, and a puffy, black bruise encircled her right eye. For hurting his grandmother, Matt vowed to see Clifford Crouch dead. "I know," he told her. "Are you okay?"

"I'm fine. Where's that bastard, so I can kill him?"

The wall adjacent to the sitting room exploded into the kitchen as the snake-tailed Amon, the demon now in possession of Clifford's body, crashed through. It skidded across the orange terrazzo tile until it crashed into the oven range.

"Good God!" his grandmother screamed. "What is that?"

"That's Clifford," Matt replied as she stared at the demon with a mixture of horror and confusion. He grabbed his grandmother by the arm and led her toward the hallway that ended in her master suite. "We need to get out of here."

Before he and the Duchess could cross to the hallway, Samyaza suddenly appeared before them. "Not so fast," he said as he swatted Matt backward across the table. "The only place you're going is with me."

"Back off, bitch!" Shane cried as he fired two rounds into Samyaza. The bullets hit him in the chest, but the fallen angel barely took note. He scowled and leaped for Shane, who stumbled backward to avoid the attack. Samyaza's sword managed to pierce Shane's shoulder, but the move had slightly thrown off Samyaza's aim.

Still, Matt's friend howled in pain. In shock, Shane fell to the tile, clasping his freely bleeding wound with his left hand.

"Was your friend worth your life?" Samyaza asked.

In response, Dee buried the butcher knife in his back. "He's worth more than yours," she replied as she withdrew the blade and stabbed him again.

Furious, Samyaza's wings swiped backward, knocking her into the hall. He advanced upon her, readying his sword. "Being a daughter of man will not prevent me from killing you," he told Dee as she struggled to get to her feet. "I'll slash your throat and drink your blood."

Amon sprung onto Samyaza, pecking at his back while his canine claws ripped free primary feathers from his right wing.

While the two demons wrestled with each other, the Duchess pulled Dee to her feet, and Matt ran over to check on Shane. "Are you okay?"

"Peachy," Shane replied through gritted teeth, his hand coated red with blood. "Never better."

"The blade cut clean through," Matt announced, tapping into his healing sixth sense. "No major arteries cut, so you should be fine."

"Doesn't stop it from hurting like a bitch," Shane complained.

Matt helped him stand as Dee and his grandmother joined him at Shane's side.

"Let's go!" Dee shouted. "While they're more concerned with killing each other."

"What are those things?" Shane asked. "Demons?"

He nodded in reply.

"And they talked about Gabriel like they knew him," Dee added. "That would make him...?"

"An angel. Archangel to be exact."

"These are the types of things you tell your best friends, especially when creatures from hell are trying to kill us!" Dee shouted at him as they followed him out of the kitchen.

As Matt led his loved ones through the hallway back to the sitting room, he regretted putting those he loved in harm's way. Shane bled profusely, and the Duchess looked crippled by shock. She walked forward like an automaton set on autopilot, and her eyes looked glassy and far away. Her mind shut down, apparently incapable of dealing with the horrors she witnessed.

The only one alert was Dee. Her eyes darted over her shoulder and through the gaping hole Amon made in the sitting room wall. She waited for the hellish creatures to stop fighting each other and pursue the four of them. Her panicked expression told Matt what he already knew. If they didn't reach the door in time, they might not make it out alive at all.

When a few feet separated them from the front door and escape seemed at last possible, Samyaza once again appeared before them. "Must we keep doing this?" he asked, leaning against the doorway. "There really is no escape."

They spun around only to find Amon behind them, its beak snapping sharply shut. "Death in front and death in back," the owl creature spoke in a mixture of a hoot and a hiss. "What will they do?"

"So, now you work together?" Matt asked. They slowly backed up toward the staircase in the foyer. A low groan of terror emanated from his grandmother's throat. "I didn't think demons were capable of teamwork."

"What can we say?" Samyaza replied, resting his sword across his shoulders. "Why kill each other when I can kill your friends to get to you?"

Shane raised his good arm and shot Samyaza in the forehead. The angel dropped his sword and fell backward. Shane then turned and fired another round at Amon. The bullet struck its beak, causing it to shriek in pain.

Matt didn't understand how their weapons were hurting these demons. Perhaps Heaven was still with him after all. "Nice shot," Matt told Shane as the four of them ran up the stairs, searching for a place to hide.

"Don't thank me. Thank a lifetime of video games."

"We'll give thanks later," Dee interrupted as she opened the door to the last bedroom down the upstairs hallway. "We need to barricade this door."

"Don't think it will help," Matt replied as he slammed the door shut and locked it. The room where they were to make their last stand turned out to be the room he occupied as a child, where he escaped the painful memories of his parents' murder and where the nightmares of their deaths first entered his dreams years ago.

Even though he didn't know it at the time, Gabriel had watched over him, protecting him from harm. He wished Gabriel was with him now, but since he wasn't, Matt understood it wasn't by choice.

Scraping sounds caught his attention as Dee shoved the dresser in front of the door and then ran for the window. "It might not do much good, but a few seconds could mean our lives." She opened the window that looked out over a ledge. "We can try to find a way off the roof."

Matt glanced at his grandmother, who stood silently staring at the closed door. Her eyes were wide, and she thoughtlessly plucked the fabric on her sleeve. "I don't think the Duchess is in any shape to shimmy down a drainpipe."

"Well, she's gonna have to be," Dee advised as she walked over to the Duchess. "Joanna, you have to listen to me. We need to get out of here. Now!"

"And what about Shane?" Matt asked. "His shoulder's bleeding pretty badly."

"I'll make it," Shane replied as he stumbled over to the window. "I have to. If we stay, we'll die for sure."

The futility of it all made Matt angry. Everyone he loved was in danger, and the heavens, not Gabriel, decided to forsake him. In anger, he screamed. "Why now?" he cried out. "If I'm to die, fine. But save my grandmother and my friends. *They* didn't break your damn rules. *I* did."

Dee and Shane stared at him in confusion. Even his grandmother glanced sideways at him before gazing intently at the door once again.

"I'll sacrifice myself if that's what it'll take. If you need a pound of flesh, take it from me. Don't take it from them!"

"Matty!" Dee cried out as she escorted the Duchess to the window. "Get a grip!"

"No!" he replied. He had enough. For far too long, he ran away from the dangers that chased him. Too many people lost their lives trying to protect him and now the man he loved was no doubt paying the price for loving him as well. It was time he stopped running and stood his ground. "I'm done with being a pawn in some cosmic game."

He shoved the dresser away from the door.

"What the hell are you doing?" Shane asked.

"I'm taking charge of my own fate," he said as he opened the door. "Go out the window—now!"

When he stepped into the hallway, a deathly white hand clutched his neck and a tail wrapped around his body. A few moments later, Matt's world went black.

CRAIG sped down the streets of Houston with the siren blaring.

Even though he feared he might already be too late, he had to get to Joanna Westlake's house as quickly as possible. Time was of the essence.

Danger waited for Matt there. He knew that with absolute certainty.

If he failed and didn't reach Matt in time, something horrible would not only happen to the man he loved, but the world would also suffer a great loss.

While he still didn't understand how he knew something so prophetic, he didn't question the feeling. It motivated him like the hunches he had followed up to this point.

"If you don't slow the fuck down, you're gonna kill us both," Ybarra screamed while holding onto the dashboard.

"We're not the important ones here," he told the detective. "Matt is."

Craig gunned the police car through an intersection and turned the wheel into the River Oaks subdivision. His destination lay only a few blocks away.

CHAPTER 31

MATT opened his eyes, but his vision remained blurry. It was like trying to view the world through a gelatinous barrier. Everything became distorted, and he couldn't discern his hands, which he held out in front of him.

Slivers of light broke through the shades of gray and black that dominated his vision, but he couldn't make out shapes. The world looked to be one amorphous blob.

The last thing he remembered was leaving his old room in his grandmother's house when Samyaza and Amon grabbed him. After that, he couldn't recall what happened.

Had he been knocked unconscious and taken somewhere? If so, what happened to his grandmother? And Dee and Shane?

"Duchess!" he called out, while using his sense of touch to determine his whereabouts. His hands rubbed across carpet, which meant he was inside a house that wasn't his grandmother's. She didn't have a square inch of carpet anywhere since she preferred hardwood and tile. He had obviously been taken somewhere else, but did that mean the others were brought with him?

"Dee? Shane? Are you guys here?"

When no response came, he began crawling forward, slowly. Every few inches, he held his hands out, trying to feel for some manufactured boundary like a wall or a door; each time, only empty space and more carpet greeted him.

Matt hoped the absence of his loved ones meant they had somehow escaped or that the demons had simply taken him and left. But as he crawled farther and farther along the carpet that apparently led to nowhere, a crushing fear sat upon his chest, making it difficult to breath.

He was completely and utterly alone.

He had never felt this abandoned before. In his dreams, he sensed Gabriel's presence, even before he knew who and what Gabriel was. Someone always stood with him, adding their strength to his and soothing his anxiety with their invisible presence.

Now, it was only him.

Gabriel had been snatched from his side; his parents, both adopted and biological, had been murdered; and his grandmother and best friends were gone—either because they escaped or had been killed.

If he were going to make it out of here alive, he would have to do it on his own.

That was when Matt realized he'd never truly been alone. He was a seventh son. Within him lay the potential for so much goodness that God marked him as the Gifted One. That meant that no matter where he was or what he faced, the heavens above remained at his side, whether he could see them or not

The warm glow of that knowledge burned the fear from his soul.

From somewhere in front of him, a door opened slowly. It let out a long creak as the door gradually swung inward.

"Who's there?" he asked the shapeless void.

When he got no response, he stopped his forward movement. He reached out, tentatively, to inspect the space in front of him, extending his arm to its fullest and rocking slightly forward on his knees until his back began to grumble from the strain.

Empty space sat immediately before him and nothing more.

He turned his head to the side, straining his ears to detect movement of any kind, but he heard nothing, not even the hum of lights or the strum of the air-conditioning unit kicking on. Inhaling deeply, he tried to catch the scent of cologne or musk, anything that would identify who opened the door, but only stale air filled his lungs.

"I know you're there," he said. "I'm not afraid of you."

Then, he heard a noise, distant and brief. It reminded him of a chirp but not the kind from a bird. This sounded more like a suppressed laugh, the kind often heard from a small child or an infant.

Immediately, he guessed what might be making the sound. Matt crawled backward as quickly as possible, trying to put as much distance as possible between him and what headed his way.

The chirp became louder, turning into a small giggle. The sound was followed by a thump and then another as something leaped straight for him.

Even though he couldn't see it, he knew what it was and where he was.

He was in his nightmare, and the giggling figure in front of him was the demonic baby clown, bounding toward him as it had in his last dream.

Faster, he scrambled backward until he slammed into a wall. He tried moving to his left and his right, but walls had grown up around him. He was trapped, and the giggling grew louder and closer, just as the thumps became heavier with each leap.

Matt raised his hands to his face, trying to wipe the haze from his eyes, but each pass of his hand distorted his vision even more.

With his hands against the wall, Matt used the leverage and stood up. He braced himself for the impact, preparing to smack the tiny hellion out of the way. He wasn't going down without a fight, but the giggling and the thumping stopped cold.

He heard only heavy breathing coming from a few feet before him.

The damned thing stood there in the darkness, watching him. No doubt relishing the thought of Matt's impending death.

"Fuck you," he cursed. "You want me? Come on, then! Do it!"

More breathing followed.

"I won't beg for my life. I won't give you the satisfaction, but if you think I'm going quietly, you've got another thing coming. I'll fight you, and I'll squash your baby head if I have to."

As if slowly being wiped away, the haze that blurred Matt's vision began to clear.

The slivers of light widened into circles, like a television screen coming into focus, and the grayish-black shadows retreated to the periphery. His hands instantly went to his eyes, where he rubbed them roughly. If he managed to clear his vision, he might have a fighting chance.

A few moments later he could see again.

He stood at one end of a ridiculously long hallway, five feet away from the doorway that loomed in front of him.

No demonic clown baby waited. In fact, there was no one.

He looked to his left and right and found only tan walls, covered in mildew and black mold. The musty stench of what smelled like rotting cedar assaulted his nostrils like a punch to the face. It made him gag, and as he stared at the walls, the mold multiplied quickly, resembling marching ants in search of more material to consume.

The mold progressed toward where he stood, as if sensing a meal more palatable in his flesh. He needed to get out of there, but there was only one way to go, down the hallway.

He didn't want to do that, but he had no other choice.

Matt took one step forward when he noticed a shadow at the top of the doorway. From the head jamb, a pair of black eyes peered down at him.

Even the black mold noticed the presence and halted its progress toward him. The fungus obviously didn't want to draw the eyes' attention either.

Matt turned around, trying to find some way out of the corner he had been backed into, when the giggling once again resumed. He looked over his shoulder, and the eyes drifted from one end of the door to the other, floating independently from a body similar to how the Cheshire cat's smile dangled before Alice in the Wonderland.

Except this was no fairytale, and the eyes belonged to something far more sinister and deadly than a character from a children's story.

As the eyes slid down the right side of the door, more of the body became visible. A pale white face, coated with layers of bone-white powder, appeared behind the black eyes. Its lips were red and slick as if fresh paint had been applied, but Matt wasn't fooled. The red tint came from blood, not paint. By the time the eyes reached the ground, the demonic baby clown stood before him in all its hideous glory.

It stared silently at him, standing on chubby legs descending from a badly soiled diaper. Yellowish stains coated the front, and brown matter trailed down its legs. It lifted one plump arm and pointed at him, accusing him of some heinous crime, and its mouth opened in a noiseless scream of anger. Inside its round mouth sat rows of jagged teeth like those of a great white shark.

Matt realized this was it. He had nowhere else to go and no other options.

"Come and get me, you little fuck," he told the little monster.

Without a word, the miniature demon leaped at him, hitting him square in his chest. Matt screamed in response as the baby's teeth burrowed into him, and with each gnash of teeth and rip of flesh, he heard the baby in his head.

"Kill them," it said. "Kill them all."

GABRIEL believed himself to be a good angel, a righteous being. Even when he had fallen for Matt and gained knowledge of the flesh, he had remained ignorant to the truth that existed just beyond his newly acquired perception.

Everything would be fine, he believed. Love healed all.

His imprudent actions would be forgiven, and the love he shared with Matt, born from love, could bear no rotten fruit among its branches.

Gabriel now realized he had seen only what he wanted to see.

Love was just like any other force in the world. Whether good or bad, it had consequences that were sometimes unforeseen, and his love for Matt proved no different.

He had hurt many people, including his family, and it was past time to stop playing the helpless victim and seek redemption.

"I feel awful for what I've done," he told Father, still on his knees. "To You, to my brothers, and to Matt and Craig. I've changed their destiny. I only pray that I can make it right again."

"Is that your wish?" Father asked as He again shifted forms. The tattooed, mohawk-wearing blue-eyed man turned into a Vietnamese woman with long black hair, a tube top, shorts much too short, and pink pumps. "To reset Matt's destiny with Craig."

"You did say Craig was supposed to be Matt's one true love, didn't you?"

The woman's kind black eyes smiled. "I never said that. Being a true love and meant to be together are two separate destinies. Think about it, Gabriel," Father said as He helped Gabriel to his feet. "Who else was there when the truck almost ran over Matthew? Who was Matthew dining with when the man named Blade attacked?"

"Craig."

"Precisely. Craig's purpose had been to serve as the Gifted One's human guardian, protecting him from earthly harm that might prevent him from fulfilling his destiny as a seventh son. You, Gabriel, were to be his divine protector, his guardian angel. Shielding him from the evil that waited in the darkness, evil that the human protector could never hope to overcome. In conjunction, the two of you would have kept Matthew safe, and his true destiny fulfilled."

"But I interfered with that by falling in love with him."

"No. It was Matt's love for you that changed everything."

"I don't understand. I thought it was my actions that set the Grand Design askew?"

"Your actions didn't help," Father said. Still the Vietnamese woman, He placed His hand on Gabriel's arm and they strolled about the throne room. "Your physical presence in Matt's life drew him to you, Gabriel. You are an angel. You possess a healthy portion of my divine love, which is strong and overpowering. Why do you think it's so easy for you to compel people to do as you wish? It's that inherent love they feel deep in their souls to satisfy what is divine."

"Did I make Matt fall in love with me?" he asked worriedly. He had never once contemplated the idea that he somehow forced Matt's emotions. All angels were aware of their power over humans. With but a suggestion, they could be made to act, see, or believe whatever an angel instructed. He had used it many times on earth, especially over the past few weeks, to avoid detection.

Had he unconsciously forced Matt to love him? If he did, then he truly was no better than Samyaza.

"Calm your thoughts, My son," Father said with a hug. "You did not force yourself upon the Gifted One. Had you done so, we wouldn't be having this conversation."

Gabriel understood the meaning. Had he used his abilities upon Matt, whether subconsciously or not, he would be enchained by his brothers and thrown into the deepest pits of hell along with the Watchers.

"I'm afraid I don't understand then, Father."

"I know," Father said. A tall, African male took the Vietnamese woman's place. Broad shouldered and handsome, Father wrapped His arm around Gabriel's shoulders as they continued walking side by side among the clouds that drifted in and out of the Throne Room. "You often used your powers of persuasion on Matt as a child. You calmed him through the many dangers he faced as well as through his dreams. Over the years, he's grown practically immune to it, not just from exposure but from his nature as a seventh son. One such as him cannot be tricked onto the path of righteousness or evil. Seventh sons must choose their way, and as part of that power, he has chosen you."

"But I was never meant to be with him. Craig was. How do I fix that?"

Father shook his head. "You cannot. Emotions such as love can't be manipulated or redirected from the path currently set."

"Then I've ruined everything? Broken the Grand Design beyond all repair?"

Father laughed, rustling His hand through Gabriel's short-cut hair. "Nothing is beyond My repair. You know that. But I can only work with the materials provided to Me through the actions of My children."

"Then there's a way?" Gabriel asked. He felt a renewed hope. Perhaps he had a chance to make this up to everyone, including Matt and

Craig. While his love for Matt still filled him with joy, he realized that their love couldn't serve as an obstacle to Matt's destiny. Matt had greatness to fulfill, and if he had to retreat back into the periphery to help Matt achieve it, he intended to do just that. "There's a way to get Matt and Craig back together again?"

"Like I said, love can't be forced. If Matt and Craig are to be together, it is a choice they must both make."

Gabriel looked down through the clouds that revealed all of creation below. "Craig loves him still. I know it. Even now, he rushes to save Matt from dangers he has no hope of defeating."

"Don't dismiss Craig just yet," Father advised. "Your actions, while troublesome, have produced some unexpected results."

"Like what?"

"Nothing is decided yet, so I will not say. I do have a question for you, though."

"What is it, Father?"

"Even now, creation works to repair the flaws your actions have created in the Grand Design. Your descent into sin has sullied your soul, and in consequence, the role of vengeance goes unfulfilled. Do you seek true repentance for what you have done and are you willing to sacrifice all that you are to bring order back to the chaos?"

Gabriel didn't need to think about the question. He had always been ready to give himself completely for the greater good. "I would sacrifice my very existence to mend the damage I've done. Whatever the cost."

Father nodded. "Sacrifices are all that can bring balance now." He placed His hands upon Gabriel's shoulders and delivered a gentle but firm kiss to his forehead. "The roles have been cast, and the players are in place. Free will determines everyone's ultimate fate."

A blinding light filled Gabriel's vision, and when the light disappeared, he no longer stood upon the cloudy floors of the Throne Room.

WHEN he opened his eyes, Matt stared at the unconscious faces of his friends and his grandmother. All three hung suspended from the bedroom wall held fast by a black, viscous substance covering their torsos and limbs. Stretching out in a web-like pattern, the tarry material covered the entire back part of the room, turning his childhood haven into a nightmarish landscape.

His hand held something. Its cool handle rested against his palm. When he tried to look at it, he couldn't move his head. He could only stare straight ahead at Dee, Shane, and his grandmother, who hung like flies before him.

"Kill them," a voice whispered. "Kill them. Now!"

The order prompted his feet to move forward, and his hand to clench around the object he held in his hand. Slowly, he drew closer, his feet walking despite the fact that he tried to stop them. He no longer seemed in control of his body. He felt more like a visitor than if his body were truly his own.

Dee opened her eyes. When she saw him, she screamed at the top of her lungs. Her cries woke up Shane and the Duchess who eyed him in terror. He tried to speak, to tell them they had nothing to be scared about, but he managed to only giggle.

Again he tried to communicate. This time maniacal laughter escaped his throat.

"Good God," the Duchess exclaimed. "Please, no."

Shane struggled against the substance that bound him. He writhed and wiggled, but all he managed to do was get the stuff in his hair and on his face. "Snap out of it," Shane told him. "Can't you see what they've done to you?"

Matt became confused. What was Shane talking about? When he turned around, his body fought him but reluctantly obeyed. He searched the room for answers, but instead found only Samyaza and Amon.

Samyaza leaned against the far wall, his face anxious and beaming while Amon sat on his hind legs about five feet from the fallen angel. A look of boredom clearly resided in the owl's huge eyes.

"Just hurry up and get this over with," Amon said to him. "We don't have all day."

"He's fighting me," he heard himself say, which confused Matt more. He hadn't thought those words. How could he have spoken them?

Samyaza crossed over to him, staring straight into his eyes. "Subdue him," he ordered. "Failure isn't an option."

Matt felt himself nod, though he had no idea why.

"Kill them," the voice repeated as he turned back around to face his friends. They hollered for help, their voices merging into one desperate plea for salvation.

"No," he said. This time it was his voice, his words. "I won't do this."

Whatever he held dropped from his hand, and Samyaza spun him around and slapped him.

"Don't let him win," Samyaza said as if speaking to him. "The Gifted One will become one of us."

"No, I won't!" he replied and slapped Samyaza, hard.

The former angel stepped backward in disbelief. He obviously had not expected retaliation. Appearing from nowhere, his black sword materialized in his hand. "I'll kill you for that!"

Amon suddenly darted between them. "Don't be a fool! This is what you wanted. What we agreed upon. You turn the Gifted One, and I get to kill him. Go back on our deal, and I'll kill you instead."

"Turn me?" Matt asked. "What the hell are you talking about?"

"He's regaining control," Samyaza said. "He must do it. Now!" He placed the sword in Matt's hands. "Quick, before he manages to slip free." He then spun Matt around and shoved him toward his friends.

When Matt turned his head to the right, he caught a glimpse of himself in the mirror. What he saw terrified him. Caked in bone-white powder, his face looked ghostly white. Huge black spots encircled his eyes, and red paint dripped from his lips.

He looked just like the demonic clown baby from his dreams.

"Hurry!" Amon hissed and hooted behind him.

Matt shook his head no and dropped the sword. "I will not!" he said adamantly.

Although he didn't understand how it was possible, somehow the nightmarish demonic clown baby had left his dream and taken control of Matt's body, just like the other demons had assumed control of Dr. Owens, Homer Rodgers, and Clifford Crouch. Matt had become the evil that had hunted him all these years, and now those same creatures wanted him to kill those he loved.

Matt didn't plan on following through, no matter what Samyaza or Amon did to him. Dr. Owens and the others might have let the demons inside them do awful things, but Matt knew he could stop the monster inside him. His will was strong enough. The thing could eat him from the inside out if it wanted, but he would rather die in agony than be responsible for hurting either his friends or his grandmother.

"Do it," the voice inside screamed as his body bent over to pick up Samyaza's sword. His feet again moved toward his friends, who pleaded with him to stop. He tried digging in his heels to halt his progress, but it had no effect.

With Samyaza's sword held high, he prepared to end the lives of those he loved in one swipe, when a voice from behind screamed at him to stop.

When he turned around, Matt saw Craig standing at the doorway with Detective Ybarra at his side, their guns aiming directly at the monstrosities. And Matt.

"I don't know what the fuck you three are supposed to be, but I'll put a bullet in each of your heads if you don't put your hands in the motherfucking air right now!"

Even though Matt knew the dangerous situation Craig just put himself into, he had never been happier to see him in his life. Craig might just be the one person able to put an end to this.

All Matt had to do was get Craig to kill him.

CHAPTER 32

WHEN Craig had first seen the creatures and the room, he expected to feel fear, but he only felt a desire for vengeance. After all, it wasn't every day he charged onto a scene to be greeted by a winged corpse, a dog with an owl head and snake tail, and some crazy dressed like a psychotic clown. It also wasn't typical to find three people he had grown to care about held to the wall with what could only be described as black vomit.

No, fear would have definitely been the correct emotion.

Instead, only a need for vengeance rose to the surface, a desire to right all the wrongs that had been committed today. It supplanted rational fear with righteous anger, and Craig knew exactly what he had to do. Above all else, he needed to protect Dee, Shane, and Joanna Westlake; all other priorities were rescinded.

"I said get your hands in the air," he shouted at them. "Now!"

"Belton, what the fuck is going on?" Ybarra asked from his immediate left. The man's hands trembled, causing his usually steady aim to shake.

"Get a hold of yourself, Detective!"

Ybarra nodded, his face wet with perspiration.

"A mere man thinks to order us around, Samyaza?" The owl-headed creature asked the corpse. Its tongue darted out of its beak like a snake's. "We should kill them and be done with it."

"Be still, Amon," the corpse named Samyaza told the owl. "There's something strange about this one."

"I won't repeat myself again," Craig ordered as he stepped farther into the room. He didn't understand Samyaza's comment, which had been directed at him. Why would such a monstrosity say there was something strange about *him*? But as he pondered the question, a new one came to the front of his mind: why wasn't he more freaked out like Ybarra? Why did this suddenly feel like another day at work?

Craig shook his head to clear his thoughts. He had a job to get done and couldn't risk any distractions. He nodded at Dee, Shane, and Matt's grandmother. Their frantic eyes begged him to hurry up and free them. Craig fully intended to do that once he subdued the three freaks in front of him. "Put your hands in the air, or I take you out."

"Me first!" the clown shouted. It sounded more like a plea than a challenge, and it stumbled toward him with a sword made of shadows held above its head. "Kill me, Craig. Now!"

Craig didn't understand how the clown knew him, but he aimed the barrel of his gun directly at the clown's head anyway. He wouldn't drop his guard based on an attempt at familiarity. Ronald McCrazy would die before it got too close to him.

But as the clown took unsteady steps toward him, Craig eyed the other two creatures. Fear reflected in their eyes. Their worried expressions told him that neither of them wanted anything bad to happen to the sword-wielding clown. Instinctively, he knew that if he took it out, the standoff would be over before it began, so he steadied his aim and prepared to fire.

But as he stared at the clown, he saw something familiar in the mad eyes that gave him pause. Beautiful hazel irises floated within the black paint encircling its eyes. They made him feel lightheaded, and his pulse quickened. Only one person ever had that effect on him. "Matt?" he asked. "Is that you?"

"Yes!" Joanna Westlake screamed from across the room. "They did something to him. Please, help him, Craig! Please!"

"Don't listen to her," the clown told him. "She's senile." Its blood-red lips stretched into a smile meant to strike terror. It didn't work. The person behind the grin looked terrified and desperate. "I'm the one who's going to kill them. And you."

A shot exploded, and Craig jumped at the sound.

Ybarra fired his gun and hit the clown dead in the chest. The clown fell backward and dropped the sword, and the move attracted the angry attention of Samyaza and Amon.

In a matter of seconds, they leaped upon the detective.

ALTHOUGH Matt knew he had been shot, he didn't feel the bullet penetrate his body. Still, the impact caused him to fly backward, and Samyaza's sword fell from his grasp. When he looked down at his chest, an angry red stain spread across his shirt, and breathing proved more and more difficult.

He had done it.

The Duchess, Dee, and Shane were safe from him, and he felt confident Craig would be able to keep them that way.

An agonizing scream drew Matt's attention, and he watched as Samyaza and Amon descended upon Detective Ybarra. Amon ripped into the detective's chest with its beak while Samyaza's wings turned razor sharp and gutted the detective in the hallway.

The detective's body shuddered until finally lying still in death.

From behind him, Dee and Shane yelled in fright while the Duchess loudly prayed.

"Ybarra!" Craig shouted as he fired twice, hitting Amon in the head. The demon hissed in pain as it fell over on its side. Its tail writhed upon the floor in agony before becoming still.

"I'm going to enjoy slicing the flesh from your bones!" Samyaza howled as he flew directly at Craig. Somehow Craig managed to sidestep the attack. Samyaza crashed into the far wall, which collapsed on top of him, burying him underneath.

"Matt!" Craig yelled as he ran over to his side. Craig cradled Matt in his arms and tears welled up in the corners of his eyes. "I'll get you help, Matt. I promise."

"Help them," he whispered lifting his hand to point at his loved ones who begged him not to die. "I'm the cause of all this. I deserve whatever's coming my way."

"No, you don't. You'll be fine. I promise." Craig dashed over to Shane and began pulling clumps of the sticky material off his hands and legs. When one hand and leg were free, Craig moved on to Dee and then to the Duchess, who all slowly began to remove the rest of their bound limbs.

"I don't deserve you," Matt told Craig as he watched him help his grandmother down from where she had been bound. "You were too good for me."

"I know, but I loved you anyway."

"And I loved you too," Matt told him as Craig crouched to his side. "I didn't show it very well, but I did. Things between us may have gotten weird, and there's so much that I've been going through, but it never changed how I felt about you. Please, don't doubt that."

Craig nodded. "I won't."

A furious bellow caught their attention as Samyaza flew straight at them. The fallen angel looked furious, his face twisted into an angry scowl. His plans to turn Matt by having him commit murder had failed. Now, he sought revenge.

With speed Matt didn't think he possessed, Matt shoved Craig out of the way and reached out to grab Samyaza's neck. Despite the blinding pain in his chest from the bullet wound, Matt's fingers dug into Samyaza's neck as he wrestled the fallen angel to the ground.

Samyaza stared at him in dismay.

Matt had accomplished something Samyaza never expected, and they both knew it.

Samyaza had hoped to use the demon to control Matt's actions, to make him turn onto the path of the wicked. Instead, he usurped control of the demon's abilities inside him and used them against the hellspawn that had sought his destruction for far too long.

"You've lost, Samyaza!" Matt told him as his fingers dug deeper into the fallen angel's neck. Blood tinted black began to pour from where his fingers slipped beneath its dead flesh. "You can't make me evil. No one can!"

Samyaza laughed. "Not even the body of the man who killed your father and your brothers?" Samyaza withdrew, and in his place, Homer Rodgers appeared within Matt's grasp. "This is the man who slaughtered your family," Samyaza spoke through Homer's voice. "He chopped up your brothers with an axe and then killed your father, who was trying to protect you. Ask Gabriel. He was there the whole time. He did nothing to stop it. Instead, he took you and flew away. Gabriel didn't help your family; your God abandoned you. Why choose the light when shadows have embraced you since your birth?"

Matt tossed Homer through the far wall. "Get out of here," he told the others. "Before it's too late."

"It's already too late," said Homer, rising to his feet with blood trickling from his mouth. From the discordant tone, Matt knew Samyaza still controlled his host. "Use that anger," he said. "Strike out at everyone and everything around you. You have the power; you can feel it bubbling like magma inside a volcano. Bring it out and rain death around all you see. Burn it down. Burn it all down!"

Shaking his head, Matt fell to his knees, for he felt the irrational rage rising from within.

"Get out. Now!" he screamed at his loved ones, but they refused to leave him.

They didn't understand what was happening. By harnessing the power of the demon inside, Matt had unwittingly embraced the evil it represented. A fire flowed through his veins like poison, corrupting everything it touched. If he didn't expunge the demon, it would gain complete control, and then he would truly be responsible for the deaths of everyone he loved.

Even more than before, they faced a far greater danger from him than they did Samyaza or Amon.

CRAIG didn't understand what was happening, but he knew evil when he saw it. The thing that was Samyaza but now appeared to be a man was as close to true evil as he had ever seen in his life.

Watching it goad Matt as he wrestled with inner demons caused Craig to cry out for vengeance. Its call overpowered him. It freed him of the hurt and betrayal that Matt had inflicted upon him until it grew more powerful than any other emotion, even his love for Matt.

Craig felt renewed, reborn into something greater than he had ever been in his life, so he charged at the man, knocking Samyaza down.

"I won't let you win," Craig told him. "Vengeance is at hand."

"Vengeance?" the man asked as black wings once again sprouted from his back. "What do you know of vengeance?" Once again the corpse instead of the man, Samyaza's wings pummeled Craig's body before grasping him in a fist-like grip. They shook him vigorously before tossing him into Amon's waiting paws.

Having licked its wounds, the owl-headed monstrosity had once again entered the fray. Its cold eyes demanded Craig's death.

"This one thinks he's greater than he is," Amon laughed. "Calling for vengeance as if he were Gabriel, when he is nothing but a pathetic, frail human."

Amon's beak plunged into Craig's shoulder, where it ripped through flesh and muscle. When it withdrew, blood dripped plentifully from its open maw.

From behind, Craig felt dozens of needles stab through his flesh. Staring down at his body, dozens of black feathers now jutted from his chest, and when Amon dropped him to the floor, Samyaza extracted his sharp wings from Craig's back.

"I sense what was happening to you," Samyaza told Craig. "But it is too late." His wings extended and pierced his body once again.

Strange warmth spread across him as his blood soaked his clothes.

Even though he wanted to do more, Craig understood his body had accomplished all that it could. It gave Matt the time he needed to again gain control and banish whatever evil resided within him.

As his body shut down and slowly turned to ice, Craig hoped his sacrifice would be enough.

MATT felt the demon clown within him, trying to force its evil to the surface. He couldn't let that happen. He had to get rid of whatever hellish seed had been planted inside him. Once that was done, he could help Craig.

While Matt appreciated Craig's bravery, Craig was out of his league.

That was when Matt realized that had been Craig's plan. Craig intended to sacrifice himself in hopes that the distraction would allow Matt time to save his loved ones and himself.

"Let's go, Matty!" Dee pulled on his arm, trying to get him to stand.

"You go," he told them. "I must get this thing out of me before it's too late. Get out of here. Save yourselves."

His grandmother shook her head. "I'm not going anywhere." She stood her ground in front of him and stared back at the demons, who were tossing Craig around like a toy.

"That's right," added Shane as he found the gun he used in the kitchen. "I've got two more rounds, and I aim to use them."

"No!" Matt screamed at them. The evil rose inside him as fast as the demon clown bounded toward him in his dream. In a few moments, it would be free, and then it would be over. "Leave now!"

Dee shook her head. In her hand, she held the knife that she had previously stabbed Samyaza with. "We've got your back."

Matt didn't deserve all these sacrifices. Too many people had died around him, and though he tried to right those wrongs by facing the demons alone, he only managed to bring more death and destruction.

"Have faith," a voice from within spoke. He knew it wasn't the demon because the demon inside him whispered and grunted when it spoke. This voice sounded like music.

"Gabriel?" Matt asked as he looked around.

"Believe in yourself as much as I do."

"It hurts so much," Matt replied. He winced as tiny claws ripped into his flesh from the inside. The demon sought escape and was scratching its way to the surface.

"You can do it," the voice told him. "I know you can. Forget the anger and the pain. Look at the love all around you."

Raising his head, Matt watched as Craig sacrificed himself. Amon ripped through his chest while Samyaza shredded him with his wings.

Shane fired the final two rounds from the gun while Dee and his grandmother ran toward those who would kill them. After emptying the cartridge, Shane charged after them.

Without fear or thought for her safety, the Duchess grabbed a handful of Amon's feathers from around his face and ripped them out. Dee again sank her blade into Samyaza, this time in his ribs while Shane brought the gun down upon Amon's head.

Howling in anger, the demons fought back.

Amon wrapped his tail around his grandmother's legs and flung her head first into the wall. When she landed, she lay limp. Samyaza removed the knife from his ribs before plunging it into Dee's stomach. While she fell in a motionless heap, Samyaza grabbed Shane by the arm slamming him down onto the floor three times before finally dropping him.

Although he wanted to feel anger for their needless sacrifice, he saw instead the power of love. It boldly faced what threatened it. In its purest form, it proved unstoppable and showed Matt exactly what he needed to do.

He dug deep, recalling all the love he had ever held in his heart. He remembered how his parents doted on him, cherishing the miracle his presence provided his family. His grandmother's selfless devotion to him in life played out like a movie before his eyes, and the demon inside howled in agony.

It crawled back down, trying to hide from the images, but Matt forced it back up. He wanted it to see the laughter he shared with Dee and Shane, two people who were more like his siblings than his friends. They did everything for each other, even when they drove each other crazy.

His stomach twisted, and his body spasmed as the demon inside fought back.

When his memories fell upon his love for Craig, the man who was drawn to him like the waves upon the shore, the thing inside him began to lose its tenuous grip on his soul. It struggled to gain purchase, but it was a losing battle, especially when Matt thought of Gabriel.

The angel had saved him his entire life, and Matt had a lifetime of love stored inside his heart for him. Matt felt cherished and special whenever Gabriel's blue eyes looked at him. When he lay in his muscular arms, a strength he never before possessed filled his body, allowing him to see only an endless future filled with hope and love, and in those emotions, he found the power he needed.

With one final push, the demon lost its hold completely. Matt screamed in pain as he brought the vile thing up and vomited the poison that infected him upon the floor around him.

The demon stared at him in defiance as it hissed in pain.

"Well done, Gifted One," said a voice from above.

Matt lifted his head and found Gabriel hovering above him, his wings keeping him aloft and his bronze aura shining its holy light upon the evil around them. In Gabriel's presence, the demon that had sought to take control of him turned to ash and blew away.

"You've done the hard part," Gabriel announced as he glared at Samyaza and Amon. "Leave the rest to me."

CHAPTER 33

ONCE Matt had forced the demon from his body, Gabriel embraced his part in this final act. To Father, he vowed to follow where the Grand Design led him. His wants and desires became secondary, and as he had in millennia past, he willingly surrendered himself to the whims of providence and trusted that all would be well.

His selfish actions had started them on the path they now walked, and Gabriel's selfless sacrifice promised to repair the flaws he helped create.

Gabriel watched as Matt, exhausted and spent from his internal battle, collapsed on the floor, no longer in the guise of the demon who possessed him but once again as the man he loved. Matt's hazel eyes stared up at him with both relief and love. He wanted to scoop Matt into his arms as he had in the past, to protect him from the dangers that still walked among them, but Matt no longer needed his protection.

Matt had made his choice and expunged the evil, which had haunted him for years, from his life. His heart proved true, and he no longer required Gabriel's constant vigilance, leaving Gabriel free to complete the duty he was first assigned—to remove the evil that strode the earth in pursuit of Matt's soul.

And though he still longed to hold Matt as he had before, Gabriel accepted that a new pattern currently formed around them, one that would likely make their reunion impossible, and if the new design separated him from the man he loved for the rest of eternity, Gabriel would cherish the love they had shared, however brief or bright it might have been.

So, standing in front of Matt, Gabriel gazed across the room at Samyaza and Amon. Their shocked expressions told him that they were surprised to see him walking the earth. They believed that like the Watchers, Gabriel would be chained and banished for crimes of the flesh.

Clearly that had not happened, for he now stood before them garbed in his bronze celestial armor. His sword rested firmly in his grip, and his previously diverted focus was restored. Now the Angel of Vengeance, Gabriel stood prepared to fulfill his function and return order to the chaos he had inadvertently caused.

Raising his hands skyward, a line of white fire sprouted from the floor. It trailed along the perimeter of the room, separating Samyaza and Amon from Matt and his fallen loved ones. Their parts in this had come to an end, so Gabriel removed them from the playing field.

The demons would now deal only with him.

"The time has come to end your stay on Earth," Gabriel told them. "Your plans have failed."

"Victory is still ours to be had," Amon replied. He attempted to leap over the holy fire, but tentacles of flame reached up and engulfed his tail. Screaming, Amon fell to the floor as the white flames consumed his form. "No," he howled. "I will win! I will kill the Gifted One!"

The holy fire spread quickly across his body. Soon, his canine fur was set aflame before the white coils made a meal of the feathers upon Amon's head. For a few seconds, the demon writhed in agony as only its wide black eyes stared out amidst the flames to Samyaza for assistance.

"Fool," Samyaza told him. He drew his sword and ran it through Amon's chest.

Amon sputtered obscenities, gripping onto the sword before Samyaza withdrew it. Black tar exploded from the open wound and splattered before him. Amon attempted to attack, but the fight quickly left his body. Falling to his knees, Amon cursed Samyaza and the heavens above before toppling onto the floor in a burning heap.

When Amon finally lay still, the holy flames burned out. Amon's body had disappeared. In its place, Clifford Crouch lay dead on the floor. The demon within the man had been vanquished and returned to hell.

"Your turn."

Samyaza grinned. "I'm not so easily defeated. I know my limits. Just as I know yours." He readied his sword, his muscles tense and prepared to attack. "You pretend to be the angel you once were, but I know better. While I sense renewed purpose, I also see the damage your sins have caused. You're a pale version of the previous archangel. Your full powers have yet to return, and I doubt they ever will. What bargain did you strike with Father, Gabriel? For I know one was most assuredly made."

Gabriel flew across the room, his sword clanging against Samyaza's. Sparks of lightning split the room and struck burning holes within the walls around them.

"You boast too much," Gabriel told him.

"Yet I know I'm right," he said, swinging his sword in a wide arc. Gabriel blocked it with his own before kicking Samyaza in the face and forcing him dangerously close to the fire. Samyaza rose to one knee and charged back toward Gabriel.

Their swords clashed, causing the house to tremble and the ferocious storm outside to reach cataclysmic proportions. Their battle stirred the elements around them and threatened to bring about destruction to all in the immediate area.

Gabriel knew he had to end this quickly or risk the lives of the innocent. Further conflict had to be avoided at all cost, and there was only one way to end this without doing more damage than he had already done.

Though he wanted to, he dared not look back. Matt held a power over him that no one else did. One word of protest from his love's lips would shake his resolve, so he stared only at Samyaza as he tossed his sword aside and dismissed the armor that protected him.

Samyaza stopped, studying Gabriel intently. "What trickery is this?" he asked. "You as well as I know that only an angel can harm another angel. Though I may have fallen, it does not change what I am."

Gabriel nodded. "Do your worst, and let Father's will be done."

With a grin plastered across his face, Samyaza dove straight for Gabriel, his sword aimed directly at Gabriel's chest.

AFTER Gabriel had erected a wall of fire that separated the demons from those he loved, Matt reluctantly rose to his knees. His body still burned in agony from expelling the demon, and it demanded at least a week's worth of rest to recover, but he didn't have the time to recuperate.

Matt needed to check on the others, to see what he could do to heal the wounds inflicted upon them by the demons sent here to kill him. Not only was he a nurse, but he was the Gifted One, the seventh son of a seventh son. He had to be able to perform some type of healing miracle, but in order to do that, he had to work his way over to where they lay.

Matt crawled along the perimeter of the flames. Though they burned white hot, he felt no heat. The holy flames licked and danced around the floor, but he knew the heavenly fire would not harm him.

Gabriel had erected them to keep him and the others out of harm's way.

Samyaza's taunts caught Matt's attention, and he contemplated finding a weapon of some sort to help Gabriel, but he knew any attempt would be fruitless.

The battle Gabriel now fought was beyond Matt.

He placed his trust in God to keep Gabriel safe. And since Gabriel had been returned to him unharmed, he believed that Gabriel's conflict with his brothers had ended well. He even hoped their relationship might be allowed to continue once the heavens realized their love was a force of good, not something sinful.

Before Matt reached Craig, who lay only a few feet from where Matt had previously fallen, he heard Amon scream in pain as the heavenly fire quickly consumed him. When the flames died away, Clifford lay dead on the floor. Although he knew he shouldn't get pleasure from someone else's death, Matt inwardly celebrated the man's demise. Clifford had tortured Matt long enough and deserved whatever fate awaited him in hell.

When he finally reached Craig's side, Matt noticed Craig's eyes were open, watching as Gabriel and Samyaza exchanged blows that shook the house at its foundation. "Craig, I'm here," he said while examining the mess made of Craig's body.

Craig's arm hung by a thread of muscle to his shoulder, and at least two-dozen stab wounds punctured his chest. A pool of blood encircled his body, which told Matt the damage to Craig's back was severe.

"He's an angel?" Craig asked, peering through the flickering flames at the battle. "Gabriel's an angel?"

Based on Craig's injuries, Matt couldn't believe that Craig was capable of speaking. He obviously had even more strength than Matt believed, but Matt knew that strength wouldn't last long. He had to act fast, so he nodded as he took off Craig's shirt and began ripping it to shreds. The first thing he needed to do was fashion a tourniquet and tie the arm back to the shoulder to stop the bleeding.

"I never stood a chance, did I?" Craig whispered. "How could I compete with a hard-bodied angel?" Though Craig suffered severe wounds, Matt still heard the playfulness in Craig's voice.

"It was never a contest," Matt told him.

"No shit!" Craig exclaimed as Matt wrapped the shirt fabric around the shoulder and tied the dangling limb up toward the body. The torn fabric quickly became soaked with blood, and Craig winced in pain but didn't make a sound.

"That's not what I meant," Matt replied. As he worked on Craig, he scanned the others, who lay a few feet in front of him. Dee clutched her stomach, which freely bled from her stab wound. He needed to save some bandages for her and apply pressure to stop the bleeding. If he could do that, she had a fighting chance. Although Shane didn't move, he heard low moans coming from the direction where Samyaza dropped him after slamming him into the floor. Bandages would do nothing for him. Based on his injuries, Shane suffered from internal bleeding caused by the blunt force trauma. Fractured ribs likely punctured his liver, lung, or spleen, and Shane needed to get to a hospital immediately.

But even as Matt fretted over Shane, his grandmother concerned him the most. The Duchess hadn't moved since Amon tossed her, headfirst, through the wall. He worried about a broken neck and a subdural hematoma. For a woman of her age, such injuries might prove fatal. Still, his grandmother was a stubborn woman; she had fight left in her.

He knew she would be okay.

After all, she had attacked a demon with her bare hands. That alone spoke volumes about her tenacity.

"I understand now."

Craig's voice brought Matt's focus back to him. "What do you mean?" Matt asked as he placed some of the remaining makeshift bandages over Craig's chest wounds.

"Why you love him," Craig muttered. "He's been protecting you all your life, hasn't he?"

"Yes, he has."

"And you've always been in love with him?"

Matt nodded. "Now I need you to apply pressure," he instructed Craig. "I have to go check on the others."

"I'm sorry."

"What do you have to be sorry for?"

"For thinking you were playing me. You weren't. I know that now."

"We can talk about this later. When you're better."

Craig turned to look at him. His eyes sparkled, and Matt had never seen them so green. "I'm not going to get better. I know that."

"Yes, you are." He refused to give up on Craig, and he wasn't going to have Craig give up on himself. "And I'm the nurse. Not you. So my opinion means more than yours."

"And the Gifted One," he told Matt. "Whatever the heck that means."

Matt smiled. "It means that when I say you're going to get better that you're going to get better."

Craig lifted his good arm and cupped Matt's cheek. His hand was cold. "You may be the Gifted One, but you're not God." Craig's eyes turned to look above, and by the way he intensely stared at the ceiling, Matt would have guessed that somehow his gaze penetrated the roof and peered into the heavens. "I think He has other plans for me."

"Stop talking like that. I mean it."

"It's okay. I'm not afraid," he told Matt. "I think I'm ready for whatever it might be."

"I said stop it!" Matt yelled. He was a good man, whose sacrifices had earned him the right to live out his days to a ripe old age.

"Don't blame yourself. This is bigger than you. Than all of us."

"Craig, I...."

Craig placed his fingers over Matt's lips. They now felt colder than ice. "It's about to happen," he told Matt. "It's so... glorious."

His hand fell from Matt's lips to the floor, and his face smiled up to the sky above. Craig's green eyes didn't close. Instead, they pierced the great beyond, and as Matt watched, they turned a shade of blue only found within the heavens above.

Matt didn't understand what that meant, but his inability to comprehend the change in eye color didn't halt the tears that streamed down his cheeks. He had failed Craig, a man who had risked everything for him and in the end even offered absolution for the wrongs Matt committed against him.

Craig was right. There truly was a special place in heaven for a man like him.

A furious scream caught his attention, and Matt reluctantly looked away from Craig's dead body out to the battle to his left and beyond the heavenly flames.

What he saw defied explanation.

Gabriel stood before Samyaza without his sword and without his armor. With arms spread wide, he welcomed Samyaza's blade.

From previous discussion, Matt knew Gabriel's one true weakness was other angels. Only one heavenly being could inflict permanent harm on another. And though Samyaza was no longer a heavenly being, he still remained an angel by creation.

"Gabriel, no!" Matt shouted as he rose to his feet.

But before Matt had a chance to react, a flash of light filled the room and immediately blinded him.

GABRIEL accepted the end of the life he had once known as Samyaza bore down upon him.

This is what Father meant, when He said only sacrifices could restore the balance. In order for vengeance to be rewoven into the Grand Design, the previous form had to be destroyed.

A fresh pattern fixed the flaws created by the old, and by embracing his destruction, he not only reset the balance but took out an old evil with it.

Samyaza's sword sunk deep within Gabriel's chest while his former brother cheered in victory. Never before had Gabriel felt such pain, but in the end it would all be worth it. He would die a hundred times over if it meant protecting the Grand Design and Matt.

For Gabriel, there were no other loves greater.

"I kill you, Gabriel, and wipe you from existence."

Gabriel smiled in reply. He wrapped his arms around Samyaza and whispered in his ear. "Vengeance is mine at last." A blinding white light exploded outward from his chest, completely engulfing Samyaza in its glowing radiance.

The light ripped through Samyaza's darkened soul, shattering it to pieces. As his body turned to dust and trailed away, Samyaza realized his mistake for the first time.

Though an angel can kill another, an angel's life force is pure light, which burns hotter and brighter than any summoned heavenly fire. By delivering Gabriel's deathblow, Samyaza unwittingly brought upon his own destruction.

The darkness within him could never survive the exposed soul of an archangel.

"You tricked me," Samyaza pitifully complained. He then turned to particles less dense than ash and blew away.

Not a trace of Samyaza or Homer Rodgers remained.

"Gabriel, no!"

He turned to watch Matt, who leaped through the fire toward him. His eyes were mad with grief, and by the time Matt reached his side, tears steadily flowed down his cheeks.

"Why did you do it?" Matt asked. "Why?"

"It had to be done. To reset the Grand Design."

As his wings ceased beating, Gabriel slowly lowered to the floor, where Matt held his dying body to his chest.

"That's not good enough," Matt told him. "I love you, and I thought you loved me. We're supposed to be together. Forever."

Gabriel reached out and brought Matt's face to his. Their lips brushed together, and their mouths once again inhaled each other's breath as they kissed deeply.

"All will be well," he told Matt. "It's my final gift to you."

"What do you mean? What are you talking about?"

Gabriel held Matt close as the light continued to flow out his body. Before he bestowed his present onto Matt, he wanted to relish in their last moments together. He ran his hands over Matt's cheek, his fingers gliding over his smooth flesh. Inhaling deeply, Gabriel took Matt's smell, a mixture of cologne and musk, into his body. It invigorated him and gave him the strength to do what had to be done.

Lifting Matt's face to his, Gabriel stole one last kiss before speaking the word that would restore all to what is should now be.

"Forget."

Matt sat up. "What?"

"Forget," Gabriel repeated. Though he smiled, his heart broke.

This was his final sacrifice. This was where the Grand Design would take over and refashion a pattern out of the shambles of the old.

Father and free will would take it from there.

MATT didn't understand what Gabriel was doing. He kept repeating *forget* over and over, and Matt wasn't forgetting anything. He loved Gabriel more than he did his own life. He had challenged Heaven and hell to be with him, and he couldn't comprehend why Gabriel would be telling him to forget anything.

"Forget," Gabriel repeated.

His words floated like music through the air, penetrating his mind and worming its way into his thoughts. The world became hazy, and his memories turned fuzzy. For a few moments, he couldn't recall the way Gabriel's stubble felt across his cheek or how Gabriel's tongue tasted inside his mouth.

Why was Gabriel doing this?

"Stop it," Matt frantically told him. He held onto his love's face and kissed him hard. He just had to make Gabriel stop talking.

"Forget," he repeated through their kiss.

Now he had trouble recalling what they talked about the morning after they had sex the first time. Gabriel told him a story, something from the Bible, but he couldn't quite recollect what it was. It had something to do with David and Goliath, or at least he thought it did.

"Please stop," Matt pleaded. Tears poured from his eyes, snaking sad trails down his cheeks. "Don't do this to us."

"Forget."

Images continued to fly out of his mind, leaving Matt completely confused. Wasn't Gabriel in one of his dreams? But he couldn't remember what the dreams were about. They had terrified him though. Hadn't they? He couldn't recall even that much.

And as he looked into Gabriel's eyes, he couldn't summon where they first met or how they met. In fact, he wasn't certain he knew who Gabriel was at all. But those sky-blue eyes struck a strange chord within his soul for some reason.

"Forget."

Memory after memory flew from his mind until Matt became sleepy. He was tired, and he didn't know why. He didn't want to sleep because he had so many unanswered questions. Who was this man who smiled up at him? Why was he in his old room at his grandmother's house? In fact, where was his grandmother? Weren't Dee and Shane here too?

But the exhaustion proved more powerful than his curiosity, and Matt curled up on the floor like he used to as a child, and closed his eyes.

GABRIEL didn't have much time left. The light that once filled his soul had all but already vanished, and he had one final task left to complete.

He leaned over Matt and brushed the hair from in front of his eyes. With one final kiss upon his love's forehead, Gabriel whispered his final word, "Remember."

PART V:
SECOND GENESIS

CHAPTER 34

MATT ran through his apartment like a crazy Martha Stewart, making sure everything was in order. The place had been picked up. No dirty socks or uniforms lay scattered about like usual. Although Matt was fastidious about cleanliness, his man didn't share Matt's fervor for a spotless living space.

Who was Matt kidding? He lived with a slob, plain and simple, but he wouldn't trade his slob for any other man.

Glancing at the clock, he grew anxious. Everyone would be here soon, and he still had tons to prepare for the celebration. As usual, Matt wanted everything to be perfect, but today it needed to be more perfect than ever.

Today, they celebrated the newest member of the homicide department for the Houston police force, and he wanted to show everyone how proud he was of the accomplishment, especially after everything they had all been through.

They had survived Clifford Crouch's final attempt at trying to kill him. His best friends and grandmother had been caught in the crossfire, but luckily, they had all fully recovered, even though it had been touch and go for a while.

Dee suffered a bowel laceration as a result of the stab wound, but surgery repaired the damage. Shane's spleen had been removed, when his broken rib ruptured the organ after the blunt force trauma Clifford inflicted, and his grandmother, who had been hurt the worst, was now once again on her feet. After being forced through a wall headfirst, the Duchess suffered a subdural hematoma and underwent a craniotomy to remove the blood collecting outside the brain.

They all owed their lives to his very own Officer Belton, who arrived to save the day. He took Clifford down before he had the chance to kill Matt and those he loved. Unfortunately, no one had been able to save Detective Ybarra, who had died on the scene.

Now, the nightmares that had plagued him since the deaths of his parents were gone just as Clifford had departed this world. He owed his life and his continued sanity to the man he wanted to spend the rest of his life with. Hopefully, he could repay the owed debt by the time they were old and gray.

The doorbell chimed, and Matt sprinted to answer it.

When he opened the door, his grandmother, Dee, and Shane stood on the other side.

"There's my Duchess," Matt said as he embraced his grandmother. "You look as stunning as ever."

"Why thank you, Matthew," she said as she entered, carrying the two dishes she prepared for the festivities—her world-famous deviled eggs and green bean casserole. "I purchased this outfit just for today. Our honored guest deserves no less."

"You got that right," Dee said as she kissed Matt's cheek. She strolled in with her scrumptious red velvet cake. "That man of yours is gonna have at least two pieces of this here cake even if I have to force it down his handsome throat."

"I think forcing things down his throat is Matt's job," Shane added with a shit-eating grin plastered across his face.

"Shane!" the Duchess scolded. "Ladies should have manners."

"Don't worry about it," Matt told her. "Shane is definitely not a lady."

Shane replied with a raspberry as he placed his mixed green salad on the table. "Anybody mind if I toss my salad here?" he suggestively arched his left eyebrow in regards to his double entendre.

"Oh, God, Shane! Really?" Dee asked, horrified.

The Duchess frowned. "I've no idea what that means, and I'm sure I don't want to know."

"You don't," Matt and Dee said in unison.

After setting out their dishes, everyone got busy helping him put the finishing touches on the decorations while Matt checked on the lamb in the oven. Dee and Shane hung the congratulations sign across the living room while the Duchess set the table.

"The lamb smells wonderful."

"Thanks, Duchess. It's almost done too."

"When's that hunk of man flesh getting home?" Shane asked. "I'm starving!"

"Thirty minutes or so," he replied after glancing at his watch.

"Does he know what he's walking in to?"

"No," Matt told Dee. "Unless Shane told him."

"Hey, I can keep a secret!" Shane pouted while jutting out his lower lip.

"My dear, Shane, I love you dearly," the Duchess told him. "But you most certainly *cannot* keep a secret."

"I can too. I haven't told anyone that Dee's been hooking up with that hunky Dr. Franklin."

Matt stared dumbstruck at Dee who walked over and punched Shane in the arm. "Dr. Franklin, Deeds? Really? He was your surgeon!"

"Was," she pointed out while smacking Shane again. "He's not my surgeon anymore, so it's perfectly acceptable for us to date."

"A date means you have to actually leave the house," Shane added before running away from Dee. He hid behind the Duchess for safety.

"Don't look to me to save you," his grandmother told Shane as Dee drew closer. "When you rile the hornet's nest, you expect to be stung."

"Oh, I'll sting him alright. When he least expects it."

"Sting him later," Matt told Dee. "I want to hear all about the doc. Spill."

"A lady doesn't kiss and tell, Matthew," announced the Duchess.

Shane opened his mouth, but Matt's grandmother gestured for him to be quiet. He was in enough trouble as it was without adding further comment on Dee's status as a lady.

"Thank you, Mrs. Westlake. I think I'll keep the details of our private life private for now."

"You must really like him then. Otherwise, you'd be telling us everything," Matt offered.

Dee blushed at Matt's comment. "Maybe."

"Well, good for you, Deidre," his grandmother said. "I've been waiting for the right man to enter your life. Not only that, but I'm glad to hear that you've been getting your freak on."

"Duchess!" Matt called out from the kitchen while Shane and Dee burst into laughter. He hated when his grandmother embarrassed him by talking so nonchalantly about sex.

"Is that not what you say anymore?" she asked. "Do you say 'hitting it' or 'getting some' instead? I hope it's not that awful humping phrase. I abhor that one. It's so crass."

Dee and Shane practically rolled in stitches on the floor while the Duchess surveyed the fruits of her labor. She enjoyed shocking everyone with her off-color comments, and Matt knew it. It was one of the many

330 | Jacob Z. Flores

reasons he loved that woman. While she might be a society dame, she had no problem getting down and dirty when the mood struck her.

"What's going on in here?"

They stopped laughing as the guest of honor walked into the living room, saying, "Sounds like a party,"

"Gabriel Belton!" Matt chided. "You're home early and ruined my surprise!"

A big smile stretched across Gabriel's tanned face that made his eyes twinkle like two stars set in the sky. "I always rush home to you."

"That's a good answer," Matt said while walking into his man's outstretched arms.

"Besides, I already knew about the surprise party, so I got here early to surprise you!"

Everyone turned to glare at Shane who immediately backpedalled.

"He beat it out of me," Shane told them as they converged upon him from all sides. "Have you seen how big he is? He's very intimidating and persuasive."

"You hold him down, Dee, and I'll take care of the rest."

"Not on your life, Matty. I plan on putting him in a world of hurt. You hold him down."

"You're both wrong," the Duchess told them. "You two will be holding him down while I go all ape shit on his ass."

Everyone burst into uncontrollable hysterics after hearing the Duchess cuss like a bad ass. When the laughter subsided, they no longer had the energy or the will to punish Shane for once again being incapable of keeping his mouth shut. Instead, they all congratulated Gabriel on his promotion with a toast of champagne, celebrating not only Gabriel's accomplishment, but also the love that brought all of them together.

MICHAEL stood across from the Gifted One's apartment. His eyes pierced through the building and observed Gabriel living out the life that Father and free will had granted him. Although he missed his brother dearly, Michael knew this was the life his brother now wanted to live.

He had chosen Matthew Westlake, and Matthew had chosen him. Intertwined through love, their souls survived the sacrifice required for reweaving the Grand Design, though Gabriel had wiped out all memories of their encounters with the supernatural.

And when he jumpstarted the new pattern by asking Matt to remember, Matt forgot about demons and angels but refused to relinquish the love in his heart for Gabriel. Providence therefore saw fit to weave the two together as men, creating a new life where Gabriel had not been Gabriel, the archangel, but Gabriel Belton, the police officer.

But the changes in the pattern didn't stop there.

Providence granted Craig a new destiny, one integral to restoring balance to the Grand Design. Reborn through his selfless sacrifice for love and pursuit of retribution, Craig Belton was no longer Craig Belton.

He was now the Angel of Vengeance.

"I'm still not quite used to this," Craig said next to him. He stretched the wings across his back and eyed them suspiciously.

Michael nodded. "You have all the time in creation to adjust, brother."

"Perhaps," Craig replied as he tucked the wings back under. "But will I forget the life I once led?"

"In time, your knowledge of Craig Belton will fade. Are not the memories of Gabriel's life as an archangel now finding a home within your memory?"

"They are," he told Michael. "Though I wasn't there when the Watchers fell, I recall every detail of Samyaza's treachery. Of how we rid the land of the Nephilim and imprisoned our fallen brothers for all of eternity."

Michael smiled as he placed his hand on his new brother's shoulder. "See, you already speak as one of us. You called the Watchers *our* brothers."

"I suppose I did," Craig replied with a grin. "Still, being referred to as Gabriel has been disconcerting, considering that I know myself not to be him. At least not the *real* Gabriel."

"You are the real Gabriel, now and forever more. You've helped to restore the flaw in the Grand Design, and you are welcomed with open arms."

"I still don't truly understand how all this was possible? How could a mere man become an archangel and an archangel turn into a man?"

"All is possible with Father," Michael reminded him. "He can make or remake any of us. He is the creator of all life after all."

"But why choose me as the Angel of Vengeance?"

"Because when faced with overwhelming odds and loss, you cried out for reprisal. You did what had to be done to ensure that retribution for those responsible was delivered, no matter the cost. That is what the Angel of Vengeance does, and when my previous brother ceased acting as the instrument of vengeance, your cries for retribution summoned the mantle to you. It wasn't a role forced upon you, but one that you accepted upon the death of your mortal soul."

Michael could still sense confusion, so he tried another approach. "Do you remember the moments before you died?"

He nodded.

"You knew something glorious waited for you in Heaven, and you embraced it with open arms. Once you did that, your soul became the immortal and living embodiment of vengeance."

"I remember that," he told Michael. "I felt drawn to something bigger than me or anything I knew before. It filled me overfull with love and purpose so that it was easy to leave the concerns of the world behind."

"Because the love for Father filled your heart and your soul and remade you as you stand before me now."

"What about Gabriel?" he asked as he stared into the apartment where Matt now threw a party in his honor. "Does he remember his past like I still remember mine?"

Michael shook his head. "He has been reborn as a man and knows nothing else."

"I envy him that, but I suppose with time this shall grow easier."

"With time and distance. Now that the Gifted One's path has been set in stone, he no longer requires heavenly intervention. He remains safeguarded from further evil and can now fulfill his destiny when it is at long last revealed."

"But what about ordinary threats?" Craig asked. "Disease, accident, human treachery."

"He must face those conflicts as every other man. His destiny is his to write, and fail or succeed, he and those he loves are now responsible for the outcome."

"It will be glorious. I have no doubt about that."

"Neither do I," agreed Michael, but as he watched Craig's expression, he noticed a cloud of sadness creep across his vision. "Are you well?"

"I will be," Craig answered. "But I just realized that I will never return here again. Do I speak the truth?"

Michael nodded. "It's time for us both to say good-bye. Our destiny lies in the heavens. Theirs lie in the events of the day-to-day. They must play their part as we must fulfill ours."

Craig nodded as his wings began to flutter, lifting him off the rooftop where they both stood. Nodding once at the life he now left behind, Craig soared into the sky with a heart no longer burdened by man's troubles.

Michael followed his new brother across the sky, but he looked back one final time. He gazed upon Matt and Gabriel, holding each other tight. The love in their hearts outshone the smiles emblazoned across their faces.

"Farewell, brother," Michael whispered before heading home.

MATT crawled into bed beside Gabriel and snuggled into his chest. The intoxicating aroma of rain mixed with sweat filled his nostrils, making him immediately want to devour the man whose strong arms wrapped protectively around him.

"How is it you always smell like rain?"

"Because I'm so heavenly," Gabriel teased while kissing the top of his head.

Matt looked up and smiled into his gorgeous blue eyes. Whenever he stared into them, he wanted to lose himself completely in their rich, luscious pools. "That you are," he said. "My earth angel sent to me by God."

"I think you're the one who's the angel."

"No. You are."

Gabriel shook his head. "No. You."

Matt kissed Gabriel and climbed on top of him, delighting in the feel of their naked bodies pressed against each other. As far as he was concerned, this was heaven. "I love you, Gabriel Craig Belton."

"And I love you, Matthew Cruz Westlake, especially since you threw me such a fabulous party."

"Is that the only reason you love me? Because I threw you a party?"

A sly grin stretched across Gabriel's face as he rolled over and on top of Matt, trapping him underneath his body. "That's one out of many."

He passionately nibbled on Matt's neck, his stubble scraping across his bare flesh.

"And just what are the other reasons?"

Gabriel kissed a trail to Matt's lips, where he stopped before pulling away to answer. "I've got a million of them, but I'll only give you one a day. Which means you're stuck with me for the rest of your life."

"I wouldn't have it any other way," replied Matt as he wrapped his arms around Gabriel's neck to seal the deal with a kiss.

JACOB Z. FLORES lives a double life. During the day, he is a respected college English professor and mid-level administrator. At night and during his summer vacation, he loosens the tie and tosses aside the trendy sports coat to write man on man fiction, where the hard ass assessor of freshmen level composition turns his attention to the firm posteriors and other rigid appendages of the characters in his fictional world.

Summers in Provincetown, Massachusetts, provide Jacob with inspiration for his fiction. The abundance of barely clothed man flesh and daily debauchery stimulates his personal muse. When he isn't stroking the keyboard, Jacob spends time with his husband, Bruce, their three children, and two dogs, who represent a bright blue blip in an otherwise predominantly red swath in south Texas.

You can follow Jacob's musings on his blog at http://jacobzflores.com or become a part of his social media network by visiting http://www.facebook.com/jacob.flores2 or http://twitter.com/#!/JacobZFlores.

www.ingramcontent.com/pod-product-compliance
Lightning Source LLC
Chambersburg PA
CBHW050033030726
47506CB00001B/253